"THE HOUSE IS GROWING, SOLOMON . . .
On its own . . . eccentrically, you could call it," Aunt Morgana said.

"Then the Borders . . ." Solomon began.

"As far as anyone can guess, the Borders have arrived," Morgana agreed. "We'd taken to watching the children. We were afraid that a child's bedroom might change suddenly in the night, leaving the sleeping little ones prey for fauns or dryads bent on a changeling."

"I see, Morgana. But why call me back from Lambeth?"

"Because it has finally happened, Nephew. It's Endymion's youngest child. Faith."

"What of Faith?"

"Gone," Morgana announced. "Faith is gone. I sent her myself for nothing more than sugar. She opened what she thought was a pantry door. The room filled with light and a choir of birds were singing. Then she cried out, and the whole kitchen rocked and trembled. And the door closed behind her, like the Borders had enough.

"That is why you have come, Solomon," Morgana continued. "To settle this maze of a house. Drive out the Borders. Perhaps you'll find out where Faith has gone in the process. . . ."

ARCADY

Michael Williams

A ROC BOOK

ROC
Published by the Penguin Group
Penguin Books USA Inc., 375 Hudson Street,
New York, New York 10014, U.S.A.
Penguin Books Ltd, 27 Wrights Lane,
London W8 5TZ, England
Penguin Books Australia Ltd, Ringwood,
Victoria, Australia
Penguin Books Canada Ltd, 10 Alcorn Avenue,
Toronto, Ontario, Canada M4V 3B2
Penguin Books (N.Z.) Ltd, 182-190 Wairau Road,
Auckland 10, New Zealand

Penguin Books Ltd, Registered Offices:
Harmondsworth, Middlesex, England

First published by Roc, an imprint of Dutton Signet,
a division of Penguin Books USA Inc.

First Printing, April, 1996
10 9 8 7 6 5 4 3 2 1

REGISTERED TRADEMARK—MARCA REGISTRADA

LIBRARY OF CONGRESS CATALOGING IN PUBLICATION DATA:
Williams, Michael, 1952 Dec. 17–
Arcady / by Michael Williams.
p. cm.
ISBN 0-451-45500-2
I. Title.
PS3573.I4536A73 1996
813′.54—dc20 95-25757
CIP

Printed in the United States of America

To the memory of Mark Gromer

ACKNOWLEDGMENTS

If a novel has many ancestors, these are some of *Arcady*'s:

William Wordsworth, Percy Bysshe Shelley, John Keats, Alfred Tennyson, Emily Dickinson, Matthew Arnold, and especially William Blake, without whose work the Text would be impossible.

Professors Robert Hill of Middlebury College and Leon Driskell of the University of Louisville, who guided me to the Text, and inspired me early and late.

Margaret Weis, whose every gesture over fifteen years of friendship has been both generous and uplifting.

My superb agent, Shawna McCarthy, and my kind and wise editor, Amy Stout, midwifed a difficult birth. It's a better book for their intelligence and sensitivity.

I also received technical advice from many and varied sources, to all of whom I am grateful:

Cass Johnson designed the first map of my world.

Professor Hollace Lawton Cox of Speed Engineering School guided me through some basic principles of optics.

Jeff Bright of the Bright Foundry answered, quickly and clearly, some questions I had about bronze casting.

Tim Nutgrass provided invaluable information on nineteenth-century prosthetic limbs, without which Diego Hawken could not have marched through Arcadian history.

Brian Beasley of Balloon Odyssey took me up for my first balloon ride and was patient with my subsequent questions.

Drs. Michael Foster and Gary Davis gave of their medical knowledge, both practical and curious.

The novelist's old disclaimer, that "the technical mistakes are mine alone," has never been more true than in this book.

Finally, the deepest thanks to my wife, Rhonda, and our boys, Shane and Josh, who have nurtured, encouraged, and delighted me through the long process of this book.

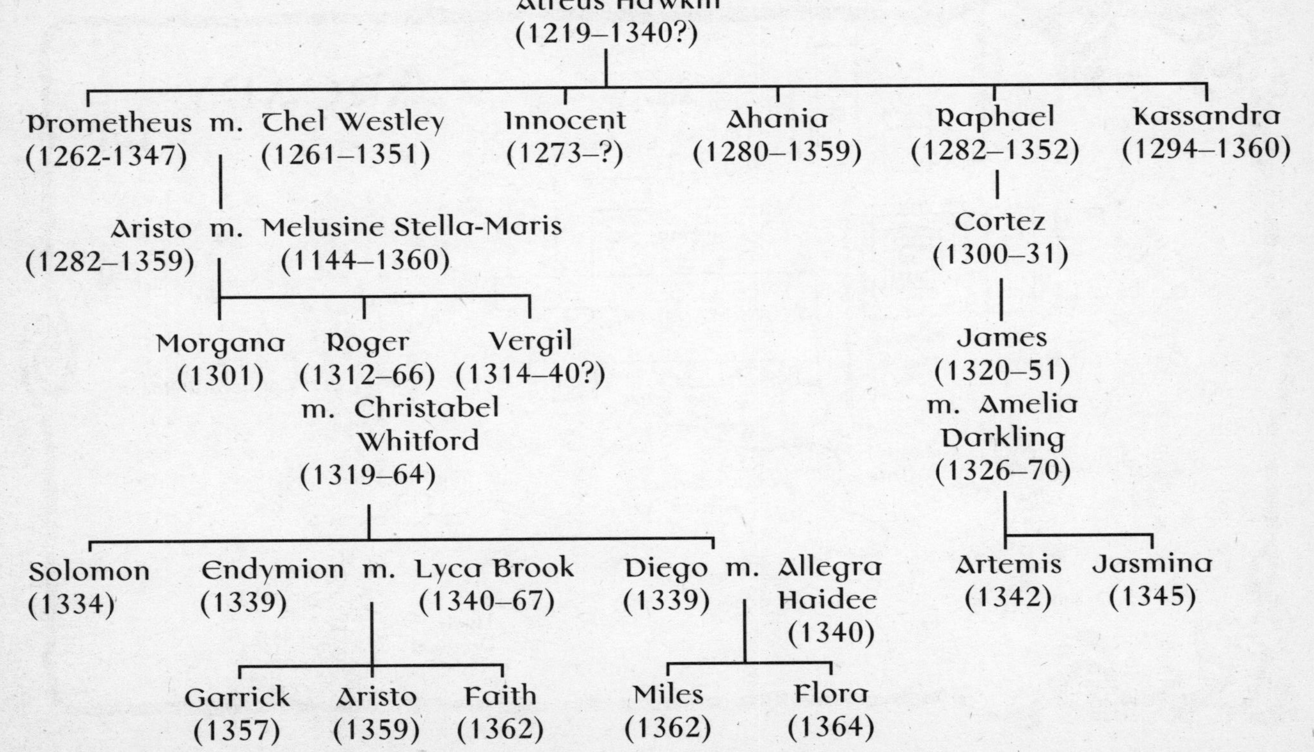
Atreus Hawkin
(1219–1340?)
Prometheus m. Thel Westley
(1262-1347) (1261–1351)
Innocent
(1273–?)
Ahania
(1280–1359)
Raphael
(1282–1352)
Kassandra
(1294–1360)
Aristo m. Melusine Stella-Maris
(1282–1359) (1144–1360)
Cortez
(1300–31)
Morgana
(1301)
Roger
(1312–66)
m. Christabel
Whitford
(1319–64)
Vergil
(1314–40?)
James
(1320–51)
m. Amelia
Darkling
(1326–70)
Solomon
(1334)
Endymion m. Lyca Brook
(1339) (1340–67)
Diego m. Allegra
(1339) Haidee
(1340)
Artemis
(1342)
Jasmina
(1345)
Garrick
(1357)
Aristo
(1359)
Faith
(1362)
Miles
(1362)
Flora
(1364)

ARCADY
Aviary
Topiary
Barn
Stable
Old Servants' Quarters
Courtyard
Carriage House
Maze
The Mansion
The Gardens
The Ancestral Gate
N
Grandfather Artreus' Lake
The Mill House
East Woods
Hemp & Tobacco Fields
Orchard
Uncle Raphael's Nut Grove

N
URTHONA
Napolis
LUVAH
Alph
River
CHARMAS
Lambeth
Ville
Shiveleigh
Ley
Station
Arcady
URIZEN

Prologue

On summer mornings, before the heat in the upper rooms became unbearable, Solomon would lie awake and listen to the house shift and settle.

He was always alone in his room. His younger brothers were scarcely more than toddlers, bedded on the first floor near his mother. Aside from the twins, the house was childless, a haunt of great-uncles and aunts.

It was an arrangement that suited the boy immensely.

And now it was no longer safe.

The sheets billowed and tented when Solomon raised his knees in the warm bed. Promising breezes passed through the upstairs windows, carrying upon them the smell of peaches and pears, the distant, muddy smell of the slow-flowing Alph.

It was the summer's sameness that delighted him the most. He knew that three strides would take him to the window, where a green shingle roof sloped to the middle branches of a sprawling maple. Beyond the tree—though he knew in this season he could not see through the thick, hand-shaped leaves of the maple—lay a red dirt path leading north along the side of the house, and beyond that path the tobacco and hemp fields that kept Grandfather's business flourishing.

Kept four generations thriving in a big house, when the countryside from Arcady to Shiveleigh was littered with peasants and precarious dirt farmers.

Unlike most ten-year-olds, Solomon knew his own great good fortune. He slept two hours later than any schoolchild within twenty miles, and his summer days were riding and explorations, ventures into the lofts amid the head-high hay, amid castles of bales fashioned expressly for him by his kindly older cousin James, a glut of fruit pies and honeycakes lavished by his great-great-aunt Ahania, the phoenix in the new aviary, and visits to Grandmother in the cool of the mill house.

Even school, at which he excelled, was adventure, the Hymns and the saints' lives stored readily in the lofts of his memory. You had to be a priest to really know the magic of the Hymns, his tutor told him, but the saints were everyone's, and a faithful, wise child would pray to the right saint for the right thing, then thank them all when those prayers were granted.

Solomon thanked those saints especially on summer mornings, when it seemed that his good fortune would stretch out forever. Oh, sometimes at night he would waken, the knots and grains in the wooden paneling catching a deceptive shaft of moonlight and magnifying, distorting, until it seemed as though the walls had tear-stained eyes that watched him enviously, greedily. And he would forget that Great-Great-Aunt Kassandra's dressmaker's model rested against the near wall outside his door, and sometimes the light would catch its frame, and for a moment Solomon would think someone scarred and caped and ominous stood at the threshold of his room.

But then sunlight would come, and a morning like this one, with larksong blossoming from the East Woods and a breeze climbing through the maple boughs. The paneling would resume its customary form, and the dressmaker's model would return to its inanimate metal and cloth and wood.

And Solomon would thank the saints that everything was as it always was.

That is, until now.

Grandfather and Father were arguing downstairs. He could tell through the boards and rafters. Bickering as they had for the last month.

Grandfather would win. Which meant things would change for Solomon.

The boy leaned out of the bed, dangling his head upside down.

If the blood rushes into the roots of your hair, it will grow more quickly. Cousin James had taught him that.

Soon his forehead seemed full, swollen. His eyes blurred and swam with dust motes and dizziness. He could almost make out what the men in the rooms below were saying.

School, Grandfather murmured. And *away.*

Solomon wanted no more of it. Quietly, covering his ears to shut out the sound of argument, he sang the first verse of a Hymn his cousin Amelia had taught him—a Hymn of joy for children and for summer mornings.

"I love to rise in a summer morn,
When the birds sing on every tree;
The distant huntsman winds his horn,
And the sky-lark sings with me."

For a moment his hopes soared like the bird in the Hymn, like the phoenix aloft over the topiary. Perhaps all would be well: he would stay at Arcady and be schooled in the soothing, familiar tasks of the estate.

No seminary. No journey far from home.

Solomon closed his eyes. Far over the hemp fields of Arcady he heard a winding, a bellowing deep in the East Woods. . . .

A huntsman's horn?

He listened closely, praying to the saints—to Saint Los, especially, who hears laments and prayers—that he would hear the sound again, that something in the words of Amelia's Hymn was magic.

Because if the Hymn was magic . . .

Then he could stay at Arcady. Something could keep him here forever, on windy autumn nights, playing with simple, dead Uncle Vergil's lead soldiers in the attic, or feeding the birds in the new aviary.

Or best of all, to stay here in the summer, past care and change, drowsing in the morning to birdsong and the murmur of bees, the sweet smell of the orchard warm through the room's western window. . . .

The distant sound of the horn faded from hearing. *School.* The word rose to him like the recollection of an unsettled dream.

Away.

CHAPTER 1

It seemed as though the gondola floated south by itself, frail on the current, offering no shelter against the damp wind and the falling temperature. The gray-green globe of the balloon swelled and rippled in the black smoke and the high wind like something large and sickly, dizzying to look upon.

Below, the Alphside Forest, Urthona's greatest woodland, reddened and streaked with the sunset. A stand of poplar glistened to the port side of the gondola, dark foliage boiling in the sunlight and soft wind. The sun settled on the western hills, its light fractured by the wetness in the air, as though it shone through a prism or through the thick walls of a bottle. Their dying leaves caught in the angled light and framed by the dark red clay of the soil, the poplars glinted a terrible deep crimson.

Two men rode in the hazy wicker basket.

One was young. Wrapped in wool scarves, gloved and booted and cloaked against the wet wind until he looked like a bundle of rags come to life, he scrambled amid ropes and sandbags, tugging open the tall rotator vent that turned the balloon in the intricate wind. He was all motion, all purpose and worry and haste. The smoky fire coughed and sputtered as he clambered around it, as he teetered dangerously on the gondola railing.

Meanwhile, his companion stared vacantly out over the darkening landscape, muttering to himself.

This one was older—forty, perhaps—dressed foolishly for ballooning in a thin greatcoat and the black tricorn hat of his clerical order.

Willie glared at the priest with rising irritation. Little help this Father Solomon had been. Brooding ballast on a dangerous and windy evening.

"More bags aft and over, I was saying, Father Solomon," he repeated loudly over the rumble of the fire. "We're sailing uncommon low into Urizen."

"Very well, Master Willie," Solomon Hawken answered abstractly, never shifting his gaze from the forests below. "Jettison whatever it is gondoliers . . . fancy jettisoning."

Willie rolled his eyes and hoisted a sandbag to his shoulder.

Solomon propped himself against the railing, out of the way. He wrapped his greatcoat more closely about him, pulled his hat more tightly down over a chaos of long, graying hair.

"Over the Lady's Land," Willie breathed. "It'll be any minute now."

No sooner were the words out than the shooting began, stuttering from the fringe of the trees behind them as they passed over the southmost edges of Urthona and sailed toward the brown watercourse of the Alph. The gunfire fluttered and cracked until the whole landscape whitened below, rattling with the snare drum sound of musketry.

"We're low, Father Solomon," Willie urged, crouching against the hard wicker of the gondola basket. "Dangerous low, mind you!"

The priest nodded, sneezed at the smell of powder climbing on the wind. At last, he laid a gloved and tentative hand on a sandbag.

"Thank you, Father. 'S much better if both of us . . . *jettison*. Now toss it, and stand back from the railing, if you'd be so kind," the gondolier warned. "Father or fiend, you're liable to catch a bullet for high curiousness. They ain't too precise from this range, if you follow me."

The balloon lurched and dropped into the smoke. A flock of ground doves surged around them. In the midst of the flurry, the high, skidding sounds of the doves aloft, a white winged horse rose suddenly out of the trees and smoke, its dark eyes wide in fear.

Too close to the Borders! Willie thought with dismay, reaching for his pistol. But the big animal surged harmlessly by, its mottled flank brushing the wicker gondola.

For a moment both men saw into the heart of the pegasus—the insubstantial translucency of the creature, as though the horse were a lantern, a specter. And something swirled in the flanks of the horse, an eddying, hypnotic whirlpool.

Light . . . winged men spinning in the light . . .

Willie tore his eyes from the creature. The doves reeled about the gondola, solid and almost reassuring in their natural panic. They soared off to the west amid the next blossoming report of the guns.

By this time, the ground fire had found its range. The first bullets whistled about the balloon, skittering like rising birds, tearing through the wind.

Father Solomon closed his eyes. For a moment he seemed to be praying. Then he lurched from the railing as a musket ball crashed through the wicker, splintering the side of the gondola with a fist-sized hole.

Willie's movements became more hurried, more frantic, the gondola spilling sand like the top of an hourglass and the balloon rising, rising beyond range of deadly fire. Still the musket balls whined by, peppering the billowing canvas. Two more rounds ripped through the gondola, and a third, spent at a greater height, struck the underside of the basket with a low, rattling thud.

The balloon rose, its fuel dwindling dangerously, to a height where most of the firing was a waste of ammunition. Soon most of the bullets fell far short of the mark. Down in the hazy forest, the red line of the army twisted like an adder.

"Redjackets," Willie announced, drawing a knife and deftly opening another bag of sand. "Citizens' Guard. Couldn't hit a galleon from this range, Father."

"Such faith in science you have, Willie," Father Solomon observed dryly.

The young man grumbled. It had been this way since Lambeth, forty miles and two hours away. He had taken the priest south as a favor to the abbot, when half of Urthona and all of Urizen were up in arms, shooting at one another across river and glade and Absence.

Shooting themselves as the Guard and the rebels chased each other through the mirror-maze of woods.

And yet this one—this Solomon—*had* to return home. Would brook no delay. Something about accident and family tragedy. All veils and whispers.

Willie was ready to speak, to tell Solomon Hawken the way the wind was blowing, but then, from the swirling chaos of smoke and scurrying guardsmen below, another volley arose, and a suspension rope of the gondola snapped as a musket ball passed cleanly through it.

The lad swore softly, poured more sand over the lip of the basket. Now the basket rocked dangerously, five hundred feet above the cloudy forest. Willie wheeled from the railing. The ropes creaked with the sudden, new tension.

What if they toppled into the forest?

We will be lost in the Alphside, where the least danger is that of soldiers. Where stands of trees float on the terrible cold swamps and flesh-eating squirrels lie in numbers awaiting the passerby. Where it is said that magnetic North moves in the branches, luring travelers into quicksand.

They had passed over the redjackets now. Instead, legions of poplar and pine lay below, occasional clearings where rock and twisted bordermetal caught the sunlight, then vanished in green and gray and tangled wood as the balloon continued on a steep and southward decline.

Suddenly, a second rope whined and unraveled, with a last snap like a bone breaking.

Willie whooped and dove clear of the shredding rope. He stumbled and lurched across the gondola, falling against the shot-fractured side of the basket. The wicker crackled, ripped, gave way beneath his weight. Willie screamed as the ground passed over his head. Whooping, clutching frantically at the railing, he slipped . . .

And seized at the last moment the rocking lip of the basket, dangled above forest and air, his legs churning desperately. Solomon clung to the opposite side of the gondola, silent, his tricorn tilted over his face.

Sparks and ash scattered from the central fire, raining up into Solomon's greatcoat, into the smoky air. The source of buoyant heat had shifted slightly, but enough to send the balloon upon a rapid descent.

"Now we're goners," Willie urged, clambering back into the gondola. "The ropes won't hold an hour. Lest you lend a hand, Father. There's something you clergymen do with mending?"

Solomon looked away. For a long moment he kept silent, then shook his head. "Sails, Melmoth," he replied. "The Form for the Mending of Sails, it is called. They used to teach it at the seminary, but it's been fifty years. For seamen and mariners, as they embark on the wide ocean. Not for balloons. Which have no mention in the Hymns or the Text. Not that we could be sure it would work anyway. . . ."

Willie staggered to Solomon's side of the gondola, the basket tipping beneath him as he moved. "What goes for sails might go for balloons," he offered through clenched teeth. "I'm not standin' on precise theology now, Father. Your abbot'll never hear from me. . . ."

Solomon nodded with almost a dizzy reluctance. "It's Second Form spellbinding, actually. For . . . for priests on the coasts and river towns, so I'm not sure I even remember the words. It was from the Commentaries, as I recall. No holy Text or Hymns. But you know that if *one word* is misplaced . . ."

"We'll be no worse off than we are now!" Willie shouted, clutching the gondola railing.

Muted by his hat and muffler, Solomon's words were scarcely a whisper in the chaos of wind and smoke.

> "The helmsman steered, the ship moved on;
> Yet never a breeze up-blew;
> The mariners all 'gan work the ropes,
> Where they were wont to do."

Old words from the Commentaries, Willie guessed. The chapter and verse a mystery to him.

But the mystery did not work.

The frayed tendrils of rope fluttered uselessly over the gondola's edge, twining like snakes as a cold breeze passed over them. The basket listed dangerously, and the downward voyage continued in the rising Urthonan dusk.

Now Willie was forced to improvise. Muttering to himself, shouldering what was left of the ballast to a far corner of the gondola, he managed to bring the craft shakily aright. The smoke and spark from the central fire now rose unsteadily into the swelling balloon and slowly, miraculously, the ground seemed to drop away, the craft rose, and the wind encircled the gondola, murmuring like a hive of bees, buoying it softly back onto its southward route and gentle descent.

"It won't last," Willie breathed. "If I have to throw out ballast, it's goin' to unbalance the gondola. And the whole northern border of Urizen is high forest made to tangle us, so we'll need to throw out ballast to clear it. The mathematics is beyond me, but I reckon I'll think up something when the time comes."

"And at that time . . ." Solomon began.

"You'd best help with the slough, Father," the gondolier urged, his wool hat pulled down over his eyes. "I'll tell you when. Not much to do but hang on, hoist things, and toss 'em over the rails. If need be, everything goes excepting the two of us."

Lightly, uncertainly, Solomon touched one of the sandbags. He blinked in the smoke, then stared out over the shattered railing.

Two sparrows flying below the craft swerved to avoid the slowly descending gondola. They chattered and swooped westward into the scarlet hills, as the balloon continued its steady flight into the thick woodlands north of the Alph.

"Just rotten luck it was the Guard below us," Willie explained. "The rebels would of quit when we passed out of range, never made that lucky shot to begin with. A weak thermal approachin', Father. The saints be blessed we can ride it, seeing as we don't have much more altitude to lose.

"Fact is," the lad continued, prattling nervously to himself, the whole reeling memory of the capsized gondola rushing back at him, frightening him, "rebels probably wouldn't of fired in the first place. What with their shortages and all."

Solomon leaned against the railing, then stepped away in alarm, remembering the precarious balance of the craft. "I see," he replied vaguely.

Now the butterflies rose from the riverland, wafting on the old smells of rot and fish and red mud.

Urizen. Willie could tell by the bend of the river, the sudden profusion of fruit trees.

And somewhere nearby lay Arcady.

Solomon lifted his hand in what seemed to be a silent blessing, and again the wind rose.

The gunfire faded behind them, the river wider and browner and darker as they neared it and passed over. As the shadow of the balloon darkened the current at midstream, Willie pointed to a deeper darkness some miles upriver.

"Absences, Father Solomon."

Solomon wrenched his nervous gaze from the water, raised the spyglass, and followed the boy's pointing finger to the patch of opaque gloom, the glittering silver cloud at the very heart of the shadows.

As always, the Absence seemed to beckon, to draw the eye and the whole landscape about it. Light bent and eddied at its margins, and several raptors—hawks or harpers perhaps, or perhaps phoenixes, too far away for the fire on their wings to be visible—flew toward the dark patch and then, wings extended, banked around it and disappeared on the other side.

The story went that whatever entered the Absence, by accident or by design—whether man or bird or wind or light itself—returned transformed or did not return at all.

"Best not steer upriver, sir," Willie warned. "Even the hawks know it."

"But not the Hawkens," Solomon replied with an odd smile. "It's moved since I was last here, Willie. It's closer to the house now."

"It's the Borders what's moved, Father," Willie replied tersely. "Absences don't move. But the Borders is back and forth like the tides. You look for the steady country, but with them moving Borders, it's harder and harder to find. And it's right near unraveling when you find it."

Solomon nodded. It was basic Border physics.

The balloon coasted southward, the Absence receding into a watery dusk. Soon they reached the deciduous forest that marked the descent toward the grounds of the estate—shade trees giving way to almond and chestnut and walnut.

Both men rested for a space, leaning against the gondola railing, balancing the shaky craft as the rope strands fluttered in the high wind over the nut grove.

Then, skimming the top of the last row of walnuts, not a mile from where the grounds of Arcady commenced, the balloon overtook a party of Blights.

Six or seven of them there were, on the Arcady side of the river.

"Fly closer to them, Willie," Solomon urged. "I'd like a closer look."

"It ain't safe, Father," Willie protested. "Well and good we're above them, but the balloon is on a sheer downward turn, and if they're armed with more than knives, we run a risk of being shot."

"Nonetheless, Willie."

"If one of them . . . produces a pistol or a bow," Willie cautioned, "then it's you what do the answering in them circumstances."

"I suppose I am prepared for that, Willie," Solomon replied after a long pause.

It did not console the gondolier.

Nonetheless, Willie guided the craft closer to the brightly colored figures. Seven youthful forms on velocipedes, on foot. Boys, they seemed from this distance.

Almost all of the Blights were boys.

Now the balloon dropped dangerously low, the gondola brushing the tip of a pine tree. Then, with a strange, quiet suddenness, the balloon caught a crossing air current and glided directly over the boys.

The Blights moved slowly at first, but hurried and dodged when they caught sight of the balloon, converging and scattering, their bright clothing splashing the somber nut grove with particolored light—yellow and black and pale, the hectic red of Arcadian autumns. No doubt they were headed toward the Absences to the northeast, to lose themselves and emerge in the Islands of the Blessed, the Den of the Seven Sleepers, in Lambeth, or at the banks of Forgetful Lethe.

"We call them Blights in Pontus," Solomon offered.

"They call 'em Blights at home, too," Willie replied, with a reluctant tug at the valve line as the balloon dipped further into the sunstruck groves, slipping perilously between two lines of walnut trees.

"Not with them," Solomon concluded quietly and cryptically, sheathing the spyglass. "No sign."

Dirty and ragged, their hair nested and matted, the long front lock a sign of their freedom and defiance, the Blights flashed in and out through the black trees, like ghosts fleeing an enchanter, their tattered jackets fluttering like pennants and streamers in the wind of their passage. The velocipedes trailed white steam through the boles of the walnuts.

The gondola was so low that Willie could smell them—the steam and the sweat and the metallic whiff of the sky after lightning.

One of the boys—an older lad of perhaps fourteen, his hair dyed bootblack and a green tattoo over his forehead—stared into the gondola and flashed an obscene gesture. Then he released the handlebars of his velocipede, steering the skeletal machine by knees and hips, reaching into the folds of his bright green jacket as the cycle wobbled through the open field . . .

Willie yanked Solomon toward the floor of the gondola. "Get down, you damned fool!" he shouted, and drew his pistol.

Flushed and frowning, Solomon slid back into the wicker basket. For a moment, the two travelers leaned against the tilting gondola, regarding one another warily.

"I expect you've a spell for this, Father?" Willie suggested through clenched teeth. "Seein' as . . . you asked to see the Blights and all?"

"Spell?" Solomon blinked stupidly. A strange, feral chattering commenced around them, and Willie craned above the railing as the balloon bellied between the last trees in the nut grove and on over level ground. "But there's really nothing, Willie. The Text never took into account . . ."

"Something to protect us?" the lad persisted. "A warding? a circle of sanctuary?"

"Where do you get such notions? By the Belle Dame, boy, the seminary doesn't deal in snake oil and illusion!"

Willie snorted and stood, aiming his pistol at the dodging boy. The others surged toward the dipping gondola, swirls of yellow and violet and red at the borders of his focused vision.

Suddenly, Willie felt a tugging at his sleeve.

Solomon stood beside him.

At least the Father had some salt in him.

"I could try another kind of conjury," Solomon offered, his gaze distant, almost haunted. "I cannot promise success, mind you, but if he thinks I'm conjuring at him, it . . . it might *daunt* him. Put away the gun. Steer us away from them."

The priest clutched the gondola rail and rose to his feet, then lifted his hands, palms facing the dwindling Absence, and began to speak.

> "The Plow goes forth in tempest & lightnings, & the Harrow cruel
> In blights of the East, the heavy Roller follows in howlings of woe."

It was Text, no doubt: the holiest of books, judging from its obscurity.

But the cycling boy didn't care. He smirked scornfully and drew a short-barreled pistol from the folds of green. Willie leveled his own gun, squeezed the trigger . . .

A bursting noise, like a board shearing away. The old pistol bucked in his hand, and the green-coated boy toppled headfirst over the handlebars of the velocipede in a spray of blood and powder. The cycle jackknifed and careened into the walnut grove, spreading a gray haze in its wake.

The dead Blight's companions scattered into the evergreens, their bright colors lost instantly in the shadows.

Willie fumbled to reload. Solomon turned to him, glaring.

"Why did you . . ."

But Willie glared back, slipped the pistol into his belt, and pulled the line that opened the rip panel. The balloon resumed its steady descent, weaving over the crests of the drooping trees, and Solomon stared into the darkness, his gaze unreadable.

CHAPTER 2

The fire and the smoke and the faceless plummeting child would haunt Solomon later, as he dreamt uneasily in his room at Arcady, but now there was little time to brood or dwell, as, skimming the black tips of the walnut trees, the gondola scraping twice against the gnarled crowns, shaking a legion of yammering black squirrels, the balloon turned homeward.

Now Solomon could see Arcady, off on the western horizon, reddened by the last touch of the sun. The towers, the outbuildings, were still several miles away, but approaching rapidly as the balloon passed over the brown, tattered fields of tobacco and hemp. The fanciful architecture was suffused in a warm red light.

Two towers, one circular and one rectangular, framed the face of the brick mansion, reflected in the pooling waters of the canal that brushed the pasture south of the house. Behind and between the towers stretched a profusion of sloping dormers, a maze of garrets, spires, and minarets, all sprouting from the foundation of a three-story mansion as though the architect or the builder had conceived one house, then shifted to another in the making, and another and yet another.

Which, of course, was just what had happened in the early times.

The mausoleum that had marked the house's beginning, built for a man who then decided not to die, still lay somewhere at the center of the house, obscured and forgotten in later attachments, annexes, and appendages.

They said that the tomb was the heart of the house, that as long as it lay hidden, Arcady would remain involved and mysterious.

But for Solomon, even the mysteries were familiar.

From the high vantage over Uncle Raphael's nut grove, he saw the mansion, and a great, incalculable weight seemed to lift from his shoulders, from his chest.

Arcady at last. Where he had grown to manhood.

Where they still thought he was a priest. And thereby awaited his coming.

Above him, the suspension ropes strained and whined as the balloon lost the last of its height in the skilled hands of Willie Melmoth. Bracing for the landing, Solomon pointed out an open field bordering the house, away from the guarded gate but within the fences of stone and iron that bordered the property. Willie nodded and steered the ungainly balloon, as best he could, in the general direction of that spot.

Suddenly, tall branches of hackberry and pin oak rose about them. One of the unbroken ropes, strained to unraveling with the unbalanced weight of the gondola, snagged on a branch and spun the craft about. The basket struck a heavy limb; the oak leaves rustled like dry gourds.

The dark ground yawned before Solomon like the mouth of a grave. Branches clutched at the wicker, at his coat, snaked quickly about his neck and tightened . . .

"No!" he cried.

Then the basket wrenched loose of the entanglement. Willie gave the last of the branches a clearing kick, and they were free and floating, the gondola tilted dangerously over Solomon's native soil, two of its ropes long severed, a third now clinging to an unraveling strand as the balloon pitched lower toward the grounds of the estate.

To come this close and then to break their mutual necks within sight of the house . . .

The lad beside him was shouting, urging him to try the spell again . . .

The boy did not know such magic did not work, he did not know . . .

Then remarkably, unexpectedly, the balloon breasted through the last of the sparse woodland, as suddenly as it had entered, leaves and needles and branches clinging to the gondola.

Willie sighed audibly, breathing a brief prayer of gratitude to Saint Palamabron, whose pity and compassion had guided them through danger.

Lower and lower the craft swooped. Then, not ten feet from the ground, the frayed rope snapped and the travelers, priest and gondolier, plummeted roughly into the field south of the house. Nesting birds took wing as the gondola rocked and lurched and the balloon drifted into the lake and settled, billowing out over the waters. Its fires hissed; its wicker basket bobbed crazily atop the glassy surface of Grandfather Atreus' last aquatic project.

Not a hundred feet away, at the edge of the East Woods, a small horned creature whimpered, rose to its hind hoofed legs, and scampered off with the fleetness of a racehorse toward a weird piping sound from deep in the trees.

Solomon and Willie lay still, dazed, and the groves around them rustled with approaching life.

Thank the saints for a timely fall, Solomon thought. A hundred yards more, and the accident might have put them in the water.

Where depth and darkness could clutch at you like claws.

He shuddered, and hobbled over to the gondolier.

"Is that gun loaded, Willie?" Solomon asked, shaking the boy, rousing him. The dull, throbbing pain in his own head subsided at the prospect of new danger.

A gibbering sound rose from the woods, and the waters of the lake opened to swallow the gondola.

Willie blinked numbly, rubbed his eyes.

"You're at Arcady, son," Solomon informed him. "At my home. Is the gun loaded?"

"I'll load it again, sir. But surely we're safe on the grounds of your estate."

"Would that it were the case, Willie," Solomon replied, dusting the grass and the sand of the last, gutted ballast bag from his greatcoat. He pushed his wind-battered tricorn safely back upon his head. "But I've a letter from my aunt that claims otherwise. Did you not see the faun in the woods? The Borders are here, boy. The grounds are . . . well, *unstable*. Ruffled, as they say. Perhaps our dangers are only beginning."

The Borders, he heard Willie whisper, as he turned toward the house.

The pale light on the grass faded and dappled, as if clouds were passing across the face of the moon. Solomon looked up, into the silvered eye of the heavens.

Which was changing as he watched, halving itself out of fullness into a half moon, halving itself once more to a quarter, then waning toward crescent and beyond that toward the simple, unalterable dark of the moon's newness.

Five steps across the grass of the yard had taken a month in the heavens.

Behind him, Willie swore softly to Saint Milton. Who traveled through Chaos.

The pistol clicked when the boy cocked it.

As the muddy globe of the balloon deflated on the water, Willie and Solomon started over the long yard toward the house. A strange, stifled outcry rose from the orchard, answered by a softer cry from somewhere along the far, veiled western walls of the house.

The air was ripe with the dark smell of rotten fruit, of something also decaying beneath the decay. Solomon clutched his walking stick more tightly at the sound, and Willie reached to the inside pocket of his waistcoat, where the pistol rested, reloaded and ready.

Above them the moon continued to change, the clouds scudding across its damaged, shifting face.

The ordered, even manicured landscape that had greeted Solomon when he last visited five years ago had vanished almost entirely, as veiled as the contours of the earlier house. Now the orchards surrounding the grounds of the estate sagged with new life and with brown moss and with overgrowth. The rich, neglected burden of apples and peaches dragged the lowest branches almost to the ground.

The house itself was twice the size he remembered. It had taken on a new and unruly shape. Two new wings stretched off to the north and the east, the fresh brick glistening next to the worn, rounded masonry of the original mansion.

Moonlit, the house and the outbuildings were eerie, almost sepulchral. Over the grounds of the estate Solomon and Willie waded, the shadows gliding around them, shifting, turning, and growing along with the phases of the moon. On the narrow dirt pathway that circled his grandfather's pond, Solomon stopped, removed his cap. With a thin, almost ghostly hand, he brushed back his hair.

"It is here. It must be."

"What's here, Father?" the boy asked, drawing the pistol, blue and deadly, from its nest in his coat.

Solomon peered at the labyrinth of new buildings. "I could have sworn the main entrance . . ."

"Don't say that, Father. Don't tell me you can't find the way into your own . . ."

"Hush, Willie."

Solomon raised his staff at the sound rising from the orchard, the whimper of something wounded, something large brushing against the heavy branches of the peach tree. The liquid sound of ripe fruit dropping.

And then it appeared, as though it arose from the ground or took form from the fog, the night, the mist . . .

Hawken Gate. The ancestral entrance. The flagstone threshold, the iron bars, and the crest.

The full-winged hawk, red sun at his back.

That, at least, had not changed. Nor the enormous, nearly unnecessary locks, into which the two keys at his belt fit with a grating, rusty sound. And the shriek of old hinges when the gates opened. With a deep breath, Willie followed Solomon into the inner yard of the estate, and together they turned, set their shoulders to the heavy iron bars, and closed the heavy thing behind them.

Now they stood where the sphinxes walked.

The monsters had patrolled these grounds for ages, learning to live along with the family, according to the agreement set down between old Atreus Hawken and Ceraphis, the great foremother of the sphinxes. Most of the time, the creatures were dormant, mistaken for statues at the far boundaries of the estate.

But when the Borders encroached . . .

"Willie," Solomon whispered, "if we chance upon a sphinx in our path to the doors of the manor house, I shall have to ask that you wash from your memory all that is said and done. Or if you cannot help but remember, I must beg of you not to tell anyone."

Willie nodded. It was as good as a pledge.

Together they crossed the yard, the moon above them shifting and reeling from quarter to new and then beginning to wax again. The grass waved westward at the crest of a low breeze off the narrow, rechanneled river.

Solomon loosened his scarf in the warmth of the night . . .

And noticed that the walls had shifted, permitting no entry now.

He must not panic. Nor show his fear to Willie, who walked as a rearguard, scanning the gate and the adjoining gardens for creatures hidden in the vines and the unkempt taxus, the yew, arborvitae, beech, and hornbeam.

Something stirred amid the deep complexity of branches and leaves. Something more than the wind.

"Father Solomon . . ."

"I know, Willie. By all the saints, do not look upon it but keep your eyes upon the house. There was always a door here upon this wall. There must be one yet, of that I am . . . reasonably . . ."

"Reasonably! Begging your pardon, Father, but 'tis hardly the time for 'reasonably' with some monstrosity lurking in the leafage!"

Willie's face was clenched.

Solomon put on a mask of courage.

"Which is why it would be most circumspect to bring forth that pistol once more, Willie, if you'd be so kind."

Willie fumbled with the weapon.

"Now steady the gun, Willie," Solomon urged, "and look not too intently in the direction of that noise, if you please. For if it's a sphinx, she will return your eyesight to you entangled and charmed, so you fancy her beauty and wait for her . . . *embrace*."

Willie swallowed nervously.

Solomon heard the firm metallic click of the pistol hammer from within the folds of the gondolier's jacket.

And now, if only out of the glow of these red walls in moonlight an entrance would appear.

Somewhere . . .

Solomon beckoned to the lad, and moved rapidly toward the tall rectangular wing, toward a shadowy place in its wall where Solomon remembered—or imagined he remembered—a door.

The wind behind them switched, carrying upon it the smell of something sharp and bloody through the sweet bouquet of the peaches, the sound of a quick, rushing movement as something broke from the grove in pursuit.

The sphinx was attacking.

Solomon pulled a dazed Willie toward the south corner of the walls, where he thought he remembered . . .

. . . as the sound closed in . . .

. . . and he thought *This must be* and *this has to be, oh let it let it* . . .

. . . but still nothing but brick. Behind him now, a growl. The snap of dried branches. He pushed Willie ahead of him, turned, began the chant before he saw her . . .

And she was beautiful, as they always were, the face and the breasts of a girl as pale as the walls behind him, pale as the moon. His voice little more than a whisper, he began . . .

"Although a subtler Sphinx renew
Riddles of death Thebes never knew . . ."

and at once he was lost in the words and the wonder, for she smiled, she slowed and began to walk toward him, her white breasts marbled in shadow and moon and shadow, her eyes dark and engulfing.

And sure in language strange she said, *I love thee true . . .*

Willie tugged at Solomon's arm, his whisper rude and vexing, disturbing this night perfumed and melodious and lunar . . .

"Father? Father Solomon? There's a door over yonder. Quickly, sir, by the saints and elementals!"

Solomon turned. The thwarted sphinx growled and whimpered, and together the two men walked through the door into a deeper, vaulted blackness.

Behind them, long claws scraped against the locked door.

Solomon leaned against the dark paneling and gathered his breath. Slowly, his eyes adjusted to the gloom, and looking about, he took stock of the front hall of Arcady.

It was still the home of his childhood. The air was calm and dim, smelling of wax and of cedar. When Willie lit the lamp at the door, the watery, metallic smell of oil mingled with an older, more quiet mustiness, as if memory needed fire to kindle.

The long hall was more than it might seem to the lad. That much Solomon knew. His memory breathed what was or might have once been into the high paneled corridor, broken by shadow and light and shadow.

The stairwell midway down the hall Father had called the Stairwell of Dreams, out of which Great-Great-Aunt Kassandra saw old Atreus' skeleton rise, and from the top of which Solomon's dear Aunt Morgana first saw the angels.

The hall itself, in which Solomon now stood, was the room he remembered from thirty years ago, not the brighter, diminished corridor, cluttered with chandeliers and tables, it seemed when last he visited.

Solomon leaned against the stained mahogany paneling. Someone or something in the house was restoring the rooms to the way they had looked in an older time, returning the lamps, the swords and antique pistols. Even the oil portrait of Great-Great-Uncle Innocent scowled out into the shadowy hall—the very painting that Father had turned face to the wall not long before Solomon had left for seminary.

Now his disreputable ancestor glared down at him from his place above the cabriolet and drop-leaf table reserved for callers and their cards. It was as though Innocent supervised the whole restoration.

Shadows hovered over the tarnished frame. From the frown in the portrait, you could not tell whether Innocent approved or disapproved.

Solomon hoped it was Morgana who had effected these changes. Though deep down he knew she would never touch this room, much less recover the way it looked when she first went away to that priory high in the eastern mountains.

Yes, deep down he knew that something in the encroaching Border had . . . untethered the house. Though for what purpose it was impossible to tell.

He turned to Willie, started to speak . . .

It was then that Solomon's mother glided down from the top of the stairs, as feathery and fragrant and young as she was when he first remembered standing at the end of this hall, reciting his first memorized passages of a Hymn for her great and encouraging delight.

She could not fade, despite the evidence of time and of what he had heard.

Surely he had dreamed her death, the long trip home from Lambeth, her funeral in the family plot—was it five years already?

Forever will I love, and she be fair.

Solomon stepped forward. "And by came an angel," he began, and lost himself in the first verse he had recited for her, almost forty years ago:

> "And by came an angel who had a bright key,
> And he open'd the coffins & set them all free
> Then down a great plain, leaping, laughing they run,
> And wash in a river, and shine in the Sun . . ."

"What is that, sir, at the end of the passage?" Willie asked nervously, raising his pistol. Firmly Solomon grasped the lad's wrist, he lowered the gun, and about her business his mother went, lighting lamps and gliding through the entrance to the Great Hall off the foot of the stairs.

Breathless, Solomon followed her. Through the open arch, he watched her drift among candles, covering the dozen mirrors of the Great Hall with dark cloth.

Someone in this place has died.

"I think you'd better stand back, sir."

"Nonsense, Willie," Solomon whispered, and raced toward his mother, his arms open. She turned to him and smiled.

For a moment he saw light through the full sheer sleeves of her blouse, and then no light as forward he leaned, stretching forth to touch her hand, her hand soft and remembered and motherly . . .

Through which his own hand passed, as somewhere behind him Willie cried out.

CHAPTER 3

Five times the balloon seemed to pass over the Lady's Land. Seemed.

Emanations, they called them. Border ruffles. The doubling and distorting and refracting of the things that brush against the lip of the Borders. Afterimages only, like the shadows over the eye when you have gazed too long into light.

Diego knew from the first time the gondola passed over his milling soldiers that he would see it again and perhaps again.

After all, he had entered the Borders that morning.

Near dawn, at the head of two companies—six hundred infantry and threescore cavalry, all red-jacketed and bannered, well armed and ill trained—Captain Diego Hawken of the Citizens' Guard had marched into the labyrinth of Alphside Forest, the woods that marked the southernmost margins of Urthona, where in the fortnight past the Borders had encroached on the evergreen and red poplar.

Where the Lady herself held court in mystery and nodding leaves.

The Guard were in search of bordermetal, escort to a dozen of Arouet's miners as the skilled technicians combed the disrupted landscape, salvaging a handful of wire and a strange rusted casing that reminded Diego of a giant's helmet.

The Alphside was perilous country even when it rested safely in the Presences—those lands untouched by the Borders and their peculiar magic. He lost two men by late in the morning—one to drowning, one to a beast of some kind. . . .

He lost the third that afternoon, under stranger circumstances.

On foot, at the head of a green squadron of dragoons, Diego felt the air tense and crackle over his face—the sure sign that a man had passed into the Borders.

He shouted to his troops, to his nephew Garrick, and to his second in command, Actaeon Peacock. Told them to be mindful, to watch for more than rebels. Being mindful himself, he ordered one lad up a tree for reconnaissance.

And the boy simply vanished. One moment his red-trousered ass slipped into the middle branches of a bright-leaved poplar. And then he was gone. Disappeared into a tangle of limb and leaf and overcast sky.

They found the poor boy's cap nestled in the fork of two branches, a white film of ash spread over the black wood. Diego blustered and stomped, cursed the woods and the Borders and the Lady . . .

Then the balloon passed over for the first and actual time.

The startled troops fired and fired again. Only Diego's shouting and threats, his brandished sword and his brace of strong-armed lieutenants, prevented the fools from firing a desperate third volley into the ponderous craft, coasting under the rising moon like a damned silk eclipse.

Diego saw the greatcoat and tricorn, even from a long smoky distance. Could imagine the hooked nose, the dry skin, and the bright emerald eyes of his older brother.

Now, an hour after that first passage, Diego tilted in the saddle and surveyed the leaden sky for the craft's return.

Oh, it would return, all right. Or at least the image of it. The Borders were as widespread, as omnipresent, as the rebels, and the Borders were a country of emanations, of mirrors.

No wonder the guardsmen were nervous.

Dull-witted, jug-eared farmboys from northern Urizen, their powder wet and their guns muddied, they combed the forest in search of an ambush, imagining rebels in trees, Blights in bushes.

Gap-toothed, gaping, some of them cross-eyed. Not one of them with even a remote idea.

They carried those blightlocks on their belts like battle trophies—long, matted strands of hair they had scavenged from the Borders, as they skirted the silvery glowing eye of the Absence, awaiting whatever it might spew forth.

And spew forth it did. Hunks of twisted metal, broken prows of ships. Sometimes an absence stone—the clear red rocks that occasionally adorned the necks and ears of the generals' wives like rubies, but more often were worthless, housing long-dead insects or animalcules, encased and preserved as though they were frozen in amber.

Sometimes the brilliant, whirling eye of the Absence would disgorge a Blight. Stunned and disoriented, or more likely dead. Easy pickings for men with long knives and short scruples.

And the Citizen countenanced such things.

In long decrees from his palace in the west, in the gallery two thousand feet long, filled with the various apparatus of mathematics and natural philosophy, Citizen Arouet, ruler of three nations, gave license to throat-cut boys at the edge of disheveled woods.

Slaughter in the name of science and mining.

She wouldn't have such a sort in *her* army, so they were Arouet's by default, Diego's by order.

His personal escort a band of hyenas.

Such were the dark thoughts attending the Captain until midafternoon, when the dryad came back.

She moved silently, difficult to notice. Diego saw the bole of the willow shift and blur before the tree took on flesh, took on the shapely form of a young woman.

It was as though willows did such things naturally.

The boys gaped and stammered and fell over themselves. The dryads were breathtaking—dark-skinned and silver-eyed—and the stories that they seduced wanderers and imprisoned them in hollow trees were always believable when you saw one.

The girl trained her glittering glance on the Captain himself. Diego coughed, blushed, and looked away.

"Don't trust 'em, Garrick," he muttered to his nephew. "They're sly and . . . and inveigling. And most always on the rebels' side."

Garrick glanced at the dryad and blushed as well.

"Not this one, sir," Lieutenant Peacock observed.

Diego snorted. "Gaze too long in her eyes, Actaeon, and you'll *canonize* her."

"No, sir," the lieutenant insisted. "This one came to us out of the trees, claiming she's seen Artemis bivouacked near the banks of the Alph. Says she could show us a back trail. Promises an ambush and a bloodless harvest of rebels."

"Too good," Diego maintained. "Too promising. There's more mazes to a dryad's assurance than even those woods can hold. And yet . . ."

Now he turned to the girl. Nodded, bowed crisply. Locked her in his most military, level gaze.

The dryad bowed in response.

Diego smiled. "And yet she's all we have to go on," he said, his voice as unruffled as though he spoke of the wind or the weather. The dryad, though she listened alertly, would hear no uncertainty in his inflections.

"Well. Let's hear her plan, Actaeon."

Lieutenant Peacock translated as the girl gave the rebel whereabouts quietly. Her language was the rustling of leaves, was birdsong, all clicks and whistles and dry stirrings. Diego kept his eyes politely on the dryad all the time.

You are never supposed to look at the translator.

But it was hard to look the girl's way and . . . remain a gentleman. A pretty thing she was, though outlandish. Her hair was white and her skin as brown as polished butternut. Her eyes glittered like dimes.

Diego's horse stirred nervously, skittish next to the smell of lilac and greenery and decaying leaves.

"She says, Captain," Peacock interpreted, "that there are 'groves of them, many on manys.' That's what she says, sir. Could mean anything from twenty to a thousand, seeing as dryads only count to ten."

"Ask her how many campsites, Actaeon."

"Beg pardon, sir?"

"Ask her how many damn fires," Diego rephrased impatiently, smiling and keeping his eyes on the dryad as more of the strange, sighing language passed between her and the lieutenant. "These pretty little monsters hate fires. They'll count 'em to the number."

"Four, she says, sir," Actaeon relayed.

Diego looked into her eyes for deception or truth, and found only something impervious and plantlike, impossible to read.

So. She was either lying or not lying.

"That'd mean about a hundred of them, Captain?" Actaeon ventured.

"Maybe two hundred," Diego guessed, drawing his eyes from the girl. "Rebels are as sparing with fires as they are with everything else."

Peacock nodded somberly at the dryad, who, her interview over, stepped back and was lost, suddenly and disturbingly, among the trees. A faint whiff of lilac remained in her passing.

"By the mustered saints, Garrick," Diego whispered. "Did you notice the legs on her?"

"I'm not a boy anymore, Uncle," Garrick replied, his gray eyes flickering to the spot where the dryad had vanished. "Legs like that don't usually walk with the truth."

"Still, it's half a chance to collar my cousin," Diego reckoned, drawing forth his spyglass. "As long as it's no more than two hundred rebels, and as long as we have surprise on our side, I expect we can take them. Actaeon, assemble the men. You will do nothing without my orders. Understand?"

As always, Actaeon understood.

Swiftly, in less than an hour, the guardsmen closed in on the reported campsite, muskets at the ready and among them the rising disquiet of green troops on the edge of battle. Less than a mile from the encampment, many of the men discarded dice and flask, reverently placing copies of the Text in breast pockets. Not from religion: there was a superstitious rumor that the Text drew and stopped bullets.

On foot, swiveling on his artificial leg, Diego directed the guardsmen into wings, into flanks. Now they stepped more softly, more slowly—heavily, as if they were walking underwater. The faint whiff of woodsmoke laced the air, and no bird sang.

The rebel fires, Diego thought. Artemis is mine.

Then, at the edge of ambush, the first emanation passed over.

It caught Diego entirely by surprise. The image of the balloon floating slowly overhead, the same greatcoat and tricorn passing silently on a silent wind . . .

Casting no shadow this time, for emanations cannot block the light . . .

And before Diego could call down the line to hold fire, the troops were at it, those big river lads too simple to be priests or merchants or farmers—too simple to be rebels. Those lads, their commanders—the whole damned Citizens' Guard—erupting with shouts and curses and shooting. Instantly the air was thick again with smoke and the smell of powder. The translucent balloon coasted serenely over them, trailing iridescent sand, its pilot and passenger glowing, winged like angels. Suddenly, the whole apparition vanished in a flock of rousted doves and an infernal humming that set the boys to aiming their guns about them, expecting the saints knew what monstrosities.

An immense, stupid silence filled the forest.

The guardsmen gaped at each other, and in rage, knowing his quarry had escaped, was escaping, Diego roared and lit into the nearest squadron of his men.

He felled two of them with the flat of his sword, one with a swipe of his spyglass, and the rest of them fled him like dried leaves before a whirling wind. All the flailing and windmilling almost spun Diego over, damn his wooden leg, and still, when the third trooper toppled senseless to the ground, put under by metal and optics, his ill-kept rifle went off into the branches of a beech tree, scattering birds and another squadron of supposedly stout-hearted men, who rushed off into the forest screaming, guns blazing.

Nobody could take an order in this damned army.

Nobody could take a punch either.

The next thing Diego knew, he was back in the saddle, astraddle unruly old Juno, whipping the mare to a full gallop toward still another squadron, which had set up under a stand of juniper and needle pine. The boys there had already launched into a regular brainless routine—five of them firing at the illusory balloon while the other five reloaded.

Young Garrick Hawken followed behind his uncle Diego, holding his breath when the Captain rode straight into the line of fire and set boot to the side of the sergeant's head. Boot and leverage and sound wooden leg . . .

. . . the leg none of them had the salt to mention . . .

. . . hit home, and the sergeant . . . broke ranks in a heap on the needled ground.

Booted and disciplined, the company grew silent. For the first time they began to pay attention, perhaps because Diego was the only officer left standing. In the lull, he struck one more boy—this time with the back of his hand—and dismounted slowly, as gracefully as he could atop his newel post of a leg. Standing in the shade and the clouds of powder smoke, he addressed his nephew.

" 'Twas your least favorite uncle, Solomon, in that airbag, Garrick. On that I'd wager. Acoast to the house, he was, at Morgana's bidding. Saw him through my opera glass, leaning over the gondola in a greatcoat and a shambles of wicker."

Garrick masked a smile. His uncle always sounded more colorful in the field.

Diego tossed the broken telescope to Garrick. Now he drew his pistol, brandished it at a flinching, quivering private. The woods around the soldiers were silent once more. Nearby a cardinal, encouraged by the lull, offered up its joyful, chipping cry, then thought better of it. Diego wheeled and fired the gun in the direction of the solitary birdsong.

The bullet clattered uselessly through the trees, as it always did with the Captain and pistols. In frustration, Diego sent his sword hurtling after it, end over end, the sharp blade flickering with green forest light.

Several of the men, Garrick included, stifled laughter.

For a terrible moment Diego reeled and tottered, leaning precariously over the whirling, leaf-strewn ground. Then he recovered balance and dignity.

"Such, of course, were my orders, Garrick," he boomed, as the armed men around him cowered, whimpered, pulled their hats over their eyes. "I *wanted* these boys to shoot at each other. To waste government ammunition and give a map of our whereabouts to *her*, or to any rebel within earshot."

The guardsmen bowed their heads in unison, scolded in a swarm there together. A solitary, fat corporal broke ranks and waddled into the woods, in search of the Captain's sword.

But Diego was not done with them.

"Reload my pistol, Garrick. Since these fools have betrayed our position with gunfire and noise, what difference will one more shot make? I'll kill one as an example to the others. Show them how to use a firearm at close range."

Garrick loaded the weapon, handed it back to his uncle. The private in front of Diego fell to the ground. He was an aristocratic boy named Peter Bell, a complainer and straggler who suffered a perpetual and messy head cold.

Diego cocked the pistol and aimed it at the groveling lad, pressing the barrel against the boy's temple.

At this range even the Captain would not miss.

Bell whimpered and sniffed, began a prayer to Saint Milton, forgot the words. Garrick sat silently in the saddle, waiting for his uncle's mock rage to settle, knowing that the tongue-lashing and the threats and the drama were almost over.

Diego smoldered in his best fierce silence, looming over the boy. His mustache and long black locks knotted and tangled with evergreen and bramble, the Captain looked like a vengeful forest spirit, fit consort for the dryads who vexed him.

Some of the men backed away, still afraid the commander might make good his threat, follow up the performance with an execution. In the hush, the cardinal began its song again, the high crisp sound of a jeweler's hammer.

Diego lowered the pistol. He stumbled, whirled, and kicked at the root of a smoke maple. The sound of wood against wood echoed about the clearing. Diego reeled, but nobody noticed or let on that they'd noticed.

Except for Garrick. He started for his uncle, then held himself back.

Diego glared at the boy. Slowly, his gaze softened. He smiled and brushed pine needles from his hair.

Good boy, this Garrick.

The best thing about Brother Endymion is his children.

Eventually this one will learn.

Through the lines a murmur rose, as baffled skirmishers returned, breasting the bramble and high undergrowth, flintlocks raised and red jackets tattered.

The rebel camp was empty. The fires were cold.

Had the guardsmen moved with the stealth of foxes, they still would have found nothing.

Diego glowered in silence. Artemis had . . . a nose for metal and powder, as Major Werther used to say. Knew when to cross swords, when to strike out of darkness and nowhere. When to steal away.

Yes, Cousin Artemis had a gift for it all.

It was as though she rode out of the heart of an Absence.

There were stories, up in Urthona and as far south as the Alph, about Artemis Hawken, the Lady, the queen of the guerrillas. That the birds told her of the movement of troops. That where there were no birds, the winds told her. Stories most popular here in the farmland north of Arcady, which people had renamed "the Lady's Land."

They called it that to Diego's face.

He knew the stories were false. Or if not false, embroidered from a thread of fact into some kind of rural myth.

For Diego knew his cousin well. Perhaps better than anyone knew her.

It had been bad enough when the two of them were young. Diego had been a strapping, stocky boy nearly three years her elder. Yet Artemis beat him in every contest of resourcefulness and agility, and even of strength, for she used her smaller size and weight more intelligently.

Bruised, humiliated, young Diego had found himself calling her constantly to tests of simple physical courage—of foolhardiness. "Who will jump off that cliff?" or "Who will stand at the edge of the fire?"

He would ask, and Artemis would back down out of good sense, and at last, in the haylofts of the estate, he won.

Far later, Diego realized that the dangers she saw readily and clearly never occurred to him. But he had learned that he could balance his strength and sheer courage against her agility and ingenuity, and that sometimes the scales would tip in his heedless direction.

Strength and courage. They were what he brought to this labyrinthine world. And though Diego Hawken was far from a fool, sometimes strength and courage were not enough, as his thoughts would entangle in the complications of things.

Even today, in the backwater of the Lady's Land, foolish courage had set victory within his grasp. And damned stupidity had let it slip away.

Now the balloon was gone, and the emanation and the rebels, and even the smoke had cleared. Diego looked about for higher ground. He found a low rise in the rocky landscape, dotted with evergreens, steep and treacherous despite its modest height. It overlooked the Alph and the rebels' best avenues of escape.

As quickly as he could manage, the Captain limped toward the bluff. The guardsmen parted before him as easily and as fearfully as they would before a charging band of rebels. Garrick started to speak, then thought better of it and fell in sheepishly behind his uncle.

Diego reached the rise and began to climb, the wooden leg sliding back dangerously over the tumbling gravel and the steep incline, as though he walked on stilts.

Garrick's warning blurted out before the boy could call back the words.

"Look out, sir, for . . ."

Diego paused midway up the bluff, gripping the rocks.

"Look out for what, Nephew?" he asked coldly.

Garrick stepped back, reconsidered.

"For . . . snipers, sir. The high rocks call them, draw fire like . . . like the gondola of a balloon."

Diego turned back to his climbing. Garrick sighed heavily, sat in the rubble at the base of the bluff.

Using his strong upper body, Diego pulled himself to the top of the rise. Climbing through juniper and taxus, through nettling webs of low cedar, he lost Garrick and the rest below him, under the screen of trees and the last of the powder smoke.

From this height he could see southward to where the banks of the Alph were shrouded in mist and riddles. To his left lay a torn and rocky landscape where the Borders had dwelt for years, for the Borders settle on no country without cost. It stretched, gray and barren, to the edge of the Absence, where the air flickered and swirled, and where all sorts of strangeness lived in the metal forests.

To his right, in country freshly covered by the same Borders, spread a green ocean of branches and leaves and needles that glistened dark under the red of the departing sun.

Impenetrable. The Lady's Land.

It would be night soon, and in the night all hopes of capturing Artemis would fail again as they had on a hundred nights before. Downriver to the west it would be impossible to find even the clumsiest rebel. There the river wound among the trees and the underbrush for miles before it emerged in the clear, sloping lands at the borders of Tharmas. If Artemis was that far away, she was past capture: the best search would turn up nothing.

It wasn't much better up the river, in the rock and metal. There the land took the shape of an opium dream and monsters walked. Diego had been there before, had been to the very edge of the Absence itself. But the situation was more complicated, the way much more treacherous, when you rode at the head of a column of debutantes, recruits, and tyros.

These boys believed that the Borders were rebel country by nature. That the rebels invented the Borders.

Whatever the truth, Diego's last hope of finding his cousin, his rival, was the freak accident, the unlikely delay. Maybe Artemis was still in the Levels directly below him—the riverland pastures of southern Urthona. Where the woods gave way to farmlands and the flowing Alph itself, there was usually a league or so of level ground, peaceful and arable, often parceled out to tenant farmers.

Part of the Lady's Land now. Diego could count on his fingers the tenant farmers who would stand by the government. The Levels were filled with sharp eyes and sharp ears, with the toughest and most honest and most clever of rustics . . .

Whose sons filled the ranks of the rebel armies. If he searched for Artemis in the Levels, he would receive no help in finding her.

Diego sat down, extending the wooden leg in front of him. It looked as if it was attached to someone else.

The mists of evening continued to rise. Below him Garrick was calling, in concern for his whereabouts and well-being, sounding despite good intentions like a fretful, worried old nurse. The rest of the voices—those of the uncertain guardsmen—mingled together like the murmur from a distant beehive.

Then the sounds seemed to fade suddenly, as something moved in the western woods.

There in the deepening evergreen was something—a flicker of light on metal, perhaps, or upon the curried flank of a horse. From this distance he could not tell. He stood for a better view, but lost the weaving light somewhere in the greenery and the rising mist of evening.

Still, the trees were moving, more distinctly and violently than if the wind alone were moving them.

If it was Artemis, she was not too far away to collar.

He turned, started to descend and muster the guardsmen.

Then, this time to the east of him, something rippled in the fog descending on the Borders. A series of lights, like signal fires, flared briefly in a line from the riverbank to a mile or so north, where it was lost in the mist. There was something processional about that column, as if the dead themselves were marching.

Diego shook his head. There could be anything out there, he figured, reining his thoughts away from death, from the abyss. Rebels, Citizens' Guard, Blight or centaur or some monstrosity working its way to the water.

There it was again: a flicker, a distant flame. All that monstrosity and procession—a winding light at the edge of his vision.

The whole thing could be swamp gas for that matter.

Slowly and painfully, Diego seated himself again. Above, a loud flock of starlings circled, banked, and fluttered off with a cry and a whistle.

He considered his strategies, and once again came up empty.

Thinking itself was bad for the balance.

Diego clutched his head. Muttered an oath that, had they heard it, would have scattered his own troops in embarrassment and dismay.

It was humiliating to feel so stupid, to be duped and cozened and wild-goose-chased to the point that your own imaginings turned against you, inventing your enemies out of mists and refracted light.

The forest was a labyrinth of mirrors, and nothing lay at the heart of the maze.

Diego shuddered. He felt rudderless, without compass or sextant in a cloudy country.

CHAPTER 4

But despite his feelings, Diego Hawken had to do—*would* do—the brash and heroic.

As he sat atop the bluff, the turn and bustle subsided amid the nearby trees. It was as though something—the Lady's passing column, no doubt, or a sudden trick of wind along the forest floor—had set the maples and poplars twisting, then died away or burrowed into the dark, cavernous limestone beneath the woods . . .

Emerging a mile upriver.

Diego shielded his eyes. There, out in the Presences, in a notch of oak just north of the edged ruins of Ley Station, the heavy, unnatural movement of branch and dried leaves had begun again.

Something was moving away from him rapidly.

Descending from the high ground, skidding against mud and gravel, wrestling himself back atop Juno with grumbles and trumpeting oaths, he marshaled his cavalry—converting Peacock and a reluctant Garrick to horsemen—and hastened west, toward the juncture of forest and river, where the blood-colored leaves thinned and vanished into the sloping pastures north of the Alph.

The column, two riders abreast, wound through the forest paths, passing a stand of bordermetal that groped like a spidery green hand into greener shadows. Diego rode at the head of the column, black cloak covering the government-issue red of his officer's jacket, his long, brambled hair tied underneath a black, wide-brimmed fedora.

He looked like a traveling priest. Like an undertaker.

Behind him, the riders filed nervously, jackets scarlet in the dappled green of the woods. Threescore popinjays, Diego thought. The Citizen's best, the brightest of moving targets.

This was not the East, where the war had begun over bordermetal, the long sunny days of Diego's childhood clouded with the first rumors of its outbreak, of the initial skirmishes in Luvah and the far-flung Hannock River. There, where Citizen Arouet had sent forth the first of the miners, their orders to gather the supple, durable metal littered like driftwood along the ravaged edges of the Absences.

If that had been all—the scavenging of a handful of government hirelings—it would not have come to war. Not then. Not ever.

Diego tugged at the fedora, drawing it more tightly down over his ears.

It was when they started to dig that the trouble began. It was innocent enough—excavation, surface mining—but a fanatical band of ruralists had objected.

They had started it all. *They* had petitioned, claiming that the Citizen intended to turn their green and pleasant land into a desert—into the desolation that you found at the very brink of the Absences, where the silvery clouds ebbed and flowed like withering tides.

Arouet had not listened. He had not bothered with them. So the rebels clamored, then ambushed the miners in their appointed duties.

Then the Citizen had paid them mind. Then he mustered the Guard—a functionary army to protect his functionaries—and ambush had turned to raid, to retaliation, to skirmish and battle, all the while the rebels fighting like zealots, like lunatics, claiming that the Citizen had

> form'd the Serpent
> Of precious stones & gold, turn'd poisons on the sultry wastes.

Diego sniffed disgustedly. It was what he mistrusted about the Text: every madman could make it read what he damn well pleased.

But the war in the East. That soon became clear-cut, unambiguous. Important folk flocked to the side of the government, to the side of the rebels. They mustered armies, fought intelligible battles on gentle sloping plains, on farmlands and plantations clear and forgiving, where you could see the enemy for miles barring night and a low fog.

Where you could even skirt the battle if you'd a mind to.

Why, the East had been almost a lark.

Diego's service on the Luvan borders in the ranks of the Citizens' Cavalry had been nothing short of valiant. Wounded six times in pitched battle, decorated by Citizen Arouet himself, Diego had seemed charmed despite his injuries, destined for high field command.

Then Nightshade Vale, and the maiming.

The Guard wanted no *imperfect officers.* And so Diego was reassigned west and home, to fruitless patrols in partisan country, leaving the Vale behind him in rueful memory.

The dream was over, far from the rebellion's great battlefields.

Sobered by recollection, Diego drew a cheroot from the folds of his cloak. He cupped his hands, mantled over the dark cigar, and struck a damp lucifer once, twice, a third time against the rough red broadcloth of his trousers. Muttering a mild oath, he stood in the saddle, his troops steering softly by, like water breaking over a rock in midriver. A sergeant—a man named Thaddeus Bacon—extended a small flame, but even that extinguished when it touched the damp end of the cigar.

Diego swore, this time more gaudily. He clenched the tobacco in his teeth and spat, reining Juno into the rear of the column.

Trailing sixty redjackets at midmorning. Nothing apparent within ten yards of the forest trail. All of Urthona like a maze of foliage. The rebels could close to intimate quarters without his knowing.

Could sneak up close enough to batter the whole damned column with shovels.

No, this was not the definite East, where the battles were clearly won and lost, and the enemy faced you over long pastures. This was a land of apparitions, of dryadic mazes.

This was war at its most uncertain—deadly, unreadable country.

Muttering, Diego reined his mare onto the widening trail. Out into the Presences the column rode, the strange surface tension at the edge of the Borders spangling the air with swirls, with reflected light.

Diego bowed his head, shielded his eyes. The Crossing was always unpleasant, going in or coming out.

Like a membrane, like a stretched and gauzy veil, the Border tightened, crackled, and finally broke over him as he and the horsemen passed out of the woods and into the Presences.

Sloping land. Natural land. Red clay and gravel. The forbidding farmlands north of the Station, just north of the river itself, where generations of dirt farmers scrabbled a livelihood in the river's embrace.

"Spread out," Diego ordered softly.

Thaddeus Bacon nodded, and motioned to three of the troopers. The men dismounted at once, handing the reins of their horses to Garrick, seated unsteadily on his unfamiliar sorrel. With Bacon in the lead, they waded up a rise, clambering like squirrels until they rested on a gray knoll dotted with hayricks and a broken harrow protruding from the hard earth like bordermetal.

Still no sign of rebels. No sound, no imprint in the dry grass. And yet . . .

"Where are the larks?" Diego asked, his eyes on Garrick, then beyond. He scanned the rise ahead of Bacon, the slope down toward the riverbank, where Actaeon Peacock now led two other dismounted troopers. "No song. No birds taking wing. Not even a jarfly's rattle."

"What do you make of it, sir?" Garrick asked, steadying Bacon's old mare with an uncertain tug on her reins.

"Somebody's passed through not half an hour before us," Diego replied, chewing the cigar thoughtfully. "A numerous somebody. Or that's what it generally means. Who can tell?"

Bacon stood and waved on the rise. For a moment in the clouded sunlight, he looked like a wraith, like a scarecrow caught in a switching wind.

We may be back in the Presences, Garrick thought, leading the horses toward the knoll and their riders as the company remounted and rode to join them. But it's strange as any Border after an army passes through.

As they weaved through the ricks on the bare knoll, the rumble of thunder approached them out of the west. Far away, where the Alph bent into a black horizon, storm clouds tumbled and boiled. Hiding in the depths of their jackets, beneath cap and quickly produced greatcoats and gum blankets, the column approached the little village Bacon had spotted from his vantage point atop the broken harrow.

Squat houses lay bunched around a circle in the dirt road, the lamps of early morning still glowing in their windows. They were little more than huts—plank houses and dugouts, smoke flaps rather than chimneys. A dark child, whether boy or girl Diego could not tell from this distance and in this light, scurried from one door to another, rattled a latch, was taken in.

Diego approached cautiously, his escort only Peacock and Garrick.

The three rode over the graveled, dusty circle, to the doorstep of the house into which the child had vanished.

Peacock called out. Once. Twice.

An old woman peeked through the open window by the door, her face unreadable as water, her eyes flat and gray as slate.

"Trouble you a moment, ma'am?" Diego asked, adopting the term of respect for an unknown older woman in these parts. She would know he was from around here.

He brushed the brim of the hat back from his face.

The old woman was as silent as the fields by the knoll.

"Have you seen . . . any hostiles . . . *ma'am*?" Peacock asked, the honorific clumsy on his tongue, dishonest in his eastern accent.

"No," the old woman replied.

A long silence followed, as another sentence rustled silently through her thoughts.

" 'Less," she continued finally, "you consider *partisans* hostile."

Lieutenant Peacock winced at the country euphemism for *rebels*. Diego masked a smile, and Garrick chuckled behind him. In some things they were all the same, these river peasants. Baffling as an absence stone, but just as clear: all of them, without exception, stood firmly in the rebels' camp.

"So where is your boy posted, ma'am?" Diego asked softly, not unkindly. It was more than a hunch: all of these crones had sons, grandsons. He smiled at her then, his eyes darting all the while from house to house, from the stone rim of the village well to a hedgerow lining the road into town—dark green holly and taxus, a nest for a lurking sniper.

"West," the old woman replied finally. "Not that it helps you none. Clear to Tharmas, in the cavry themselves. Whitefield's Irregulars."

Diego leaned forward in the saddle, winked impishly at the pale face in the window. "Then you wouldn't be harmin' them to tell us . . . whether we run a risk of *partisans* by, say . . . followin' the river west."

"Wouldn't be helpin' 'em either," the old woman declared impassively. "And I'm inclined to help 'em."

Garrick chuckled again.

Diego stood unsteadily in the saddle, peered over the thatched roof of the cottage, over the green and a brace of gardens, a pigsty hard against a squat mud dwelling, and beyond these a makeshift smithy and livery at the westernmost end of town. The dirt road snaked around these farthest buildings, then sloped south toward the riverbanks, losing itself in a copse of young cedars.

Still no sign of Artemis. No sign of the passing rebels.

"I could have sworn . . ." Diego began, speaking softly, leaning toward Garrick. Then he noticed the brushmarks, thin and whorling, scoring the dirt with elaborate, parallel designs.

"Someone has swept the road," he muttered, suddenly alert.

Garrick frowned.

Diego's eyes followed the grooved dust, the twigs and dried leaves. Sure enough, the road had been smoothed by brooms and branches, the dirt grooved and manicured as it broke from the village circle and followed the road west out of town.

"Bacon!" the Captain called. The sergeant, waiting in the ranks at a distance, approached the cottage, a dozen horsemen following close behind.

"No! No!" Diego urged, waving his arm. "Bring the rest of them, dammit! We're not twenty minutes behind 'em!"

It was an old trick, older than the Wars of False Doctrine. Diego was astonished that he had not noticed it at once. If a cavalry unit keeps to the roads on a dry day, it takes no more than three troopers armed with branches, trailing the column and sweeping away hoofprint and wheel groove, to cover their path so that their pursuers, following only an hour behind them, may lose their trail altogether. It took discipline and road-savvy, swamp-smarts and order, but a skillful broom could brush three hundred riders from the memory of earth.

Especially when those riders followed the sly and insubstantial Lady.

Diego, however, did not stop to dwell on possibilities. At the head of his threescore troopers, he rode recklessly past the copse of cedar, guiding Juno skillfully over the narrow riverside path where horses could pass in single file only, then forking north to where the brushed road gave way to churned, damp dirt and the mists of approaching rain. He goaded his troopers, encouraging, guiding, until a dark, hovering cloud seemed to stand against the horizon like a deep mirage, green and wavering, receding ahead of him.

Artemis. The green of rebel cavalry.

Diego crouched in the saddle against the moist wind, calling back to Peacock, to Bacon, as the horses broke into a canter, then a gallop. Bacon pulled abreast of him, his cap discarded and his long, thin hair fluttering as they rode out of the mist and impending rain, into full sun and warmth and light and the rebels receding, a farther and farther green in the sunstruck west.

* * *

The sun was suddenly, intolerably bright, a space between the foretaste of rain and the rain itself. Heat rose off the road until the fences far ahead of them and the road itself seemed buried in water and light.

Border weather, Garrick thought sullenly. If you don't like the climate on the banks of the Alph, just wait an hour.

They had turned back at midday, giving up the chase when the rebel green vanished on the western horizon. They rested only an hour in the dried grass by the road, the smoke from a dozen small fires and the smell of the coffee still in the air amid the smell of powder and dust and honeysuckle.

Halfway back to the village, their horses slowed to a walk, Diego had sent his nephew up the column with Sergeant Bacon. Now Garrick rode near the front of the cavalry, raw in the midst of a dozen raw troopers. All of them rose in the stirrups and stretched uncomfortably, their backsides sore from a morning's hard ride.

"You've about got a purchase on that horse of yours, Hawken," Bacon conceded, his eyes flickering over the woods before them. "Better than most of these, though they have five years of riding on you. Must be the Hawken in you."

Garrick sniffed bitterly, thinking of his scholarly, distant father. "The principal Hawken in me," he grumbled, "has burden enough just keeping a pony beneath him and pointed in the right direction."

Bacon said nothing. What could he say?

Garrick regretted the harsh words instantly. He started to explain to the sergeant—explain that his father was more . . . speculative. More . . .

But then someone ahead of them, a young trooper at the very head of the line, called nervously down the column.

"Pickets!" he shouted, pointing toward the woods off to their left, where the foliage stirred and dark shapes weaved in the shadows.

The Citizen's prized cavalry sprang clumsily to life. Most of the boys around Garrick scrambled and tumbled off their horses. Two of them, wrestling the big animals over to where Garrick still sat stupidly atop his horse, handed the reins to him and scurried off into the high brown grass, crouching and falling and fumbling with their weapons.

Then the woods were blooming. White smoke sprouted from a line of trees to the left of the road. Garrick flinched at the sound of something like june beetles diving with a sudden *whick whick* around him, and then in their wake a sound like ice cracking on the distant branches.

The smoke weaved itself into the trees in fire and whiteness. Out of the high grass someone yelled, *Get offn that sorrel, yer damn fool!*

Then, with a surge of great power, one of the horses Garrick was holding jerked the reins from his hand and galloped off up the road as though it intended to arrive in the village before the sound of battle.

The smell of powder rushed over the guardsmen who had dismounted, as they returned fire into the woods. By this time Garrick understood the moment . . .

this is for real by the assembled saints someone is shooting at me . . .

And at the same moment, the old horse Nimrod beneath him must have drawn the same conclusion. The creature's eyes rolled, hoisting white, and he jerked and snorted.

Garrick looked around him. The rattle of musketry and the haze of gunsmoke addled his senses, but he could tell he was the only man horsed on the road.

He figured he had done poorly. He was supposed to watch over the mounts entrusted to him, and two of them were spooked and lathered while the third had galloped off back up the road.

Suddenly, recklessly, he decided to make amends.

"You stay put!" he hissed to the big gray shivering beside him, then kicked at Nimrod's flanks in an attempt to get him started after the fleeing horse, now engulfed in fog and distance. The gray galloped off, back toward Diego and Peacock: Garrick pivoted in the saddle, groped vainly for harness and reins.

Now he was entirely alone, Nimrod jittering silently beneath him.

Then the road spouted up in dust. The paling of a roadside fence split in two, as if someone unnaturally strong had taken a dull ax to it.

It was strong persuasion to Garrick that he made too clear a target. He slipped one foot from the stirrup, prepared to dismount . . .

And at that moment it seemed to dawn on Nimrod that he had been goaded and urged not ten seconds earlier, and for the first time in a rough acquaintance between boy and horse, the horse decided to oblige the rider, taking off at a gallop.

Somehow Garrick got his foot back into the stirrup. The road in front of him was clear of everything but smoke. Nimrod soon recovered his senses and slowed to a canter, though horse and rider still passed through the fringes of battle. To the right of the road, some of the guardsmen had drawn away horses, and to the left, beside him and behind him, a red line of boys crouched and fired into the woods. All around, the dry grass was tearing, spouting up into the air as if wind were blowing it straight from the ground.

Soon Garrick had outstripped all of these, the fire and tumult of the skirmish, the horses and guardsmen smaller and smaller on the road behind.

But then, through the cornfield to his right, the high dry shocks left stripped or fallow, a soldier on horseback rode with a rush and crackle. Garrick saw him ahead, bareheaded and a neck above the brown shocks of the field like a storybook giant.

When he burst clear to the road, Garrick saw for the first time the horse beneath him, and the uniform he wore . . .

Greens and browns. Colors of the rebellion.

It was the first rebel Garrick Hawken had met in hostile country.

And this, of course, was the time that Nimrod picked to slow to a trot, then a walk, then stop to graze.

The rebel rider pivoted his horse on the road, clearly as surprised as the guardsman boy before him. With a sharp whistle, he steered the animal back into the cornfield, looking over his shoulder and firing a pistol as he turned.

When he heard the *whick* of the bullet pass over him, Garrick drew the shotgun from his saddle holster and brought it to his shoulder. Somewhere between anger and fear and relief, he raised the weapon and fired into the stalks after the dwindling green form, and at that moment something struck or seemed to strike him full in the shoulder.

He cried out and toppled from the saddle, lurching backward toward the dusty road. Something grabbed at his ankle and gave, and he hit the ground and slept, slept between autumn and a strange, imagined spring.

He awoke on the River Road to Nimrod licking his face like a block of salt. He was on his back, facing the Alph and shouting something about aviaries.

He blinked, the horse vanished, and the midday sun dazzled him until a shadow passed overhead.

Sergeant Bacon crouched above him, asking him if he was hit, and the dreams of the aviaries—something of phoenix and angel and burrowing gnome—vanished entirely. Garrick moved his left hand easily to his right shoulder where the pain was, full expecting to find his arm wet or ruined. He felt the arm, sore but unbroken and unbloodied.

Sergeant Bacon winked. "How many times," he asked, "have you fired the shotgun . . . in question?"

"S-sir?" Garrick stammered, flushing, struggling painfully to his feet.

It seemed he had been kicked from the saddle by his own weaponry.

Garrick stood, and the road weaved, and he saw the redjackets weaving through the hovering smoke, darting like bright birds through the dark boles of poplar and walnut.

* * *

The rebels vanished as quickly as they had appeared, green light flickering into the labyrinth of trees.

Diego, solitary on horseback, led a dozen dismounted cavalry along the fringe of the woods. Deep in the tangle of walnut, oak, and evergreen, the occasional musket fire sputtered. Smoke and distance muffled the noise, and squadron called to squadron across a hazy net of branches.

He was about to lose them again.

Desperately, Diego looked over his shoulder, as Garrick and Sergeant Bacon rushed to join him over the uneven ground. The young man vaulted to his horse gracefully and, following the sergeant, guided his horse nimbly across a fire-shattered fence.

Assured of his nephew's safety, Diego peered with his spyglass into the farthest recesses of the woods.

A column of horses dodged briefly into sight. Smoke on a roan flank.

If he did not hurry . . .

I'll catch her yet, Diego told himself. Like in the old days.

With a whistle, he spurred old Juno toward the flickering green in the woods' depth. The mare surged under him, and together they galloped toward the smoke and the fading rebel column. Garrick and Sergeant Bacon followed quickly, desperately, in the breakneck wake of the Captain.

Into the woods Diego charged, the rebels receding ahead of him like foxfire. The smell of cedar and powder rushed to meet him, and the noonday light tilted through the branches, bottle-green and smoky.

It is her country, he thought, as somewhere to his left a horse whickered and a dark branch snapped.

Diego reined in a heaving Juno, stood in the stirrups.

Suddenly Bacon crashed into the clearing beside him, raised his carbine, then lowered it as quickly.

"Gone, Cap'n," he announced, his deep voice alien and raspy in this strange woods. "She's taken 'em back into the Borders, I'd wager."

"If she was ever there," Diego replied, smiling despite himself. "Where's Corporal Hawken?"

The sergeant motioned somewhere off to the left. "Comin' in on a flank, sir. As I told 'im."

Diego nodded. The smoke ahead of him pooled and rippled against the surface tension of the Borders.

They could always follow. It was only slightly more uncertain, more perilous, than the Lady's Land.

For a moment he reckoned the costs—the pure mathematics of tactics and strategy.

"Muster the men," Sergeant," he began. "The Lady isn't far into the Borders yet, and we've half a chance . . ."

But Thaddeus Bacon stared beyond him, at a knot of cedars not fifty feet away. Where a young rebel emerged from the screen of dark needles, half veiled in smoke, his roan horse at a steady walk over the branch-littered floor of the forest.

Bacon raised his gun, took careful aim. The young man had not seen him: he reached up absently, stripped a dried leaf from an overhanging poplar.

"No," Diego said quietly. Something in the boy's movement, in the way he rose in the saddle . . .

Then "No!" more loudly, more emphatically, his hand flashing out, catching the barrel of Bacon's carbine.

The gunshot echoed through the trees, and the rebel looked up, stepped out of the smoke . . .

And was transformed, as the air flashed and glittered around him.

In a dodging light, the green of the boy's cloak muddied to the brown of fallen leaves, to red as the young man pushed back his cap, as Garrick emerged from the mask of smoke and Border.

The gun barrel shook in Diego's gloved hand. "Border ruffles," he whispered.

Sergeant Thaddeus Bacon closed his eyes and shuddered.

"Let us . . . return to camp, Sergeant Bacon," Diego commanded, his order shaken and tentative as a soft wind muttered through the branches. "It's all her country, wherever you look. Absence or Border or Presence, we are strangers here."

CHAPTER 5

Absence, Border, and Presence.

A logical progression at the core of nature.

In the seminary they had explained it simply.

The Absence is a hole in the world. A void where the fabric of reality unravels. It is nothing—an emptiness difficult to imagine but nonetheless *there*, and empty . . .

And nothing.

It is a region where the laws of physics vanish. A world abandoned by the senses, by sense.

The Absences are always at war with the Presences, with our daily world—a dark, festering confusion blotting our bright countrysides, our forests and villages.

And the strange no-man's-lands between Absence and Presence are the Borders.

If the Presences are being, and the Absences, well, absence . . .

Then the Borders are becoming and undoing. Are the changing of things from *nothing* to *something*. Or *something* to *nothing*. The place where matter transforms and transmogrifies in a flux between void and existence.

They also fit together well.

Again, the seminary explained it through analogy.

Let the Absence be the stone striking the surface of the lake, and the Presence the rest of that lake. The Borders, then, were the ripples sent out by the impact of the stone on the surface of the water.

And though the Absence lay always in the same place, as stationary as stars, the Borders moved around it, in a state of constant movement and flux, like a spill of oil on that water's surface, anchored eternally to a single spot, but stretching far afield, spreading and contracting, ruled by no recognizable physics and changing by the hour.

What lay within the Borders changed as well—it, too, ungoverned by the laws of cause and effect, by the simple principles those in the Presences took for granted.

This was all the science they taught at Lambeth. All the science that *any* seminary taught, for that matter.

As one of the late Commentaries said, it was all ye know on earth or need to know.

And it was all Solomon Hawken knew of the way the world worked.

Absence, Border, and Presence.

Oh, and optical transmission lines.

Optical transmission lines is what Endymion had called them, years ago, to puncture Solomon's wonder when the two of them sat in the Great Hall and marveled at their receding reflections in old Grandfather Aristo's multiple facing mirrors.

Optical transmission lines, he had whispered then, his older brother in an albert overcoat, his bags packed for the coach back to Lambeth. *All they are, Solly. No magic in 'em.*

No magic in the flippin' world.

That's *all ye know on earth.*

But on this night, on the night of Solomon's return to Arcady, when the gaslamps sputtered and erupted with light, the Great Hall was again an infinity of mirrors.

Twoscore of them hung at regular intervals, facing each other and flickering across the ballroom, each containing the room and a thousand other mirrors in its shimmering heart.

Solomon's mother vanished in the light, and he looked instead into the heart of a mirror, at himself facing himself facing a countless number of mirrored selves. The great dance hall of the mansion lay shrouded in dark draperies, its furniture covered as though it had been abandoned for the season.

Solomon sighed, tumbled into a draped chair.

Cautiously, Willie put away his pistol.

A noise from the stairwell. The brushing of a moth's wing.

Solomon turned as Cousin Mina descended drowsily from her bedroom, phoebe lamp flickering in her pale hand, her auburn tresses loosened and dull in the muted light. He leapt to his feet, strode over the wax-encrusted floor to the foot of the stairs, lifted her as though she were a small child.

"Little cousin!" he whispered, drawing her into the Great Hall, dancing with her—with a thousand of her—in the mirrored light of her lamp. "Aren't you a sight, now?"

She smiled, tensing in his arms, her skin papery and pale. "I suppose I am, Solomon. Put me down now."

Solomon set her down gently, as if he had picked up porcelain by mistake.

The death's-head moth had spread its dark lines on her face. A mottled flaring of red, like clouds in a soft-dying day. Catarrh and chilblains, they had called it at first, but they knew better now, or worse . . .

Maw of the wolf, the lupus no doctor could remedy or forestall. Spreading rapidly, like ripples in water, the disease was flourishing, thriving.

Her body was eating itself away.

Solomon had heard all the symptoms from his aunt Morgana: the weariness in the mornings, the aversion to sunlight, the numbness of extremities—especially the blunted, clumsy feeling at the tip of her fingers. Sure enough, Mina's fingers were clubbed, reddened, and cracked at the tips. Her arms were hot and dry to his touch.

Willie, still shaking from the sphinx in the courtyard, from the refracted light and a thousand apparitions, bowed perfunctorily to the young woman and stepped into the shadows, vanishing as though he had stumbled into the heart of an Absence.

Solomon's hands lingered on Mina's shoulders, his blue eyes misting. She smiled and averted her gaze, slipped softly from his grasp.

Through the years, Solomon had envied the girls their parents. Artemis and Jasmina, born late and more fortunate, blest daughters of a cheerful marriage, a doting father.

Solomon remembered two faces—one framed in dark hair, the other in auburn, peering through the dirty window of the mill house as he, a decade older, had ridden by. They did not seem to have much, but caught in a tide of his father's expectations—the oldest son, the heir, the promising student at the seminary—Solomon had imagined them untroubled, even happy.

The only son of Solomon's cousin Cortez, James had been carefree, a lackland, dwelling in the Arcady mill house by his cousin's good graces. He was radical, a painter; he was perhaps a heretic, though the Hawkens never spoke of the faith's particulars, of the Text or the Hymns or the Commentaries.

It was rumored he smoked a concoction of hemp and tobacco, blended from his great-uncle Prometheus' money crops.

Yet James' daughters had not flourished. Through the years Artemis had moved farther and farther from her family, leaving Arcady in a cold and mutinous fury to join the rebel army, to destroy the way of life embodied in this house. And Mina . . .

Well, Mina leaned over a hooded table now, exhausted by a brief turn over the dance floor.

Following her with his eyes, Solomon sighed and sat on the lowest step of the stairwell.

And then, from another point in the hall, another light, another lamp.

Aunt Morgana shuffled from the drawing room into the big, mirrored dance hall. She was holding a candle, her white hair yellowed by worry and rushlight and neglect.

Morgana looked older, ten years less at ease than when Solomon last had come to Arcady, and even heavier than before, her stockiness now bordering on enormity. Her broad, open face seemed to sag, and her eyes—always large and owlish—bulged with a new and unexpected seriousness.

"Solomon," she murmured, her old woman's voice a croak, a throaty whisper. "Welcome home."

Solomon took his old aunt's knotty, sinewy hands. The strength in them was extraordinary; clay was embedded in the clubbed fingernails. Their eyes met, aunt and nephew. Together they waited a long moment, listening.

Upstairs a chair groaned across the floor. Something dropped up there, muffled by walls and ceilings.

Endymion, as usual, was in no shape to join them.

"You've ridden hard, Nephew," Morgana said finally, placing a dry kiss upon his forehead, steering him back toward the drawing room. "And the balloon has . . . arranged your hair most curiously."

Solomon lifted his tricorn, brushed absently at his unruly mop.

"But come in," his aunt urged, steering him toward light and warmth.

"Sit down by the fire. Mina will see to the gondolier. You must be sore and weary."

They moved toward the drawing room in a flicker of muted candles. Solomon looked back once in concern as his little cousin rose and set about the tasks that Morgana had ordered. Quickly, as though a moment's rest had restored her entirely, Mina lifted her skirts and crossed the floor toward the shadows and toward Willie Melmoth. Mina's faint smile catching on the mirror's surface, reflecting in yet another mirror and another . . .

Solomon turned his head, and the whole scene, the lovely girl, the stalwart young man, and the shadowy darkness that surrounded them, vanished as Morgana ushered him into the drawing room, into firelight and the water-smelling dust of three decades of clay.

An airy, windowed chamber off the main hall of the mansion, the drawing room lay exactly as Solomon remembered it: an old receiving room from his grandfather Aristo's day, appropriated by the women as a studio when Aunt Morgana established her pottery. Morgana's wheel sat in front of the fireplace, moved closer to the flame and the warmth since her arthritis had flared. At one time she had supplied the entire house—the extended community of dirt farms and river docks that encircled Arcady—with tableware and crockery, her art an extension of her love of fellowship, of binding together household and household in the friendship of daily tasks. But that old community had fragmented with the war, and the wheel itself had fallen into disuse, covered in dry shavings of clay, littered with abandoned tools and dried sponges and rags.

A generation of greenware covered the sprawling benches, dusty and whitened with the years' neglect—the more recent pieces less practical, more fanciful. Winged vases in the abstract shape of angels, and large bowls, adorned with white concentric swirls of slip in a spreading whirlpool pattern.

Absence bowls, the family called them as a joke.

All of this ware lay untouched, unfired, left to harden and whiten in a thin envelope of dust. The furnace that once had fired the pottery was now used only for Mina's bronze statuary.

On the other hand, in the far corner of the room, under a large bull's-eye window, the room was alive. An obelisk of wax rose vaguely from what was no doubt Mina's table, its moist smell mingling with woodsmoke and lavender. There Solomon's younger cousin prepared another statue, her role as family historian thriving, as she translated the remembered form of no doubt another Hawken into abiding bronze.

In a slow, strained gesture, Morgana swept shavings from her workbench and motioned for Solomon to sit. She grunted as she settled beside him, straddling the wheel she no longer used, and looked into the depths of the fire.

"So you came, as I asked you to come," she observed. "And may the saints bless your speed and devotion."

Solomon looked into the fire as well. He was uncomfortable with blessings.

"You've a task ahead of you, lad," Morgana continued, "that would tax the spirit of the strongest priest. Let me tell you what has happened here in your absence."

In this family, as in many families, talk shied naturally from the real subject at hand. It turned back on itself and receded like mirrored light, tunneling into old stories and side issues until even those in the midst of conversations had forgotten the original subject.

So alone at last, Morgana and Solomon did *not* begin with why she had called him home, but with his absent brother Endymion.

"Three days now I've passed his food through the door," Morgana explained, scraping the clay-crusted edge of the wheel with her broad, yellow thumbnail. "I wouldn't even know if he was alive except for the cleaned plate outside in the morning. And the times I can overhear the talk inside his room."

The fire ebbed a little, and the shadow of wheel and kiln and distant wax investment lengthened until they almost swallowed the room.

Then Morgana laughed.

"Morgana?" Solomon asked, rising and walking toward the fire.

"Endymion," Morgana replied, folding her hands in her lap as the prioress had taught her nearly sixty years ago. They were hands Solomon had never remembered as proper or delicate, the clay embedded forever in her fingers along with the arthritis and the craft.

"What he says to that bird," she chuckled. "And what he . . . *thinks* the bird says back." She became suddenly serious. "Of course, we've known the bird longer than he has. We know it doesn't talk."

Solomon leaned gravely against the mantel. "But *Endymion* does. What does he say, Aunt Morgana?"

"Oh, he talks metaphysics, machinery. Talks about that village of teakwood and coral he builds in a bottle. About all of you, sometimes."

She looked mischievously at Solomon, who smiled wanly, masking his eagerness to know what had been said about *him*. Now Mina glided into the room, bearing a tray upon which rested a bottle of whiskey and two glasses.

She set the tray on the potter's wheel and faded into the shadows, as insubstantial as . . .

As mist, Solomon told himself. As mist.

"And about the angels," Morgana murmured. "Sometimes Endymion talks about the angels."

A darkness passed over her face, the owlish eyes widening.

"That is all behind you now, Aunt Morgana," Solomon reassured her. "Being punished for imagining angels is . . . is a thing of the past. You are here to stay, remember? None of us would *think* of . . ."

"I'm not afraid any longer, Solomon," Morgana replied, waving her large hand. "Too near dead for that."

As her nephew started to protest, a smile spread across the potter's wizened face.

"When you're seventy, you'll know. It's not the angels anymore. None of you listen. You write them off as Endymion's gin, as Border ruffles, as my decrepit dottiness. That way you don't have to reckon too closely with . . . the way they're behaving."

She looked over her shoulder, as though she were looking back a century.

Solomon swallowed his portion of the whiskey, started on Morgana's.

"You mean you're seeing . . . I mean . . . the angels are back?" he asked, turning his cold blue eyes toward Mina briefly, then back to the fire.

Morgana nodded. "They told me to call you."

"The angels," Solomon declared softly, with another veiled glance at his cousin. "I've been called twenty leagues in a windy autumn to . . . see about . . . the angels."

Mina smiled opaquely, removed the whiskey tray with a chiming of glasses.

"It's not twenty leagues, Solly," Morgana chided, falling into the old nickname Solomon despised, that he had told them all not to use. "Don't be dramatic. And it's not just the angels, either. It's Arcady as well. The house is growing, Solomon. On its own . . . *eccentrically,* you could call it."

Solomon turned the wheel, the glass and bottle spiraling slowly toward his hand.

Arbitrary growth. An expanding house.

It's what they always claimed had happened when the Borders encroached. He had seen it himself once, with Cousin Amelia.

"Then the Borders . . ." he began.

"As far as anyone can guess, the Borders have returned," Morgana agreed. "The house was expanding to begin with. We added a wing three years ago, a summer kitchen last spring. It's as though the Borders . . . rushed to meet it."

"It wasn't just appearances, then," Solomon murmured. He fell silent in the dusty drawing room, motes nodding and swirling in the firelight.

"They're moving again," Morgana said, "and they're moving this way, as they did when you were twelve, and again when you were thirty and away at Lambeth. We've taken to watching the children, keeping a closer eye as the rooms shift about us. We were afraid that a child's bedroom might . . . change suddenly in the night. Might blend into adjoining rooms—to the drawing room or a pantry or the Great Hall itself. Or worse still, open onto a courtyard or garden or the fields west of the house, and leave the sleeping little ones prey for fauns or dryads bent on a changeling."

"Or for a wakened sphinx," Solomon added with a shudder. "I see, Morgana. But why call me from Lambeth?"

"Because it has finally happened," Morgana declared flatly. "This is the reason I have called you, Nephew. The reason you have come from Lambeth at this late time of the year."

Solomon listened intently, his eyes never straying from the fire. If he could do something . . . anything . . .

"It's Endymion's youngest child. Faith."

"What of Faith?" Solomon beckoned to Mina, and again, as though they winked into being at his command, the tray and bottle and glasses appeared, set carefully on the mantel. The glasses, adorned with a white Jacobite rose, brimmed with the amber liquid.

Good. He knew he could use it. For he already suspected what was coming next.

"Gone," Morgana announced. "Faith is gone. She . . . opened what she expected to be a pantry door and vanished entirely inside. I watched it all from the kitchen, Solomon. I sent her myself, for nothing more than sugar."

"It's not your fault, Morgana. Go on."

"She walked to that door cheerily, and I remember thinking that at last she was loving to *do* something, no matter if she made pastry rather than pots or poetry or sculpture. In a faded blue dress—one of Mina's castoffs—powdered with flour and yeast from the crown of her auburn hair. Ribboned in pink as she always insisted, down to her sandaled feet. She opened the pantry door, and the room filled with light and a choir of birds singing, like she was being . . . *assumed*, or *raptured*, the best I know."

Solomon frowned. Morgana was given to ornament and drama.

"Then she cried out," Morgana continued, "and the whole kitchen rocked and trembled. Downright seismic it was, Solly, and it sent me skidding away from the oven, sliding myself toward the door and the light and the birdsong. I remember I was thinking it could not be all that bad because the whole thing was so beautiful, with the music and green light and all, and a single pink ribbon settled on the threshold. But the door closed ahead of me, like the Borders had enough. Here are the scrapes on my arms to prove it."

She showed her elbows, purpled and raw with abrasions.

Solomon swallowed the whiskey and turned to the fire. The room was warm, uncommonly bright. He reached for Morgana's glass, still full on the tray.

"It was after this," Morgana said, shuffling next to him, holding her aching hands to the fire, "after the visions and the changes, after Faith was gone and Endymion locked himself in his room. Then I sent for you. Called you from Lambeth and . . . from your eternal duties."

Solomon turned away.

"Maybe she can be found," Morgana soothed, her gaze resting upon her nephew's unreadable face. "Maybe she is still even on the grounds. Or safe with her brother. Among the Blights."

Solomon turned the glass in his hand.

"That is why you have come, Solomon," Morgana continued. "To settle this maze of a house. Drive out the Borders. Perhaps you'll find out where Faith has gone in the process."

"Why me?" Solomon asked. "You know the house better than I do.

Know its changes through the years. Know what the Borders have changed, what they've dislodged. I . . . I remember Arcady from childhood. Nothing more."

"But you have the priesthood in your judgment," Morgana urged. "All that anointing. Like . . . like silver on the water for a drowned soul."

"That's foolishness. Superstition, Aunt Morgana. Where did you hear such . . ."

"From the nuns."

"At the wish sanitarium?"

"They told me there that the priests had power. That they could cleanse a house, or grounds, or a whole landscape itself, by the words of the Text and the magic that was in them."

"The nuns say many things," Solomon muttered. The warmth of the room had settled on his shoulders. He was drowsy, bleary, irritable.

"*Nuns, fret not at the contents of* . . . What is it the Commentaries sayeth, Solomon?"

Solomon laughed harshly. "Not *that*, Morgana. It's *Nuns fret not at their convent's narrow room,* is what it says. Nothing to do with truth or falsity. Only their contentment."

He turned from the mantel, sidling into the shadows, bumping his leg softly against the rim of Mina's wheel. The old sorrows, it seemed, continued unto several generations.

Mina and Morgana, cousin and aunt, the best souls and minds of all the Hawkens, were unraveling before him. The crimson moth of Mina's disease was spreading, furling its dark wings across her countenance. And Morgana . . .

Well, it was the angels again.

Endymion, as well, was still killing himself, no doubt, with mourning and gin. Diego and Artemis were roaming the woods north of the house, intent on killing each other.

And the house itself was dismantling. The wretched sprawling house that beckoned him homeward in every line of Morgana's letter, that held him here now, regardless of his strength or desire or nature.

There was something to do with Arcady that demanded, Morgana had decided, "the attentions of a priest."

And now that he knew what it was, only two things remained clear in the cold half-light of the dusty Arcadian drawing room.

If she wanted *the attentions of a priest*, some power beyond counsel and consolation and literary lectures on the holy Text, she should have asked someone else. Someone with a gift for deep magic, if there were any left—had ever been any—in all of Urizen, all of Urthona.

He had never been a priest. A postulant once, then later a lecturer in Poetic Theology. But never the man of spirit and power his old aunt imagined him to be, the nephew she needed at this time of fragment and danger.

No, Solomon Hawken was not that man. And he feared he would never find the courage to tell her.

CHAPTER 6

Solomon sat on the bed in the high chambers. The lamplight shone through the half-empty bottle he had snatched from the tray as he lurched up the stairs to his bedroom.

He had scarcely heard Morgana's warnings not to open doors suddenly, not to turn down unfamiliar halls. And for the most part, the second floor of the house was as he remembered it: an angling corridor lined with a dozen rooms.

His old quarters had changed by more natural means. His bedroom was layered over with the leavings of two later inhabitants: Aristo's steam engines and lead soldiers, inherited from Uncle Vergil (who had played with them, childlike, until his death at twenty-five), had given way to Faith's drawings and dolls, so that Solomon's spare, scholarly room was scarcely detectable behind the remains of childish belongings.

Nonetheless, it *had* been his room once, a quarter century ago.

When he was young and prone to sparks and illusion.

Whiskey-drowsing on the bed, aloft in a bedazzlement of mirrors, Solomon looked deeply into the mirror facing the bed—a cracked one with a chipped plaster frame.

"The attic," he murmured. "It was last in the attic, with the salt and the seared floor."

The broken face of the mirror reflected three, four, five faces. Somewhere in its depths was the Arcady of old—the house in which he was born and spent his childhood.

Solomon stared into the darkened glass, remembering. . . .

* * *

Old Arcady was a child's paradise.

Long late-summer days Solomon would ride, when he first learned how to ride, on the fringes of Uncle Raphael's nut grove. The warm ground lay littered with the soft, green hulls of walnuts, and Lucy, his late uncle Vergil's gentle mare, would tread softly on the husks in the shade, unknowingly freeing the shells to dry.

The mansion was smaller then. The third story of the house was new, and the round southwestern tower had yet to be built, still a dream in the architectural fancies of Solomon's great-grandfather Prometheus.

Four generations of Hawkens lived together on the sprawling estate, from Prometheus down to Solomon's younger twin brothers, and aside from the jostling and volume of the dinner tables, from the pontification of an ancient patriarch, the questionable sanity of his aunt Morgana, and the vaguely unsettling presence of his hapless cousin James in Melusine's mill house not a hundred yards from the mansion, Solomon's was a fairly normal Urthonan childhood.

A normal childhood set in an abnormal place.

For Arcady had been brushed by the Borders twice before. Once in the building of the mansion, and again in '14, in the aftermath of a fierce electric storm. None of his elders spoke of the events—not even Great-Grandfather Prometheus, who had seen it happen twice—but the Borders were said to bring odd things.

Disturbing things.

Still, the last encroachment had been over thirty years ago, three lifetimes to a boy on a gentle mare who rode at the brim of the forest where dust motes swam in the bright Arcadian air.

On this particular summer day, the thick smell of peaches beckoned Solomon from the westernmost grounds, and he steered Lucy accordingly, guiding her over the sunstruck southern pasture toward the orchard. Old Atreus' lake stretched sluggish and brown beside him.

He took great care to give the water a wide berth. Solomon was no swimmer. The possible depths of the lake, the prospect of drowning, daunted and chilled him.

Beyond the lake sat the mansion, its upper stories lost in a blind of noonday sun.

Solomon looked away. He reined in the horse and squinted southward. The field rolled in a shimmering haze toward the bronze statues of the sphinxes at the farthest fringe of the grounds—figures so worn, humped, and blue-green with verdigris that the boy found it hard to believe they were sphinxes at all.

"Much less come to life," he whispered. "Cousin James and Amelia are both elfshot."

He glanced skeptically at the horizon beyond the sculptured sphinxes. The air flexed and shimmered in the distance.

It was all he'd ever seen of the Borders.

With a low whistle to Lucy, Solomon set off in a canter toward the shade of the orchard. Ducking beneath a low-hanging bough, he guided the horse into the fragrant shadows, wasps humming drunkenly over the fallen, fermented peaches.

From here he could see the mansion much more clearly. The rough western walls blocked the sun from this angle. Above them loomed an array of spires and gables like darkened lighthouses on a disorder of rocks.

Solomon brushed away a persistent wasp. Looked again.

A third story of the house rose out of the attic above the nursery of his twin brothers. The walls jutted up from a simple slanted roof, then inexplicably seemed to change their minds and settle once again into a strange windowed compromise between loft and dormer.

Solomon had never seen it before. He had not even heard the builders.

Through the ancestral gate he rode the little mare, around the western face of the mansion, passing the parts of the house built within his own memory: Prometheus' great chimney and bay window, Aristo's north wing. His father's summer kitchen.

Dismounting at the stable and tendering his horse to the groom, he stalked through the topiary, raising a long dozen of larks from the juniper and taxus. Startled, the birds rose and scattered in the morning air, and the boy, his mind jostled from the excitement of the new building, leaned against a carefully sculptured bush and watched the larks rise.

"An *exaltation*," Solomon whispered. "That's what they call them. A raising up."

Over the courtyard he raced and up the worn steps of the main entrance, through the large double doors and into the hall of Arcady. Still whispering the word to himself as he ran, because words were the wonders, the germ of the magic itself.

"Mark well my words!" he quoted, his thin boy's voice ricocheting through the long, sparsely furnished hall.

"They are of your eternal salvation," a girl's voice replied from the top of the stairs, completing the quote from the ancient Text.

Solomon startled, backed against the wall.

Then his cousin Amelia descended the steps, and as always, his words scattered like larks.

Amelia was the bride of Solomon's cousin James and the mother of an infant daughter, Artemis, though in all honesty she was little more than a girl herself. In a green robe she stood above Solomon on the flight of stairs . . .

In exaltation, he thought . . .

Her red hair radiant in the sunlight through the landing window. She was beautiful and thin and mysterious, her countenance hinting at the rumored dryadic blood of the Darkling family, of which she was the youngest and dearest daughter.

"Th-there's a new floor to the house!" Solomon blurted, and Amelia paused, leaning over the balustrade, her hair a cascade of autumn leaves, the faint odor of woodsmoke and rosemary showering over him, leaving him breathless.

"Is that so?" she asked.

Solomon nodded stupidly.

"Well, then. We must see this addition." She wiped her hands on the loose green robe, her fingers tracing the prominent swell of her belly. "Suppose you lead the way, then, young cousin," she suggested, extending her hand to Solomon.

Amelia had been his partner in adventure of late. It was she who had showed him the charred foundation of the first aviary, mysteriously burned years before his birth, and the rutted marks of old Atreus' wheeled bed in the mud beside the Alph. There as well she had showed him the last known footprints of his great-great-uncle Innocent and remarked, with an odd, abstracted stare, that she had seen almost identical prints by the stored mirrors in the attic.

She had showed him those prints as well, seared scuff-markings that dragged and shuffled ten feet across the dusty floor.

Solomon could not see the resemblance.

But this was clear adventure. The new floor had sprouted unbidden from the same attic, an alcove off the long, musty ogee roof that covered the mirrors and velocipedes, and Solomon was eager to see it.

In his brothers' room, the ladder leaned against the far wall. Solomon, staggering through a confusion of toys and discarded clothing, wrestled it to its proper place beneath the trapdoor.

"Are you sure you should be climbing and all, Amelia?" he asked, steadying the ladder and setting foot to the lowest rung. "I mean, with the child due in winter . . ."

"Nonsense, Solomon," Amelia replied, handing him the lantern. "You wouldn't want me pent in a daybed for half a year, would you? I'm not an egg or a porcelain granny."

Solomon smiled and scrambled halfway up the ladder, the shadowy vault of the attic yawning to meet him.

Branching from the attic like an improvised alcove, the new room smelled of sawdust and light. A solitary window, which overlooked the pond and the fruit trees beyond it, was frosted with a strange, opalescent salt that came away at the touch and tasted . . .

Tasted of the air after a thunderstorm. The faint, watery odor of lightning.

"The Border's come again," Amelia whispered. She arched one beautifully tapered eyebrow and spread the glittering salt over the back of her hand. With a laugh, she blew the granules into the close attic air, and they shimmered as they fell like a spray of snow over the hatracks and trunks and cedar chests. An old velocipede whistled and spun its jeweled wheels.

"The Border?" Solomon frowned. "But I thought it was *out there*. Beyond the statues. Beyond the grounds."

Amelia sat on one of the cedar chests. "For the time being, it is. But the Borders never stay still. Ask Prometheus. He's seen them over this house twice."

"Great-Grandfather never speaks of the Borders."

Amelia rolled her eyes. "Just like the whole mess of Hawkens. If you don't speak of something, maybe it'll go away. The Borders have spooked 'em for fifty years."

"Spooked?" Solomon traced his finger over a Saratoga trunk. The salt glittered on his hand. "What do you mean, *spooked*?"

Amelia laughed. "Oh, Solly, surely you don't think that this is a *nor-*

mal family?" Then her face darkened. "It's high time you knew about the house and the Borders."

And with Solomon rapt and attentive in the stifling summer attic, this is the story she told him.

* * *

It began for them all with Arcady. Before the time of Solomon's return, before his time and the time of his father and grandfather, before the wars or the seminary or even the wish sanitarium in the mountains. It began with the house and with Atreus Hawken.

Great-Great-Grandfather Atreus was the first of the line of Hawken and the founder of the house. He had set the first boards and bricks on the grounds almost a hundred years before, when the countryside was as wild and unsettled as war and the Borders were now making it again.

Atreus settled Arcady when Urizen was genuine frontier, strange artifacts and twisted scraps of old metal the only clues that someone had been here before and long since vanished, and the countryside so pure that someone could walk for days through vines and moss and undergrowth without stumbling across village or farm or even a dwelling of any kind.

Old Atreus was a brigadier general in the Citizens' Guard and a Priest of the Text—the first Hawken to be educated at Lambeth, one of the last great warrior-priests of Urthonan history. And a century ago, he had decided to come south to die.

For the General had explored the banks of the Alph during the Third War of False Doctrine, in his last campaign against the army of the heretic Ezra St. Ezra, who had rebelled when the Book of Manfred was purged from the Commentaries. There in the northernmost tip of Urizen, chasing heretics amid the vines and the cedar and the endless tangle of reeds and wild hemp, Atreus fell in love with the wilderness and its beautiful unruliness. Years later, when he felt the first pain of what he thought were his final days, he announced his plan to build a mausoleum by the banks of the Alph. Like any patriarch, he intended to employ his entire family in the building of it.

Thus began the labors of his three sons and his two daughters—Prometheus and Innocent and Raphael, Ahania and little Kassandra. Together, the family set the foundation and began a small brick mausoleum, which, as far as anyone knew, still lay somewhere at the center of the present mansion.

Atreus' children set the bricks, clumsily at first but with increasing skill and speed, around their father's tent in a parcel of land he had staked out for himself at the edge of a wild orchard. They had to chase off the occasional centaur and gnome, and Innocent Hawken, the second son of old Atreus, was wounded by a sly dryadic dart, after which he was never really the same.

From the beginning, old Atreus was disappointed: somehow the mausoleum should have been larger, of marble, not brick. After all, it was *his* death he imagined approaching, and when he closed his eyes the final time, naturally the world would end—birds would vanish on the wing, and the ancient stars of Los and Rintrah would wink out in the southern sky, leaving a dark void like that of the fist-sized punctures in the air he had occasionally come across in the Arcadian woods, swirling and shimmering and drawing the light into their midst.

So reluctantly the old man lay in his new brick tomb, awaiting a death that now seemed a little shabbier than he had bargained for. His five children visited him daily, bringing him flowers and kind words and thin soups and water, then left him every evening as though it were the last time, with weeping and fond goodbyes.

After the mausoleum was finished, it still took a month for the younger Hawkens to realize that their father was not about to die at all. Apparently they were a trusting sort, although family history has it that after his wound, Innocent became retiring, surly, and suspicious—a ghostly presence amid the ground lime and mortar.

But all of them wondered and suspected when, instead of wasting into nothing, old Atreus asked for brandy.

Soon after that the children's sorrow became manufactured and the departures became ritual. Atreus lay there, basking in the tears of his offspring, in their goodbyes. Whether those tears were ritual or heartfelt did not matter to him, as long as all five of them wept and wailed, stroked his long gray beard, and set the brandy decanter by his bedside.

The children were at a loss as to just what they should do with the old man. Supposedly Innocent suggested privately to his brother Prometheus that they proceed as planned, walling up the old moneygrubber as everyone had expected to wall him by this time.

It was an idea, as family history said, that was *rejected with horror*.

Finally, one of the more tenderhearted of the children—versions of this story vary, but most say it was Ahania—concluded that if Father was about to die, at least it should not be of starvation. From that moment on, after almost a month of liquid diet and leave-takings, the children began bringing the first of the solid food, which old Atreus devoured, immediately and downright eagerly, having forgotten how much he missed bread and pigeon and potatoes and, now and again, a little gin and cigars.

Soon, of course, the old man realized that dying was not what he wanted at all. Instead he preferred the inviting prospect of being waited on for the rest of his mortal days, while he lay in state and did absolutely nothing. He asked Prometheus to tear down one of the walls in the mausoleum and erect in its place another wall—one with a sunny bay window. After this, he promised, there would be no more errands, no more fuss. The window was "the dying wish of an old man," he added pathetically, cunningly.

Soon the "dying wish" included various rooms added onto the mausoleum, and wheels on his bed so that he might visit those rooms he had so finally and so piteously demanded.

After he was up and about, Atreus' wishes became more ambitious. He demanded topiaries, a carriage house, northern pastures, and eastern fields of hemp. Under his specific instructions, Uncle Raphael had built the first and most lasting of the many orchards on the estate.

It was about then that the children began to tire out.

All five of Atreus' offspring had taken up residence in Shiveleigh, a town some five miles northeast of the mausoleum. Daily they had gathered in the bed of Raphael's wagon and trundled the distance through the woods and heath and occasional spreading Borders, making a pilgrimage for parting words and final comfort to the dying old man. Now, all of them suspecting what Prometheus had suspected after a month of Atreus' lying in, they got together and nominated baby Kassandra to go to their father with a request—that among these dying wishes he consider chambers for the rest of his family so that they would not have to make the long daily journey to kneel at his final bedside.

"Of course," Atreus had agreed, always delighted to be plied by the baby of the family. "Have my children ever suffered on my account?"

So the first of many versions of Arcady took shape. Quarters for the children arose in the southern wings of the house, followed by a library and a kitchen and a drawing room.

Atreus remained attentive to whatever of his children's wishes pleased him. Or he could be made attentive if they sent him messages through Kassandra. He built an aviary when Prometheus took to raising talking birds—an aviary filled with perches and megaphones so that the speech of the creatures was greatly amplified and Atreus could hear it while at rest on his bed in the middle of the sunny mausoleum. The aviary burned when Solomon was an infant, and Atreus restored it immediately, because the birds had become his most enduring entertainment. At night they spoke to him of the passage of years, and sometimes, when one of the phoenixes muttered in its sleep, Atreus would waken, listen, and wonder if he had been spared so long in order that he might receive some visionary moment in which he would come to understand the dreams of birds.

Nor was the next generation of Hawkens any less demanding on time and on architecture: Prometheus' son, Aristo—grandfather to Solomon, Endymion, and Diego—brought home his bride the mermaid, and old Atreus soon saw to it that the mill house south of the Alph, used at first only for channeling the river into the paddles of its enormous wheel, now contained an outbuilding of its own. Into this building a steady stream of water tumbled before rushing out the other side, cleverly directed so that Melusine Stella-Maris Hawken, mermaid and bride, could swim untroubled in the currents of the Alph under the delighted eyes of her father-in-law, her firm breasts flushed in the river foam and a solid roof above her auburn-tressed head.

Great-Great-Grandfather Atreus died—or *passed away*—when Solomon was six. At the doddering age of 120 he was fishing by the banks of the Alph, accompanied, or so the story goes, by Innocent and Vergil. The three of them were pondering a way to divert the course of the river through the center of Arcady, so that Atreus would not have to travel as far to fish or to watch Melusine ,Stella-Maris swimming.

The old man, so the story goes, was leaning dangerously toward the riverbank when the wheels of the bed unlocked and he rolled—sheets and pillows and huge mahogany lap desk and all—instantly into the water.

Or he was pushed by Innocent, as some family traditions had it.

For Innocent vanished that very night and was never seen again in

Urizen, or anywhere else, for that matter. His portrait hung uncomfortably in the front hall of Arcady for another seven years until Prometheus' death, glaring down on all visitors, the scar from the dryadic dart purple along the left side of his neck. Then Aristo, *the* Hawken now, patriarch of the family and flushed with his new power, ordered the painting turned face to the wall, confirming what everyone had secretly wanted done all along, but in family fair-mindedness had lacked the sheer self-righteousness to do.

Whatever the cause of his tumble into the waters, the old man's final voyage was dramatic stuff. Atreus swept westward on the current, screaming and struggling as he floated downstream. For the first time in years he admitted he did not want to die after all, his confession fading into the roar of the river and the rising night.

On the near bank Vergil plunged into the water to save his grandfather. Twenty-five and a strong swimmer, he floated beside the daybed, struggling vainly to steer it toward shore—either shore.

He was still struggling when the night and the river swallowed them both, somewhere near the Tharman border.

The new aviary was restless and loud that evening, and though Solomon was only a child, he remembered his father saying on the next morning that the birds were mourning the old and the young, that whatever search the family could organize would end up with nothing. Though the family dragged the river, though they threw bread and silver on its surface and watched for where the bread rose from the water, though they fired cannon to bring afloat the body itself, they found neither Atreus nor Vergil.

After Atreus was gone, Arcady continued to grow. In each generation, the head of the family had added a structure. And other expansions rose unexpectedly, sprouting, it seemed, unbidden from the frames and foundations of the ever-changing house, drawn forth by the Borders as, almost tidal in their ebb and flow, they washed over the grounds and manor, then receded for years, even decades, as Arcady settled into *peace* and *normalcy*.

But each time, the Borders left oddities in their wake.

One of which was the mysterious third floor of the mansion.

All of this Amelia Darkling Hawken told her young cousin, who realized in the telling that he was come into his inheritance. For the story was his legacy, as much as the Hawken name and the Hawken grounds, and as cloudy and Border-transfigured as both.

"Tell me more, Cousin Amelia," he pleaded. "About the Borders and the house and . . ."

The girl raised a pale and warning finger. Framed by the light from the single window, she seemed shadowy, a figure of smoke and mirrors. More dryadic than ever before, and for a brief, unsettling moment Solomon thought he heard the rustle of leaves in her voice, the roll of forest brooks in the consonants and vowels.

"Not telling," she murmured. "No stories now, Solomon, and few words. I will show you what the Borders do to the things we say, and what the things we say can to do the Borders."

Solomon frowned. It was double-talk. Words in a mirror. But words were the wonders, the germ of the magic itself. And Amelia was so lovely and kind that he listened through the confusion, watched as she knelt in the salt-dusted attic, as she gestured and intoned a verse—something obscure from the Commentaries, he guessed:

"On a poet's lips I slept
Dreaming like a love-adept
In the sound his breathing kept;
Nor seeks nor finds he mortal blisses,
But feeds upon the aerial kisses
Of shapes that haunt thought's wildernesses . . ."

As she chanted, the white grains on the floor and on the sill of the frosted window stirred and eddied, as though awakened by her breathing.

This is not happening, Solomon told himself. *Do I wake or dream?*

Amelia continued, her voice muffled now, as though he heard it through a stretch of water.

"He will watch from dawn to gloom
The lake-reflected sun illume
The yellow bees in the ivy-bloom,
Nor heed nor see, what things they be;
But from these create he can
Forms more real than living man,
Nurslings of immortality!"

And the grains began to hum and whine, a chorus of bees in the closeness of the summer loft. Amelia's fingers dripped with honey, her eyes were hooded, sleepy . . .

And for a moment Solomon lost himself in their fathomless green.

He remembered stammering something to her as he scrambled down the ladder to the nursery. Something about light and air, about needing to be at the business Father had set him to on that sunstruck afternoon. Shortly afterward, seated amid the toys of his little brothers—Diego's hobbyhorse and wooden soldiers mingled with Endymion's alembics and stuffed birds—Solomon was suddenly aware, for the first time ever, how truly *odd* this house was, how odd its architecture, its furnishings, and the toys themselves.

It was like a moment when a traveler returns to his home country after long years of absence, and finds that things once familiar have become suddenly, irrecoverably estranged.

CHAPTER 7

He was that traveler now, and his home country was a maze of glass and illusion.

As below, so above, he thought blearily. For mirrors lined the bedroom, as they lined the Great Hall downstairs. Faith had set them there, no doubt, as she tested her growing beauty, and the mirrors faced each other, as they did in the Great Hall, so that Solomon could see himself sitting on a score of beds, staring into an infinite regression of images and light.

Optical transmission lines.

Only the curtains were the same: the black velvet that blocked the sunlight at all hours.

Solomon lifted the bottle.

As above, so below.

When Amelia had shown him the power of the Borders, how the great verses of the holy Texts could channel the energies of those changing, chaotic regions, acting as spells, perhaps, or prayers or incantations, he had believed her at once.

Believed her, despite what he said.

Never had he doubted the evidence of his eyes, nor entertained the possibility that the bees who rose from the woodwork of the mysterious third floor had been just what he called them when he fled the room and his cousin—beautiful illusions. Or that they were something to do with her dryadic origins—a sleight of hand her people used to deceive, to inveigle.

The doubts came later, when the seminary had sown the seeds of doctrine and high theology.

* * *

He went to Lambeth as a student all those years ago.

A boy of eleven, fresh from the southern provinces, the smell and the accents of Urizen still upon him, passing through the sacred gates of Lambeth, the chief seminary of mystical Urthona, hard by the great lake known as Pontus Tarn.

When autumn turned to winter that first year, the northern boys of the seminary, toughened against wind and snow, laughed at his shivering and delicacy. Called him the Hothouse Lily, the Deciduous Scholar, whose leaves fall before the first frost.

Solomon endured Lambeth nevertheless, from that early and awkward time, despite the weather and the teasing of his classmates. After all, old Atreus was its proud alumnus, as were Cousin Cortez and Great-Great-Uncle Raphael.

So Solomon sat in the classroom, close by stove or brazier, hands gloved against the crisp air even when he was writing. Lulled by four layers of clothing, his breath misting and the tips of his fingers numb, he awaited eagerly the outpouring of magic and poetry promised by the priests from their high lecterns.

The Text was the heart of the faith, the Divine Word—the first book found by the Forefathers in the mythical Time of the Veil. The Hymns were the inspired songs of the Bard, illumined as well with colorful engravings, but less in stature because they were the heart's or soul's brief outcry and not the timeless story of the faith. The Commentaries were only teachings: the best of earthly wisdom, of faithful thought by faithful men—priests, prophets, and lesser bards; though wise, these texts were wholly human and anchored in what reason and intelligence reveal and allow.

Solomon was in love with the Text. Enraptured by the Hymns and the Commentaries, but in love with the Text and a dozen generations of interpretations.

The Text, they told him, was from the Absence but not of the Absence, arising from the dark times when it had been hidden secure in seminaries and towers, in the skeletal country of bordermetal and rock.

Long ago, when the Text was first written, Absences had covered the world, though many of the priests, by this late date grown figurative and unorthodox, maintained that this Time of the Veil, of the Absences, was never historical, only a way the ancients had of describing the watery roots of history, where fact and verifiable account fade into conjecture and rumor.

At any rate, the Text was an old book, a long poem illustrated by colorful engravings. Despite the obscurity of the poetry and the complexity of the drawings, the Text bore a simple central story.

After an account of creation, the poem introduced the figure of the Bard. He was not only a character in the poem, but he *wrote* the poem as well—a combination of circumstances that had occasioned volumes of theological debate. The Bard told an ancient story of struggles among powerful, semidivine entities. It was a confusing history, this quarrel of the saints, punctuated by the famous and urgent warning of the Bard,

> Mark well my words! they are of your eternal salvation.

and introducing the figures of the great saints of the Text: Los the Poet and Palamabron, who pities the oppressed, Rintrah of the Just Wrath and Ololon the Feminine Principle; also the four saints for whom the nations of the continent were named—Urizen and Tharmas, Luvah and Urthona—and dozens of other lesser saints, understood as symbols by most seminarians, but invoked with devotion by less tutored folk, by miners and gondoliers, chimney sweeps . . .

And backwater Urizenian hemp farmers, it seemed. Young Solomon was astonished that many of his classmates prayed to no saints. Did not pray at all.

Whatever the nature of the saints or their quarrels, these obscure and early passages of the Text sounded momentous and frightening; puzzled by this part of the story, Solomon took great assurance in the knowledge that his teachers themselves disagreed, not only on the meaning, but even on what happened in them.

But after this account followed the Great Story, the myth that had inspired generations of readers and worshipers—the Bard's tale of Saint Milton, a man of considerable gifts and virtues, who, in his earthly life, had mistakenly taught a theology of judgment, condemnation, and denial. In his afterlife among the quarreling saints and the Angels of the Presence, Saint Milton realizes his error and returns, through chaos and through many hardships, to earth. There, the Bard claims, he and Saint Milton become one:

so Milton's shadow fell
Precipitant, loud thund'ring into the Seat of Time & Space.
Then first I saw him in the Zenith as a falling star
Descending perpendicular, swift as the swallow or swift:
And on my left foot falling on the tarsus, enter'd there:
But from my left foot a black cloud redounding spread . . .

The *black cloud redounding* was the Absence. Or so the seminaries taught. It was a dangerous place, and yet when the time came, Saint Milton and the Bard would join within it, unite as proponents of a new faith—compassionate, imaginative, and renewing.

Separately, Saint Milton and the Bard were incomplete. Together, they were wondrous: Creator, Incarnation, and Inspiring Word gathered in one.

Deeply Solomon loved the story, which was a wild and mysterious adventure for a boy who loved tales of peril and heroism. But the Text was more: it spoke to him of his own weaknesses, of ample time in life and in eternity to correct them, and to a forgiveness in which all faltering things, himself among them, nestled and took solace. Solomon took it upon himself to learn more about the Text, and about the Hymns and Commentaries found with it when it was first discovered. He would be a priest, he resolved joyously; and though Lambeth offered all kinds of theological learning, it was the priesthood to which the most capable and gifted of boys aspired.

But with seminary study came exposure not only to the Text itself, but to texts about the Text, and texts about *those* texts. From the most basic of agreements, the theories forked and branched.

Orthodoxy understood the faith in simple, millennial form: Saint Milton would return—some said *soon*, others pointed to an indefinite time in the future—and when he joined with a Bard yet to be born, the division, fragmentation, and intolerance which flowed over the world like the cresting tide of an Absence would be swept away, and the world returned to the *green and pleasant land* of prophecy.

The Post-Millennials disagreed: Saint Milton's return had already taken place, the Text itself was a record of that event, and as the Bard had urged in that ancient time, we should mark well its words, which were of our eternal salvation.

Those were the old theologies, imbued with magic like that of which

Amelia had spoken in the new, Border-built attic of Arcady. But Orthodox and Post-Millennial had clashed over whether this New World of tolerance and compassion was in the wings or among us already, waiting to be found.

Over that issue they fought three Wars of False Doctrine and unpeopled the landscape.

Nowadays old theology had all but vanished from Lambeth. There were those at the seminary who believed that the Holy Writings were holy only by mutual consent. Better, it was said, not to revere the Text as much as respect it as poetry, as metaphor. After all, was not Saint Milton's voyage the voyage of all men—to return and correct our former misunderstandings, thereby creating life anew?

This new philosophy was daring and wonderful. Free of superstition and the hard intolerance of old times, it left an untutored southern boy breathless and warmed in the vaulted rooms of First and Second Theology.

And yet it offered no magic. It was not Amelia's enchantments, no bees magically rising from the silica of the Borders' wake. Where the old theologians had believed that words—from Text or Hymn or Commentary—changed the shape of the Borders, altering things or bringing things into being, the Lambeth of Solomon's day taught more figurative magic: that the spells of old were objects of contemplation, and that within them the adept might contemplate the relation of order to chaos and might emerge, through that contemplation, more serene and wise.

Able to counsel and teach from that serenity and wisdom.

Solomon believed everything the seminarians told him, his nose in the Text and the Hymns and the Commentaries for seven years of snow and ice and youthful loneliness in a place far from family and homeland.

But that first winter became less lonely, less cold, with the first warmth of friendship.

Marcus Chatterton was the name of Solomon's friend. Second child of the Luvan Chattertons, Marcus was two months Solomon's senior, but years his senior in knowledge and knowing. Short, dark-haired, with gnomish features and a certain patrician shagginess, he was an Easterner, from Canaan in Luvah, and thereby subject to the many jealousies the raw Urthonans bore toward that older, more refined province.

Under the Luvan boy's tutelage, Solomon survived the perilous second year of seminary. History and Border Physics he plodded through without distinction, and Absence Theory was a fathomless nightmare. But in Incantation he actually showed a peculiar talent, interpreting and applying the Holy Writings in manners that his instructors considered correct but quirky.

A promising, if erratic, student.

It was Marcus who sat on a stool in the corner of Solomon's cubicle and, clearing his throat quietly, prodded his lumbering companion farther—first to a basic understanding of his studies, then to more sophisticated concepts. Finally toward something beyond what the seminary offered: a strangely ancient theology that eventually drew all that Lambeth did or had done into question.

Magic was alive, Marcus claimed. It was the hearts of the mages that were dead.

So he claimed, despite the assertions of lecturers and divines that such things did not work—that Border magic was mainly superstition, what the common folk called "ruffles," a complex and uncontrollable physical displacement of time and space and matter.

And, with Solomon as his assistant, he set about to prove it.

"Theirs is a hodgepodge of bad science," Marcus insisted one spring night, hands shoved into the pockets of his corduroy jacket, flannel scarf wrapped around all of his face but his hooked, protruding nose.

The boys were on their way to the boat docks. From there it was a brief voyage over the easternmost reach of Pontus Tarn.

"Great metaphor," Marcus continued, "but no meat. I don't buy old Father Ezekiel's physics any more than I do the ecstasies of Blights."

Spring was unseasonably cold in Lambeth, and the mud on the banks of the little lake was crusted with a thin glaze of ice. The vesper bells rang crisply at the end of the lengthening day, though the darkness still fell before supper, and scarcely a bud peeked from the branches of the dormant trees.

Prime nights for heresy, Marcus had proposed with a laugh. Prime nights for magic.

Bundled like polar explorers, the boys circled the chilly water together, Marcus' short legs churning to keep pace with Solomon's irregular, cranelike strides. All the while, the southern boy listened to his companion, as Marcus shot holes in everything the lecture halls had propounded that morning.

A fur-lined tricorn pulled down over his ears, Solomon barely heard the last phrase. His breath congealed on the scarf around his mouth, and he muttered a mild curse against the wind, the cold . . .

Against Marcus, who had insisted on this night for conjury.

The shorter boy motioned to Solomon, parting a lakeside tangle of branches to reveal a narrow footpath that followed a soft declivity down to a clearing where a dozen or so large stones lay tilted against each other, covered with dried grass, brown moss, and mud.

"Some sort of dryadic leaving," Marcus explained with a wink. Solomon didn't know whether to believe him or not: Marcus' sly eastern irony would bypass him on occasion, and he knew for a fact that the Luvan boy had little respect for things dryadic.

Marcus crept to a moonlit spot in the clearing, where the shadows of three stones crossed in a curious gray-white darkness. With a clownish grin at his companion, he placed his hand among the crossing shadows.

The air around his fingers crackled with green lightning.

"Borders," he whispered. "The real thing. It's a little crease in the edge."

"A crease?" Solomon asked, squinting skeptically as the light flickered again around Marcus' hand and sputtered off into the shadows.

"Remember your Border physics?" Marcus prompted. "Sometimes as the Borders ebb and flow, an edge catches on an outcropping of rock, or in a thicket of thorns. This little whirlpool is like a Border, more or less. Does the same thing to all the physics at hand."

Solomon squinted at the shadow. It looked little different from the shades the other stones cast across the clearing—a little darker, perhaps, its center dappled with a silvery gray shimmer, with flickering forks of green and red.

"The Blights *do* have part of the truth, though," Marcus said, his fingers lacing over the shadow, drawing green, then crimson fire from its swirling depth. "It's a place of magic, not of chance. I wouldn't be surprised if the Blights have it all over our teachers. After all, some of those boys have been through the Absences and lived to tell. And you have to travel the Borders to reach the Absences."

Solomon frowned. "But that's a myth, too, Marcus. Blight legend and folderol. It's what—"

"What do you accept of it, Solomon?" Marcus' brown eyes, customarily soft and kind, were suddenly intense. "You've been studying here for two years. What do you *believe* about what you've learned?"

He lifted his right hand, cradling a matrix of purple fire.

Solomon frowned, cleared his throat. "Wh-what about you, Marcus?" he asked.

Marcus grinned, brushed the fire into his left hand, then back again, juggling a will-o'-the-wisp in a moonlit clearing. "I believe most all of it," he said quietly. " 'Cept for some of the Commentaries."

Solomon gave out a low whistle. New Orthodoxy. A maze of heresies. Old Ezekiel Gordon would birth a heifer to hear it.

"Now watch," Marcus whispered. Flinging his hand as though he were sowing seed, he scattered the fire against the surface of the Border.

Purple flame spread like burning oil on the face of a pond, like shimmering salt in the dark air. The fire spread rapidly, defining a narrow pocket of swirling cloud that had anchored itself among the stones. In the purple light, the green and red flickers of lightning flashed deeper gray, flashed black.

"And this is the manner of the Daughters of Albion in their beauty," Marcus began, his raspy voice savoring the words.

> "Every one is threefold in Head & Heart & Reins, & every one
> Surrounded with fires unapproachable: but whom they please
> They take up into their Heavens in intoxicating delight."

Solomon flinched. He knew that Marcus was casting for visions, for a glimpse of a beautiful dryadic woman—one of the Daughters of Albion.

After all, it was all they talked about at fourteen.

Marcus waved his hand across the roiling cloud, a sleight-of-hand artist's dramatic flourish that both boys knew was unnecessary but that both accepted as part of the moment. For a moment, green fire flickered again through the cloud, and the air crackled with the smell of juniper and ozone.

Then the girl stepped from the mist.

Naked and pale, with a greenish dryadic tinge to her skin, she wafted toward the tense transparency that divided Border and Presence. She regarded the gawking boys with green, unruffled eyes, then extended her hand toward the Border surface.

"See?" Marcus whispered, and extended his hand to meet hers.

"Marcus!" Solomon shouted, but it was too late.

Their fingers touched in a web of fire and ether. Solomon stood back as a green, dryadic skin cast raced up Marcus' arm, and his fingers, twined with those of the girl, greened and branched and sprouted like a springtime of desire.

Marcus cried out and pulled his hands from the coursing flames. They were intact; indeed, they were the same hands he had thrust into the Borders.

It was the lad himself who had changed.

It was not evident as they returned that night, but in the weeks to come, Solomon realized that his friend had been touched by more than a dryadic hand—that something alien, not altogether ill nor good, had reached for him out of the Borders.

In the months and years that followed, Marcus never preached to Solomon. He was far too courteous for that. In the same courtesy, he never defied, out-and-out, the teachings of Lambeth's sophisticated divines. Nevertheless, he applied himself to unorthodox, even heretical studies, convinced that the dryadic girl was no dryad at all, no ruffle at the Border, but a divine Person in which power and love had come to dwell.

Solomon followed his friend, but only at a distance. He tried the occasional spellcraft, the occasional conjury at the Border crease and in a neglected bower the boys had discovered, but his own magic was erratic and volatile.

Sometimes Solomon wondered if it even worked at all. If even Marcus' conjury was no more than a blend of Border ruffle and wishful thinking.

Marcus' examinations suffered. The lecturers boded and scrutinized, though they were pressed to offer arguments against his assertions. His standing in the class slipped considerably, but a sweetness had come over the lad, one that Solomon had seen in no other person except, perhaps, his baby cousin Jasmina.

Marcus traveled the walled grounds of Lambeth in a sort of wondering ecstasy. Students and lecturers paused as he passed, and some marked the odor of incense and an abiding sense of peace that followed in his wake. Once, Solomon, catching a glimpse of his friend in a certain angle of light, noticed a cloud—violet and gold and white like the feathers of a phoenix—following Marcus as he ascended the chapel steps from a sojourn in the bower, the afternoon sun spilling generously upon his stocky shoulders, his shaggy hair, and the beak of a gnomish nose.

A phrase from the Commentaries took Solomon by surprise. *Not in utter nakedness,* he thought, *but trailing clouds of glory do we come.*

And trailing clouds of glory, his good friend vanished into the chapel door, as surely as a light winked out at the edge of the Absence.

So it went until the autumn of their sixteenth year, when the storm struck the lake, and the world changed forever.

It was the last best time for boating, late in the ninth month before the first frosts and freezes made uncomfortable the passage on the lake. Marcus, as always, was eager to go: as always, he preferred a midnight voyage to the students' customary day boating.

Solomon went along reluctantly. A river lad from infancy, he trusted the powerful moving water simply because, on the river, you could keep the banks in sight at all times. Pontus Tarn was tricky: the lakeshore was lost under reed and undergrowth, and at midnight sometimes the shoreline seemed to vanish, leaving the boater alone on the lake, far from help or solace.

Neither of them thought of the dangers that night. As always, Marcus had whistled by Solomon's window and the southern boy had climbed out dutifully, his foot precarious on the sill for a dizzying moment before, as always, he clutched the welcoming branch of the ancient poplar that wound its way up the side of the Students' Tower and, his face pressed uneasily against the smooth bole of the tree, descended amid the blood-red leaves to the ground, where his companion waited in the shadows, oar in hand.

"It's always better this way," Marcus insisted mischievously, his breath clouding in the moonlight. "Heretics sail by night, old Ezekiel says, and the tarn is more of a venture in dark water."

Solomon did not agree. As always, he regretted being drawn from the safety of his book-lined room by Chatterton's midnight summons. And despite its serene surface, the tarn was deceptive: the summer before Solomon arrived at Lambeth, two student boatmen had vanished in a sudden storm sweeping down from the Mountains of Albion. But scarcely a ruffle of breeze disturbed the waters when Marcus and Solomon rowed over the moon's reflection on a voyage to the lake's southernmost shore, where the dolmens still held tatters of the Border pocket.

Marcus was bent on seeing the green woman again. Over a courtship of six months he had wooed her religiously, returning to this spot from all corners of the compass, as though seeing her from a thousand different angles would only complete his adoration, give him some understanding that the first encounter had not afforded.

He had brought wine for the boating, and pulled sullenly on a bottle of Tharman Amber as Solomon, his eyes on the dwindling northern bank, rowed toward their destination.

"She will look the same from the north," Solomon scolded. He tired of ferrying Marcus to this metaphysical tryst, but the Luvan youth was preoccupied, finishing the last of the Amber and peering at Solomon ironically through the distorting green glass of the bottle.

"You look green yourself from this vista," Marcus proclaimed. "Seasick, perhaps?"

Solomon muttered and rowed.

Above them, a flock of black birds, caught unexpectedly by the moonlight as it drifted from behind a bank of clouds, wheeled and plummeted toward the trembling surface of the lake. Solomon watched them in fascination.

Fishers. Riding a rising wind.

For the clouds moved more rapidly, scudding the face of the moon. The dried leaves swirled from the near shore like ghosts fleeing an enchanter. Marcus set the bottle in the bottom of the boat and leaned forward, regarding his classmate confidentially.

"She is all there is," he whispered. "Ultimately, there is no more than that girl."

Solomon snorted, redoubled his rowing. The turbid waters rebelled against his efforts, and soon the little rowboat turned athwart in the middle of the lake.

"She's all there is," Marcus repeated. "Nymph of the forest and rising waters. This tempest will blow over, and again we can go to her."

"Nonetheless, we'd best find a way to steer this tub to the nearest shore before the storm takes us in," Solomon said through clenched teeth, as he wrestled the craft toward a shadowy, tree-lined cove. "Whether it blows over or not, we are in for it now, and an hour on the lake is passing deadly."

Solomon redoubled his rowing, but it was already too late. The midnight sky blackened to a color darker than black itself, and all the luminaries—moon, stars, and the halo of torchlight from the distant seminary—vanished in a scud of storm clouds. Marcus' little lantern was a feeble light on the vast stretch of water, and soon the lads lost the shore, rowing steadily in what they thought was a southern direction.

In the brief illumination of the first flash of lightning, Solomon's spirits sank. No shoreline was visible: water and cloud stretched as far as he could see through the brackish light.

Lulled by wine, Marcus reached into the pocket of his frayed corduroy jacket and drew forth a flask. Brandy or whiskey—Solomon knew from their previous festive outings. But tonight it seemed unwise, reckless even for wayward students.

Solomon kept rowing, while Marcus drowsed in the stern of the little boat. Now the lightning was furious, crazing the sky above the lake, reflected on the trembling surface of the waters until it seemed like a Border's edge, as if beneath the lake's surface an Absence roiled and summoned.

The rain and the wind swept in together, and the first wave washed across the gunwales of the boat. Marcus sputtered and sat upright, then the boat itself was engulfed in darkness as a second wave doused the little lamp.

A sudden surge of water off the port side wrenched an oar from Solomon's hand. A sick, sinking feeling rose in him as he looked out over the violent waters, watching helplessly as, briefly illumined by a flickering red thunderbolt, the oar rocked serenely away into far water.

Solomon turned around. Marcus, groggy from the liquor, was trying valiantly to bail the craft with his cap. The boat was taking on water, and each furious tilt of the vessel and more furious slap of the waves filled it further and further.

Marcus stood, bailing yet another capful of water. For a moment, as lightning framed the sky once more, his form was defined, teetering in the stern of the boat. Then, in a flicker of green light, he tumbled over the side.

Solomon shouted, scuttled aftward in the listing craft. Marcus' pale hand, then his shaggy head, burst the surface of the water. He came up sputtering, grasping desperately for the side of the boat, but a huge breaker passed between hand and gunwale, drifting him farther and farther from safety.

"Solomon!" he called out, as the current's embrace dragged him toward midlake.

Solomon called out, groped and splashed in the bottom of the boat for a rope, a rod, anything to throw to the drowning lad. Marcus wheeled slowly in a quickening eddy, his eyes desperate in another lash of crimson lightning. Frantically, Solomon tried the magic. With distracted urgency he mined his memory of the Text. Nothing of drowning . . . nothing of *shores* nor anything of *lifeline* at all. Drowning himself in panic, he tried a spell Marcus had fashioned from the Thirty-ninth Plate of the Text. Closing his eyes against the stinging spray of water, Solomon remembered the facing print. The couple wrapped in each other's arms, the eagle of storms above them.

Ololon and Marcus. Nymph and drowning boy.

His spirit plummeting, Solomon began an invocation—*any* invocation.

> "Loud the enemy thunder'd; loud & dark upon mild Felpham shore,
> Not daring to touch one fibre, he howl'd round upon the Sea."

He opened his eyes, breathing a prayer for calm. But Marcus had vanished in the turbulent water.

Solomon remembered little else of that evening. Someone rescued him—one story claimed it was three nuns by the lakeside sharing a secret bottle of wine. Solomon recalled only the empty, forbidding face of the lake as he trudged his years through seminary, as he lost spirit, inclination, and finally a vital spark that, somewhere in his soul, extinguished like a rushlight in a watery storm.

He remembered Marcus at Lambeth, at Arcady.

And now, as he sat in the mirrored room of his youth and remembered, the waters seemed to close again over the boy's head, and like a bitter wave his memories rushed to embrace and cover him.

CHAPTER 8

Afterward no priesthood came his way, no matter how much he had dreamt it and wished it and yearned for it over the best part of a decade. Instead, he received a lectureship, a teaching post which he lied about at home, calling it *priesthood* in the presence of Aunt Morgana and to soothe the expectant ears of his dying father.

Despite his lies, despite what they called him in Arcady, he was "Master Solomon," not "Father" or "Brother." He would teach forever the Second Form, the recalcitrant students who continued to linger, like himself, at the spiritual outskirts of the seminary.

Despite his disappointments, his lessons progressed comfortably if not reverently, in the very classrooms where once he studied. He taught the Holy Writings to boys from Urthona, from Luvah and Tharmas and western Elysium—boys who sat glumly and sleepily where once he had sat ardently and devoutly.

Text, Hymn, and Commentary. He taught them in the way he had been taught, from a lectern in the eastern wing of the seminary, lower rooms that seemed to capture and hold the morning light, purpling and greening it in the awful stained-glass windows installed by old Father Athanase in his stormy tenure at the helm of Lambeth.

"Joy's Grape" it was that adorned those windows in homely clusters climbing the oval frames.

In front of those purpling monstrosities Solomon stood, every morning for twenty years. There he calmed his great unease, forgot his failures, his warring family, his divided house and useless magic in days of uninterrupted lecture and meditation.

Slowly he gathered himself into a safe and numbing custom.

But finally, even the seminary walls were neither high nor thick enough to keep out the world forever. Between the wars and the rumors of war, between upheaval and discontent and poverty, the terrible world outside Lambeth was determined to intrude.

The Borders intruded on his ancestral home, and Aunt Morgana's letter came.

Arcady called him. And he returned to the labyrinth of his childhood.

Now, in a room at the heart of that labyrinth, Solomon started awake on his childhood bed. He had fallen asleep atop the blankets, whiskey glass tilted in his hand. Now he surfaced from unsettled dreams—dreams he could not remember, except that they traced his long history at Lambeth from one failure to another.

The lamplight mounted up the black curtains, and despite the confusion of lace and mirrors, the wilted balloons and cobwebbed steam engines, he remembered at once where he was.

"Home," he whispered. "Arcady. How often have my thoughts . . ."

Then the curtains moved, and the two men stepped from the darkness, their long robes dusted with light, their swords aflame like candles.

It was a moment before he saw their wings.

"Morgana's dreams are infectious," he murmured.

The two men regarded him with calm, brilliant stares.

Solomon knew at once what the angels wanted. It was their wings that did the speaking, choiring as the breeze passed through the feathers like breath through a reed, and their language was music that danced on the edge of words.

Breathless, Solomon listened. It astounded him that, as a man long accustomed to words and the knowing that words provided, he could understand the creatures so readily.

Perhaps they were only his dreams.

Whiskey. Border ruffles.

The curtains nodded behind them in what seemed to be a directionless wind that coursed through the high chamber scattering drawings, tilting the mirrors, sending Aristo's toy balloon aloft in a last, silent flight to the bedroom floor. The angels seated themselves at the foot of Solomon's bed, the warm dark breeze riffling their long hair, their feathers.

And he knew at once what they were saying.

At his feet, the glassy, melodious music continued, fanned by the angels' wings.

"I cannot perform such miracles," Solomon admitted. "If Morgana imagines that I can stalk through the house spouting the Text to dispel the cowering Borders . . . well, then, the nuns in the East have garbled her more than I imagined."

He leaned back in the bed, casting a nervous, skeptical glance over the bright forms sitting at the foot of the bed. Their wings, palpable and translucent as thin smoke, wavered in the still air of the room.

"Why did I bother to come?" Solomon asked. He told himself these were only apparitions, illusions, and yet he felt his anger rising.

To be challenged by dreams!

"This is *my* house," he insisted. "More than it is Mina's, or even Morgana's. More than Endymion's or Diego's, for I am, after all, several years their elder. After all, I *am* the head of the Hawken family, and when one of them calls, I . . . I . . ."

The angels regarded him, their dark eyes brilliant.

"Granted, there *are* things I could do. Provide counsel. Knowledge of Border physics. Spiritual guidance. But not this dramatic exorcism Morgana expects. Why, there's not a seminarian anywhere who . . ."

The angels' stare was unwavering.

Solomon cleared his throat. "At any rate, the Borders will recede. Sooner or later. It's like a tide or a season: they encroach, they disrupt things a little, they go away."

He linked his hands behind his head. But he was not satisfied with his rationalization.

Nor did the angels move.

"I know," he conceded. "Sometimes the season lasts . . . for years."

They had found him out, those bright uncompromising eyes.

Solomon slipped beneath the coverlets and pulled them to his chin, like a child hiding from eyes in the grain of the wooden door or imagined bugbears in the bedroom's darkness. He was no Saint Milton, tumbling from Paradise to redress the wrongs of a benighted, wounded world.

He was only a lecturer, and an unconvincing one at that. For the angels regarded him calmly, their expressions unchanged and skeptical.

"Then . . . what would *you* have me do?" Solomon asked.

The music welled in the high chamber. He was sure the rest of the house would hear it.

As one, the angels held aloft their swords and vanished. Solomon drew uneasy breath in the moonlit room, the darkness attendant as though he had dreamt his visitors out of mirrors and moonlight.

"I . . . I *can't*," Solomon replied huskily to the vaporous air, to the vanished angels, to no one in particular. "I can't do what Morgana asks. There is no magic that can push back the Borders. None I've heard of. It's too momentous a task. Besides, there are other things more pressing, other things to do. . . ."

He set his feet on the cold floor of the room and dressed, eyes averted, blushing before imagined, inscrutable eyes. At last, hoisting his coat over his shoulders, he stood at the door of the room.

The night had scarcely turned. He could be through the gates in an hour. To the Alph by dawn. He'd a better chance, he told himself, at finding Faith on foot than conjuring through a shifting house.

But that was not true. He was not after Faith, not really.

No. He was leaving because of himself.

Because his failure to employ the Text in a Border-haunted house would announce one thing to all his family—to Morgana and Mina, to Diego and Artemis, who were far afield and warring each other but would no doubt hear the news, and even to Endymion, who held no stock in the Text, but would use the occasion to an envious younger brother's advantage.

For all of them, it would mean that Solomon had failed—not just this time, but always. That his life had been spent in fitful pursuit of . . .

Of nothing particular beyond sweet sound and fancy.

This way was better. He could dodge through the night, mysterious and incomplete. They could make of him what they would in his absence, which is what each of them had done all along and would do again if he gave them no evidence, no surety of his weakness.

In the faint light Solomon buttoned his coat, the pistol secreted in its inner pocket. A fur hat of Aristo's adorned his head crazily, and a red silk scarf—the boy's? Faith's?—was wrapped about his neck to ward off the cold Urthonan wind.

There were coach lines not far from the river. One was at a shallow ford—an old, ill-kept inn where he could spend the morning. Two days, three at most, would see him back in the seminary, among bell towers and stained glass and dim, inattentive students. He would be safe again in the world of his choosing, in docile quarters, reading a docile Text.

He would be far from Arcady, from the altering, drunken halls and the afflictions of memory.

Silently, resolutely, he ran from the shifting house.

CHAPTER 9

From the upstairs window Endymion had seen a gray form weave through the moonlight, through the dark and the dappled topiaries. Crossing the grounds and vanishing behind the northern wing of the house.

And Endymion was afraid.

Now, scarcely two hours later, he stood by the window, watching as the garden's green animals—the taxus hare, the juniper hawk—took life from the wind and the cloudy, shifting light.

Endymion blinked. The topiaries seemed to move.

Khole perched at his shoulder like an oracle. The phoenix's feathers were muted by shadow, but the smell of incense, casia and balsam, wafted off his wings.

"Could the house I contain withstand the house that contains me?" Endymion muttered, eyes on the thick, undulating foliage.

Khole laughed softly. "Each time you ask, your questions tie themselves further into knots, farther from the answer. I can't even *follow* them. Don't confuse yourself with all this asking."

Endymion shrugged, ran his fingers through his iron-gray, thinning hair. "What do you know of questions, bird?"

The phoenix shifted his weight in an odor of ash and myrrh.

"I know that . . . it is more important to find answers," the bird replied. "And you have never done well on that account."

Endymion scowled at Khole. Slowly, he lifted himself from his seat by the window and, unsteady with gin and sleeplessness, weaved back to the littered table at the center of his attic room.

Shorter by a head than his brother Solomon, Endymion was plagued by a dozen scholar's maladies, by paunchiness and pale skin and reddened, weak eyes. In a red nightshirt and black baggy trousers, he looked like a dance-hall comedian, like a clown in a fly-by-night carnival.

All around him the chamber sagged with shelves. To his left lay the rusted machineries of a dozen years' discovery and collection—a pipe organ, a rusty cannon, a spectroscope—all discarded when the gadgets disappointed rather than delighted. To his right, stacked from floor to ceiling, were books, swimming in candlelit dust, casting enormous shadows over the narrow room. A dozen copies of the Text lay open to different passages, where Endymion sought for contradictions, for flawed cross-references in the holy book. Beside them lay a single copy of the Hymns and over a hundred of the Commentaries, their pages notched and dog-eared, bookmarked with phoenix feathers, letters, gin labels—all the respected sources, from the standard catechisms of the Urthonan grammar schools ("*What* do we thank?" "*What* is a joy forever?") to the heretical analyses of Ezra St. Ezra and the obscure meditations of Saint Hyperion Perkins.

Endymion knew them all. Though he had never gone to seminary himself (never been favored, he claimed, like his brother Solomon), he had studied the Holy Writings, memorized them and analyzed them. Had collected them like the hundred mechanical inventions that littered the room with wheels, cogs, levers, and treadles.

Endymion searched for all the places where the Text unraveled. Where it contradicted itself, or history, or the laws of physics. Where, most important, it made no sense to his sharp, analytical mind—to the intelligence that had inspired Grandfather Aristo to call him "the fox among my grandchildren."

The Text was a puzzle, and Endymion Hawken was out to pick it apart.

With a sigh, Endymion copied yet another contradiction into his thick notebook. Then, closing its leather cover in a flurry of dust, he turned to other things.

In the center of his room, propped on a table, braced by three discredited Commentaries, lay the enormous bottle.

"It is hard to believe," Endymion announced, "how a gin bottle houses a world."

"Why hard to believe?" the phoenix asked, spreading his mottled wings. "Everything possible to be believ'd is an image of the truth."

"And you scold me for *my* obscurity!" muttered Endymion. " 'Tis a fine pair we are."

Khole fell silent. Together, the companions regarded the model city that lay upon the table encased in glass. The faint odors of juniper and glue wafted through the air of the dusty chamber, and the books nodded on the shelves along the left and windowed wall.

When Endymion had begun the first of the tiny teakwood buildings, the bottle itself had not been empty. Faith had been gone two days and two nights, and Morgana and Mina were busy drafting the letter to dear Brother Solomon, asking him to come, to lift the manor out of the Borders.

Endymion was lifting himself out of the Borders as well, the gin half finished in his childless hands. They had brought him the news of his daughter's vanishment as he contemplated the fifty-five Commentaries of Saint Adonais, a short, elegiac text filled with an abstract yearning for vanished youth. He had buried his head in the pages and wept, trying vainly to remember Faith's face through the glaze of gin.

Remembering at last, the pink ribbons.

Like an emblem, a frail memento.

Khole had come to him then. Out of the old aviary, last of a surviving line of phoenixes that included the legendary Jechonias and his son Salathiel, the birds whose transforming flames had driven old Ezra St. Ezra from the banks of the Alph in a time when the heretic threated to conquer all Urizen.

Jechonias and Salathiel. Jesse and Bathsheba. The illustrious line that ended here . . .

As Endymion's line was ended.

For Faith had vanished, and Aristo had gone to join the Blights.

And Garrick . . . had never really been a son of his. Had never stood by him.

Now, in the dark nights of drinking and building, Khole perched on Endymion's shoulder, violet feathers dappled with gold and with white. And the bird had advised and boded.

Khole had told him once again to *find a purpose for the work*, or some other moralizing foolishness. Said that he would be of no help to Faith while awash in his cups.

As if sobriety kept the pantry door closed. Kept the Borders away.

Khole was proving to be a schoolmarm in his inner regions.

So instead, Endymion ignored the bird and built the bottled city. It was an intricacy that challenged his wits—a landscape of geometrical, almost abstract buildings glimpsed through the thick green glass of the gin bottle.

A city without people. Therefore, without pain and disappointment. It was his art: distant, mathematical, and complex.

He could not understand why Morgana and Mina, the resident artists, did not love it as he did.

The first pieces—the teakwood, the Elysian coral—fit together unsteadily, the tide of gin remaining in the bottle a constant threat to wash over them, to wash them away. And yet the long needle with which Endymion first assembled the little buildings was surprisingly steady, the detail magnified through the bottle glass so that intricacy was no problem, the foundations and first stories rising out of nothingness, as though like Great-Great-Grandfather Atreus and his hoodwinked children, he were building a dwelling place from the ground up.

"Your troubles will fly there, and your troubles will return. 'Tis too small a city for refuge," boded Khole, his long bill at Endymion's ear. Now the phoenix smelled of orchards and sleep.

"Hold your tongue, bird! This gives to airy nothing . . ."

"I know, I know," Khole continued. "I have heard that poetry before. And where is Faith while your ship-in-a-bottle city flourishes and thrives and prospers?"

"What would you have me do?" Endymion asked, the flutter of startled wings at his shoulder.

"Listen, Endymion," Khole replied, his voice melodious as a choir of doves. "I would have you begin by listening. Listen before you speak. And look closely, closer than you do through the glass. In short, pay regard and pay attention."

* * *

Upstairs, in the servants' quarters of the attic, Willie Melmoth said his prayers to Palamabron and to Tharmas, "the mildest son of heaven." Then sang a childlike song from the book of Hymns:

"Sweet sleep with soft down,
Weave thy brows an infant crown.
Sweet sleep Angel mild
Hover over th'happy child."

But then he slept fitfully on a hard cot, his dreams troubled by angels and by the faint smell of incense and woodsmoke in the stagnant air.

Twice he awakened in the night. On the first occasion, the pale moon rose into the roundels that dotted the attic roof, and the light poured through the dusty glass, illumining the room suddenly, completely, as though a flash of lightning lingered over the darkness.

In the new light, the contents of the attic spilled into view—hatracks, trunks, a bellows, a velocipede with costume jewelry adorning the spokes of the wheels. A dressmaker's model leaned against a portmanteau, and three cedar chests, stacked in a squat pyramid, breathed fragrantly from the shadows. A birdcage lay empty, skeletal, in the far western corner of the room, and against the eastern wall, where the sloping roof touched the dust-littered floor, a pile of rags—source of a spicy, smoky odor—seemed to glitter and smolder for a moment, as though something in the moonglow had ignited it, and it awaited only a moment, a turn of the dazed gondolier's head, to burst into full and consuming flames.

Willie stirred uneasily, closed his eyes, and tried to sleep. For a time, he drifted in and out of wakefulness, his drowsing punctuated by dreams he could not remember. A faint flapping noise, like a bird startled in a cage, stirred deep at the edge of his hearing.

* * *

Meanwhile Endymion sat and regarded, paying attention as the night turned and the dark hours of morning crept.

Sometimes the moonlight twisted and dappled across the magnificent statuary in the yard—little Mina's memorials to family history, in which the ancestral Hawkens stood resolute in bronze, littering the disheveled northern grounds.

Here was Atreus on his deathbed, with pen and plumbrule beside him.

There was Prometheus behind the plow, honored as the Hawken who raised Arcady to its financial splendors of tobacco and hemp.

Kassandra was there as well, blindfolded, her hand uplifted in the traditional stance of the prophet.

There was also the bare pedestal, which stood mockingly for the missing Innocent.

Endymion sighed. At night, especially in cloudy moonlight and even more especially since the Borders had returned, it was almost as though the statues moved, grew like the topiaries. Sometimes of late a mist would settle on the empty pedestal, and for a moment the cloud would fashion itself a human form, shoulders and arms and perhaps a head out of the shifting haze . . .

And Endymion would say to Khole, "This time. This time we'll see old Innocent for sure, see by the look on his face whether he lives up to his name or is a parricide come home to roost."

"Why do you care?" Khole would ask. "You cannot blame everything on Innocent: the war, Faith's and Aristo's disappearances, whatever it is that you hold against Garrick. Innocent did none of those things. And if his was *not* the hand that pushed old Atreus into the water, clearing his name of old crime will not make the world safe. Whatever the answer, you will still be here, in an upstairs room of Arcady, drinking gin and building a dollhouse world in an empty bottle."

Endymion sniffed and stared out the window, his bleary eyes intent on the vacant pedestal.

But nothing ever took form. Not quite. Nothing more than cloud and a churning movement. Endymion could look at the yard for years awaiting proof and revelation. And still the empty pedestal would shimmer and darken, for a moment promising that revelation, only to deny it with a passing gust of wind, the voyage of the moon out of the covering clouds.

So for a month the time had passed. Clouds in the bottle and on a bronze pedestal among the topiaries. Until tonight, when in the halls below his family gathered to decide his future, Faith's, the future of them all.

* * *

It was the noise that awakened Willie, completely and for good.

At the turn of the night, the noise increased until it seemed like thunder outside the roundel windows. Willie sat upright, the attic dappled by a shifting light, hatrack and cage and fragrant nest vanished in the shadow of wings.

An angel stared into a skylight window, his golden eyes beckoning, dark hands clasped fiercely against his struggling wings.

For a moment, dazed by the sudden wakening, Willie thought that the hands were the angel's own. But they were too dark, they were . . . were . . .

Not even hands. A black swirling nothingness gripped the bright creature, who wrestled back the darkness again and again, crying out in a high, plaintive voice—a sound musical, even in duress, as the chiming of crystal.

And by came an angel who had a bright key. . . .

Willie vaulted to his feet and shouldered a Saratoga trunk to a spot underneath the window. Then, climbing onto the arched, ribbed lid of the container, he grasped the latch of the skylight, wrestling, pulling, the light arm of the angel pressed against the panes by the swirling mass. The boy tugged frantically, dangling by the latch, wiry legs waving in the dusty attic air. Breathing a prayer born of the Text, of folk song, of gondolier's manuals, he braced his feet against the attic ceiling and, with a swift, desperate turn, opened the window.

A bright wind enveloped him, lifting him, turning him about and hurling him . . .

Lightly atop the ashen nest in the far corner of the attic.

And a cracked mirror beside the dressmaker's model, mate to those arranged in the long hall below and stored up here for its damage, shimmered a moment and went dim, as a faint chiming of bells tumbled through the attic and out of hearing.

* * *

Meanwhile, the conversation downstairs lasted until the early hours of the morning, when the chime of the great clock in the anteroom had struck two.

Only Morgana's voice, and Mina's. Sometimes the murmuring that arose from the first floor as they spoke and muttered to one another almost took shape in names or in words. Yet it was like the mist on old Innocent's pedestal, their talking—ill defined and teasing.

In the morning dark, someone climbed the steps below the attic room, passed beneath Endymion's room, brushing against the ladder that rose through the trapdoor, and continued down the hall, the candlelight showing vaguely through the cracks in the floor.

Was it Mina passing? Morgana?

Why did he concern himself?

Once again Endymion turned to the bottled city and began to build, the long needle knitting teakwood to coral and wire.

Golgonooza he called it ironically, after the fourfold city in the Text through which travelers to eternity were said to pass. Its buildings rose slowly like a dark reef in the refracted light of the glass.

Golgonooza. Way station in the midst of chaos.

Endymion reached for the flask in his pocket, for the fire and juniper. Khole rustled at his shoulder.

It had come to seem inhabited sometimes, the city. If you held it right, tilting the neck of the bottle as if you sought to empty the last drop of gin from it (though all of the gin had been emptied these several weeks passing), then the light would catch the base of the bottle and tumble downward, until it filled of a sudden the dark toylike city with silver wisps—silver shot through with red and green. A bright cloud continually moving between the windows of the little buildings.

And *Khole*, he would say. *Look, Khole.*

But the phoenix seemed uninterested, perched by the window, the moonlight spangling his white feathers. Khole was waiting for something else.

But this night the bird regarded his handiwork. And they both listened at the stirring out the window, at someone moving through the fenced grounds toward the East Woods and the fields beyond.

"Hist!" Khole whispered, and they both paused and listened.

"Who is it, Khole?"

The phoenix cocked his head curiously, fiercely, in the manner of predatory birds, all birds. He looked intently through the bottle into Golgonooza.

"Not your aunt nor your cousin Mina, for the two of them have begun to dream. I can see their dreams rise through the bottle. . . ."

"And you're sure it is dreams you see?"

Khole peered across the room into the bottle in Endymion's hand.

"Dreams, indeed," he repeated. "Dreams have a green-and-golden cast, like moonlight on the floor of the forest."

"But, Khole, what . . ."

"I see no more," the phoenix cautioned. "They have invited me no further."

"I, on the other hand, stand on no invitation," Endymion proclaimed. With a quick, unsteady lurch to the right wall, he lifted the spectroscope from its cobwebbed place on the shelf. He turned ominously, ironically, to the bird.

"Hist!" he cautioned. "And pay attention, signior."

Khole fell silent once again, ruffling his wings. The air in the attic filled with jasmine.

Endymion peered at the glass through the glass, and under the lens of the spectroscope, the light in the bottle began to dapple and move. The reef of tiny buildings was awash in mist and in glowing, and from among them, from a single high room in a coral tower, a light shone forth, as if the bottle no longer refracted the light of the moon or the lamp or the candle, but was a source of light itself.

Indeed there were curtains on the tiny window—dollhouse curtains Endymion would never have placed there, for it would have been too cunning, too precious, and far too painstaking.

Like Arcady, Golgonooza was growing on its own.

"Gin," Endymion said scornfully, dismissively. "But as long as I am here . . . I shall part those curtains and look inside." He winked at Khole, then began to declaim in a voice uncannily like that of his twin, Diego, a parody he had mastered in childhood.

"No curtain can daunt me, for I am dauntless!" Endymion boomed. "I shall behold the divine interiors of Golgonooza and my aunt Morgana at rest. Sleeping she is, and I shall look even more closely, and part the curtains of her dreams."

It was always wayward, this spying on the family.

Khole did not approve.

Endymion, on the other hand, was most always willing. How his family's dreams had entered the bottle he had never understood, never figured, never even cared. Sometimes he suspected he had dreamed the whole matter out of sorrow and gin. But generally he used the mystery for espionage and intrusions.

He wanted to know and then to know more. It was in knowing, Endymion felt, that his power—all power—lay. If the family was like an equation, like a long geometrical proof, then every theorem and fact must be known, must be factored in.

Then there would be no surprises. No children vanished or estranged. No shifting house.

When the mind encompasses all, it can predict what is to come.

Oh, Endymion would scold himself after he dipped into the family's dreams. He would mouth all the nice, proper words about *privacy* and *regard*. But the phoenix's bemused glance told him he fooled nobody.

So leaning forward, forgetting the glass that enclosed the buildings, the room around him, forgetting Khole and the nodding light and the wanderer in the hall below—Endymion entered the tiny room in thought and imagining.

* * *

Morgana slept uneasily, a cloud dappling in mist and in light above her head. And as she tossed nervously in the bed, out of the cloud came a quartet of angels—three young, the fourth immeasurably old.

Each of the angels turned in an amber light, each for a moment bearing the countenance of men, of lions, of oxen, of eagles. They turned without seeming to turn, the change in appearance fluid and dazzling, like sunlight breaking over moving water.

Standing above Morgana, they sparkled like burnished bronze, and spoke to one another in the untranslatable language of angels. It sounded as though someone, at a great distance, was running his finger across the lip of a crystal wineglass, or as though Uncle Raphael's grove, scarcely a mile from the house, harbored a navy of doves. For the angels' language is wordless exchange of music and pure tone, and at its sound Morgana sat up in her bed.

As she began to listen, the song changed. Beneath the piping and cooing the sound of breakers arose—the rush of waves against shorelines far to the east. The room smelled of verbena, of wax and stale clothing—an odd smell Morgana remembered from her youth, attached like legend to the ancient females of her family.

Now the angels took other forms. Her mermaid mother, Melusine Stella-Maris, complete with fishtail and kelp-green hair, shrouded in soggy linen and swimming in the candlelit mill house south of the mansion . . .

Ancient Great-Aunt Ahania, the very bricks of Arcady in her hands, and Kassandra prophesying and gesturing . . .

And the piping and cooing changed to the wordless song of women.

* * *

"They are starting to call her," Khole whispered.

"As they do each generation," Endymion agreed sorrowfully, peering into the bottle. "To all our women. Morgana will be going soon."

"But not yet. Morgana will not answer for a while. And she knows that she has much left to do before the yearning is too powerful."

"To set her house in order?"

"Her house. And yours."

Endymion watched through the glass as the waters of Morgana's dream spread before her, in a ship manned by a faceless crew, their backs to her, their heads bowed, attentive to the oars.

And in the dream they rowed his aunt to an island bathed by waves and by a steady orange light. Upon that island stood a chorus of angels, singing and beckoning.

The light shifted. The pull of the tide toward shore became stronger, and the crew lifted oars from the water, content to ride the low urgent waves into the bright and singing arms of the angels . . .

Who were changing again.

Whose long robes soiled and thickened with the dark waters, with algae and kelp. The darkness of the robes wedded itself to the bright ethereal bodies, shifting, roiling, until the robes themselves fell away, revealing a discordant choir of lamias, women above and pythons below, who beckoned the boat ashore with the same gesture, but a gesture that now seemed corrupt, hungry—even obscene.

Endymion gasped. The faces of the lamias were those of his grandmother, his aunts and cousins. Among them also sweet Christabel, sweet Mother.

Khole creaked at Endymion's shoulder. Under the spectroscope, the light of the bottle turned green, then amber. They were no longer afloat, but once again seated in the large brown overstuffed chair, in an attic room smelling of gin and of old things and the damage of rain and neglect.

Endymion blinked, his eyes smarting with lamplight. Again he must have been weeping. All these losses, and his children into the bargain.

"Enough," Khole warned. "Do not turn all loss into your own, Endymion. 'Tis one reason why the dreams of others are dangerous."

"Mina," Endymion breathed. "I shall see . . . what Mina is dreaming."

The phoenix fell silent again, as Endymion peered back into the swirling country of the bottle. Now before him, in the small world of Golgonooza, in a miniature drawing room trapped in glass and in green-and-amber light, Mina continued her sculpture, atop a low stool where she might give closer attention to its still mysterious face.

"Am I dreaming, Khole? Or is she?"

"It makes absolutely no difference, Endymion," Khole declared dryly.

"Whose face will it be, do you know?" Endymion asked the phoenix. "On the statue, I mean."

Khole was silent.

"Don't stonewall me, bird. I know it's Solomon, and that the continual dream of the sculptor's hand has brought him here more surely than any letter—than any distress, for that matter."

Endymion knew no such thing, but through probing and espionage, question and cajolery, he was generally right about family secrets. He kept quiet, looked into Golgonooza as again he proved prescient, satisfied himself.

For indeed, the head of the dream-statue assumed the shape of his brother's—the long gray hair given birth from its source in the wax. The map of the face itself—hawklike and proud and yet defeated in the depths of the eyes—rose unexplainably from the dream of Mina's hand.

Just before he could be sure, before he could see the face and its features, the head of the statue began to glow—the red, the white, the yellow of flame arose from the green and amber. A livid, purple scar, unlike any Endymion remembered on his brother, traced up the statue's neck like a crazing in crystal.

Mina stepped back to regard her work and was lost in the swirl of light at the edge of the bottle. A huge death's-head moth circled the head of the statue, drawn by the light and the warmth into the center of its fire, where it was consumed, crackling like meat on a spit.

The glow of the bottle faded. Endymion felt dry and his head hurt grievously. Again he reached for the flask, settled into the softness of the chair.

"Why am I seeing these things, Khole?"

"Your eyes are red and terrible," Khole observed. "Look not into that glass."

A moth, very real this time, settled on the surface of the still-glowing bottle. Khole hopped to Endymion's shoulder as though regarding the thing hungrily. He rumbled, then thought better of the whole venture.

"But what of the visions, Khole? I am an engineer, not a prophet."

"And not much of an engineer, for that matter," the bird observed wryly, dropping sullenly to the arm of the chair and gazing ironically at the bottled city.

"*That* is none of your concern," Endymion huffed. "Confine your architectural commentary to . . . nests and stone baths. Meanwhile, I shall see what my brother dreams."

"Nothing," Khole declared.

"Nothing?"

"That much I can tell you. He is already gone."

CHAPTER 10

There in Endymion's bottle lay the image of the very house Solomon was leaving, an image formed in slow time from teak and from coral. The house and the surrounding grounds: Uncle Raphael's grove, the Stella-Maris mill house, the endless sprawl of brick and stone and frame and window arising, taking form, behind and above them the rush and the swirl of violet air . . .

"Whose dream?" Endymion asked, squinting to make out the rooms in the assembling upper stories.

As always when it came to dreams, Khole refused to answer.

"Solomon's," Endymion answered himself ironically. "But no longer. For Time is bending. The Borders have seen to that. As a bottle contains old air, this Golgonooza has captured the edges of Then. It is Then we are seeing, for Now is invisible, rushing away into night, toward the end of the story. If you understand."

"Too convoluted," Khole observed. "So much fury and feathers and high drama and gin. Stop philosophizing and pay attention."

Endymion peered into the bottle. There the violet air turned gray, glittered and boiled behind buildings fashioned of teak and coral. Then, as suddenly and as completely as the air had turned, the outbuildings were no longer, swallowed and dissolved in the approaching, swirling darkness.

"The Borders," Khole whispered.

Now two angels stood at the edge of the moving cloud, on the oldest pillared porch of the house. Burning swords they carried, and as they raised the swords, the house gave way behind them, toppling into the terrible reeling darkness.

“What dreams this brother of mine has!” Endymion squinted, tired with the hour, with the blue ruin in the flask.

“His dreams are as they should be,” Khole boded, and his companion glared at him hatefully. “For he is awake as he imagines this. But hist!”

“Another ‘hist’ at this early and godforsaken hour? By the Caves of Saint Alastor . . .”

“Enough of the bottled theatrical. To the window, Endymion.”

Endymion rose unsteadily, Golgonooza in hand. He clutched the table for support, and suddenly, abruptly, the window stood in front of him. So violently had it moved or seemed to move that for a moment his knees gave at the sill, he was falling over . . .

Until strong hands at his shoulders drew him back. Or strong hands it had seemed, for he turned unsteadily to find no one but the phoenix in the room.

Endymion shrugged, and looked again. The house was moving. By Borders or by gin.

For a moment he forgot why he was standing there.

The window. Outside the moon raced into shadows. Khole fluttered briefly in the air, came to rest once more upon Endymion’s shoulder.

Again the bird began to sing—divine verses this time, a passage from the Hymns in a ruined, melodious voice like an old door creaking:

“The night was dark, no father was there;
The child was wet with dew;
The mire was deep, the child did weep,
And away the vapour flew.”

Endymion tilted his head, frowned at the phoenix.

“He should be coming from the house,” Khole declared, on his breath a faint, oriental smell of balsam. “Look to the window, and below.”

The clouds, as the song suggested, covered the face of the moon. Suddenly the courtyard below was gilded and framed in light and as suddenly dim once more, as whoever stepped out into its shadows closed the main door behind him. A lantern bobbed toward the path through the topiary, its deep orange light catching and glittering on polished metal.

"Diego?" Endymion asked the silent bird at his shoulder. "Diego arriving at last?"

"Solomon leaving," the phoenix corrected. "Bound for that country where his dreams are hiding."

Glittering in the moonlight, the lantern receded among cedar and taxus and juniper. Endymion followed his brother with the eye, then with imagining, as somewhere near the stable, perhaps fifty yards away, the trail broke into open country, and Solomon was off in the saints knew what direction.

And from on high, the bottled city still and quiet in his hands, Endymion watched out the window until the topmost leaves of the poplars reddened at the edges. Suddenly, surprisingly, the shapes in the topiary and the things of the courtyard were manifest, defined in light, and he realized that he had been watching them for some time now.

Again, in the first red ascent of morning, he was afraid.

* * *

Morgana was restless, rising in the dark before the dawn and descending the stairs to the drawing room, the wheel, the clay she began to spin and shape, joined by an equally restless Mina. Together the women worked, each at her separate station, until sunrise, as outside, unknown to them both, Solomon stalked off into the shadows.

No doubt the restlessness, the inability to sleep more than an hour's running, had come from Morgana's stay in a wish sanitarium. It had been her misfortune to be born in a time when visions were not merely ignored, as they often were now, but punishable.

Crimes of Vision, they were called then. Seeing things in the Presences. Things others did not see.

And Morgana, of course, was a woman. Thereby, under the strange masculine agreement of priesthood, prophecy, and bardic wisdom, her visions were that much more threatening.

Still, she was a lucky one, if you could call it that. Some of the women never returned from the mountains.

To this day she thought twice before telling a man about her angels. Three times before telling a priest.

"I knew they were here long before I saw them, Mina. *That,* at least, I haven't lost: it's like drawing a vase or bowl or bottle from a lump on the wheel as though I know its whereabouts in the dark life of the clay."

"And yet you told Solomon, Aunt Morgana. And see? You are still here. Still living. And Solomon a priest and all. So what was the big ado?"

Morgana glared at Mina, who meant no flippancy, and yet said harsh and addled things. She must move that statue from the west side of the room, Morgana thought: her best light is at sunset, and the nuns said . . .

But enough of the nuns' pronouncements. Throughout the mansion, it was not only the waning sunlight that crazed and distorted the work of your hands. Lately the vases and bowls and bottles came to life off-center, or more off-center than usual, so Morgana had known, weeks before, that the Borders were coming, that the angels would herald, and that their visit was nigh.

Known, but would not admit it.

First came the breathlessness, the light-headedness she had not felt since the mountains. She thought it was death approaching. Even now, she saw death looking back at her, cold and gray-faced in the wet clay on the wheel.

That would not do.

Morgana winked at the hooded visage and laughed nervously.

Mina rose, circled the distant statue, the phoebe lamp aloft in her delicate, swollen hand. Somewhere in the recesses of the house a clock chimed twice, then growled, then chimed again, and something fluttered nervously.

No, death would not do.

She had too much work to tend to in this dispersed family, too much to smooth over among nephews and nieces as confused and as lost as a bottle hidden in the clay.

So each night she said no to the death approaching. No, and then the dizzy spells were over. Morgana thought she was winning, then, that she was beating back whatever it was that had set itself upon her, whether sorcery or curse or charm or merely seventy years upon this earth—whatever it was, she hoped she had set it aside.

Meanwhile Mina circled the evolving sculpture, surrounding the wax figure with the clay investment, preparing the mold for the molten bronze of her statue.

There was a human shape trapped in it, the girl had discovered. It would take most all her energies to draw it out. The boys—Solomon and Endymion and Diego—had never understood how made things came to be. Thought it was silliness, that rock or earth or a certain sound in the garden would open unto you and show you its mystery.

But they understood how the clock worked against their cousin, was woven into Mina's disease: the death's-head moth spreading across her face, smothering her slowly . . .

And, of course, Endymion just as ill above, locked in an upstairs bedroom with memories and loss and a bottle and a bird. With imagined slights, a daughter vanished, a young son running the Borders, and an eldest son he suspected was not his own, not really.

And now, there was more.

Missing rooms. Vanished windows.

At first Morgana had feared for her sanity. Yet she had noticed Mina and Endymion checking doors before they entered or left a room, watching the light twist about in a window above them as though somebody were dragging a shade across its face. Even now, her back to the heart of the room, Mina glanced around herself at the shadows in the firelight.

Morgana had known when the house had crossed into the Borders. But she had not spoken. After all, it could have been the visions again.

When she was a child, before the angels, the house in which Morgana had grown to adolescence was the same house, more or less, in which she now lived (give or take the sudden shifting of rooms). All the Hawkens had lived there, too—the grandparents, great-grandparents . . .

And more strangely, to hear Morgana tell, those long beyond the sound of earthly voices, the far more interesting ghostly relatives she watched wander through the halls of Arcady. Old Atreus, with his intricate foolish blueprints of an ever-growing mausoleum, floated ethereally through the hall on his wheeled deathbed, his ghostly great-grandson Vergil paddling beside him. Her grandfather Prometheus wandered the rooms with the first of the talking birds perched on his shoulder, the first of a hundred generations of raven and roc, parrot and phoenix . . .

Of whom Endymion's Khole was the last of the line.

The numerous others, both Hawkens and brides of Hawkens, dwelt in the burgeoning house until its many rooms were a dense labyrinth of arrivals, residences, and departures which nobody followed, noticed, or even concerned themselves with except for Morgana herself.

Innocent she had never seen.

One simple day, after she announced the presence of ghost and angel, her brother Roger had smuggled her into a coach and driven her east.

She remembered the black crepe curtains on the coach window, Cousin James staring dolefully out of the eastern tower as the coachman carried her away. She remembered the rough road and a sense of rising.

Now, back at home and safe these forty years, she feared that her reason crumbled as the walls of the house shifted, collapsed, and vanished entirely.

Then there was that unwelcome lightness again—the dizziness that had signaled the arrivals of departed relatives some sixty years back.

The Wish Disease, the sisters at the sanitarium had called it, as they gave her the black syrup.

Remembering the syrup, the long stay in the mountains, Morgana rose heavily from the wheel.

It was dawn. The pot she had been making was grievously off-center, leaning like a willow in a high wind. Already Mina had left the drawing room for bed, silently slipping out as her aunt crouched over the wheel, caught up in work and revery and perhaps for a moment in sleep.

Still, it was morning, and the shifting of the house more mute and somehow safer. Now Morgana moved sluggishly, pained by the stiffness in her ankles, toward the door to the courtyard, behind which lay light, fresh air, the sound of birds, and a seat on the stone bench in the garden, from where she could watch the water arch and tumble from the mouth of the marble dolphin Grandmother Thel had commissioned from the famous sculptor Praxiteles Bell—his last work before he passed into the Borders, never to return.

The very Borders that were approaching, Morgana was sure.

She turned, looked back fondly at Mina's work. No Bell, to be sure, but learning—the clay and wax pliable and talented beneath her fingers and tools. Mina was learning, provided she had the time.

Morgana looked above her, distracted by the sound of something falling, of high laughter from a room upstairs. Was it the bird's? Endymion's?

She shook her head, reached out, opened the door.

Opened it not into the garden she had expected, but into a drawing room that mirrored the one she was leaving, except it was massive, its appointments twice the size of those in the room behind her. She felt threatened, felt the old fear of open places that first had seized her in the airy vistas of the mountains. As the first impulse to panic ebbed away from her, Morgana marveled, wondered if somehow, like Faith, she had opened the wrong door.

But the house had changed again, of course. It was only mirroring itself in some monstrous and chaotic way.

Room upon room upon infinitude of room.

What was it Endymion had called it?

She felt a draft—cold air descending—and looked above, where the ceiling of the room had been torn, as though by a high wind or by cannon fire. For the first time in months, she stared directly at the sun, which had risen blindingly from the heart of early morning.

Quickly she turned away, her vision darkening and spangling with shadows of deep green, the old dizziness doubling until she staggered in its power. Again, she looked where the dazzling light from the break in the ceiling was broken now by crouching, dark forms that bent over her, the sun at their backs. A cloud passed over the hole in the roof, blocking the sunlight, and at last Morgana could see clearly.

There above her, at the top of the walls, perched amid rubble and the jagged edges of the broken roof beams, seven angels stood, their wings a brilliant and merciless amber, their hair cascading like the spun gold of the fairy tales. Calmly they regarded her, their wings fanning in a chiming, musical language that sounded to her bewildered ears like something that was not speech at all, as though those above her passed messages in runes or in hieroglyphs or in numbers—in something a step removed from words and from voices.

And the last thing she remembered was when they turned toward her and caught her in their glowing eyes. For a moment she understood it all—the arrival of the angels, who warned her of something in the movement of the house, in the cruelties of her past, in everything leading to this new and sudden encroachment of the Borders which was not like all the ones that had preceded it.

It seemed to have a purpose, a malign intention.

But her thoughts were too small. She forgot it all at once. Swiftly the vision swept her into a deep sleep in which she dreamed, for the second time, of the sea.

CHAPTER 11

It was the High Moon, when the banks of the river flooded and turgid water wound between the boles of the cedars like a great snake, devouring itself and all who ventured near.

And now, of course, was the time Solomon would pick to return.

Scarcely beyond sight of the campfires, the hoofbeats of Diego's mare muffled and splashed in the green dark of the forest. He was bound for Arcady, for the family council Aunt Morgana had called.

Solomon's arrival meant the long ride home. Diego had trusted the troops to Lieutenant Peacock, if you could call it trust.

If you could call them troops.

"There is no telling what monsters they'll imagine in the undergrowth," he advised the lieutenant, as they both stood in Diego's lamplit tent, the sound of the woods muffled by the coughing of a sentry, the stirring of horses tied in the distant dark. "Sphinxes. Centaurs. Everything a fool's believed in they'll fashion out of Borders and night."

Peacock nodded soberly.

"But with all your military schooling," Diego continued, standing at the tent flap in a slow eddy of cold autumnal wind, "maybe you could keep half of them alive until tomorrow evening."

The lieutenant frowned, then smiled suddenly, recognizing the joke.

Diego had stalked through the camp, Garrick filing crisply behind him. As he walked from firelight to firelight, the Captain heard the Lady's name brush the conversation like the soft, ominous flutter of a bat's wing. Most of the men slept lightly now, recruit and graybeard, muskets no longer stacked but nestled beside them in their blankets like lovers.

"At least by this time," Diego muttered to Garrick, to nobody at all, "the bastards know enough to be afraid."

"Fear's a wakeful tonic, Uncle," Garrick replied. He never ventured to call Diego anything but *Captain* in the presence of the men, but it was night, and they passed so rapidly from campfire to campfire that they seemed to be alone, moving in smoke and darkness.

"It'll keep 'em awake, all right," Diego agreed, gesturing toward the farthest fire, where a solitary boy stood, clutching the reins of a little mare. "But it's just as like to rout 'em through bramble and river and even into the Absence, with all those imaginary rebels barking at their heels. Oh, don't laugh, Garrick. I've seen it before. I've had to bluster and coax and strong-arm enough routed soldiers to know that fear's no reliable comrade.

"And the Lady's Land is no place for government troops."

Above, in the obscure notches of an enormous cedar, something rustled and slipped, crashed through a web of branches, grunted and lay still on a thick low limb.

"They have enough on their hands to hold to their posts in a wind," Diego grumbled. "Don't laugh, Garrick. By the saints and assembled ancestors, do *not* laugh."

* * *

He was still muttering three miles from camp.

Diego leaned forward in the saddle, ducking a drooping cedar branch. He was half an hour from the fires and the bivouac where he so passionately wanted to remain, an hour or so from Arcady and home and all this foolish business of Morgana's summons.

He had dawdled in the camp until he could wait no longer.

About the only good Diego could make of this whole sticky and inconvenient visit of his brother's was that it would bring Artemis home, too, as the family gathered to tend to the perils of the house. At least the Lady would not take the field against these boys, her rebels like owls in the trees.

And he could see her there, in Arcady. In lamplight.

But mostly, the trip home would be like going to school, pent up among all those Hawken intellectuals and Hawken artists and Hawken clairvoyants without a good hunting dog on the grounds or passable whiskey in the pantry.

Diego drew an old gum blanket from the saddlebag. It smelled of mud and sweat and wet horse. He slipped it over his shoulders and clicked soothingly to old Juno, who waded uncomfortably in pastern-deep waters.

The Alph had risen to meet them halfway.

They called the river sacred in the Commentaries, and for good reason. It flowed in and out of death, and back in again, past the ruins of pillared Riverfront south and west to the ruins of Ville, flowing thick with rubble and refuse, and mystery out in the dark midcurrent.

"Through caverns measureless to man," Diego whispered. *"Down to a sunless sea."* As always, the Commentaries, or what little he remembered of them, seemed right.

Diego had been trapped once by the Alph at high water. With his sister-in-law Lyca in a sturdy barouche. They had waited out the night wordlessly, he on one side of the coach, she on the other—for after all, what had he to say to the bookish bride of his brother?

In the months that followed, Diego wished more than once that the waters had drowned them both. Drowned him, at least. Or perhaps, for everybody's sanity, drowned Endymion.

And now it was the drowning season again. The rain swelled and the clouds settled, obscuring the fragmented moonlight and rustling the pine needles, the cedar branches, the clinging dry leaves of the poplars. The water dripped down on Diego, rose to the steady flanks of his mare. Diego steered old Juno mindfully through the sluggish waters.

Faintly, as though it was memory or imagining, the smell of a watchfire wafted through the trees, the dark smell of dry wood burning.

Rebels, obviously.

Where they got the dry wood, especially in the midst of high water and rain, was beyond Diego. But not, of course, beyond his cousin.

Not beyond the Lady, who rode with the rivers and rains.

Keeping the fires downwind, the blanket steepled over his soggy head so that he looked like a tent on horseback, Diego guided Juno into the brimming riverlands. He listened, alert to movement, to the sound of anything rushed and sudden in the trees. But the path was confused: the darkness took away the edges of things—the trees, the undergrowth, the tall, drooping branches—until the greenery blurred into something downright cavernous.

Measureless to man.

In the deeper dark to Diego's right, something coughed. Steadily, quietly, he drew his pistol, thought better of it, and slipped the gun back under his belt. Producing his long knife instead, he peeked from the blanket and waited.

Juno stood still in the high water as torches bobbed green and distant among the branches.

Torches, and thirty or so ragged riders, their horses steaming from a long ride and a rising rain.

Diego knew them for rebels instantly. No government troops could move that quietly. Not even Polidori's Dragoons, the best government cavalry on the Tharman frontier.

He bent into the dark blanket as the column passed by within sight, within pistol range. A line of gaunt and bearded horsemen, men who looked three days from a meal and six from a bath. Shotguns, sawed-off muskets, a pistol or two: no blade, no foolish lances, or anything that would draw them into a close-quarter fight where, as usual, they'd be outnumbered mortally.

Diego knew these men from the aftermath of battle. There he would find them, one or two fallen among a dozen dead guardsmen. The green uniforms a decade old now, tattered into fringe and ribbons and banners.

So little fat on the men that the corpses kept for days, while the guardsmen ripened in the humid river air.

Their priests were as gaunt as the privates, and welcome in the rebel columns, where over half the men carried copies of the Text, despite the fact that few if any of them were booked enough to read it, taking their religion, as most did, from childhood schooling in the Hymns and the instructions of the clergy.

Diego had found the holy fathers dying on the battlefields as well, armed like mercenaries and whispering Hymns with their last breath.

The rebel horses were ragged as well, the evidence of fine bloodlines and Urizen pasturage worn thin over miles and months. Forced to live by grazing, by what they could muzzle from the badlands. Still, they were twice the horses the government issued.

Diego shifted slowly in the saddle, his movements veiled by shadow, undetectable to any but the best of rebel scouts. But the passing column stared straight ahead, bound for a vanished point to the north where commander and staff ranged in green shade and descended night.

Who led this company?

Artemis, perhaps, if Morgana hadn't got word to her about the gathering at home. Black hair hooded against the rain, green eyes aglitter in this green and witching light.

His lovely cousin, his rival.

His better.

Gabriel ben Ezra, perhaps. Great-grandson of the famous heretic and the most senior of the rebel officers in the West, around whom rumors of murder and conjury had circled for years.

Or Marion L'Overture, the defrocked priest and military genius, as skilled with a line of horsemen as he was with the silver flute he played in the concert halls of his youth and on the battlefields of his prime.

Whoever led these rebels, whatever they carried, and how many rode in the column Diego could not tell from this remove. The horsemen passed, and he slipped the long knife back into his belt. There in the darkness he waited atop Juno, as the torchlight drifted south and away. Then slowly he turned southward, angling east to steer away from outriders.

Then another noise stopped him in his tracks.

Nearer, this time. Crashing though the underbrush like a boar or a tyro. Like the greenest recruit from the Citizens' Guard. When the man came into view, Diego could tell by the silhouette against the fractured moonlight that this was no boy, no youngling, but an old fool bound for disaster.

Wrapped in a long cloak, the traveler breasted thorn and fern alike, setting his own clumsy trail through the woods as though he were the first explorer, as though none had ever marked track or measured the depths of this small but deceptive forest.

Something about the man was familiar. Inexplicably, Diego thought of the house. A dark shape at the edge of his memory teased him like the face of one of Mina's sculptures emerging from the clay. Then the darkness enveloped the wandering, lurching figure.

"Whoever it is," Diego muttered to Juno, "he's bound for an appointment with the rebels, if his path don't steer him otherwise and he don't quiet down to a roar. Artemis' lads won't sit in the darkness and watch him pass."

The traveler blundered off into the dark net of the Alphside, and Diego soon forgot about him. It was getting late, and Arcady beckoned from beyond the river.

As the night turned, horse and rider breasted midwater, the brown, fish-smelling current thick and cold around them. Even in the darkness Diego could see the Borders to the east, the swimming, shivering air and the river cresting white a hundred yards upstream as though the water itself breathed easy, now that it was free from the bedlam behind it.

Juno snorted wetly and shook the water from her flanks. She waded in the shallows near the south bank of the river, then climbed up toward dry ground.

Diego himself relaxed. They were two leagues from Arcady at the most. In country where he knew the dangers like the floor and the walls of the house where he grew up.

He rode, approaching his ancestral home, and the forest opened before him.

The southern gates of the grounds were guarded by four bronze sphinxes, relics from the days of old Atreus and the covenant with Ceraphis. Worn by winter and rough weather, green with verdigris and dying moss, they looked like the blurred statues in the far background of a painting, like something old Atreus Hawken must have dragged years ago from the ruins of metal and stone some half a dozen leagues upriver.

Diego approached them heedlessly, slipping his pistol absently into his yellow sash. Details of the house emerged from the shadow now—the twin towers, the row of stained-glass windows high in the first story's southern exposure. Moonlight pooled on the surface of the lake, and for a moment Diego stopped, rose unsteadily in the stirrups, and stared admiringly across the flat expanse of pasture toward the mansion.

Right pretty thing by night, was Arcady.

Then the bronze of the statues began to ripple and move.

At first Diego weaved in the stirrups, fumbling to keep his balance. Old Juno rustled beneath him, and only a quick grasp of the tightened reins kept him from falling out of the saddle.

"Damn!" he breathed, and spurred the mare toward the orchard at a gallop, just as the sphinxes' eyes began to emerge from the gray-green metal. He was off like a shot over the pasture, guiding Juno with a skilled rider's hand as the mare hurdled a rock fence and weaved gracefully around a capsized wagon, racing swiftly through the rain-soaked hayricks toward the westernmost edge of the lake.

Then three more of the creatures emerged from between the peach trees, lumbering slowly as though they labored to free themselves from their heavy bronze bodies.

Diego cursed and wheeled the horse hard right, headed now on a broken path between the lake and Uncle Raphael's nut grove. The sphinxes followed, picking up speed in pursuit, as the Border passed over them, changing their substance from metal to flesh and sinew.

Diego heard the snarls behind him, heard the creatures gaining ground. There was a story about them—something to do with a riddle.

He cursed himself for his childhood hatred of fable and lore. Had he listened to that tutor for a moment, ever, he would have known what to do.

Whistling to Juno, Diego ducked beneath a spreading oak, and out of a tangle of branch and shadow the mill house seemed to vault—a dark little cottage at the juncture of darker waters. Diego spurred the mare again, and with another heroic leap, Juno cleared the mill stream, stumbled, and found footing on the gravelly far bank and lurched up into the night, leaving the sphinxes whimpering and snuffling at the margins of the water.

Diego shuddered and drew his pistol. The night was suddenly haunted.

Carefully, he guided his horse through a gap in the ancient wall and around the circular tower, heading along the western wall of the mansion toward the courtyard, the main gate, safety. On the gables and spires of Arcady, Diego could see bright wings flashing. He could hear elusive birds cooing and gibbering to each other in a language that sounded like the rubbing of crystal. Juno snorted, and to the left, by the old ancestral gate, a pillar of darkness rose from the ground as though the lawn were sprouting night. As he rode past the pillar, Diego held his breath once more and fired the pistol twice at the looming shadows, for whatever good it might do.

The shots, as usual, went far wide. Cold, subterranean air washed over Diego, carrying with it the faint, ruined smell of death.

He held his breath and spurred the mare. Even at home the rules were changing.

Now Diego clattered recklessly into the circular courtyard at the front doorway of the house. In the darkness behind him something was lurching, nearing, and for a moment his fears propelled him, the thought of abandoning the mare to the pursuer rushed over him . . .

And shamed him.

I abandon no one, he told himself. As long as my strength holds up, I will never leave anyone behind.

Swiftly, pivoting in the saddle, Diego drew his pistol from beneath his cloak, turned, and leveled it at the approaching darkness, which widened and expanded and deepened hungrily, as though it opened to receive him . . .

"Sir!" a voice called from the lamplit doorway. "Over this way, sir!"

A ragged boy, not much larger than a child, held the huge double doors of Arcady open and beckoned Diego into the hallway. With a shout, the Captain spurred Juno, who surged beneath him ably, responsively. Together horse and rider lurched up the wide slate steps and into the front hall. Diego tilted in the saddle and ducked, his shoulder brushing against a crystal chandelier, scattering glass lusters dramatically like a rain of ice as the boy closed the door against the rushing darkness and Juno muscled down the corridor, churning scatter rugs beneath her skidding hooves.

With a leap, Diego dismounted, toppling into a delicate drop-leaf table as his wooden leg slipped from beneath him. Grasping desperately, his hand found Juno's reins, clutched them, steadying himself and the horse at the same time.

Pulling himself to his feet, he shouted for Morgana, then turned to the boy, who leaned with his back against the door, hair like a parted curtain above wide and startled eyes.

"Thank you, gatekeeper. 'Twas witty of you to make the house a paddock when that *thing* come up in the courtyard."

The lad nodded. "You reckon 'twill be gone by the morning, sir? I've a journey to make at sunrise. On foot, since my gondola's logged and busted."

Diego grinned, for the first time since he handed command to Actaeon Peacock. "I reckon *nothing* when it comes to Arcady," he admitted. "What in the hell of hells has happened to those statues? And who are you, sir?"

"Melmoth, sir," the lad replied, stepping away from the door. "Willie Melmoth."

The boy was a bundle of rags, his sleeves smoke-stained and the cuffs of his jacket singed.

"Well, Master Willie," Diego drawled, "if you must depart in the morning, then may the assembled saints walk with you. You're a likely lad."

Willie frowned at the strange, military ruffling of the stranger's speech. "That may be, sir," he observed. "But I pray that some of them saints might lend a little more hand in a place like this, what with the shifting and sphinxes and all."

"Hitch the horse in the hall, if you would, Master Willie," Diego requested, shuffling the sad remains of the leaf table with his foot. "I expect you're right. Whatever's afoot here has little to do with the saints."

CHAPTER 12

Diego's shouts and the racket of the mare in the hall awakened the household. Morgana, bleary in the collapsed anteroom, lurched out of the chair, the sound of tides receding in her ears. Into the hall she came, to find her nephew standing over the remains of the antique leaf table, in somber conversation with that rumpled, omnipresent boy who had guided Solomon into Arcady on the previous evening.

Solomon was nowhere to be found. A search of both stories and the dormer high above the nursery revealed that her eldest nephew had deserted Arcady on the previous night. All of a sudden it made sense to Morgana—the sudden and furious movement of angels, the unbidden music, and the transformation of a dozen shifting rooms.

"Our last chance," Morgana warned, seated on the pedestal beside Mina's sculpture. "He *has* to say the words over the house. Whatever the words are. And if he is beyond recall, we must still find a way to recall him somehow."

Silently, Mina laid hands to the wax.

"Mina? Perhaps you don't understand the . . . urgency of 'last chance,' " Morgana scolded gently, instantly regretting the words as she looked into the face of her niece.

For the moth was there. The flush and inflammation.

Last chance. The girl knew it in her blood, to the roots of her thinning hair.

Unfazed, Mina circled the wax investment, setting the first layer of clay around the translucent figure, the echo of a smile on her lips.

Diego entered the room, cloaked and capped against the night, glass lusters tumbling from his coat like shaken snow. "I've settled the mare," he murmured. "The courtyard made her skittish."

"Warm yourself, Nephew," Morgana urged, her back to Diego. "I've some stratagems to fashion. Regarding your brother's disappearance."

"Disappearance?" Diego asked, removing his gloves. "Then you're certain the house hasn't swallowed him? like it did my niece?"

"I'm certain of nothing," Morgana replied wearily. "What do you believe has happened to Solomon? And where should we look?"

"I'm no more sure than you are," Diego offered. "But I *might* suspect something . . ."

A dark stumbling form wrapped in a long cloak . . .

Painfully, Morgana rose and shuffled to the pottery wheel. "I spoke to Endymion," she said. "He claims to have seen Solly blundering off into the night."

Diego seated himself heavily by the pottery wheel. "It will be difficult," he said, "to raise a patrol to find my brother. The rebels have been here first. No doubt they've taken the best of the men, as they always do."

"No doubt," Morgana agreed, splashing the wet slip over the wheel, moistening a year's worth of crust and sediment. "They have great allies."

She dropped a wedge of clay onto the wheel. Then seemed to think better of it.

"Where do you think a *patrol* can find your brother?" she asked, the wheel spinning slowly to a stop.

Diego shifted uneasily.

"North," he challenged, his voice a little loud, echoing in the large drawing room. Above him, birds stirred in the damaged rafters, and the lamplight seemed to bend to follow him. "Where else could Solomon have gone, Morgana? Into the Absences like a Blight? No. Grown men don't vanish into chaos. Abstract he may be, but he ain't addled."

Diego caught himself. Blustering like a field commander to an old woman who was not listening.

"Solomon is going back," he concluded wearily. "To hole up in that seminary."

In a long silence Morgana leaned over the wheel, nudging the wedge of clay into its still center. Then, spinning it slowly, cupping her hands against the damp, twisting surface. On the other side of the room, weaving slowly through the slanted light, Mina redoubled her work on the statue.

In the midst of that large, uncomfortable silence, something shuffled at the top of the stairwell.

"Then again," Diego said, his smile ironic, "perhaps *Endymion* knows it all. 'Twould be momentous stuff." He rose, tottered, made for the drawing-room door as Morgana rose from the wheel and followed, wiping her hands on the tattered apron, the potter's wheel spinning slowly with its lump of unformed clay.

Together, the two of them crossed fifty feet of shadowy floor and stared up into the cavernous darkness of the stairwell. A pair of booted feet descended one step, and then another . . .

"If it's finding a brother you're after," called a voice from the shadows, "then you will need no lamp in the darkness."

"Endymion!" Morgana exclaimed, tempering her surprise and delight.

Diego gaped as his twin descended the steps, dressed in a threadbare greatcoat, a large, cumbersome bird perched on his shoulder, a large, cumbersome book held aloft in his shaking hand.

Endymion looked ancient, gray and glittering in the failing lamplight. Lifting what seemed to be a bottle, he began a strange incantation, in a language Diego could only assume had been spawned in the depths of the Borders.

Diego turned away. Thank the saints this brother resembled him little, if at all. Another precisian, smelling of ink and lamp oil.

And unlike Solomon, this one on the stairs hated him.

"*Sed veritati interea*," Endymion concluded triumphantly, the phoenix surging from his shoulder and perching upon the railing, "*invigilandum est, modusque servandus, ut certa ab incertis, diem a nocte, distinguamus.*" It was all gibberish and smoke, as complex and useless as his hundred collected inventions, and yet Diego felt the same old envy, the rising anger.

" 'Meanwhile,' Endymion said, smiling blearily at his twin brother, 'we must be vigilant for truth and keep balance, so that we can distinguish the certain from the incertain, the day from the night.' Roughly translated."

"And no closer to common sense," Diego snapped, and Morgana stepped between her nephews.

Diego rumbled. Always, in its depths and its entrenched foolishness, the family had valued gobbledygook over gallantry and vapors over valor.

It was why young Garrick had not returned to Arcady in a year. The *real* reason, not some fabricated biology Endymion had discovered halfway down a gin bottle.

Diego knew. It was the same reason he had joined the Guard at seventeen.

"So you're awake, dear?" Morgana asked merrily, beaming up at the favored twin.

Endymion lurched to the bottom of the stairs, smelling of ink and mildew, wax and juniper. Diego staggered forward to catch him, and the twins met on the bottommost stair, looking straight into each other's faces, where once again they saw the resemblance they constantly denied.

Face upon face.

"Optical transmission lines," Endymion whispered with a sneer.

Diego turned away.

Khole fluttered to the railing and spread his variegated wings. The feathers caught the lamplight and blossomed with bright color. The bird rumbled and coughed, and Endymion cocked his head, almost birdlike in his attention.

"I . . . I am going west now," he announced, standing to his full height, reeling, assuming the exaggerated dignity of the masquerading drunkard. "Prepare the wagon . . . accordingly."

Morgana looked to Diego in alarm.

"*Now* you expect me to say something," Diego muttered.

"It's here," Endymion announced urgently, pointing to the weathered Text in his hand. "It's all here, Morgana. Solomon's flight. His whereabouts. His destination."

"Prophecy is fled, Endymion," Diego insisted. He had no idea where he had heard the phrase.

"I was speaking to Morgana, Diego," Endymion replied.

Diego leaned against the balustrade, glowering, as his brother continued.

"It's simple detection, actually. What is the word? *Ratiocination.* Yes, that's it. Where the mind ventures forth and around the puzzlement, tying it up neatly and splendidly in a simple, decipherable package. Our brother is a priest, is he not?"

Dumbly, Morgana nodded.

"And as a priest, is he not guided by the contents of this book?"

"No need to lecture and puff, Endymion," Morgana cautioned, but Diego could hear it in her voice. She was intrigued. Charmed and delighted at the prospect of wit, of a clever solution to Solomon's departure.

Of this *ratiocination.*

"No lecture is necessary, Morgana," Endymion said, steadying himself against the balustrade. "Simple anticipation, this is. Predicting Brother's movements by the map he will consult. He will use the Text to guide him, and I . . ."

He leaned precariously over the railing. Diego stepped forward, but Endymion righted himself, waving his brother away.

"I shall follow in Solomon's supposed footsteps. It's as simple as that, Morgana. Khole and I are westward bound, and I shall need the following things transported from my quarters and placed in the wagon. The velocipede. The bellows, the faceted spyglass, and the hurdy-gurdy. Most of all, the bottle. Send the servants to retrieve them."

"The servants have fled, Brother," Diego reminded him. "And doesn't it make more sense that Solomon would . . . go back to seminary? Rather than on some western goose chase . . ."

Endymion raised his hand. "It *might* make more sense," he conceded, "but it would be less interesting. Our older brother is a man of learning, of scholarship. I believe the road he takes is . . . a bookish one. One that would intrigue a *more than ordinary mind.*" He looked pointedly at Diego. "And I believe I have a map of the road," he concluded.

Endymion waved the Text above him triumphantly, but stopped when the phoenix ruffled its variegated feathers. He turned, lurching back up the steps.

"He's mad," Diego declared to Morgana. "Mad with gin and mourning."

Morgana leaned in the drawing-room doorway.

"Mad," she said, "is never a word . . . to my choosing." She glanced furtively at the phoenix, who continued to watch her calmly from the balustrade.

"Sometimes at night," she confessed, her voice scarcely above a murmur, "two voices fall from Endymion's room upstairs—his and another

I do not recognize, full of thought and music. And then the air is thick with balsam."

"Illusion," Diego muttered. "Scientific sleight of hand. One of Endymion's contraptions."

Morgana settled herself heavily into a chair, which creaked as it received her weight. "I am less certain of that," she replied. "In fact, Nephew, I am less certain of all things."

Her skin was pale, mottled against the dark wood of the chair. The smell of stale verbena and wax washed over the room like unbidden memory. Khole murmured again, his soft, muffled gabbling like the prattling of an infant in a room upstairs. Diego, standing at the foot of the stairs, winced and disentangled a solitary glass luster from his rain-damp collar.

She would follow Endymion, and nothing he would say could shake that certainty.

CHAPTER 13

Morgana *was* certain of one thing: that Endymion, left to his own resources on the western road, would be prey to most anything that wandered there. Either of the clashing armies might seize him, bandits or Blights might waylay him. And there were always the Borders, shifting over the Tharman roads like clouds on a passing wind.

Morgana had not planned to leave Arcady again. Not in the declining year and at her declining age. Not onto a road perilous and strange, where disasters waited to happen and her only possible protection was a melancholy nephew with a penchant for gin and machinery. Certainly not while her niece faded into a slow consuming disease.

Nonetheless, by the afternoon, when Endymion had sobered up and begun to load the wagon, having consulted the Text and the Commentaries and his makeshift astrolabe in the hope of finding his brother's possible route of escape, Morgana was thinking second thoughts.

She watched from the tower window as Endymion, gnomelike and small from her giddy perch above the mansion, seemed swallowed by the broad hurdy-gurdy he hoisted to his shoulders and deposited in the paneled bed of the drummer's wagon he had discovered the saints knew where. The slogan on the side of the vehicle—*Doctor Immaculo's Famous Oils and Nostra*—scrolled across the wings of a gaudily painted phoenix as though the bird towed a banner through the stationary air.

"You want to go," a voice declared behind her. Morgana turned as Mina glided ghostlike into the circular tower room.

With brilliant dark brown eyes, the ailing girl regarded her aunt.

"You want to go with him, Aunt Morgana. With Endymion, to whatever western destination he has determined. You believe you would be of greater help outside the grounds."

"But the house . . . but *you* . . ." the old woman objected. Mina waved away the objections.

"We will be here in your absence," she assured Morgana. "There are other Absences that threaten us more."

Morgana nodded. In the courtyard below her, Endymion had placed two more of his inventions—a fragile faceted telescope and that gin-bottle city of his midnight speculations—carefully on a mattress of blankets in the wagon bed. In a heavy, lurching flight, the phoenix swooped from the tower window to the seat of the wagon, the gray air spangling behind it, and Endymion vaulted up to a place beside the bird, seizing the reins in his gloved hand.

Suddenly, Mina stood beside Morgana. The sunlight played through her pale, translucent skin, and the old woman startled.

She is vanishing, Morgana told herself. *My niece is fading away* . . .

"Go," Mina urged her again. "And trouble not."

She was not like Endymion, incapable of remaining in half-knowledge. Mina could survive the mystery of the house. She would lose herself in her work, and scarcely notice that Morgana was gone.

But it was still with reluctance that Morgana consented. Heavily, as though the pain in her wrists and knees had shackled her, she descended the wide front steps of the mansion and, hoisted by a straining Willie Melmoth, mounted to the driver's seat beside her nephew. Settling her ample backside onto the leather-padded bench, the old woman looked back once into the dark of the wagon bed, inspected the exotic array of machinery.

Illumined by a hurricane lamp, Khole returned her gaze from his new perch atop the hurdy-gurdy. His shadow, large on the far inner wall of the wagon, seemed for a moment strangely human, as though the bird had stepped behind a looming giant, his wings lost in the dark silhouette of enormous trunk, shoulders, and arms.

Khole whistled, and his songbird's voice trilled a version of one of the early Hymns.

Or so it seemed to the old woman's hearing. She stopped, listened, but the song drifted into disorder, then silence, leaving only the echo of the Hymn in her recollection.

Mildly irritated, Morgana turned to receive the reins from Endymion.

It was as though the bird's eyes questioned her, followed her movement, bored relentlessly into her back.

Then a strange attar of incense rose from the cluttered wagon bed behind her. The smell washed over Morgana, and she knew—with a certainty even deeper than that of her angelic visions—that the only way to save her niece, or at least to save Arcady, was to do just what she was doing.

To risk losing both and travel with Endymion.

Morgana blinked. What had just happened?

What was the source of her knowing?

She pivoted slowly on the driver's seat, peering over her shoulder into the wagon bed. For a moment, Khole himself seemed to glow with a soft, ethereal light.

Then the feathers were merely feathers again, gold and metallic green, and the phoenix hopped restlessly from the hurdy-gurdy to the long, faceted maintube of the telescope. Khole hid his head under the shadow of his wing, and instantly began a soft, tranquil snoring. Morgana looked back upon the bird, upon the strange opalescence of his wings, in which, for an odd moment, she caught her own reflection staring back up at her.

It reminded her of the morning that the aviary burned, and she sat there in the wagon, rapt, recollecting.

* * *

Even as a small girl, before the visions began and the angels settled in Arcady, Morgana had been cautious when she passed the aviary. Just north of the topiary it sat, a large gazebo fashioned of wooden frame and bordermetal mesh. Indeed, to a child the whole north grounds seemed haunted, between the occasional prowl of old Ceraphis and her brood and the constant, melancholy sounds of a dozen species of exotic birds, the collection of her grandfather.

Nightingale and phoenix. Roc and cockatrice, skylark and hoopoe. Even then she had mouthed the names ecstatically, watching from the entrance to the stables as the morning sun reddened through the dark mesh, and the winged shapes—some of them small and flitting, some almost man-sized, ponderous on perches—came to slow wakefulness. The feathers, red and green and white, flashed in the early light. Then the chorus would begin, and Morgana would feel the sadness of caged things in the music.

Khole was the last of his line. Or so the family claimed, and Morgana had no reason to doubt them. He would last a thousand, two thousand years, renewing himself each century in the ashes of his nest.

The bird would change again, old Grandfather Atreus promised. And it did in the spring of Morgana's twenty-fifth year.

In the previous winter, the Hawkens had endured uncommon snow. The Luvan Mountains were still impassable in the topmost regions, and the March thaw had been slow to come along the Urizenian banks of the Alph. All the midlands awaited spring with special yearning.

One day, late in March, Morgana sat at the spinet in the topmost floor of Arcady's solitary rectangular tower. The windows were open, and the faint, earthy smell of the Alph rode the moist air through a flicker of curtains, ruffling the pages on the music stand.

Under that watery smell lay another, the ever so slight hint of incense.

Morgana lifted her hands at the keyboard and listened.

It was the aviary. The usual melancholy sound from the gazebo beyond the topiary gardens was spare, downright mournful for a March afternoon, the skylark's song scarcely a whisper and the pair of brown doves old Prometheus had gathered from the south chiming in a soft, despondent chorus.

Morgana set aside her music, and, dangling her feet idly over the piano bench, breathed in deeply and opened her senses. It was something she had been able to do since childhood, heightening sight and sound, touch and smell, with simple relaxation and attention. Suddenly the room swam, as it always did for the briefest of moments. Then the dust motes in the air glittered and danced, and her sight and hearing and smell were assailed by a thousand stimuli.

The hum of a wasp in the topiary.

The rustle of waters in the mill house, as Mother stirred in her sleep.

The pacing of Uncle Innocent in his room in the tower below.

Vergil's loud, simple laughter as he chased after Cousin James through the topiaries, playing at a game for which Vergil, at least, was far too old.

The odor of green peaches from the far edge of the orchard.

And the sound from the aviary deeper and more complex than she had thought before, the rustle of feathers and the stirring of birds on their perches mingling with a new sound.

The low, sonorous thrum of the phoenix as it settled the spices and grasses into its nest.

Morgana slept well herself that night. The faint whiff of incense hovered in her room in the new north wing, and near dawn the rumbling of the phoenix rose in volume, in intensity, until the pottery on the girl's shelf quivered and scooted with the vibration.

The rumbling woke her. She rose, and tiptoed to the window.

In the north, above the topiary, rose a halo of yellow light, creating a false second dawn on the still-shadowy grounds of Arcady.

The phoenix haze. The cool, brilliant fire that heralded the transformed bird.

Morgana held her breath, wrapping her night dress tightly around her bare shoulders. Over the topiary the light grew. The lovely fire of rebirth and rekindling.

But only a moment later, the cry arose from the stables. The aviary was burning, in a riot of white-hot fire.

All the household poured forth, buckets and rakes in hand, to meet the rising disaster.

Fortunately, the grounds were wet with the moisture of spring. The bucket brigade of servants and relatives circled the house from Atreus' lake through the ancestral gates and over the courtyard and topiary. Fire darted from the wooden frame of the aviary, and the shrieking birds battered against the wooden latticework that caged them.

Morgana stood between her aging great-uncles Innocent and Raphael, passing the brimming oaken pails toward Roger and Vergil and Father. She was shocked when old Innocent set down a bucket and lowered himself to the ground.

"Let it be," he declared, rubbing the long livid scar on his neck left by the dryadic dart. His sooty fingers streaked his pale neck, and Morgana caught the faintest hint of oil in the air. But Innocent's cold blue eyes looked weary, haunted, and Morgana concluded that her poor uncle was fire-sick, smothered by ash and the gaseous smoke of burning night soil.

"Let it be," he repeated quietly. "Something inside is burning out of control. Too late to save the lot of them.

"They let the fire in to begin with."

It was obscurity. It had nothing to do with the aviary.

Morgana shrugged, hoisted the discarded bucket, and delivered it, splashing, into the waiting hands of Cousin Cortez. Little Cousin James closed the ranks bravely beside her. Together, they wrestled three more buckets to Uncle Raphael, as black smoke billowed through the topiary and the acrid smell of burning wood covered them, brought tears to their eyes.

Through the pall of smoke came a cry, a cheer from Vergil, Morgana thought. The rough wood of yet another bucket tore at her hands, and as she handed it to Uncle Raphael she heard Vergil—or she thought it was Vergil—cheer again.

"The phoenix busted through, Roger!" he shouted. "The birds is free!"

Sure enough, the sky darkened further with a tumult of wings, the loud, hysterical cries of twoscore, threescore birds. Free in the smoky air, they sailed away toward the East Woods and liberty. Khole, however, perched atop the stable, his new feathers brilliant, resplendent, edged this time with a rare and immaculate white. He glared down in Morgana's direction, his black eyes glittering.

"He has much to answer for," Innocent said, nodding at the phoenix.

For a while, Morgana agreed. After all, had it not been the fire of his transforming that ignited the aviary, letting loose Grandfather Prometheus' prized collection of birds? As the fire died down and the exhausted Hawkens scattered themselves throughout the topiary, coughing, sneezing, falling to their knees in gratitude and weariness, Morgana glared back at Khole, wishing him trouble and as stern punishments as a sheltered young woman can imagine.

Perhaps it was the smoke. Her own weariness, perhaps. But as the haze scattered and the noonday sun emerged, it seemed for a moment that the phoenix's shadow . . . lengthened. That the broad wings cast a human shade, as though a tall man stood behind the bird, his shadow swallowing the smaller silhouette of the phoenix.

Seeing things again, Morgana told herself.

And seeing things was bad.

Yet she was not surprised when Cousin Cortez, combing through the rubble of the gutted aviary, found blackened splash patterns on the earthen floor and smelled the unmistakable odor of kerosene.

The fire in the aviary was no phoenix haze, but wrought by human hands.

Only then did Morgana remember the faint whiff of oil around Uncle Innocent, the powdery ash on his thin, tapered fingers.

They let the fire in to begin with.

* * *

Now, nearly a half century removed, Morgana blinked as she stood at the same spot from which she had watched the aviary burn, the phoenix rise. Suddenly, surfacing from the past, from the memories of burning and of Innocent, she found herself in the courtyard, surrounded by nephews and nieces, the ashen fingers of her great-uncle vanished, replaced by Endymion's thick-fingered hand as it traced along a line of text in a book opened before her, impatiently held up to her face.

An illumined book. It was the Text her nephew showed her.

"The clues are all here, Morgana," Endymion urged. "Here in the Text itself."

Morgana held the pages at arm's length. She could make out a few words. *South* and *fire*. *World* and *end*. Words retrieved from the fragmented, swirling ink, amid the whirling shapes and the drawings—the rooted man on the page facing Endymion's pointing finger and the six women at the top of that page, three basking in sunlight, three cowering in shadow.

Morgana frowned. They had never taught her letters at the wish sanitarium, nor at home in Arcady, and her nephews were prone to forget it.

"Read it to me, Endymion," she said. "My . . . my *eyes* are not what they used to be."

Her nephew hovered over the page, as intent as a hawk mantling. In clipped, almost military intonations, he began to read from the sacred book, and Morgana closed her eyes, following the words with study and regard.

The ancient words raced into the foggy air, and it seemed that the landscape itself stilled to hear them, as Endymion intoned and chanted. . . .

> "All falls toward the Center in dire ruin sinking down.
> And in the South remains a burning fire: in the East, a void:

> In the West, a world of raging waters: in the North, a solid,
> Unfathomable, without end."

" 'Unfathomable, without end,' " Morgana repeated, after her nephew's voice had died into the foggy morning air. "Beautiful words they are, Endymion, though they're somber enough to my ear. But why *this* passage, Nephew? Saint Agnes knows there's a score of 'em like it, with boats and coaches and travel."

"But look at this one, Morgana!" Endymion exclaimed. " 'All falls toward the center'! Like here, among the Borders! And the only passable direction to the west, amid the raging waters. And by what watery western route would he go save the Alph itself, fair Ololon of the Text? He's seminary-trained! No doubt he has chosen this very passage!"

Morgana frowned. It seemed less obvious to her.

"To what end?" she asked.

"He's looking for Faith, is Solomon," Endymion explained, gesturing widely. "As I knew he would be. West into Tharmas under cover of darkness."

Endymion paused dramatically. Morgana lifted her spectacles from the chain about her neck. Solemnly, she stared at the book once more.

How Endymion could draw a western route and rescue and Faith from a solitary passage that mentioned none of them was beyond her. How did he know Faith had gone toward Tharmas?

How did he know that she was alive at all?

It was all beyond Morgana. But as she saw her nephew's eyes brimming, scanning a hope in the faded, illumined text beneath his gliding finger, she was not sure.

"Read it again, Endymion," she coaxed. "This time more slowly."

Endymion cleared his throat and again began to read, his high thin voice raking the morning silence. And Morgana whistled once, twice, softly to the team of horses, shaking the reins above their dark, undulating flanks, as together the great beasts surged into slow life and the wagon crept unsteadily down the brick drive toward the battered western gates of Arcady.

* * *

Diego stood at the doorway as the wagon passed through the gate and out of sight.

It seemed far-fetched to him. Each time his brothers came up against a hard place, they buried their noses in books until they emerged with an answer, like metaphysical ferrets. On rare occasions, they found the truth—a sort of accident of detection, as he understood it. Much more often, though, they surfaced with a course of action that left them worse off than when they began.

And no matter the policy nor strategy, neither Solomon nor Endymion ever listened to *him.* Endymion, in fact, was downright hostile to his twin, nursing a longtime grudge.

And Morgana? Morgana had hopped in the wagon.

What do they expect me to do? he thought indignantly. *Post guard on this forsaken place?*

The young gondolier in the courtyard dusted himself off and made for the steps. A bit winded from hoisting Diego's aunt into the carriage, Willie Melmoth stood on the front steps as Diego leaned in the doorway above him and pondered.

"A curious sort, your brothers," Willie observed, as though he had divined Diego's thoughts. Diego pivoted on his wooden leg and regarded the young man warily.

"Melmoth, is it not?" he asked in his best drillmaster's voice.

"In the natural, sir," Willie replied with a slow grin. "And now that I've brought one brother in and seen one out, I expect I'll be on my way back home to high Urthona."

"And I," Diego said, rising to his full height on the steps above the lad, "expect otherwise."

* * *

The red jacket fit Willie awkwardly. Bright colors appalled his gondolier's judgment, as he imagined himself floating above the forest, a scarlet target for anyone with a gun and a passing inclination. Apprehensively, the undergrowth a tangle of green before him, he followed Diego through the noonday forest.

Pine branches, bent back by Diego's mare Juno as she breasted the foliage, whipped across the stiff, waxy surface of Willie's blanket as the lad hunched in the saddle, miserable in shadow and greenery and more miserable still atop a docile swaybacked plug of a horse—the only mount available at Arcady after the thievery of rebels, the hunger of sphinxes.

It had not taken much to persuade Willie Melmoth to accompany the Captain into the woods. There was no safe passage through the Alphside Forest, and the river itself was treacherous water, and further woods on the other side of the Alph made it downright dangerous for a solitary traveler, on foot or on horseback, and Willie's gondola lay at the bottom of Arcady's muddy pond.

Diego had promised Willie safe conduct past all attendant peril, and an escort of government cavalry to the outskirts of Lambeth—after all, the Captain was headed that way in search of his wayward priest of a brother. Willie's balloon and belongings would be sent to the seminary by the next week's coach, and he could forgo lugging the heavy silks through rough and brambled country.

It was a reasonable offer, Willie reminded himself. Kept reminding himself, for these woods before him were shadowy and windless, heavy with green light, as though the two men traveled in a faceted bottle. Time and again Diego dipped from sight in the green shade, as though the trees had swallowed him.

Willie was no coward, but each time his companion's vanishment startled him. Stories, there were, about the groves of the lost, where the trees dripped blood and cried out in solitary pain as though children were trapped within them, imprisoned by dryadic magic.

And there were always the Borders. Ever-shifting, and if you believed the runaway priest, moving steadily west along the banks of the Alph.

"Up ahead, I know," Diego muttered, appearing almost dryadically beside a brace of black poplar. "Not far."

Willie was not accustomed to following, to dense country. He drew the gum blanket about his shoulders, with a prayer that its gray drabness would shield him from vigilant eyes.

They were headed toward the mining camp, Diego told him. Toward the Captain's own company, where he might handpick a squadron for a venture north into disputed country.

Of course, Diego had guessed that it had been Solomon, that blindly rushing form that crashed by him on its way north. It was quite likely that the rebels had caught up with his brother, and that Solomon lay in a rough encampment, tethered and blindfolded, protesting his relation to the interrogating army but forgetting which one—brother or cousin—served at its head.

He would need serious rescuing, Diego said.

"Now, Mr. Melmoth," Diego called softly over his shoulder. "If I can find thirty good men in my army, if Actaeon hasn't killed the lot of them . . ."

The rest of his words were lost, trailing into leaf and shadow.

Willie muttered at the reluctant horse beneath him. Diego dodged before him like a scarlet specter, flashing from bracken to deadfall as the woods thinned at last and the land rose toward a misty knoll.

The two riders emerged into sun-spangled cloud, onto a breezy slope that smelled of moist hay and late honeysuckle. Diego reined Juno in a tight, smooth circle, and Willie, gasping from the effort, wrestled his resistant mount out of the undergrowth.

Diego rose in the saddle. "Top of the rise," he whispered. "Our guardsmen on vidette."

Willie followed the Captain's gesture. Two men—or more: it was difficult to tell in the thick, hovering mist—sat on horseback, deeper shadows against the hazy white of the air.

With a soft whistle, Diego hailed them.

There was no reply.

Instantly, the Captain reddened, his face indistinguishable from his uniform coat in his sudden, inexplicable anger. He drew his pistol.

Uneasily, Willie followed suit, remembering too late that his own gun was still unloaded, neglected in his swift departure from Arcady. He thought to tell Diego, then changed his mind.

The Captain was already dismounted, Juno grazing tranquilly on the slope as Diego crept toward the shadowy sentries, pistol in one hand, a long, wicked knife between his teeth.

We're in for it now, Willie thought, struggling from the saddle. *Saint Milton protect us both . . . all.*

Diego dropped the pistol, sprang into the saddle beside the dozing sentry, and yanked back the boy's head. The sentry cried out, a brief, doleful bleat stilled by the Captain's hand over his mouth.

Roused by the noise, the other sentry pivoted in the saddle, crying out and fumbling for his gun. Willie surged from the mist and shadows, grabbed the guardsman by the leg, and wrestled the boy to the ground, sealing his silence with a quick blow from the pistol butt.

"See?" muttered Diego through clenched teeth, steadying his wriggling captive, nodding to the hazy spot where the gondolier knelt over the fallen sentry. "*That's* in store for you if you've a mind to struggle. I ought to . . ."

He settled the blade of the knife against the boy's throat.

"One little tug," he menaced softly. " 'Tis an odd thing, lad, how the life dangles from the thin strings of the arteries."

Willie shuddered. Diego thrust the sentry from the saddle, facedown onto the grassy slope.

"Take me to Actaeon, boy," ordered Diego.

The sentry gazed up at him stupidly.

"To Lieutenant Peacock, dammit!" Diego exclaimed. "Why . . . I ought to hang you for desertion right on the spot!"

The boy scrambled to his feet and, as Willie dutifully gathered the horses, made off over the rise on foot, Diego pacing the horse behind him.

The other sentry they left dazed on the grassy hillside.

As Diego and the sentry approached the camp, Willie Melmoth caught up with them. At the sight of the first circle of watchfires, the gondolier held his breath, for indeed, the Citizens' Guard and the whole countryside itself was filled with stories:

There was Commodore St. Milton Marat, who drowned off the starboard of his own steamboat, midstream in the Alph, in an accident so foolish the Citizens' Admiralty had claimed that it could not be an accident at all.

Closer to home, there was Major Hyperion Werther, cannoned by his own men in a sorry attempt to gun the rebels out of the western corner of Nightshade Vale. The artillery had killed the major outright; his brother, as well, died the next day of wounds.

That escapade, Willie had heard, had cost Diego his right leg.

And of course there were rumors of even worse. Command in the Citizens' Guard had become dangersome at best.

So Willie's alarm was justified, when his Captain . . .

. . . his sole companion in indecipherable country . . .

. . . passed in front of an aiming line of government troops, his intention the tent of his drowsing lieutenant.

* * *

Lieutenant Actaeon Peacock dreamed of battle. Of a blinding surge of red light, of a thousand clamoring voices and long, incessant gunfire.

Something about this clearing, the jagged branching of metal, the old and watery smells of petroleum, troubled his sleep.

In his dream, the clearing was inhabited, crowded and ruinous. Smoke and alarms weaved through the air like the outcry of a bird—perhaps a wounded phoenix—and for a moment he thought he had awakened in the Borders.

Fire, he told himself, and started dreamily to his feet.

Then the cold pressure of metal at his throat—bordermetal? he asked—awakened him in truth.

Diego's knife rested on his windpipe. The Captain knelt above him, dark hair cascading over his shoulders, mustache drooping over the angry mouth of a prophet.

Actaeon tried to speak, but the blade pressed him more closely, menacingly.

"And *this* is what you call vigilance," Diego declared.

CHAPTER 14

Still muttering at the drowsy vigil kept by his sentries and lieutenants, Diego Hawken picked thirty of the best soldiers to search for his brother.

These were dragoons trained in the west, in Tharmas beneath the shadows of the great Doradian city itself, beneath the watchful eyes of Citizen Arouet. Guard regulars, they were, and older—some of them graying and bearded, their red coats tattered with five years of riding the Urthonan woods.

They espoused no ideology, these guardsmen. When the Citizen sent miners into the Borders, raising metal from the ravaged land and hard words from the country folk of Urizen and Urthona, these men had been the first to come to his aid. Their inspiration was simple: it was a man's duty to defend his government, and all philosophy began and ended with that notion.

Duty had kept them going when the first rebel armies slipped out of the woods to raid the bordermetal expeditions. Kept them going for nine years now. Before Diego's arrival, before the Battle of Nightshade Vale, and his wounding and recovery, these men had stalked the Lady along the turgid riverbank. And though she had eluded them, had passed through their snares like riverwater, they had crossed swords with her forces a dozen times and they all were alive yet.

Their reward for seasoning and vigilance had been further bordermetal patrols, the most thankless assignment in the Citizen's army, the principal target for all rebel assaults. They guarded the parties of miners and gatherers who scoured the country over which the Borders had passed. Receding like tides, the Borders left the land behind them turned and altered, sometimes unearthing metal girders, metal wires—worn but still useful to build the Citizen's machinery, his mills and looms and engines. What was left was melted in the smithies, fueling the war effort against the rebels.

All of the bordermetal guards were wary and Border-seasoned. Men who could catch a glint of iron in a foot of leafmeal, a green coat in a thicket.

Surely *they* could find a wayward brother in the shifting woods.

* * *

In the dark of the woodland morning, fully rested from a night's sleep around the muted campfires of the bordermetal mines, Willie rode in the midst of the column, beside Diego and an old Tharman mercenary named Peterbell Maddalo. The Captain had mustered the company into the saddle shortly after the night turned, while many of the green boys were still sleeping. Silently, their horses' hooves wrapped in canvas because sound carried in the southern woods, they rode off northward, led by a thin dryadic guide, bound for the river and the Lady's Land.

Willie squinted into the darkness. Ahead, the point men combed the shade-dappled woodland. All that guided the rest of them, drowsy soldiers in the saddle, were the jack-o'-lanterns of torchlight somewhere ahead and the sound of men and horses grunting and snorting and breathing heavily.

The dryad moved in a flicker of fractured light at the very edge of his vision.

On precious occasions the moon drifted out from behind the clouds at just the time when they all crossed through a clearing. Then Willie could see the men in front of him bent over the back of their horses.

Leave it to me, he thought, *to find myself in the midst of them, holding to the reins of a horse I do not trust or even fathom, riding down in the shadow of the valley of death with the owls watching.*

* * *

Sestos Bend was really a notch between two bends, where the Alph circled back upon itself and cut an island out of the woods. As the light grew in the eastern sky, Diego's troops came in sight of the clearing that led up to the banks, to the island and the bend itself. Right beyond it, the videttes had told them, was a place where the scouts had heard the rebels working late into the night. The sky grew red to their left, a watery light filtered through the branches of the poplar, and slowly the insects awakened, busy in the last weeks of their lives.

The morning promised unseasonable warmth after the night of accustomed cold.

The fishy smell of the river and of wet mud reached the guardsmen at once, but mostly the air was thick and intolerably still, a silence and heat and cucumber smell that made Willie think of snakes.

And then, beyond the brown crook of the river, a wall rose into view out of the haze.

Chevaux-de-frise, the books called it. *Abatis.* A tangling wall of spikes and bordermetal wire interspersed with felled trees. A fortification named by a language lost in the Wars of Heresy.

Scrambling up the thin bole of a bare osier, the dryad crouched in the low branches and surveyed the rebel defenses. Her brown legs blended with the bole of the tree. Suddenly, she seemed to vanish, wedded to the branches and the still air.

Diego took the broken spyglass from Maddalo and scanned the works on the island. The cracked lens fragmented the light, doubled the image, wall upon wall.

Shadowy forms dodged among the white vapors above the wall.

Rebels. Even aided by optics, his eye could not tell how many. If there were more than a handful, it would be fruitless to attack them. An assault would carry the guardsmen across open terrain to the riverbank, then through the sluggish waters of the Alph onto the opposite shore and up to the abatis itself, all the while in easy range of the rebels' musketry.

"What do you think, Garrick?" Diego asked softly.

Willie watched as a lad, a full three years his junior, stood in the stirrups and squinted over the drab expanse of plain and river.

Diego's nephew, he understood. Somehow estranged from his father, who was the drunken inventor riding west in the nostrum wagon.

"We can take 'em, Captain," old Maddalo offered from his seat atop a weathered red stallion, pointing at the hazy abatis. An enormous regimental ring, worn on his middle finger to commemorate the Battle of Blackheath, caught the slanted sunlight. "By Saint Milton, we done it in Nightshade Vale."

"Not without losing half the men," Garrick cautioned. "So then, so now. And we're after Uncle Solomon, Captain."

Diego fell silent. It was obvious to all that he could not resist a clash with the rebels.

"But if we're planning to move against them, you might ask the dryad for particulars, sir," Garrick prompted. "I can translate a mite."

The Captain glared at the wispy form in the tree, as the dryad took shape from the bark and the twisting branches. "Can you translate lies to truth, Nephew?"

In the distance, the shadows at the abatis shifted and swirled.

"Burn the brush," Diego ordered. "We'll go in under smoke and ruin."

The dryad looked down at him with bright, unfathomable eyes.

Willie said his prayers as Diego assembled the troops at the woods' edge. Cedars brushing against his face, the lad besought all the saints he could imagine would come to his aid: Saint Palamabron, who pities the oppressed, Saint Milton, who willingly descends into danger and darkness, and the Sweet Shadow of Delight, Bride of the Bard, who lifts dreams out of deathlike vision.

But it still seemed dreamlike, visionary, as the woods darkened when the smoke from the covering fires passed over. To his right a horse snuffled, and Maddalo nodded at him through the fitful glow of the fires. Together, at Diego's call, they rode out into the light.

For a moment, brief and disorienting, Willie was dazzled, all caught up in the sun and the hot wind like a sudden emergence from ancient cellars. In a wide column the horsemen made toward the forking river and the abatis.

Suddenly, like the ground falling away from the gondola of a rising balloon, the trees were behind them entirely.

Diego set the pace yards ahead of his troopers, blustering and much too endangered. Crouched in the saddle, his pistol raised to still the small-arms fire until distance and angle were right, he sang as he rode in a low, daunting baritone,

"Bring me my Bow of burning gold:
Bring me my Arrows of desire:
Bring me my Spear: O clouds, unfold!
Bring me my Chariot of fire."

Some of the men took up the song, but soon it was drowned by the first volley from the abatis and the whooping and gobbling of the rebel troops.

The shots came all in bunches now, and the bullets whiffled by Willie as if they were tearing the air open. Low in the saddle, clinging desperately, he thought, *Merciful Saint Palamabron, we are no place near the water already, we are not moving fast enough.* He gave his pony a good kick in the sides, and the horse surged forward as a man in front of them said *oh* so quietly then fell back over his horse as the charge rushed by.

Warm dark drops speckled Willie's neck and his hands.

Then the abatis appeared again, bigger and bigger through a haze rising out of the ground until the logs and spikes and bordermetal seemed afloat on a river of fog and fire. The horses breasted the river, the Alph washed over Willie's legs, and then the abatis was to his side, then past him . . .

And the rebels were completely, inexplicably gone.

In a daze the score or so remaining cavalrymen wheeled their dripping horses in the high grass. The last of the charge vaulted and skirted the broken abatis, and Diego holstered his pistol in disgust.

The enemy troops who had fronted them not a minute before, who had taunted and shrieked and killed ten of their number, had vanished entirely, as though they had passed like Blights through a shifting Absence.

Diego swore softly, muscling Juno toward a gap in the trees behind the abatis.

"They *must* have gone this way!" he exclaimed. " 'Tis the only path that—"

The sentence broke off abruptly. For a moment the air in the clearing seemed to stiffen and still. The guardsmen gaped at one another. One young soldier whimpered, fumbled to reload his pistol . . .

And at that moment, the rebels rose like gnomes out of the ground with a flurry of gunfire.

Diego shouted and, grabbing Willie by the sleeve, pointed to the trail, motioning wildly as the deafening first round of musketry riddled the air. The bullets whined by them, invisible and angry, as the young gondolier spurred his horse toward the gap in the trees . . .

Then, not fifty yards from safety, reined in the frightened horse.

For out of a stand of poplar arching over the broad passage through the forest, a dozen more rebels emerged, a tall handsome black man in the vanguard, green bandanna wrapped about his head like a gypsy's turban.

Marion L'Overture.

Again the rebels had won.

Willie wheeled about his panic-stricken horse with a loud oath. L'Overture whistled, and the rebels raised their weapons and fired.

Suddenly Willie felt it, white-hot and burrowing beneath his shoulder blade, the wind escaping him in a sudden, precipitate rush, and he was falling falling, the shadow of his horse in flight passing over him like a solitary storm cloud. Somewhere he heard answering gunfire, the Captain's bellowing command, and the ground rushed blindingly up to meet him.

He awakened in the night to the sound of a man screaming.

The forest was black, illuminated by occasional flurries of gunfire. The skirmish, it seemed, was not over.

From his place upon the ground, Willie could smell something turned in the air and turned too soon—a smell he had never encountered before, but that he recognized instantly with a knowing older than learning, older indeed than wisdom.

It was as though the guardsmen had died before they crossed the Alph, before they had left the mining camp, even before he had brought the balloon to an ungainly landing in the pool beside the Captain's ancestral mansion.

It was as though these boys had died back then and did not know it, and now that the dying was over they wanted to hasten the rest, to be free of the terrible business.

It brought to mind his own wound. Willie turned painfully onto his stomach, felt his back.

His shoulder throbbed, but his hand came away dry.

Spent bullet. Gondolier's luck.

He smiled grimly.

Luck was losing ground, though. Pinned down by enemy fire, the guardsmen had a few hours to settle what affairs they could settle from forest undergrowth and scattered abatis. Sunrise would give the rebels sufficient light to aim, lock sights, and fire.

And if it was true what they said about L'Overture . . .

He reached out for his pistol in the darkness, but his fingers closed upon another's hand. With a low, suffocated cry, the young gondolier pulled away, but he knew by touch the lightness of the hand, the wet stickiness congealing at the wrist, the huge ring on the middle finger . . .

Maddalo had not fared as well.

Willie looked up into the wind-shifted branches of the trees, a deeper darkness silhouetted faintly against the night. A passage from the Text came to him—something from one of the early chapters—but he forgot it almost instantly as it seemed to float into the dense powdery air.

He wished he knew the magic of the Text, how the priests mined the Borders with words and imaginings and breathings. More than that, he wished for a priest: for a seminarian trained in the incantations of rescue and peace.

Even the strange, abstracted Solomon would do.

* * *

That man, however, combed the southern banks of the Alph, his intentions on the north and clear ground and the seminary beyond.

Quickly and stiffly he ran through the cryptic night, outstripping the overgrown grounds until Arcady vanished behind him. He ran until he outstripped thought. Trees flashed by him, their dark boles menacing, as Solomon loped along the fringes of the shadowy grove. The mourning doves rustled in their sleep as the gangly, lurching form passed them and passed them again.

Finally, stone sober and exhausted, surprised by sudden morning, he lay on an outcropping of rock at the edge of the Alphside Forest, the lapping of the river against its banks faint but within earshot.

Back through the darkness he stared, where the roof of the mansion was a dark silhouette over the tops of the trees in Uncle Raphael's nut grove. A solitary light shone in the topmost window of the circular tower, and below it a light more dim, bottle-green—the lamplight of Endymion's room.

For the first time he regretted his flight from Arcady.

It had been too easy. At every moment he had expected to be seized, brought back, scolded and chastened and exposed for the charlatan he was certain he was, for the fraud that his running acknowledged. But nobody had followed him, and now, on the woods' edge, he stopped and reconsidered.

Was it only his supposed magic Morgana had needed? Or was it something further she asked of him, that she was unable to ask for in words—the consolation and the standing with the family that was more brotherly than priestly?

Solomon smiled cynically. It seemed *that* was a magic as far from him as any Textual conjury.

Until now. Here, for a moment, he had outraced his own fears.

Solomon pulled his greatcoat tightly about him, settled the fur hat snugly on his head. It was deeply embarrassing, this panic and hysteria.

I'll go back, he told himself. Back to Arcady. The least I can be is some solace to my family . . .

Though even *the least I can be* is beyond my reckoning.

Nonetheless, he climbed down from the outcropping, losing sight of the mansion in the overhang of woods, and guessed a path back toward Arcady, guided by scanty astronomy and even more scanty memory. His whiskeyed family tended to sleep in: perhaps he could be back before sunlight, his flight unnoticed. And then . . .

He would find some way to tell Morgana. And some way to be of help.

Then suddenly, stretched over a line of maple like a transparent netting, the edge of the Borders loomed before him. Here the air rippled like the surface of a wind-shivered lake, and beyond it the forest seemed blurred, fragmentary . . .

And even more perilous. Solomon remembered the sphinxes.

Slowly, warily, he skirted the wavering air. He would keep to the Presences as long as possible—to country familiar and assured, where nothing . . . unnatural awaited the unwary traveler.

The less time spent in the Borders, the better.

But even the Presences were no safe terrain. Not, at least, in the Alphside Forest, tricky country at its most sunlit and clear. A brief venture into the wooded ground south of him produced nothing. Arcady had long vanished in a veil of leaves and contorted branches, and after an hour's circling, skirting the Borders, listening for the sounds of the river and searching vainly for the dark outline of the mansion's towers, Solomon found himself at the spot he had left, Arcady no doubt as far away as it had been before.

"I *must* return," he whispered. He was uncertain whether concern for his reputation or for his family was the force that moved him. But it kept him going through a night of false trails raucous with the distorted cries of birds and wild animals.

His wandering continued long after sunrise. Indeed, into the next evening and the morning that followed. But a day and a night of circling the grounds brought him nowhere, brought him back to the same landmarks, the same spots—the outcropping of gray and weathered rock, the shadowed bank of the river, the wavering line of maple.

It was as though Arcady would not let him return.

A band of horsemen, passing in the distance under torchlight, he had taken to be patrols of one side or another. Neither guardsman nor partisan could be trusted not to shoot trespassers on sight, so he had fled them, the whole forest crashing with his clumsiness and panic. And later, when he had stumbled across a solitary rider, dark and forbidding and yet somehow strangely familiar, standing a horse in a narrow clearing, he had again lurched wildly into the darkness, shivering, expecting the worst.

But the worst had not come.

And yet, perhaps, the worst *had* come to pass. Solomon found himself again among the same bare rocks, the Borders stretched tauntingly before him, the prospect of circling here forever playing absurdly over his thoughts.

Then slowly, inexplicably, the air turned wintry around him. A chill and an icy wind pursued him into his fortress of coat and blanket, and his fingers felt numb even through the ragged leather gloves. The scarves layered over his mouth—to filter the frozen bitter air before it reached his throat and lungs—were crusted with ice from the moisture in his breath, and the air felt glassy on his face.

Wearied, Solomon sat amid the outcropping, hard by a circle of trees. The shadows of walnut and beech meshed over his head. Caught in his confusion, in his desperate thoughts of return, he was not ready for the Blights.

The boys dropped from the trees around him, landing as softly as cats or as alighting birds. There were four of them, and in the mist and the cold and the strange glittering moonlight reflected off the ice and the smoke of his breath, Solomon thought for a moment they were angels, Morgana's angels . . .

Then he saw their feral eyes. Saw that they carried knives.

The Blights were clothed in tattered light cotton, impossibly open to the weather. They circled around him as though it were the first time they had seen a man, as though they had been raised by wolves, by owls. They chattered to one another in a fallen language that had passed through the Absences and no longer made sense to safe and priestly ears.

Solomon fumbled for his pistol, but his arms were entangled, bound to his side.

He decided at once against incautious bravery.

Hugador de mannos, hichicera, one said. Or something like it. For a moment they circled cautiously, sniffing the air like predators.

Danameck mannos, one said, pointing at Solomon with his knife. His breath was stale, carried upon it an undersmell of decay.

"I beg your pardon?" Solomon's voice shook with both cold and fear. He sounded foolish, he knew—schoolmaster's manners in a place where human kindness had sunk into ice and mist and frozen air.

'E say come wiv' us, idleman, one of them said—the youngest, the smallest—in words that were slurred but unmistakable. Then the little one scrambled into the low, bare branches of an apple tree, staring hungrily while his comrades crouched and closed in.

Solomon stood as they approached, an obscure passage from the Text arising sketchily to his thoughts—whether as prayer or spell he could not determine, but the passage was one he had prepared, had memorized when young for times such as these. His mind burrowed for the words, but he could not recall them, what with the time and the suddenness and the fear arising.

"And . . . how and why . . ." he began, but the words resisted.

The largest of the boys looked to the small one, the interpreter, who egged him on with nods and hisses. Solomon tried again, but the text had vanished, and he could remember only the cold air, geese on the wing . . .

And regardless of words or memory, the Blights were on him.

They pulled Solomon from the rocks, kicked him as he tumbled to the ground whimpering in fear, whimpering in shame that his fear had overtaken him again, that he was whimpering. One of the boys gestured at his legs with a knife, as though he intended to hamstring him. One gestured toward places higher, even more frightening.

Why did no steam rise from their breathing? It was dreadfully cold.

For a moment Solomon wondered if they were dead already.

Then ropes tumbled lightly onto the shaken priest, weighted by rusty sinkers of bordermetal. As the cords clinched tightly about him, Solomon tried vainly to rise, tumbled, fell back to his knees.

And then more boys. Five, six, seven of them, dressed in bright tatters like fierce, ragged birds. Their long forelocks tied back for battle, they stepped into the clearing, surrounding the rock where Solomon lay. Their young faces were anatomies of menace, grimy and scarred with livid tribal markings.

The Blights encircled the trespasser, raising their crossbows, their blowguns, their hooked and razored knives. Nine of them in all. Solomon raised his hands slowly, with difficulty, cords lacing his fingers. It was a sign of peace . . . of surrender.

His hopes sinking, Solomon scanned the faces. Like those in the classrooms at Lambeth. Vacant, almost lifeless. Eyes like slate.

Then a tenth one stepped from the shadows, and Solomon's heart rose and tumbled in a second's span.

Aristo. His nephew. Endymion's younger son.

But he gazed at his uncle with a look blank and forgetful and pitiless, as though he examined a fish drawn from the eddying waters.

CHAPTER 15

They had first appeared ten years ago, these feral boys who roamed the twisted Borderlands. Around the great ruins of Napolis and Ville they wandered like strangely painted street urchins, on foot or mounted on steam-powered velocipedes.

Citizen Arouet was the first to call them Blights. As in *blights upon our green and pleasant land.*

At first, many thought that the boys were somehow born of the Absence. They had the whiff of nothingness about them, the odor of ash and ozone. Rumors of vandalism followed them, rumors of worse crimes.

Of a strange and fanatical theology.

And though it was never certain where the first Blights had come from, or what took place in their ranks, those ranks soon swelled with adolescent boys from Luvah and Urizen, from Urthona and Tharmas—youngsters who ran away to the vagrant, savage life as blithely as a boy in another time and a safer country would troop off to the circus or the merchant ships.

And yet it was more than simple adventure. It was the glamor and rebellion of outlawry and destruction that overwhelms the young, especially adolescent boys, when something tense and unsettling in the air tells them their civilization is fragmented, botched.

Even those who stayed at home followed the Blights in their imaginings. The most tame and settled of boys—honor students and heirs to property who were too civilized, sensible, or afraid to join the growing legion—began to dress like guttersnipes and pikers. Even the safest of these children, the future leaders of Urizen and Urthona, adopted ragged, particolored clothing, rode breakneck on velocipedes through their respectable hamlets and market squares, on the grounds of their manicured estates.

Most of them sported the blightlock—the long, matted tresses that had become the insignia of the dangerous raiders they mimicked. But the blightlock itself had become dangerous: in recent days, the Citizen had offered a goodly bounty of fifteen guilders for each forelock, and complaints were beginning to rise from good families that the guardsmen were seizing and shearing *respectable boys.*

And yet up close, the real Blights—the ones in whose custody Solomon traveled now—were not the romantic figures of adolescent myth and story. They smelled of worse than ash and ozone, and several of their number, especially the younger ones, seemed to swim in a dazed bleariness as they guided their captive toward the saints knew what destination.

Their path through the forest was involved, intuitive. The large, ash-smeared boy at the head of the party—Constantine, they called him—slipped through the undergrowth gracefully. He parted the branches with a thick metal rod, carried half as insignia, it seemed, half as weapon.

Constantine guided his followers along a trail of rags through the maze of poplar and cedar and undergrowth. Long streamers of torn cloth hung from the branches like banners, and knots of scarlet and green and silver adorned the thick clumps of evergreen. The Blight leader took account of them all, steering a crooked course from tatter to tatter, gently, almost paternally helping smaller boys over the intricacies of branch and slippery rock. Perhaps a half-dozen of the older boys, riding on sputtering velocipedes, served as outriders, herding these younger Blights into a ragged line behind Constantine and his bordermetal scepter.

Once Constantine stopped at the edge of a clearing. He raised the rod uncertainly as he examined the overhanging branches. A long strip of black silk lay coiled like a snake on a bed of dried leaves, and vainly the Blight leader searched for a break in the canopy, for the snapped limb that would signal the branch from which the cloth had fallen. Several of the younger boys huddled behind him: one grasped at his coat with a mud-crusted hand and whimpered *lost lost lost* until the Blight leader silenced him with a soft touch on his shoulder.

"Waitin' here, Molton," Constantine said to the boy. "Waitin' for the vision."

A great sigh and shouting arose from the company when a fierce, squat felon the other boys called Luther pointed to a shadow-stunted willow at the clearing's edge, around the bole of which someone had tied a blue sash studded with costume jewelry.

"Luther has the vision," the Blights choired. "Thanks to Saint Milton, to Saint Allalong."

Again the velocipedes spat and rumbled, and in a haze of steam the pilgrimage began again. Rough hands pushed Solomon forward, and he found himself in a warm fog smelling of oil and sweat, following the shadowy form of a boy not ten feet ahead of him.

On two occasions as they passed through the maze of woods, Solomon tried to catch Aristo's eye. He cleared his throat, gestured, but the boy regarded his uncle blankly, adopting the slate-dead stare of his tattered companions. Solomon soon gave up the effort, turning his thoughts to keeping pace with his ragged captors.

As the band of Blights weaved through the forest, Constantine held forth his metal rod like a wand and in a high, incanting voice rattled off ancient passages from the Text, some scarcely recognizable from their corruption. He spoke the words with neither understanding nor feeling, recited them in a monotone above the parting branches.

"I return!" the boy began, and Solomon strained to listen, to make sense of the tricked and converted words.

> "I return! Both Time & Spay sobey m'will.
> Ein Six Towson dears walk up and down; for natwan Moment
> Of Time is lost, narwan Eventa Spay sun pernint . . ."

Solomon deciphered the passage.

"From the Twenty-second Plate," he whispered, to nobody in particular. "Where the Shadowy Prophet falls from his station in Paradise and enters the Bard, who waits on earth in the *black cloud redounding*. Where Saint Milton returns to correct the Great Error. But this . . ."

A velocipede rammed into Solomon from behind, and he fell forward into the dry needles and loam of the forest floor. Luther, straddling the steaming cycle, ordered him along with an oath so obscene that the falling poplar leaves rustled distressfully in the vault of the forest high above.

Solomon coughed and nodded and pressed forward, following Constantine through the knots of undergrowth, for the first time in twenty years observing and noting everything.

Observing and noting, he knew at once when the Blights crossed into the Borders.

Constantine repeated his hocus-pocus, tirelessly and tiresomely, every hundred yards or so. Each time it was the same distorted passage from the Text, and as he chanted, he lifted the bordermetal rod and waved it slowly, dramatically before him.

At last, the party stalked into a clearing where the air bristled and crackled at their passage. Constantine stood at the threshold, the end of the lifted rod suddenly bathed in a soft beam of light, incanting as each of his followers stepped into the shifting, altering country.

Of this, Solomon took note as well. Pausing as he passed the Blight commander, regarding the rod with sudden, scientific scrutiny.

Then Luther's tattooed hand rested roughly on his shoulder. Solomon gathered himself and followed the glowing rod into the Borders, as the mist subsided and the tense air crackled around him. Then a push and another oath from Luther sent him stumbling reluctantly into the very Borders he had dodged for two nights and a day.

It was as he had expected, Solomon thought, gathering his breath and nervously brushing the evergreen needles from his sleeve. Constantine's scepter was a simple artifact, remnant of the men of Old Eden.

When prophets and machinery were wed.

These occasional contraptions, as odd and as useless as those in his brother Endymion's collection, surfaced with the deep bordermetal at the very fringe of the Absence itself. Only the most intrepid of travelers had seen them, and fewer still had returned with the likes of them. The illuminant rod, the growlers and rattlers—all were glamorous and flashy and virtually useless devices.

Old Eden must have been a country of the trivial, where trinket and ornament prevailed over thought and spirit and substance.

And yet such gadgetry could be useful *this* time, Solomon speculated.

To free myself. To get back to Arcady.

On through the Borders they trudged, for an hour or two, as fitful clouds passed over and a strange, untimely dusk settled on the road ahead of them. They were bound for a distant building, dark and twisted on a barren knoll.

The house to which Constantine led them had been uninhabited for years, Solomon guessed. Tilted slightly and pushed from its foundation, no doubt when the Borders had first passed over it.

They called it Bowlahoola. The absurd name for the human body in the Text. Its windows bulged with waterlogged wooden shutters, and the old gabled roof was honeycombed with tattered holes, its rafters peeking through the shingles like a skeleton.

Unceremoniously, each boy slipped to a separate spot in the huge roofless hallway, where ruptured mattresses, bales of hay, pallets of rushes lay ready to receive them. Two of their number—boys Solomon had not seen before—awaited them there, tending a low and smoky fire.

The walls of the hall the Blights occupied were as tattered as their clothing, singed by a dozen fires they had no doubt abandoned and forgotten. Scraps of paper—torn book pages, fragrant stationery, occasional faded newsprint—dangled from nail and hook, scrawled with almost illegible writing, wafting eerily on the breezes in the drafty ruin.

Like an elaborate network of veins, a web of rope and mesh and cord lay stretched and knotted through the charred rafters. Within this webbing, outlined in the light of the rising moon, a dozen or so of the boys hung like colorful spiders, armed with bow and sling, with pistol and with long, menacing knife, their tattered clothing flapping in the current and the midmorning light.

The boys milled around the fire, gloved and grimy hands extended toward the fitful warmth, the smoke encircling them as though they rode from the heart of the mist, or were half composed of Absence themselves. Constantine mingled among them, whispering to one, joking softly to another.

For the first time, Solomon looked at his captors with a calm and scrutinous eye.

None of them over fifteen.

It was the way with their kind, he had heard.

The Blights gathered their numbers from the schools and the countrysides, from the spacious, aristocratic farms of southern Urthona and northern Urizen, from the marbled, discontented cities of Luvah, and even from the seminaries. From the same places that Arouet drew his guardsmen, his miners.

But the Blights, as a rule, were younger. Fourteen, thirteen. Some as young as ten.

These were children. Wearing slogan hats—old, battered fedoras adorned with slips of paper containing the scrawled names of deceased comrades, sayings from the Text or the Commentaries or the Hymns, most curious because few of the boys could remember how to read and write. Solomon had heard from his seminary students, who played at Blightlore in their more rebellious moments, that the slogan hats were the Blights' attempt to preserve their memory, the messages scrawled in an early time before the lettered among them forgot how to read.

The costumes were a bright motley of the Absences' leavings, of the litter of war and abandoned mines. The fur-lined capes popularized by the Tharman cavalry blended with white miners' shirts, the red braided jackets of the Citizens' Guard, and old rebel greens. Like walking quilts the boys seemed, a patched and implausible company.

At an order from Constantine, Aristo approached his uncle, handing Solomon a ladle of tepid water. In one of Diego's infantry jackets, the boy was. A field coat that swallowed him like the lip of a whirling Absence.

Solomon took the ladle with a scarcely audible thanks. Still no recognition in the boy's eyes—no acknowledgment of the uncle who, when Aristo was a toddler scarce more than decade past, had nuzzled and dandled him, had taught him the first of his letters and songs.

Letters and songs. Perhaps . . .

Softly, Solomon began to sing the first of the Hymns, the childhood chorus, in a desperate hope that the words and music would jostle the boy, that in the midst of Border and oblivion, he would turn, remember, and cast light . . .

"Piping down the valleys wild,
Piping songs of pleasant glee,
On a cloud I saw a child,
And he laughing said to me . . ."

"Fugoff," Aristo muttered, letting the half-empty ladle drop and spatter at Solomon's feet, turning back to the fires, to his new and oblivious family.

* * *

Nasty, brutish, and short.

What his teachers had told him about the lives of these wayward and feral children was true. The fire-damaged shelters, the fissures and scales of pellagrous hands, the gaunt, haunted look in the eyes of the older boys.

And the *voids*. The damaged, addled Blights—generally younger boys—who followed the others witlessly, now crouching at the firesides staring vacantly into the low flames, gaping and drooling.

They smelled of sweat and ozone. Of ignited water.

The voids did not listen when Constantine told the stories. But they were the only ones.

Constantine was an odd one among oddities—remote, yet unusually considerate of the comfort of the younger boys, even of his hostage. Now, as the night began to deepen over Bowlahoola, the Blight leader dipped into a wealth of stories that wound loopily through gaps and cul-de-sacs, fragmentary accounts from the Text connected intuitively, by bizarre metaphors that Solomon could scarcely follow.

Sometimes not connected at all.

Lacunae, they had called the Absences at Lambeth. The erasures in the Text, the gap in the telling.

Aporia. The place of uncertainties.

The Black Cloud Redounding.

And here in the ramshackle house of the Blights, the tales complied with the telling.

"When the new age is at leisure to pronounce," Constantine began, the words sonorous in his young voice, "all will be set right, and those Grand Works of the more ancient and consciously and professedly inspired men will hold their proper rank, and the Daughters of Memory will become the Daughters of Inspiration."

Solomon's eyes widened.

It was the beginning of the Text. Tattered, but surprisingly undistorted, given Blight memory and the story's transit through word of mouth.

How did they preserve it?

And more important, why?

"Rouze up, O Young Men of the New Age!" Constantine urged, the metal torch waving in his grimy hand. "Set your forelocks . . ."

Foreheads, not forelocks. But wait . . .

". . . against the ignorant Hirelings! For we have Hirelings in the Camp, the Court and the University . . ."

You have that right . . .

". . . who would, if they could. for ever depress Mental and prolong Corporeal War. There is a Class of Men whose whole delight is in Destroying. We do not want Models if we are but just and true to our own Imaginations, those Worlds of Eternity in which we shall live for ever . . ."

On the lad traveled, through a Text holed and holy, through the great Hymn at the book's beginning.

Not content to rest in the Hymns and the Text, the Blights, it seemed, had bent the great story to their own mythology, filled with their own saints, with passages and vanishments, with looting and perilous escape, and with the prospect of hidden countries lying through the hazardous portals of the Absences.

And yet it all led up to a simple, millennial theology, as best Solomon could understand.

Saint Milton was returning, the boys believed. Returning as the Text had prophesied, to unite with the Bard and usher in the New Age.

But as Constantine spoke and gestured, whistled and sang in the smoky interiors of Bowlahoola, it became clear to Solomon that the end of this theology was stranger than any he had encountered in seminary. For though the Blights awaited Saint Milton's arrival, they believed that the Bard was among them.

And Constantine was that Bard.

Now Constantine ascended the winding, truncated stairwell of the house, high to a point where step and banister broke off, neatly sheared away so that it seemed to be a stairwell into vanishment itself, leading nowhere but into the smoky air. There, atop a landing that was no longer a landing, the boy began to speak, drawing slogans from the band of his hat, reading lessons from the Text and from the Border-distorted air.

"You know the story of Saint Milton," the Blight leader began. "You know how he come from the mazes of Providence . . ."

"From the intricate mazes," his followers replied in unison, sitting and crouching in a broken circle about the foot of the stairwell.

Now Constantine smiled for the first time in Solomon's recollection, revealing a row of yellowed, crenellated teeth. "Oh yes from the mazes Saint Milton come," he continued. "He come for the salvaging, to his people who wait for him in the Borders."

And again, as a thousand people told it in hovel and hut, on farm and riverdock, in the mines and mountains, Constantine recited the Great Story, the central, defining myth of the Text. How Saint Milton traveled from "ardorous Heaven" into the deep to rescue his Sixfold Emanation, to be one with the Bard though it meant that he himself would perish.

At the seminary they had talked about its symbolism, its allegory, how each of the six women, known as the Sixfold Emanation, had stood for a part of the mind, a part of the soul.

Here, among forgetful boys, the story had shifted and altered. Though the Blights' version varied in detail from what the Text originally said and intended, it was obvious that they believed it as *history*, as *fact*. Now, the smoke rose from a half-dozen fires and Constantine, obscured in the haze, droned on about the salvaging, the harvest.

"He come for the salvaging, to harvest the six little girls."

Solomon looked up. Something stirred at the edge of his thoughts. There was something he should connect with this, should remember . . .

"Out of the harvest, Saint Milton clean up himself."

"He become the Bard, and he clean it up," Luther echoed. Twoscore forelocked heads, bent over the smoldering fires, nodded in agreement.

"At dawn," Constantine continued, "Saint Milton the Blight come out of his travel as the larks are rising, and he fall into . . ."

He waited with a gap-toothed, vacant smile.

"He fall into the Black Cloud. Then into the Left Foot of the Bard!" Aristo exclaimed, and a chorus of shouts and whistles followed the words.

"Yes, he fall there, into the Left Foot of the Bard, the foot of visions, 'cause he give the Bard the visions, and Saint Allalong is there in her twelve years and her askings for Saint Milton."

Ololon. Solomon fidgeted with the ropes.

The girl's name in the Text was Ololon.

"Twelve years old is Allalong," the boys chorused. "Sweet River of milk and liquid pearl."

“First listen,” Constantine urged. “Then talk. It is the bestest rule.”

“First listen,” the Blights echoed. “Then talk.”

Suddenly, through the veil of rising smoke a thin light shone. Constantine’s staff was glowing.

“But Allalong is not alone, she ain’t!” trumpeted the Blight leader, as though the source of light itself spoke out of the darkness. “Saint Milton’s Shadow come, too.”

“Arouet!” Luther exclaimed. “Come out of the mills! Out of the clouded hills come Arouet! And all the ones who keep Saint Milton away!”

The light staff swayed in a mystery of cloud. The Blights murmured in assent, in approval.

Solomon coughed, his eyes smarting. It was not woodsmoke now, but hempsmoke stale and sweet and nutty, wafting through the enclosed and ruined air. Around him the mutterings of the boys died into silence.

“Here come Arouet!” Luther announced again, and a dim light shone at the entrance of the house. The smoke itself became a dark and swirling screen for a panoply of light whose source seemed to be Constantine’s light staff. The Blights murmured and gasped again, as a pale and luminous man, his countenance thin as a tendril of smoke, stood at the threshold of Bowlahoola.

Solomon peered into the smoke. Surely it was not the Citizen. Surely . . .

“Saint Milton’s Shadow!” the Blights cried again, from the oldest boy to the youngest. “The Covering Cherub! The Citizen!

“The Enemy!”

By a dozen names, by a dozen fragments of Text and Hymn, they called and summoned the luminous image of the man as he stood before them expressionless and vague, his face obscure in the melding of cloud and light.

“Yes, it is Arouet,” Constantine proclaimed, the cool assurance of legerdemain in his voice. “I see him now, where you show me he is! He is in the way of Saint Milton.”

Camera obscura, Solomon thought. The simple resources of lenses and light. He had seen it before, exposed at Lambeth as spiritual skulduggery, the sleight of hand of a mountebank.

These children would believe anything. And belief was a powerful thing. If the Blights could be gulled by simple optics, then other things . . .

"What do we say to the Arouet?" Constantine bellowed, his audience answering, lifting hands in the rising smoke. One boy—Solomon did not know his name, only that he traveled in the party vanguard, his red stocking cap gaudy and visible in the brindled forests—rose now and danced through his arrayed companions and the shifting smoke, casting spark and ash as he pivoted in the midst of a dying fire, coal-walking in his ecstasies, dancing back into the roiling shadows.

"We say to the Citizen these words," the Blights choired. "We say to the Citizen, There is an Arouet, and there is a Saint Milton: the Arouet must be destroy'd to redeem the Saint Milton."

"And when we have said so," Constantine declared, his lightstick waving above his assembled followers, "*she* come to us. Saint Allalong. The girl, the river, the virgin in my garden. Nor time nor space is to her perception, for time and space is the Citizen's delusion.

"And when Saint Allalong come . . . Saint Milton and the Bard be one!"

Solomon blinked. His thoughts raced to follow the Blights' ritual. As methodically, as ceremoniously as anything that had come before in word or dance or song, the feral boys trained their weapons upon the glowing, fictional form in the doorway. In a chorus of shouts and whistles and wails, they fired pistol and slingshot, hurled stone and dagger and assegai at the wavering shape, which vanished instantly in a thunder of powder, a clatter of weaponry.

The smoke cleared and the light faded. A boy lay wounded at the doorway. The red stocking cap lay riddled on the spattered ground beside him, and his wounds smoked with powder and the remnants of coals he had gathered in his final, frenzied dance.

Silently, the fingers of his left hand stretched and convulsed, but the body was dead as it grasped at the sticky dust.

The smell of powder mingled with the woodsmoke.

Solomon rose and rushed to the lad, to attend him in any fashion, from benediction to rite, but Luther and Aristo restrained him. Constantine descended the steps, raising his lightstaff ceremoniously, almost regally. He knelt before the body and whispered softly, almost lovingly, in the dead child's ear.

Solomon gasped at the prospect. What had transpired in the ash and smoke had been a holy play, based upon the firm, unshakable belief that the Text the boys could not read was entirely true, entirely factual, and firmly, divinely inspired.

And that they still knew what it said.

The killing was a sacrifice. A homily, a rehearsal.

When they had killed the Citizen, the Blights believed, the last obstacle to Saint Milton's return would fall. Somewhere in the Borders or the Absence, the saint would descend into the Bard Constantine.

And the New Age of peace and tolerance and forgiveness would begin.

But meantime, they would act in their holy play, decimate their innocent numbers . . .

And live like animals at the edge of the Absence's chaos.

Solomon twisted his arms, trying vainly to free himself from the taut ropes. His wrists smarting, his fingers numb from the wringing attempt to escape, he gazed through a shattered window onto the grounds outside the manse, where the smoke dissipated and the sunlight laced through the fading tendrils. The overgrown lawn, the topiary given over to chaos and misrule . . .

Almost everything in this rite seemed barbaric and horrible. Almost alien.

But he knew from the gesture and theater, from Constantine's ceremony and lightstaff, that what had taken place could, if he was wise enough to understand it, offer him an avenue of escape.

Escape to Arcady. To stand with his family against the cresting chaos.

CHAPTER 16

They woke him after midnight. The fires had fallen to a red glow in the ashes, and the moon tilted high overhead.

Rough hands seized him, wrestled him to wakefulness. Blearily, Solomon sat up.

Constantine and Luther. Both in tattered greatcoats.

Constantine brandished his lightwand and beckoned.

Solomon struggled to his feet amid whistles, soft, plaintive outcries, rustling in the dark.

The whole camp was wakening in the recesses of Bowlahoola. Softly, filling the air with muffled grumbles, occasional and distorted snatches of Hymns, the boys assembled. Swiftly, they dressed in long black coats, masked in darkness and shielded against the night air. Solomon tried to make out Aristo among the milling crowd, but the gloaming edge of the firelight was a chaos of shapes, of black draperies and wings, as though dark angels had risen from the shadows of the mansion itself.

Luther jostled him once, needlessly, muttering a vague anticlerical oath. But a sharp word from Constantine sent the tormentor back into the darkness. Then a louder command—this time to the dark assemblage of Blights—set the whole column moving.

Shrouded by darkness, the velocipedes rumbled and sputtered. The Blights afoot began to stir and move, following Constantine's dim light until Bowlahoola was looming in the distance, darker still against the fractured shadows.

Full light caught them in a tangle of metal and stone.

Scarcely a mile from Bowlahoola, Constantine guided the party of

Blights onto a level plain, bare of leaf and foliage. In the moonlight, cable and beam and wire jutted grotesquely from the hard white ground, as though overpowering hands had wrenched an enormous cage from its foundation.

Solomon, held in a sort of watchful escort until this time, startled as rough hands pulled his arms behind him, as gritty fingers bit against his fingers. Luther glared at him cruelly, a wide smile forming on his flat, swinish face. Solomon looked away, scanned the wreckage of metal and stone.

So this was the Deep Borders. The desolation at the lip of the Absence itself.

"Is it like this always?" Solomon asked.

"Herenathere," Luther muttered, wresting the rope manacle, drawing it tighter, painfully tight. "The last you'll see it, annaways, idleman."

His breath was coppery, smelling of blood and neglect.

"Thank you," Solomon declared, wincing at the constricting binding. "You have been most helpful."

Now in the moonlight, black hooded forms weaved between the broken beams and black, turgid pools that covered the bleached floor of the plain. The Blights headed for the far side of the field, toward a looming geometry of honeycombed stone. Eerie rock formations jutted at the horizon's edge, beveled and fashioned into enormous cubes, into a strange, almost funerary architecture. Behind the shaped stones, glimpsed like sunlight through a thick stand of trees, a gray cloud swirled at the very edge of Solomon's sight.

He shuddered. He had never been this close to an Absence.

For the first time in his hearing, a grating, metallic sound carried over the field, rising in pitch and volume as though it had issued from the heart of the distant gray chaos.

" 'There Chaos dwells,' " Solomon whispered. " 'And ancient Night and Og and Anak old.' " He scarcely knew what he was saying.

"No spellcraft outta ye, idleman!" his captor muttered, jostling him harshly. "No twistin' the Text."

Solomon stared out toward the gray, swirling cloud of the Absence.

Long ago his thoughts would have been of magic, as well. But this time he thought of nothing—of a nothingness as shallow and flat and lifeless as the eyes of a Border-rapt boy.

The magic had passed over, leaving a void in its wake.

He was standing on the edge of nothing.

"Clear o' the pools, idleman," Aristo warned flatly. "They'll swallow ye, tha' will."

Through the damp, fetid landscape Solomon hastened, prodded by the relentless Luther. Wires arched from the ground like serpents, encased in wax and gum, and twice the priest stumbled—once over a staircase that descended suddenly into the ground, then a surprising curb, littered with the detritus of a hundred years' exposure.

The wind sighed through a rusted grating in the floor of the plains, and Solomon caught a whiff of old water rising from somewhere under the mortared earth.

Caverns.

Solomon closed his eyes, committed the darkness and the cold smell to memory. A shove from Luther ushered him back to the steaming, hard plains of the Borders, but he had it now—in the clear, tenacious recollection that allowed him long ago to memorize the Text . . .

And there it would stay, Solomon assured himself, because his one consistent talent was that he forgot nothing.

Meanwhile, to his increasing alarm, the Blights made for the horizon, for the distant, thrashing heart of the Absence. Like molting animals, the vanguard of the party stripped off their greatcoats, their motley, multicolored garments revealed like flowers in the bright Urthonan dawn. The dark outer garments they left where they had shed them, gum blankets and black-dyed canvas littering the stony landscape.

The boys were distracted, singing garbled Hymns.

At the head of the wandering party, festal in a red fedora, Constantine ordered three of the younger boys to drop to the back of the traveling throng, and with rush brooms to sweep away the trace of their passage.

"Why?" Solomon asked, but the leader paid no notice, surging to the foremost of his followers, a red-capped beacon in the steaming distance.

"Concealin' us," Aristo explained, the flatness unchanged in his voice. "Concealin' from the stalkers."

Instinctively, Solomon turned around.

A hundred boys shedding garments, unfettered from their coffins of black. Three little dark things sprinting among them, brooms held aloft. Velocipedes circling at the edge of sight.

No sign of stalkers, of pursuit.

"Stalkers? Who are they, Aristo? Who's after you?"

The boy fell into a sullen silence.

"Stalkers," he muttered at last. "All ye need to know."

His company sped across the desolate flatlands.

Whoever the stalkers were, and whether they followed or not, the Blights planned to elude them, it seemed, by traveling through the center of the Absence. In the shadow of the geometrical stones the procession ceased, the Blights gathered, and the youngest among them, their faces a mystery of mud and ashes, struck fires amid the stagnant dark pools.

Their greatcoats already discarded, many of the boys stripped to breechcloths, stripped naked, their pale skin stippling in the brisk autumn weather. Several among them carried ashes and woad, marigold flowers and walnut hulls, and as their fellows discarded the last of their clothing, stood beside them like ministrants, painting body after body with swirls and circles and broad, nonsensical runes.

All the while they sang rhymes from the Hymnal. Paternally, Constantine watched over them. Solomon tried to follow the singing, but could discover no logic in the assemblage of Hymn after Hymn. As the sun rose higher and then sank past noonday and the shadows of the hulking stones lengthened, the singing became more scattered, more erratic. Hymn built on Hymn, song doubled over song, and each lad sang a different word, a different melody.

As the sun plunged over the Alph toward awaiting Tharmas, the ecstasies began.

It was unobtrusive at first. In the midst of the strident singing, one of the boys—a small lad whose name was Lake or Locke, Solomon could not remember—knelt and extended his gritty hands toward the Absence. He beckoned to the gray, swirling cloud, and his words passed from Hymn to distortion to nonsense. Luther knelt beside him, and a third lad—a tall, lanky specimen named Swedenborg—fell onto his face, convulsing, gibbering, his eyes rolled in rapture beneath sunken, pendulous lids.

Preparation, Solomon guessed. Fueled by laudanum, perhaps. By the hempsmoke back at Bowlahoola. So if the Absence does its worst, they will feel nothing.

Constantine, painted and naked except for the red hat now thick with slogans, hurried to assist the writhing Swedenborg. Others broke from song and adornment to stand beside the remaining ecstasts, steadying them with a fierce, almost imprisoning grasp.

Solomon sat in the midst of this frenzy, leaning against a bare bundle of greening copper wire. He strained at the constricting ropes on his wrists, but they did not, would not yield.

Aristo leaned across the edge of the fire. He streaked his uncle's face twice, perfunctorily, with the dark ashes. Solomon gazed desolately at the surface of the nearest standing pool. In his reflection, discolored by the water and distorted by the slightest breeze, Aristo's marks showed livid as scars on a frightened face.

Not only were the boys headed for the Absences. They seemed intent on taking Solomon with them.

Quietly, desperately, the priest murmured a spell of loosening, a dryadic device taught to him by Amelia in the days before Lambeth. It worked no better than it had then. Up against chains and ropes and tethers, metaphorical magic was useless, irritating. You were on your own with key or knife or dexterity, and luck, not the saints, would guide your hand.

Solomon smiled bitterly, straining yet again against the taut, biting ropes. Why fool himself that the spells were magic? Better to steel himself, like a Blight or doomed and obedient guardsman, to suffer what would follow regardless of vanishment, shift, or unraveling.

As the turmoil of the camp subsided and the exhausted ecstasts sank into sleep, Solomon drowsed awhile, awakening roughly to the whistle and cry of a sentry posted deeply in the ruins.

He looked around him at his captors and took stock.

Travelers through eternity, it seemed, were much the worse for the voyage. Despite the poetry with which the Text described passage through the Absences—the vortices, the folding suns, the heavens and earths—many of the boys were scarred, burnt, aged unnaturally.

He had seen the seared flesh beneath the kohl and ash.

A sharp smell settled over the campsite. Ozone and sweat and scorched hair. Solomon leaned toward the distant fire, where Aristo and Luther and the ecstatic boy—Lake or Locke?—lay sleeping. Solomon breathed in the more familiar, less unsettling smell of woodsmoke.

Perhaps it would not be bad, this traveling. Only a little pain, and then . . .

Suddenly, as though emerging from the heart of the Absence, a wizened, apelike thing crouched on the bundled wires and stared menacingly down on him. A child the size of a ten-year-old, but with the wrinkles and white hair of a man of eighty.

Nasty. Brutish and short. His breechclout steaming as though it had passed through fire.

The boy *was* fire, a genie entangled in borderwire. Menacingly, he extended a finger, swollen and red, toward the captive.

Instinctually, Solomon breathed a warding charm against the creature, a charm of cold and ice. He clutched the thick strands of wire behind him, the verdigris crumbling into his swollen hands.

The naive little incantation died on his lips.

What am I becoming? he thought. *Running from Arcady? Cowering before pellagrous boys?*

What is it that fear is making of me?

The Blight leered toothlessly from atop his ruined vantage point, his dark eyes shallow and lifeless as shells.

* * *

The midmorning sun seemed larger, almost scarlet here inside the Borders.

The last of the Blights wakened blearily from the ritual carousals of the previous night. Staring stupidly at their companions, at the wide swirls of paint and ornament, they tried to remember what had come to pass.

Meanwhile, Solomon raced through his own memory for a means of escape.

For this time they were serious. The loud preparations of the day before had given way to a silent readiness. Two of the boys—the one called Lake or Locke and Solomon's menacing, wizened guard—had been chosen for a special duty. Now, tied to one another by a long strand of the copper wire, they paced restlessly in the shadows of the honeycombed ruins, still singing snatches of Hymns.

The long wire, twisted and black, was strung with paper slogans, from clear directions and snatches of the Text to the drawings and symbols and scrawls of the Absence-damaged voids.

Solomon was sure that something of great portent was about to happen—that the boys were preparing, or being prepared, for travel through the Absences. He would have to act quickly now. Act quickly, or go with them.

He could appeal to their nonexistent mercy, argue with their flawed and tattered logic, or . . .

"*This* is all your protection?" Solomon asked his nephew.

Aristo, who was scrawling something on a paper scrap, lifted his head and regarded Solomon flatly.

"Slogans and wires, idleman. Stick 'em together and give 'em the memories."

But he was no longer certain. A single question had seen to that. Aristo set down the charcoal, regarding his slogan skeptically.

Solomon craned to see what the boy had written.

Two vertical lines. And, in a shaky script, the word *Bahar*.

It was nonsense. Gibberish.

"No spells?" Solomon asked, dangling the lure. "No purities of water for the journey?"

Aristo avoided his gaze, mantling like a hawk above his incoherent scrawls.

"Purities of water?"

Constantine approached, his hat aflutter with a score of paper banners.

"What of this purities?"

Solomon smiled faintly, inventing as he spoke. "I trust you know the passage in the Text. The prophecy that foretold this very moment, this intersection of time and space and spirit at the edge of the Abyss."

Constantine frowned, and removing his hat, crouched by his captive, thumbing through the slogans as though in search of something—perhaps the very prophecy that Solomon spoke of.

Solomon's imagination raced, improvising on the spot, fashioning from fragments and scraps as the campfires ebbed and the boys, having prepared for dissolution, now gathered around him, expecting a song in a strange land.

"I don't know that prophecy," Constantine replied finally, his eyes averted, the quaver nearly masked in his voice. "Supposin' . . . that *you* tell *me* what you makin' of it."

"Very well." The Lambeth lecturer's tone, all trace of his old accent, its music and its humor and its heart, seminaried out of his voice, so that what was left, he knew, was the flat, nasal tones of the Lakelands. "Very well, Master Constantine. Then I shall explain."

The Blight commander met his gaze.

Solomon cleared his throat, launched into obscure seminarian double-talk. "There is a passage in the Text I suspect you know. On the Thirty-fifth Plate, it is. Glossless and intact, the lacunae excised by the Commentaries of Tyburn's Brook."

It meant nothing. But the Blights would not know it.

"I know that part," Constantine declared, a little too hastily. "Tell me . . . the *other* part."

Good. The boy was bluffing as well. Covering his ignorance. This would not be difficult.

Solomon cleared his throat. " 'They stood in a dark land of death,' the Text reads, 'of fiery corroding waters, where lie in evil death the Four Immortals pale and cold, and the Eternal Man, even Albion, upon the Rock of Ages.' "

He paused, soaking in the drama. "So as you can see," he continued, "the waters in question are altogether lethal, dispatching all, even the Immortals—whose mortality is not otherwise *possible*—into 'evil death,' as it were. Cessation, Master Constantine. The absence of being. The waters that contradict all sense and reason."

"Ain't no waters," Constantine observed, and Luther and Aristo murmured their agreement. "Ain't seen 'em."

"Had you seen *me* before you captured me?" Solomon asked, that sly, triumphant questioning of lecturer to a particularly dull and resistant student. "Had you seen . . . the *others* before you . . . well, before they joined you?"

Constantine's gaze returned to his slogans.

"Well, then. Well. Let us propose that the corroding waters *do* exist, but perhaps the reason that they have . . . heretofore *eluded* you is the simple fact that they reside not in the Absences themselves, but . . ."

A wide, dramatic sweep of his hand, cut short by the taut rope binding.

"But here in the Borders," Solomon muttered, inventing wildly as he spoke. "That is where they are. The waters."

Constantine squinted skeptically at his captive.

Solomon was losing his initiative, his power. He felt it, the almost palpable transfer of energy from himself to the surrounding Blights. He had to act, and to act now.

"Untie my hands," he ordered, the authority scrambling back into his voice. "Untie me, and I'll show you."

Surprisingly, Constantine complied.

The cords were loosened, so readily that Solomon rebuked himself for not asking for freedom earlier. Luther and Aristo jostled him to the middle of the encampment, opportunely between a banked fire and one of the stagnant pools.

Solomon breathed deeply, inhaling smoke and the fusty odor of stale water. The Blights encircled him, painted and wired and papered like a savage mobile, keeping a distance, no doubt in respect for the reputed magical powers of the priesthood.

He was suddenly cold. If what he was planning failed . . .

A hundred depthless eyes fixed on his movements as he knelt before the standing pool in a silence of feigned meditation. Despite himself, Solomon breathed a childhood prayer, one taught to him by his mother, Christabel, now dead and vanished except for the lost light in the mirrored recesses of the great Arcadian hall.

And the prayer itself came to him out of lost light, reflected from the four compass points of memory and intuition. The image surrounding the little Hymn on which the prayer was based returned to him, and here, surprised at the edge of deception, he found himself strangely and genuinely moved.

The picture in the Hymnal had been that of a star, couched on the forest floor, glowing with an amber light. A child paced toward the star out of the gloom of the woods, its arms extended and raised to embrace the light.

For a second, perhaps superstitiously and surely sentimentally, the priest's eyes smarted with surprising tears.

"Father, father, where are you going," Solomon breathed,

> "O do not walk so fast.
> Speak, father, speak to your little boy
> Or else I shall be lost."

He knew the ending of the song was sorrowful, that the little boy who sang it was abandoned in the depths of the woods, unaided by the amber light or the painted angels drawn in the margins of the Text. And yet the first verse was free of a final despair, and it spoke to him deeply, of a hope faintly glimmering like the engraved star.

But enough. Now to deceptions.

Still kneeling, the priest trailed a strand of copper wire into the dark water. Now, standing and backing carefully across the clearing in a show of reverence, he extended the strand, dropping its other end surreptitiously into the fire.

One end of the wire lay in water, the other in the heart of the flame.

Conduction or convection. Endymion would know.

Now for the ceremony, for the words that would validate the invented magic—the saint's legend in which the revered Saint Milton reconstructed his own body from the icy water of ancient rivers.

"Silent they met," Solomon intoned, "and silent strove among the streams of Arnon, even to Mahanaim, when with cold hand Urizen stoop'd down and took up water from the river Jordan, pouring on to Milton's brain the icy fluid from his broad cold palm."

He knelt by the pool and bowed forward, his gray hair skimming its fetid surface. Anointed by bilge water, his locks gamy and dripping, he pressed bravely to the next stage in his little drama.

"But Milton took of the red clay of Succoth," he announced, "moulding it with care between his palms and filling up the furrows of many years, beginning at the feet of Urizen, and on the bones creating new flesh on the demon cold and building him as with new clay, a human form in the valley of Beth Peor."

So having spoken, Solomon bent down, and gathered a handful of gravelly dust from the hard ground, and, returning to the lip of the pool, dipped his brimming hands into the water.

Which was warm already, the heat conducted down the bordermetal wire.

Good enough.

When the dust had dissolved, Solomon lifted his hands from the water with an assured, triumphant cry.

"Though all things vanish and are seen no more, they vanish not from me and mine. We guard them first and last. The generations of men run on in the tide of Time, but leave their destin'd lineaments permanent for ever and ever."

"Whassit?" Locke asked warily, his blightlock fallen across the forehead, masking his dark eyes.

"Saint Milton," Constantine explained. "The idleman maketh a body for the Emanation and the Shadow."

Solomon nodded. It sounded as good as anything else, and Constantine's belief that *he* understood would convince the others readily.

It was not far from lecturing in theology, actually.

Now, if what Solomon remembered of the other sciences applied . . .

Steam rose off the stagnant pool, and the woodsmoke lurched above it as though caught in a fetid updraft. Heat. Convection? No, *conduction*.

It helped not to forget. Solomon lifted his hands, drawing the stares of the Blights to his waving fingers.

Soon. It would be soon enough, as the heat passed down through the copper wire into the steaming water.

As if on cue, the pool began to bubble and boil.

And now, the words that would seal the magic in the eyes and ears of the credulous Blights. Solomon stepped toward the roiling waters, shouting the obscure, vatic passage from the Text. He had learned it by rote three decades ago, with not even a clue as to what the words meant. But they returned to him in the necessary hour, swiftly and readily.

"This is a false body!" he cried. "An incrustation over my immortal spirit, a selfhood which must be put off and annihilated alway. To cleanse the face of my spirit by self-examination, to bathe in the waters of life, to wash off the not human, I come in self-annihilation and the grandeur of inspiration, to cast off rational demonstration by faith, to cast off the rotten rags of memory by inspiration, to take off your filthy garments and clothe you with imagination!"

The first of the standing Blights knelt at the murky edge of the fire. "Saint Milton!" the boy cried. "Saint Milton come, like Constantine said he come!"

"Is the Bard!" Luther shouted ecstatically. "The idleman is the Bard!"

Heads bowed in the rising steam and smoke, the boys began a chorus of admiration, a song that wafted over the head of the astonished Solomon, past the Blight encampment and to the very edge of the Absence itself. Most of its words were lost at the edge of that swirling, shimmering void.

But not all of them.

There, unbeknownst to their speaker or his intended listeners, Solomon's first words in the false incantation—the words of *cold hand* and *icy fluid* and *broad cold palm*—bent around the swirling nothingness and, turning white and freezing in the bridled air, rained down on the distant forest like a shower of ice.

There, in the midst of false rite and hollow prophecy, the autumn turned suddenly to winter.

CHAPTER 17

They freed Solomon in the dead of night, kneeling to him as they had to Constantine, painting him in the gray swirls they told him represented the Abyss. Encircling his eyes were the dark rings which, they told him, represented the rugged covering of the diamond in the mine. When he opened his eyes, shining and pale green, their sight was the hallowed center, the orb that held the heavens of bright eternity.

All of this passed for protection, though Solomon would have far preferred a gun, a fast horse.

A map of the shifting country.

Or somebody with an eye to Constantine, his role as Bard-to-be usurped, who gazed at the ceremony from the edge of the firelight, his expression lost in the shadows.

Solomon was seen off to the edge of the camp, to the edge of the Borders themselves, for after his display of legerdemain, Solomon, now recognized as the Bard by the gullible Blights, had explained that his path lay in the outer forest.

Where, he promised, he would enter the Absence alone, and await the coming of Saint Milton.

It was all chicanery, all twisted Text and double-talk. Solomon averted his eyes from the worshipful gaze of little Lake or Locke as his escort took him north through the woods, following a trace of red rags.

The moon rode heavy in the northern sky, and at the edge of its white corona, a solitary star seemed to beckon the priest home.

Not to Lambeth. To Arcady.

To the ruins of his ancestral home, which, simply by being a Hawken, he had somehow promised to uphold. Now, after the Blights' great love for Text and Hymn, marred though it might be, Solomon had come to understand that it was not his calling to leave fragmented and broken things, but to restore them, and even more important, not to force upon them the terms of restoration.

What *if* I must reveal that I am neither priest nor spell caster? he asked himself as the party of Blights led him through the deepening woods, as the light of the campfires dwindled behind him.

I have been . . . too proud. And for no reason.

Solomon felt the crisp, electric surface of the Borders as it broke across his uplifted face. Outside, back in the Presences, the air was dense, more humid. The smell of smoke and ozone that permeated the Borders gave way now to the thick odor of evergreen and rotting leaves.

His escorts waved as he passed from the torchlight. Waved, and scrawled his name upon their slogans. None would accompany him any farther than the Borders, wary of patrolling armies.

And after all, was he not the Venturing Saint? Awaiting Saint Milton, who would fall precipitant, loud thundering into the Sea of Time and Space?

Solomon smiled ironically.

Who would dare accompany him? And why would he want or need their company?

"Not yet," a low voice announced, its source lost in a swirl of darkness beneath a cluster of taxus.

Solomon froze. "Who are you?" he asked. "Step forward and let me see you."

And Constantine emerged from the welling night.

At once Solomon thought, *It serves you right. Masquerading as the Bard in front of him and the others. He thought he was the one. Was chosen.*

And now, he is come to settle these things with you.

But instead of violence, of fire or the fiery cast of his bordermetal rod, Constantine, the leader of the Blights, bowed to Solomon Hawken.

"Things I don't know," he said, his eyes humbled and averted. "Mebbe you the Bard."

"Constantine—" Solomon began, but a wave of the boy's hand silenced him.

"Things I don't know," he repeated. "I wanted to be the Bard, I did, but wantin' ain't belief."

"That's true," Solomon said. "You don't know *how* true it is, Constantine. But . . ."

The Blight leader waved his hand again. "But maybe *you* are the Bard. Workin' the magic. Saying the Text."

He paused, looked at Solomon quizzically. "I think y'are."

Solomon stepped toward him. "Constantine—"

The boy moved away. "And *if* y'are," he said, choosing his words slowly, carefully, "it means there's one thing I'm sposed to do. And that's whatever you say."

He extended his hand.

Solomon clasped it, touched by the gesture. Such had been the faith he wrestled to keep when all of his Lambeth schooling had struggled against it. And yet Constantine's was no glamorized ignorance: he believed, not so much in Solomon, but in the Great Story—the account of Saint Milton's perilous, compassionate descent into chaos.

The same story that had inspired a young seminarian two dozen years ago, that twenty years of self-pity and foolishness had shelved somewhere in the back of his brooding memory.

To be brought out here, at the Borders' edge, in the simple allegiance of an innocent, murderous boy, who, in the midst of violence and rage and delusion, had managed to get one simple thing solidly, gloriously right.

Once you embrace a belief, you do what it says.

Solomon would not go back to Lambeth, where he had learned to set that faith aside. Instead, he would try again to reach Arcady, where his aunt Morgana, along with the dear dead figures of his childhood, Ahania and Amelia, Christabel and Vergil, had nurtured his faith in the early years.

"Thank you, Constantine," he breathed. "And may the saints speed you."

For the first time in a long time, those saints took flesh in Solomon's imaginings, as this dirty, appalling child, both monstrous and mysterious, graced him with a yellow, jagged smile.

"One thing more I know," Constantine urged, clinging to Solomon's hand as the older man tried, softly, to break the clasp. "First listen. Then talk.

"It is the bestest rule."

For scarcely a hundred yards as he walked away, Solomon could see

Constantine's uplifted lightstaff, wavering in the green canopy of spruce and cedar. Then the forest engulfed it, and Solomon was left directionless in the maze of greenery.

Again, as when he had lost Arcady at the river's edge, Solomon Hawken circled about and was lost.

By now the night had turned, and the starlight and moonlight were obscured by the clouds. An uncertain guide before, the heavens had become downright slippery, and twice, doubling back toward what he assumed was north, Solomon caught the thick, fishy smell of the Alph.

He wished, not for the first time, for a tattered trail of cloth of his own—scraps and ribbons dangling all the way back to the gates of Arcady.

Exhausted, Solomon sat beneath a bare poplar, cupping his face in his hands. Faintly, as though his fingers and not his thoughts remembered the scent, he smelled Mina's perfume, the coarse odor of Morgana's clay and standing water. He realized he had not bathed since he left Arcady.

Solomon laughed softly.

Then he felt the crackle of the Borders' edge pass over him.

Quickly, Solomon sprang to his feet. Too quickly, because the air eddied and swam about him, and he weaved on his feet, clutching the bole of the poplar for balance. Uneasily, he sought the Borders' edge, the wave of light, blurred like heat rising off a hot road, that marked the surface tension of the gathered air.

Nothing. The edge was far past him now. Veiled by foliage and forest.

He started to follow in a general, guessed direction, but changed his mind at once. To wander in that maze of greenery would court all kinds of ambush. Gnomes lurked in the earth, fairies and nymphs in the air and water.

It was the way and the danger of the Borders.

No. He could wait here. Simply being stationary seemed safer. Here he could see the danger coming, see the form it took. And eventually the Borders' edge would wash over him like a wave, leaving him free from all this peril and confusion.

But it was not to be that simple.

Almost at once, at a great distance, moving toward him with a wild churning of trees, a thrashing sound like a reaper, a cloud darker still approached, roiling and churning like a whirlpool in quicksilver.

The Absence itself.

If the Borders were deceptive and dangerous, Absences were far worse, dissolving, addling, or destroying all things that passed beneath their glittering, swirling mantle.

But it did not make sense. Absences were supposed to be stationary.

All at once Solomon noticed the fatigue in his legs, how even walking became laborious. Trees bent low toward him, their large branches spreading as if to embrace the approaching cloud, and light branches, evergreen needles, and the last dried leaves from the oaks fluttered swiftly toward the summoning dark heart of the thing.

Solomon turned, fled the Absence, running in the face of a cold, stinging wind, stumbling over ferns and vines, a felled and rotten water maple. Plashing through a brook, slipping on the rocks that lined its sloping bank, he skidded into the icy water, cracking a thin rime with his fall.

Not water not drowning oh please by the saints no . . .

. . . Father, father, where are you going? O do not walk so fast.

He flailed through a thicket of thorns, tearing his cloak, almost losing his priestly tricorn in the fork of an alder's thin branch. The nettles slapped and raked against his skin like a swarm of stinging insects. He reeled across another creek—the same creek?—and fell to his knees in the mud. Surely he had outdistanced it. Surely he was safe now, if only for a moment's rest and breathing.

But ahead, another dark cloud—the same cloud?—swam toward him angrily, thrashing and grating and grinding.

Solomon staggered to his feet again, wrestling against the impulse to lie down, to let go. A drowsiness came over him that was not weariness as much as a dark indifference in his soul: from Blight to Border to Absence, it had all been too much, and he was sleepy now, ready to give up and in, surrendering . . .

And yet he set foot ahead of foot, stumbling wearily away from the Absence, careening from tree to rock to underbrush until he burst from the forest, arms thrashing, onto a level, grassy bluff, its edge beetling a hundred feet above the icy, turgid Alph.

Behind him, the dark whirling crescent drew nearer still, not fifty yards away, glimpsed occasionally through the shifting trees and always, incessantly audible.

On three sides now. And his back to the sheer bluff and the river.

For a moment Solomon reeled at the edge of the cliff, his thoughts desperate and far too athletic for a man of his age and conditioning.

No, the Absence itself would be better than a vault into space, into distant waters. But the Absence was no less threatening. Inexorably it closed on the cornered priest, now thirty, now twenty yards away. Faced with the leap or the whirling, dismantling mystery at his back, Solomon took a short, tentative step onto the cliff face, lowering himself between two jutting rocks.

His hand closed around the last parcel of turf at the bluff's edge, then slowly, reluctantly, as though he were setting aside the world itself, Solomon relaxed his grip and began the climb down the steep escarpment, breathing incessant prayers to cover his precarious escape.

And so I hazard it all, he told himself, swinging out over a narrow escarpment as his feet stretched for balance, for a landing.

"I hazard it all," he repeated, this time aloud. For a moment he saw his flight from Arcady in new colors, as though he glimpsed it in the redoubled recesses of the facing mirrors, reversed and transformed and reversed again until, oddly, it had come to resemble its truer self.

He had forgotten why he had run in the first place, what could have been worse than cowardice and flight.

"Why, if I had it to do again," he whispered, "I would never have left."

And in that moment he was at peace.

Then his hand slipped, clutched for the outcropping where he had just lost purchase, groped vainly for a hold. The wet rock slipped from his grasp, as, with a flutter of rag and cape and flying gray hair, Solomon Hawken fell a hundred feet, through the ice and into the gray, surging whirl of the river.

CHAPTER 18

With cold and heat Solomon had conjured, and his magic, though to him nothing more than sleight of hand and inflated words, had been enough to fool a gaggle of illiterate boys and their commander.

It was power, but not power enough. It was not even clever enough to pride himself. And yet, despite what he believed, or rather did *not* believe, about his spells, they had not returned in vain.

And it was not long before Solomon's family knew it.

* * *

When the cold rushed over the clearing where Diego lay, he knew that some sort of deliverance had come.

For the rest of the pitch-black night of the ambush, his guardsmen had huddled at the foot of the abatis, pinned down by L'Overture's rebels. Willie, still breathless from the blow to his back, burrowed his face into the leafy floor of the forest, praying and praying again as the musket balls whined through the heaped branches like hornets.

Sometime before sunrise, a strong arm had jostled him from exhausted, drowsy prayer.

"Follow me," commanded a voice from the darkness.

Diego.

The Guard was moving.

Slowly, illumined by the occasional flicker of rebel musketry, Diego crept along the ragged foundations of the abatis. Where the branches had been stripped from the new-felled trees, a last, ill-starred flourish of leaves had sprouted grotesquely, completely out of season, out of the nature of things.

Diego slithered through the low shade and borderwire like an adder, pistol clutched in his mud-spattered hand.

Willie followed uncertainly. There were others behind him. He could tell by the shallow breathing, the occasional flicker of gunlight in which they all froze, mimicking the ruined immobility of the dead.

Groping in the darkness, his hand found Diego's wooden ankle.

Ragged. Splintered by a rebel musket ball.

Circling a little sinkhole at the foot of the abatis, masked from the rebel pickets, the guardsmen crawled toward the far side of the barricade. The air was loud with the cries of catbirds, the trill of the mockingbird—not the true, diurnal birds, but their voices, imitated by the rebels in the trees.

In the branches above the abatis, green light erupted, as for a moment the trees seemed to flower in foxfire. Exposed in the eerie, heatless light, the guardsmen shielded their eyes, cried out, shivered. Diego fired a shot at a shadow crouched in the low branches of a poplar: the shot was far wide, as usual, and the shadow flitted away into a deeper darkness.

Finally one boy, a farm lad named Bolingbroke Norwood, scrambled to his knees—whether out of impatience or panic—and hurdled the piled branches, clambering for the far side of the abatis, for darkness and thicker cover.

For a moment the birdsong around them stilled. The grassy light flared harshly.

At the top of the abatis, Norwood paused, stepped cautiously and fearfully, seeking a foothold to descend. The rebel lights caught him framed against the whole ambiguous woods, a solitary shape on a precipice of metal and branches, outlined by gloom. The volley that sheared away the top of his head was smokeless, flameless, the sound following the impact of the bullets like the distant crackle of a large branch breaking.

Then the green light winked out, and a warm, sticky rain descended with the darkness. Willie covered his head, his frantic prayer resuming as the smell of powder, blood, and burned hair mingled with the dark shower.

"Now!" Diego commanded, tugging at Willie's outsized green rucksack. The Captain lurched over the abatis, dragging the gondolier with him, the rucksack breaking open on the tangle of branches, and a handful of the boy's gatherings, from smooth Arcadian peaches to a daguerreotype of Mina to a spare silver serving ladle from Christabel Hawken's tarnished collection, tumbled into the borderwire.

The rebels opened fire, musket balls splintering the dry wood at the crest of the abatis. Another man straddled the barricade, falling face-first as another sniper's shot crashed between his shoulder blades, and Diego pulled Willie to the ground, crouching beside him as another volley battered the rickety wooden wall.

They lay there, motionless through the morning.

The screams of the wounded guardsmen faded by midday.

As the night fell on the abatis, there were only six of them left.

Willie's back ached mercilessly, a sharp pain that banished most feeling, most other thought. Garrick, exhausted, leaned into a dark clutter of wires. The others—three wall-eyed boys from Urizen, virtually indistinguishable from one another—gaped and shivered at the prospect of a rebel charge.

Only Diego seemed intact.

Occasionally the Captain would peek over the unkempt brim of the abatis. Mindful of the sharpshooters' habit, Diego would crawl up and down the row of branches and brush, bobbing up at a different spot each time, firing his pistol twice and cursing elaborately when the bullet failed to find its mark.

Green shadows at the edge of the clearing flitted from tree to tree, and occasionally the soft needles of an evergreen rustled against the current of the wind.

Diego leaned against the dry wood of the barricade and closed his eyes. They were out there. Outnumbering his forces maybe five, six to one.

Then the doleful, solitary sound of a flute rose out of the green shadows.

L'Overture. The silver flute confirmed it, the music falling like freezing rain upon the exhausted men at the abatis.

The huge black man with a woman's name, a bent for music, and a decade of sheer genius in cavalry command. A raider so daring and heartless that the Tribunal had ordered Major Werther, Diego's late commander, to refuse engagement with him. The Guard all along the

Alph had been told to let L'Overture do whatever he pleased, since if they tried to stop him, he would simply do whatever he pleased and kill as many guardsmen as he felt like in the process, playing afterward a sweet and plaintive dirge above the bodies.

L'Overture was as famous for his doggedness as his brilliance. If he was waiting, rehearsing his strange, discordant melodies over the smoking field of skirmish as though he had no place better to go, it would take a miracle to lift the siege.

Diego rested against hard bordermetal at the base of the fortification. The soft notes of the flute trembled expectantly, almost hungrily, through the wires.

And the music continued past midnight, when the fires began.

As the stars shone through the gaps in the trees, L'Overture played yet another song—a minor melody bearing a heretical lyric from the Commentaries. Their voices rising out of the undergrowth, the rebels joined in their leader's song.

The first torch fell into the clearing. It sputtered with a green fire, and hissed out. But a second torch followed, then another, until the entire clearing blossomed in an eerie firelight.

Willie peered through the branches. The rising moon cast a freakish light through the smoke; maples seemed to reach and grope across the open ground, and a green smoke gathered on the ash- and blood-spattered grass.

"Set to burn us out," Garrick muttered.

"Just like 'em, too!" Diego spat, his back against the wall of felled timber. "Luddites and know-nothings all of 'em. All bothered because the Citizen mined the Borders, as if the Borderlands had anything to save or salvage in 'em. Naturalists all, the rebels. But they'll burn their *green and pleasant land* to the damned roots for a shot at a guardsman."

Another torch, and yet another, fell nearby. After a stuttering of flame and spark, the grass leading up to the abatis began to smolder. Firelight brightened the clearing, and about the abatis the branches of the trees started to sag and darken, and their shadows came nearer the timber walls.

At first Willie figured this movement, this shifting light, was just a trick of the fire, or that the music had lulled him into imagining a shifting forest, hot and bright in the middle of the woods. But part of the nearing shade was the shadows of birds, who had come to roost in the nearby trees as if a storm were rising and they had come to the battlefield to wait it out.

The branches began to sag with the creatures, darkening with crows and jays and owls and birds unnamed and unnamable. Beyond them the woods were black as a root cellar.

Beneath L'Overture's soft and menacing music, dark things snuffled and called and rose up in the space between notes. The Hymn was echoed by watery, inhuman voices, and the ground rumbled a dissonant bass, in a language of consonants and stones.

Someone has to be on guard here, Willie thought with rising alarm.

A great cloud of birds rose from the gray, autumnal branches with a tumult of wings, and for a moment the forest was absolute dark, moonlight and firelight blotted by smoke and feather. One of the lads—it was not Garrick—whimpered in the darkness. Then a faint light flickered on the Guard side of the barricade.

Diego growled and, with the long thin lucifer in his hand, recklessly lit a green cigar. "Enough of the dirges," he muttered. "Even L'Overture can't pin us down forever."

Willie looked about, at his unnerved, weary comrades.

What was the Captain planning, anyway? There were six of them remaining. No match for two dozen hidden rebels who had shown they could handle rifles like backwoodsmen.

"If you are about to order a charge, sir . . ." Willie began, his shoulder throbbing angrily from yesterday's wound.

He lost the words.

His black eyes glittering in the matchlight, Diego regarded the gondolier icily.

Then a blistering chill fell into the forest air, as the overflow of Solomon's counterfeit spell, cast among the Blights in the bordermetal fields, reached the company at last. Willie felt the cold, and clutched dramatically at his shoulder.

"It's . . . it's gettin' cold, Commander," he muttered. "D'you reckon the death is comin'? For I've heard it told that the extremities go all icy and numb in the time before your passin' and that . . ."

Diego extinguished the match. "Don't be a fool, Melmoth. It's cold as a granny's nip in this clearing. If it's the death, the world is dying. Look out there."

Diego pointed to the corpse-littered glade, where the fires shuddered and winked out at the approaching cold. As the smoke scattered and vanished, a thin steam, rising from bodies dying and dead, replaced it in the icy air.

Still the temperature plummeted, and instinctually, almost unconsciously, the guardsmen slid together for warmth.

"Peculiar," the Captain observed, his breath misting over the abatis. "Border ruffles, I'd wager. Now all we have to do is find a way to play the change in the weather."

Diego was right. It was no natural cold.

The spellfrost issued by Solomon's chant at the edge of the pools overwhelmed the forest, so profoundly that the graybeards of fifty years hence would refer to it as the First Frost of '74.

Nothing the likes of it, they maintained.

Blew up the trees.

For the sap in the pines and maples froze solid and expanded, bursting the boles of the ancient trees with the sharp, cracking report that people heard as far west as Shiveleigh, as far south as the ruins of Ville.

Like the sound of riflery. Which was what the rebels mistook it for, when suddenly the woods erupted around them.

The guardsmen, too—Willie, Garrick, and even the seasoned Diego—took the eruptions as rebel fire, but as they crouched among the clustered branches of the abatis, they heard movement in the trees beyond the clearing. Shouts, and the whinny of horses.

L'Overture was in retreat.

So when the first of the gathered wood exploded beside him, splintering an old maple bough and knocking him sideways and dazed onto the hard forest floor, Diego scrambled laughing to his feet, wobbling for a moment on the fractured wooden leg. Below him, huddled in cover, his troopers regarded him with alarm.

It was not until an hour later, when they crossed the solid face of the Alph on their way back to refuge in Arcady, that they believed him.

Willie, crouching on the surface of the great legendary river, watched the current pass brown and sluggish beneath three inches of ice, surfacing fitfully in midcurrent, spilling through and freezing as it spilled, ice redoubling on ice.

Willie could not believe, as he wrapped his greatcoat tightly about his bony shoulders, that his company had been spared bullet and bayonet. That here, in the most profound cold in the history of Urizen winters, something in the core of them all had remained intact amid the explosion of a hundred trees.

"Only science remains thro' mercy," he breathed, reciting remembered Text to the torpid, ice-channeled waters.

* * *

The cold wind rushed out of the forests above Arcady, over Endymion's paneled wagon, rustling through Morgana's long quilted dress.

They were on the road, by the banks of the Alph, not twenty miles west of the old ancestral grounds, following the vague directions of Endymion's abstruse reading.

When the weather caused by Solomon's spell reached them, Morgana believed it was another sign of her rising insanity. First she had followed a harebrained nephew who used obscure Textual scholarship as a road map, arguing all the time with the indecipherable calls and whistles of an attendant phoenix. Now she was imagining an unseasonable early winter, complete with frosty winds and broken ice on the river.

She had outlived her faculties. Her family was right.

Morgana tightened her grip on the reins and guided the horses into a little copse, to ride out the wind. Longing for hot tea, for rum, for anything to take away this sudden, unexpected chill, she reached into the wagon bed for Endymion's flask.

It lay on a bed of fresh straw, her sleeping nephew coiled about it protectively, like a guarding dog.

Above the snoring Endymion, in a dull cage, Khole shivered and flapped his wings.

So the cold *was* real.

Endymion stirred at the smell of juniper, reached glumly for the bell jar under which lay Golgonooza in its bottle and a swim of amber light, untouched by wind or temperature.

"Where, Morgana?" he muttered. "How far?"

"Three miles at most since you last lay down, Nephew," the old woman informed him curtly, setting down the flask. "But if we'd a sail at our backs, we'd be halfway to the end o' the world by now. The wind and the cold are downright uncanny."

Magic, she told herself, the gin spreading like warm silk down her throat. Even along the river, weather was not so capricious, so unfriendly.

Solomon was somewhere mining the Borders. He was rescuing Arcady from afar.

The thought warmed her more than the liquor.

"I'll take the reins, then," Endymion offered. "After all, I'm the one who guided us this way." Brushing the straw from his cloak, he stepped to the driver's seat of the wagon, crop and Text together in his hand. Morgana shifted her wide bottom to the edge of the bench, accommodating her nephew, his reading, and a fetor of gin and old straw.

"Look!" Endymion proclaimed, tugging at Morgana's sleeve. He pointed at a passage from the open Text on his lap.

For a moment the cold wind lifted and surged, and the astringent smell of the distillery scattered. Morgana breathed deeply, gazed over her nephew's shoulder, and pretended to read along with him.

All she saw was the swirl of color on the page, the red-and-yellow sunburst emanating from its lower right-hand corner. No pictures—not like the cottage on the next page—to suggest what to expect.

Endymion read to her, his excitement scarcely bridled by his voice. "It's obvious, if you know where to look."

Morgana yawned.

"See?" Endymion persisted, his ink-stained finger gliding along the page like a black wind over ice. "Here, where it talks about the Moment . . .

> " 'There is a Moment in each Day, that the Enemy cannot Find,
> Nor can his Watch Fiends find it; but the Industrious find
> This Moment & it multiply, & when it once is found
> It renovates every Moment of the day if rightly placed.'

"See, Morgana? It confirms my suspicions all! It's why my brother is so hard to find. He's looking for that Moment, that place where the enemy can't find him and from where he can renovate all moments, all places."

"Moments and places?"

"The place from which he can try his spells to restore Arcady. Not that they'd work, Morgana. But we can use his belief to find him. See? The Text goes on."

He pointed to other lines, farther down the page. Morgana watched his finger glide stealthily over two lines. Vainly, she tried to decipher the neglected words.

Milton was in them. And *track*. What she thought might be *South,* though she hadn't the letters to be sure.

But Endymion was reading. And why would he lie to her?

" 'Just in this Moment,' " he continued, his voice wondering and triumphant,

> " 'Just in this Moment, when the morning odours rise abroad
> And first from the Wild Thyme, stands a Fountain in a rock
> Of crystal flowing into two Streams: One flows thro' Golgonooza
> And thro' Beulah to Eden beneath Los's western Wall:
> The other flows thro' the Aerial Void & all the Churches,
> Meeting again in Golgonooza beyond the Enemy's Seat.' "

Wide-eyed, he looked to his aunt expectantly.

"West. He's gone west to search for that place. One of the two Streams is bound to be the Alph, and wherever Solomon is . . . Golgonooza *has* to be there."

Endymion patted the gin bottle triumphantly. The teakwood city inside the glass tilted and chipped beneath his heavy hand, and quickly, contritely, he nestled the bottle in the dark blankets on the wagon bed.

"Not that . . . its presence would make any difference," he added, almost apologetically. "But if Solomon thinks it does, it might make it easier to get him to return with us."

Bored and baffled by the obscurity of Endymion's cherished Textual passages, irritated that he believed not a word he cherished, Morgana turned to watch the river. From far upstream, pieces of gray-brown ice flowed by on their way west, to the great convergence of waters in Tharmas.

Crystal waters, indeed, Morgana thought.

As Endymion prodded her, badgering her with the cryptic Text and his even more cryptic glosses, shouting back at the cooing phoenix, whom he believed was arguing his strategies, Morgana set her gaze to midriver, where a dark floe of ice carried an object darker, small and frail. Not a hundred yards upriver the current eddied and broke toward the near bank, and the ice slid into a closer view.

What is it? she asked herself. Fumbling for her spyglass, she drew it from her portmanteau, trailing kerchiefs, wool stockings, and a pair of outlandishly knitted mittens, images of the martyrdom of Saint Palamabron embroidered on their palms.

Khole muttered on his perch. A more susceptible listener might have mistaken the noise for laughter.

Her telescope retrieved, Morgana peered out over the water toward the broken ice, the dark object riding on its mottled surface. She leveled the glass, and the mystery lurched into view.

A tricorn hat, wet and crusted with rime.

Swept along by the dark water, it rushed by the wagon, a dark speck on the merciless river. It vanished into the uncertain west, as Endymion continued to speak his airy nothings, and the bird in the cage moaned once, tenderly, as if his voice contained the key that held back the night.

CHAPTER 19

The lights of Arcady were never so welcome.

Mina's candles and hurricane lamps, her Chinese lanterns and phoebes, illumined each window of the towering house and reflected brilliantly off Grandfather Atreus' artificial lake like drowned stars.

It was close to dawn, the last darkness punctuated by the first diurnal birdsongs, and Diego was glad for once that his cousin labored through the night on her statuary.

At the southern gates of the estate he stopped. Garrick and Willie Melmoth, who had followed closely through the darkness, collided with him like clowns in a musical. Garrick cried out, and the gondolier grabbed him, slipping a grubby hand over the loud boy's mouth.

Wheeling on his splintered leg, Diego flogged away the startled lads, staggering once as he lost purchase on the gravelly road in front of the gate. "Stand back o' me, dammit," he rumbled. "Before I shoot the brace o' you!"

Willie and Garrick backed away from Diego, colliding with one another again and reeling to a place near the brick wall that encircled the grounds.

Now the Captain opened the gate. The iron hinges, weathered by years and mist and neglect, creaked in the ominous, prohibitive way they had done since his childhood. But for once he did not feel guilty, as though he were sneaking back after a night of excesses.

Diego had made peace with the grounds, set aside his father's contempt for unversed sons, Solomon's indifference, and Brother Endymion's suspicions and practical jokes.

None of them were factors. Old Roger was a decade dead, Endymion gone on a wild-goose chase across Tharmas, hauling Morgana and the bird and his petty suspicions.

And Solomon?

Diego crossed the grounds, his nephew and brevet aide-de-camp advancing warily in his footsteps. At the edge of the pond, rising like herons from the reeds and the red mud, flitting shapes parted and scattered before him like a low mist on the battlefield. Within the fog he might have made out faces, gray cerement and tarnished tiara, had he been looking. Indeed, the boys behind him shuddered at the shapes of phantoms, trapped on the grounds by Borders and by other, unfathomable forces.

Diego saw no phantom, no revenant, as he skirted the brimming pond. He had little time for phenomena. He was bent on the house, on the entrance, on reunion with a cousin he had pursued and wrangled with for months. After the abatis and L'Overture, the ambush and the ice storm and the long trek home, the petty ambushes and wearisome detachments of his family were almost welcome.

He paused, though, as the tarn bent north toward the sprawling brick towers of the house. Crouching in the pondside reeds, Diego watched the men move through the lamplight of the main door of the house.

Men in green.

Palmetto leaves, rushes in the hatbands. Muskets and long knives rather than pistols and swords.

A rebel party if he'd ever seen one.

Garrick and Willie crept into the water and crouched by the Captain.

"L'Overture, d'you think?" Garrick asked, his gloved hand resting on his uncle's shoulder.

Diego snorted. " 'Twas L'Overture, we'd never've reached this far. Pickets would've taken us, one by one, before we even screeched the gates back yonder. Skinned us alive in the evergreens."

Willie's imaginations reeled. For a brief, terrifying moment he fancied himself pale, intangible, afloat in the algae-thick waters of the pond. It was a vision of doleful emptiness—of a vast place, cold and wet, that imprisoned him in its great horizons.

"No. It's Artemis," Diego concluded. "My cousin is home."

The lads exchanged uncertain glances.

"And we'd be safe enough if Herself was on watch," Diego continued, his deep voice spilling out of a whisper with his thought and excitement. "She'd give us safe passage. But sometimes her men act . . . on their own authorities."

Willie watched the big commander as he straightened his scarf and ran his fingers through the long, black curls of his hair.

More than strategy, this was. The gondolier scratched his head.

"You're not going to charge, are you, Captain?" he asked. "I mean, you like to done so back in the forest."

Diego shook his head. "The last thing I want," he muttered, "is to fall before her rifles. On my own back lawn."

"Leaving a widow and a son behind you?" Garrick asked.

The commander glared at him.

Willie shrank into the reeds. He had not known that Diego was married.

"Still," Diego said, thinking aloud, "we've a need to get in there. Morgana and Mina will know where my brother is. Surely Endymion's wild-goose chase has raised no feathers, and surely they're home by now. Maybe Endymion himself can find Solomon with one of those damned machines of his—the saints know all that gadgetry is of no other use. Whatever happens, I'll be boiled and divided if Artemis gets to Solomon first."

Parting the thick cane, he peered out at the sentries.

"There's a window open upstairs," Willie offered.

The commander turned slowly, regarding the young man icily, calmly.

"A window, you say."

Willie nodded. "I left it ajar when I let in . . . some air. Yes, some air."

Diego had turned away. With a tactician's swift reasoning, he was already arranging a shadow-covered route to the wall, a means of ascent, a tower-darkened path over three gables to the window in question.

"It's a roundel in the roof of the house," Willie offered. "A skylight in the attic."

The attic. Diego remembered at once. One floor above the principal bedrooms, two above the Great Hall. He could find it easily, even with the sprouting architecture.

His plan unfolded instantly.

It was pure Hawken swashbucklery—the kind of bravado he had

studied in his childhood bouts with Artemis. Why, if the rebels didn't get him, Diego Hawken might well fall a hundred feet . . .

Into the welcoming bosom of his family.

* * *

Diego was lighter than Willie Melmoth had imagined.

Perhaps it was the missing leg, or perhaps the prodigious upper-body strength of a man conditioned by fighting ten years from horseback. Whatever the reasons, Diego hoisted easily to the first low windowsill. From there he did the rest, scaling the brick wall like some cloaked and hairy spider. At last, framed in the pale, shifting moonlight, the Captain cast his good leg over the eaves of the house and pulled himself silently onto the roof.

He was on his own henceforth. Diego intended a quick, acrobatic jaunt across the roof of Arcady, culminating in his dramatic descent from the attic skylight. All of this even though the house had many entrances, doors and transoms and dormers and bulkheads. The mansion was honeycombed, as porous as the far buildings on the stony edge of the Absence itself.

But Diego was one for production, and solitary production at that: Willie and Garrick were to wait for his signal, his summons to enter the hall under the saints knew what arrangement of truces with the rebels. But if the sun preceded the signal, Diego had told them melodramatically, if dawn still found them stationed by the pond, they were to emerge and surrender to the guards on the doorstep.

Willie watched Diego ascend with a rising uneasiness. Up there on the eaves, despite his strength and courage and incessant bluster, the Captain looked frail against the dark outline of the morning sky.

Again, Willie offered up a prayer to Saint Milton, and for himself. The famous prayer of Saint Palamabron, it was:

Protect me from my friends, that they have not power over me.

* * *

Diego sat on the shingled roof and recovered his breath.

The ascent had been dizzying. Twice his grip had faltered, and once the damaged wooden leg had slipped on the moss-covered face of a brick, threatening to send him plummeting into his grandfather's overgrown garden.

But now, for the moment, he was safe, and he suppressed the childish impulse to give thanks to the saints . . .

Who had nothing to do with boosting him over the eaves, when strength and resolve seemed at their limits.

No, he had made it himself to these heights. It had been his hands that clutched old Prometheus' grape-cluster frieze, his good leg that pushed him the last story to the cool slate, the misted air, the vantage from which he could see the entire grounds.

From here he could see the far orchard and the gates north and west, the dried eastern hemp fields. Below, the rechanneled Alph branched into Atreus' mill house and out the other side, pooling in the lake at the foot of the house.

She would know it. If nobody else understood, his cousin Artemis would respect his acrobatics, at least.

* * *

"You must leave with me," Artemis insisted. "Arcady is no place to be ill alone."

She stood by the fireplace in the studio, where her reluctant cousin had stood two nights before. Muddy from the long ride and the crossing of the Alph, she was nonetheless beautiful, dark hair brilliant and wild beneath a veil of leaves, the bowed lips of the angels, the supposed dryadic blood resurging every three generations.

A palmetto leaf brown and dry lay interwoven in her cataract of black hair. A last hint of green touched its edges, touched her eyelashes, until she appeared like an angel drawn at the top of a map.

She looked like a disguised queen. The Raider, the Lady, the Great Horse Thief. Her name changing like a rumor depending on the company, the country.

Morgana's summons had brought her as well. Two days late, because an elaborate chess match with the Guard in Urthona had delayed her passage.

Yet she had come.

Arcady beckoned her like an imperious mother. Once she stood at the mill-house window, a little girl with elbows rubbed raw in sliding and play. Now, in the field, she dreamt of the mansion burning, of white flame in the third-story windows, purging and purifying the house. In her dreams the smoke circled and hovered over the collapsing towers, raced along the rooftop like an avenging, living thing.

Then the smoke billowed into the brilliant skies of Urizen, taking on human shape as it rose. Figures stepped from the smoke like sound from a distant cannon—maid and gardener, gamekeeper and cook, the threescore men and women who had carried the mansion on their submissive shoulders through five generations of Hawken masters.

They were free in smoke and air, she surmised.

Only the burning could make them free.

In her dreams Artemis held a phoebe lamp and watched the conflagration from the mill house, the cool, metallic smell of water rising around her as the smoke erupted and the mansion burned. She watched in assent, in approval, but the time came, as it always did in the dream, for her to set torch to the ignited building, to add her flame to the cleansing blazes. Instead she doused the lamp as she always did in the flickering waters of the Alph, as the mill wheel turned like history behind her.

She would awaken in tears, sometimes. Sometimes in a chill sweat. Once to a burning pain in her hands, to blisters on the tips of her fingers.

But despite the dreams and the anger—despite it all—she had come when Morgana summoned her. Come to find her sister feverish and alone, preoccupied with the silly statuary that sapped her youth and health.

"You *must* return with me," Artemis insisted, leaning against the cool bricks of the studio furnace. "This place oppresses the nerves, damages the spirit. There are ghosts here, Mina, and not only the charming, eccentric ghosts Morgana and Endymion fashion from those bottles there . . ."

She gestured widely at the tray, the emptied whiskey glasses.

"But the ghosts of those who built this place, tore the farms of Urizen and south Urthona from the wilderness, made this country habitable and harmonized it with the landscape like a topiary garden, like a twisting of nature . . ."

Mina gave her sculpture a yearning glance. Artemis was lecturing again.

"Those ghosts are here as well," Artemis added, a strange note of bitter triumph in her voice, "and they'll be restless until the Citizen stops tinkering with the Borders."

Mina rolled her eyes.

"Each time the land is torn," Artemis concluded, "each time we dig and mine, rechannel and mechanize, it unravels something else—something we don't know about or haven't noticed. It's like the dart in old Uncle Innocent's neck . . ."

"I know the story, Sister," Mina protested quietly.

"Then you know how a small wound scars and spreads and touches a body in bewildering ways, Mina. Who would've thought that little sting would change him forever?"

Artemis paced around Morgana's pottery wheel, spinning it once and gracefully with the absent touch of a solitary finger. "The turning world is a body, Sister. Every part's kin to every part, and when Arouet sets off charges in the caverns underneath Napolis and Ville, we feel the tremors here and now and in ways we never understand. He poisons us just like Innocent was poisoned, and we sicken alone when we could heal together."

"Sounds like a revolutionary slogan," Mina observed quietly, standing painfully and shuffling away from the fire.

"It's for your good," Artemis insisted. "Each day that you remain here, this oppressive house bears down on your sickness. Come with me. There are those in my company who can help you."

It was enough.

"Come with you?" Mina asked teasingly, as she rose and circled the wax statue, clay molded half up its base. "What place is ideal for lonely sickness, Sister?"

She looked back yearningly at the statue.

The form was emerging from the amorphous pillar that had sat atop her sculptor's pedestal for a month now. It never ceased to astonish her how the figure emerged from raw chaos, not as though she had discovered it in the midst of the material, but more as though it sought her out, asked her consent to emerge, to *be*.

Nothing short of the miraculous.

Her thin knife glided over the sculptured hands, because for some reason the hands had come first, veined and knotted like an older man's.

It would surprise the rest of the family when the wax opened to reveal Cousin Solomon's face.

"So will you come with me?" Artemis asked. She did not know. Could not know.

Mina could not leave. Not now. Perhaps not ever.

Again she circled the pillar of wax, dropped to her knees by the incipient greatcoat. It had to be perfect. Perfect, and swift. Solomon's shape raced against the hourglass, as Mina herded it to life. But indeed, he *was* emerging. Dressed as he was three nights ago, in a thousand reflections of mirrors.

"Mina? Mina?"

Artemis was beside her now, standing over her. A shadow on the pedestal.

Artemis smelled of moonlight and cypress. Was it true how men died for her?

Mina brushed her thin hair back from her forehead. The hem of the waxen greatcoat sprang out of her lively hand.

Good. The line was right. In the smallest detail the illusion of movement, or movement waiting to happen. . . . What was it Endymion always said?

A local habitation and a name.

"Mina." The voice beyond questioning now, edging toward scolding, toward the chastising older sister that lurked beneath all masks of concern.

"I will not go with you, Artemis."

There. The words in the studio, settling like the dust on Morgana's wheel. Artemis stalked to the fireplace, sat, and warmed herself, even her sullenness lovely, almost dazzling. Mina lifted her eyes from her work, regarded her sister.

Yes, in that light men would die for her.

It had been no blessing for either of them.

* * *

The years in the mill house had schooled them both in the same lessons.

Often, her nose pressed against the dirty window, her gaze fastened on the roof of the mansion, which, through the dusty glass, seemed smoky and ruinous, Artemis had thought of the old stories—the fairy tales in which the less favored son had brought home the treasure, the bride, had prospered in some way unimagined by his elder brothers.

But James Hawken, the only son of Cortez, an unfavored son in his own right, lounged on the banks of the trace, smoking hemp and sailing toy boats merrily up the rechanneled Alph. Her father labored toward the perfection of a green rose, hybridizing and grafting his plants, while his daughters dressed in flour sacks and looked out the dusty windows as their cousins passed to and fro on horseback, from their stately rooms in Arcady unto the blossoming grounds they would inherit.

Artemis held out hope for Diego. But after all, Diego was the younger of the twins by a quarter of an hour. The third son in the anointed half of the family.

Mina, on the other hand, had no use for tales and rich relatives. Early on, she had lost herself in the muddy bank of the rechanneled river. Lifting the red clay wet and dripping from the water's edge, Mina had begun to mold another estate—a replica of Arcady, doll-like and intricate, in which the mill house dwarfed the spreading mansion, and statues stood in the midst of the topiary.

Mermaids, old men on wheeled beds, a curious statue with three figures, two incomplete and the third angelic, red wings sprouting from his thin, attenuated body.

All of these before she knew the family stories. Before she had figured the curious dynamics of blood that had placed Roger in Arcady and dear dead Cousin Cortez's son James . . .

In the mill house.

Once Endymion had dropped by to speak to her father. Had seen the toy city and no doubt taken notice. For it was Endymion's nature to collect, not create, and Golgonooza must have been born on that day, in imitation of a girl who played where a river flowed through a fertile darkness.

Mina molded another statue as well, the story of which neither Artemis nor James could recognize.

A disheveled man, clutching a book in his left hand, his right hand raised in a gesture of admonishment or blessing.

Even then, it had made no sense to Artemis. It was not history. It was not oppression or containment finding heart in the molded clay. Yet it was the statue that Mina loved the most, onto which she lavished the most and the best of her growing talent. And now, as though it had dwelt for twenty years in her spirit, seeking its final shape, it was coming forth in the wax.

She would cast the sculpture in bronze, would set it . . .

On a pedestal in the house itself. Or so it seemed.

Artemis cast a worried glance at her sister, who crouched intently at the base of the statue. It was as though she looked at Mina through glass and at a distance, and a strange fire danced over the ailing girl as her deft hands shaped a stranger.

* * *

The roundel window was shut and bolted.

Diego muttered a curse upon Willie Melmoth's fate and family, all the while tugging vainly at the casement. Sitting at last on the roof, he gazed glumly through the glass into the darkened attic.

To have come this far, only to be blocked by the thinnest of partitions. It baffled him, enraged him.

Then he realized that a closed window was no impediment at all.

Diego set wooden foot to the glass and pushed.

The window gave way in splinters, showering the attic floor with broken glass. Diego kicked out the remaining shards, then lowered himself through the roundel, dangling awkwardly from the attic ceiling as a faint light paled the easternmost window, illumining the abandoned contents of the room. Hatracks and trunks, Aunt Kassandra's dressmaker's model and Khole's first birdcage. And there, just below the wall, below the light, a pile of rags and a smell of spices, and something at rest, asleep, on top of the mound of refuse.

He had not time to reckon with these leavings. Diego dropped unceremoniously to the floor, wobbled, retained his balance, and made for the trapdoor and ladder that led down to the upstairs hall.

He had forgotten the layers of house between himself and Artemis, like a dozen windows preventing dramatic entrance. Muttering to himself, Diego hobbled down the ladder, then the first flight of stairs to the landing.

From there, shrouded below him in the morning darkness, he could see a form standing at the foot of the stairwell. Female and slight. Armed, as best he could tell.

Artemis, no doubt. She would have heard the glass break, heard him stomping about the attic like an unleashed bull.

Yet there was still time for dash and chivalry, for an entrance that partook of acrobatics and bravery. Even if the properties were not altogether there—no ropes to swing from, no chandelier to drop from nor balcony to vault—there was a banister, long and smooth from years of childhood use and fit for an arrival of sorts.

Besides, his cousin would appreciate it. Remember the old times.

With a laugh, Diego sprang to the banister and slid into the darkness. The figure below, stationary no doubt with surprise, seemed to rush toward him from the angle and velocity of his descent, and he laughed again, thinking how something this sudden, this reckless, had always surprised her, how despite her superior wits and agility she had been left breathless a hundred times by his bravado, his stupid boldness.

Into the dark Diego tumbled, crashing into the bronze statue of Melusine Stella-Maris, his mermaid grandam, moved only yesterday by Mina on its eventual path to the topiary garden.

CHAPTER 20

Solomon awoke beneath a swirl of late stars, on the border between night and morning.

He was lying on his back in the bottom of a boat, his clothes still damp beneath an ice-encrusted blanket, so that even though he was not uncomfortably cold, he felt as though he was made of sleet.

Vainly, he scanned the sky to determine his whereabouts. These were stars he had not seen before, or had not noticed, and his sketchy seminary astronomy could place them nowhere in Urthona or Urizen.

He could not tell if he was in the Borders or out of them, whether he had passed through an Absence or stayed safely at its edge. But he knew that he was moving, a slow, steady float upstream as the stars moved westward over him. Solomon took a deep breath, gathered his thoughts . . .

Upstream?

Floating upstream? Away from Arcady?

He remembered the fall, the water, the panic . . .

The surety he was drowning.

But where was he now?

Only then did the sound of oars reach him over the rush of the water against the bow.

With a gasp Solomon sat up in the boat, looking back at the stern. The woman faced him as she rowed, but her eyes were fixed beyond him, on the dark eastern waters of the sluggish Alph.

Solomon frowned. He had seen her before.

The round, ordinary face with its little red-rimmed eyes was strangely bovine in its broadness and docility.

Somewhere to the north. Around the seminary he had seen her.

Solomon cleared his throat, and the small eyes turned to him at once, a surprising intelligence flickering in their brown depths.

"So at last you're awake," she said. "You slept almost from sunrise to sunrise."

For a moment Solomon did not believe her. Never had he slept that long before. But then the memories returned—the brief, sunstruck fractures in his sleep, the rush of water, once the twilight call of an owl when he climbed toward wakefulness in a sea of night . . .

Always the sound of the current brushing by. And the sound of oars in the water.

He shivered, reached for another blanket—a dry one, closer to the woman. "Thank you, whoever you are," he muttered.

She nodded slowly. "Enith," she said. "My name is Enith Moneta."

Solomon introduced himself, ransacking his memory to identify the woman. She was a good fifteen years older than he, and rawboned like a farm wife. Her costume jewelry—from paste earrings to a dark, inexpensive cameo—suggested a pack rat's indiscriminate appreciation for glittering things.

Enith, he repeated to himself. *Enith Moneta.*

It would come to him soon.

They had entered a part of the river he did not know, where the wooded banks gave way to steep gorges or to rocky inclines accessible only through ancient stony stairways, carved in the rock face but worn smooth by years of weather and travel.

Enith Moneta rowed north and east. When they were clear of the Borders, she maintained, they would hitch the boat safely on the Urthonan side of the river. From there it would be clear passage north, away from Absence and army.

High above the passing boat, old piers, their wood rotten and dilapidated, hung over the cliffs' edges like grotesque balconies. Abandoned now, so high as to be useless, they were the mute evidence of a civilization long before Border and Absence, Urizen and Urthona, perhaps before the Text itself was salvaged in a time before the first records of history.

"Where are we going?" Solomon asked at last.

"Around the Absence," the woman replied laconically.

Solomon started to protest, to urge Enith Moneta to turn around the boat, to head downstream toward Arcady.

He tried to sit upright. But a surpassing weakness washed over him like the waters, and he lay back, propped his head against the gunwale, and watched the gray sky reel overhead.

Something in the fall, in the immersion, had weakened him.

He steadied himself in the flimsy rowboat, trying to recall his own uneasy childhood times on the river, something that might guide him or ward him as the river narrowed and the banks grew more steep and menacing.

What good was your youth when you could not remember a thing you were taught there?

At that moment, his gaze flashed back to the woman and settled there. Suddenly he remembered Enith Moneta from his earliest days at Lambeth.

Enith Moneta. The Dirty Nun.

* * *

The Daughters of Albion Nunnery, a convent adjoining Lambeth Seminary, was a small one. Its inhabitants, carefully screened by the faculty to avoid untoward disruptions to the exclusively male student body, were either dismantled with age or extraordinarily plain.

Enith Moneta had been the youngest nun. And the plainest.

She had served in the adjunct role in which many of the sisters supported the abstract, intensely patriarchal faculty, teaching the younger children their letters and fundamental theology. Though Solomon had never been assigned to her classes, he had attended them on various occasions, hidden behind Joy's Grape in the Great Hall of Esthwaite, along with dozens of curious boys from his form and older. Seated together and snickering, he and Marcus Chatterton would listen to the poetry of the Dirty Nun as she recited exultantly to her students.

Her baubled fingers fluttered in the air as she rendered the verse in the urgent, pausing monotone taught in the Urthonan schools.

Poems about her breasts. Her nether parts. Her acrobatic desires.

For the plain Sister Enith Moneta was as mad as the inmates of the wish sanitarium.

Though she was clearly harmless, her poetry had supplanted what the elders considered *more substantial instruction*. Within a month after she had convened her first class, the Dirty Nun was gone—some said to the wish sanitarium herself, while others maintained she was simply parked, sent down, placed on the road to wherever it was in Luvah she had first come from.

Solomon had thought about her twice, maybe three times since, all of which took place in the first rush of puberty. But in nearly thirty years Enith Moneta had not crossed his mind.

Until now, in the borders between Absence and waking world, night and day, Urizen and Urthona. In a place where all things seemed to converge.

* * *

"So you knew me at Lambeth?" Sister Enith asked.

Solomon could only blush and nod.

"Has it changed much since my departure?"

Solomon averted his eyes, shook his head. "No. Nothing changes in Lambeth."

"Don't be shy, lad." Sister Enith's voice was coaxing but not unpleasant. "Tell me what *has* changed. I remember well the rest."

So Solomon told her of the new, more theoretical schools of thought that had entered the seminary since his youth. Of the experimental physics and natural theology that invaded, defied tradition, and were picked up by the younger priests fond of invasion and defiance. Of the new conjectures concerning motile Absences and unminable Borders, and their implications regarding magical precepts.

None of the faculty believed in Textual magic anymore. *Really* believed.

Oh, the most brilliant skeptics would concede that Text spoken in the presence of the Borders shifted circumstance ever so slightly. That was their phrase, "shifting circumstance": when leaves scattered at the speaking of a dozen words or a lamp ignited to the sung verse of a Hymn. But with a rake or a lucifer match, the enchanter could do the same thing, and so was the case with all the achievements of magic. The shift was more psychological than physical.

The enchanter became what he beheld.

It was all for the best, to know the truth about our ancestors' foolishness. It was as his brother Endymion said: all knowledge was for the best.

Sister Enith listened quietly to Solomon's explanations. Nuns were taught from girlhood to listen and nod while the priests went on, and it was a habit apparently hard to forget.

But then, when Solomon had finished, or when his theory and philosophy had reached a polite stopping point, she asked him those things about Lambeth she really wanted to know.

"Is the light in the library the same, Master Solomon? And the cracked bell in the chapel of Saint Ololon, does it still ring with the sweet deadened echo? And do the snows come early in fall, then go away until the brink of winter, this time of year?"

Solomon could not answer. He gaped at the questioning woman, who asked him other things, little things, as though they were large, imponderable questions.

Which they were because he could not answer.

She no longer sounded like the Dirty Nun.

"You don't believe what you were just telling me, now do you?" Enith Moneta asked. "This business about *magic is foolishness* and *shifting circumstance*?"

"I don't know," Solomon admitted. He waved his hand dismissively, as his sentence died into the river's murmur, the soft treading of the oars. "Part of me does, but then . . ."

His voice trailed into the plash of the oars, the slow lapping of the Alph.

"I know what you are thinking, Master Solomon," Enith said finally. "It is far from poetry about nether parts, these things I am asking you. But on the road after I was sent down, other things happened to me. I saw things as well."

"Things?" Solomon asked politely. But he dreaded the story. Guiltily, he wished that his rescuer had been someone more esteemed, more suitable. Enith Moneta had always been a fool.

Enith regarded him calmly. "When the Lambeth gates closed behind me, it was like something in me had vanished. I was convinced that I had been suppressed, silenced. Kept from enlightening the young men in my charge."

"We went on to laugh at other things," Solomon replied cruelly, impatiently.

Enith Moneta smiled, and skimmed the oars across the flowing water. "I know you laughed. I know that I mistook your cheers, the swaying of curtains in the lecture halls, as aesthetic sensibility rather than adolescent heat. But the faculty at Lambeth recognized it, I believe, for what it was."

"They are famous for recognizing . . . the *limits* in folks," Solomon remarked icily.

"Then why do you care what they see?" the Dirty Nun asked quietly.

The boat passed a bare parcel of land on the port side—a piece of Urthonan woods carved or burned or otherwise laid waste. A white crusting of sand or salt covered the clearing like a thin and desolate snow, and a cold steam rose in eddies from the white surface. Far inland opposite, on the Urizen side of the river, the first lark song of the morning chimed like a cascade of silver coins, and the Alph itself hung between vibrancy and life, between music and silence.

"They released me, you remember, at the turn of the year," Enith continued. "In the winter, when it was hardest to travel the country around Lambeth."

"I remember only that we returned to find you gone," Solomon said. He remembered the winter evenings in Lambeth, the icy waters of Pontus Tarn. He shivered.

"By the first night," she maintained, "I was in danger. For you know how the badlands south of the seminary are a highway for winter winds. Coaches capsize, balloonists rise two thousand feet to steer above the prevailing currents and storms."

"I know," Solomon said. "Nothing lives there. It's like . . ."

"The wake of an Absence," Enith prompted.

Solomon lifted his eyes. The *wake* of an Absence? Obviously, she had meant "the wake of a Border." But in that case, the comparison was far-fetched, inaccurate.

Even for a bad poet.

They *really* should have taught the nuns more thoroughly.

"It was wintry and desolate," Enith continued, "and more in that year than it was ten before or twenty hence."

She shipped the oars, and the boat turned sideways in the slow current.

"Where did you go?" Solomon asked. His thoughts were not altogether on the question. Something troubled him—something out of place in this encounter, this journey, this conversation.

He still could not place it.

"South," Sister Enith answered, righting the boat with renewed and steady rowing. "I went south with an ice storm at my back. All of my clothes were on me. I was layered with jackets against the weather. And still, it was zero to the bone, as the old meditations say . . ."

It was a quote obscure and nunnish. For once, Solomon did not know the Text.

"And the ground littered white with thin snow, birds fallen, frozen on the wing."

Solomon gasped, startled by the image. Vainly he grasped for a connection, a memory.

The banks. Silica- or salt-encrusted.

Desolate.

"As you know, there's almost no living in the snow plains south of Lambeth."

Solomon blinked. The image, the memory, slipped away again.

"So I sought in vain two hours, maybe three. Over my shoulder, when I could stand to face the wind, I could still see the seminary. The four spires, the black wall against the gray of the horizon . . . the gates. Regardless of what they say in Lambeth, of *the gates that open for all, the bright Gate of Larks* and all that sentimental double-talk and foolishness, they build a gate to keep you in and us out.

"Then the first lights of the evening shone on the gates, on one of the towers—Tharmas, the western one, I believe—and I thought about turning back, throwing myself at the foot of the walls, begging for mercy. For Mercy has a human heart, Pity a human face."

"I know!" Solomon snapped. The Hymn she quoted seemed mocking now, almost ridiculous. He looked at her calflike face and softened. After all, she was part of the story, too.

"I know you went . . . away, Sister," he soothed. "I know you did not return to the seminary."

"That was a year without mercy," Enith said dreamily. "The accident. The boy drowned in the tarn in the spring. Should've never happened. What was his name?"

Marcus. His name was Marcus. How had she remembered?

"You're right," Solomon confessed. "It should never have happened. That night on the tarn was the closest I have come . . . to hell."

A scuttling along the shadowy banks, something large and furtive sniffing in the night, startled him to silence.

Enith peered at her passenger knowingly. "Doesn't the Bard say something about a 'Hell of our own making'? You should know. They let you read the Text in Lambeth, don't they?"

Her eyes returned to the rippling midriver, and she resumed the story.

"The storm shifted my path, drove me steadily east. The seminary seemed to drift away from me, like a city afloat on a sea of dreams. It was not long before I knew that I could not make it back.

"But by the grace of the saints, a cottage appeared then, as if the snow and wind had shaped it out of nothing."

"Cottage?" Solomon jostled from his thoughts of a boat like this, an early morning clear and cool, the last glint of moonlight on a placid lake.

Marcus at the helm. Always at the helm, where he belonged.

The memory was too sharp, too close. To return to it was hell again. Solomon pushed it away.

Cottage. Sister Enith had spoken of a cottage. But he remembered no houses within miles of the seminary.

"Oh, yes," she insisted. "A draftsman's cottage. A print shop once for the seminary. Abandoned and boarded, it was. The glass of the windows was old but unbroken. The wind and the snow seemed drawn toward the windows, as though a current forced the air inside. And yet the glass was silvery, reflectant, spangling the exteriors of the cottage with light.

"I tapped on the first window, the one nearest in reach. Like a mirror it was, rather than a genuine window. There was no response, not that I had expected a living soul this far from proper shelter and in the midst of snow and wind the likes of this.

"I removed my outermost jacket. A sequined spencer it was, purple and crimson like the robe of a queen."

"I remember the spencer," Solomon said. "Saint Palamabron knows why. Maybe you recited your poetry in it once."

Enith did not seem to notice the interruption. "I wrapped the jacket about my forearm and broke the pane in the window. The wind surged behind me. It seemed to lift me, to carry me through the window.

"The next thing I knew I was on the banks of this river."

"Seventy miles away?" Solomon asked incredulously.

"Seventy miles," Enith replied. "Through an Absence. I found myself here . . . around here . . . with the layers of clothes dusted, layer after layer, with a white salt. I could not remember any of my old poetry. Nothing except . . . well, a stanza or two.

"It was as though something had come down from the air and . . . and shaken me."

They sat in silence for a moment. The Alph churned by, and the lonely plash of the nun's oars echoed in the steep gorge behind them. Quietly, the rowboat slipped into level country—a morning country where a thin, sunstruck haze hovered along the banks.

"Forgive me for asking," Solomon said finally, "especially if you'd prefer not to talk about it. But I want to know. What is it like in the Absence?"

"You'll find out soon enough," Enith Moneta began. "But I think you already know that."

CHAPTER 21

"The poetry that I recited to you . . . long ago and up in Lambeth. Well, it began and ended with myself." Enith blushed, the pink flush of embarrassment strangely suitable on her wide, simple face. "It was about me even when it *wasn't* about me."

"I don't understand," Solomon said, still unsettled by the nun's ominous prophecy.

What is it like in the Absence?

You'll find out soon enough.

"I wouldn't expect you to understand," Enith said, shifting her grip on the oars. "Your journey begins and ends with you, as well. Not a sovereign's difference between 'em. Even down to the getting home."

Solomon startled. Talk until now had been of Lambeth. How did the woman know that he was trying to return to Arcady?

"I know," Enith said quietly, her bland face unreadable now. "I was that way in the storm."

Solomon trailed his hand in the water, watching the gray-brown ripples. He was uncomfortable hearing this. He was still not sure he understood.

"It is not about you," Sister Enith said. "The poetry, the casting of spells, the spiritual pilgrimage—whatever you want to call it. You can never make it that way. The world has more of the Borders in it than you think, and everything you know about yourself changes, slips away, refuses to be . . . defined."

"I know that," Solomon replied irritably. He drew his hand from the cold water. An icy strand of moss had wound like a ring over his index finger, and he thought of drowning, of the deep net of deep water.

"I was at a juncture," Sister Enith added cryptically. "How was I to know that my poetry was . . . well, not poetry?"

Solomon set his hands to the gunwales. "But we were talking about the Absence . . ."

"Poetry has everything to do with the Absence," the nun insisted. "You have to listen! Listen before you talk. It is the first thing that you learn there. Listen!"

Her sudden note of urgency surprised Solomon. He had trouble following her next words, for they seemed spoken out of the depths of the sea or from the black recesses of a cavern.

"My poetry changed inside the Absence," Enith said. "Or I changed it, rather. I changed it. It was in a silver cloud where I walked. It was a void, Solomon—as near nothing as you can imagine, and then some.

"All of a sudden, up against that nothing, the old poems didn't mean a thing. Oh, all the while a voice inside me still told me it was folly to change, that sooner or later you boys and the whole world would catch on to my . . . my *genius*. That the poems would make sense about breasts and harnesses. But there was nothing in the Absence, and something deeper than my vanity told me there was nothing in my poems as well."

"You listened to the better part of yourself," Solomon explained piously, as though he were advising a child in the Second Form.

"Oh, but it was more than that," the nun insisted with a frown, regarding her passenger with wide and skeptical eyes. "It was like . . . magic lanterns throwing light on the silver, swirling mist and showing me my past . . . the long wails of the sisters in the windowless halls of the convent and the white veils hanging from the doors like tethered ghosts. It showed me the purple light of the seminary halls, and something else I never quite placed about white clover on a raised knoll. It was south of somewhere important, that little hill, and the sun was warm and delightful . . ."

"But the Absence, Sister Enith," Solomon interrupted, sensing that the nun was off again, ranging through her old scattered memories. "What about the Absence?"

"You are hearing everything I know of it, Solomon Hawken," the woman insisted. "All I saw in it was what I brought there."

It was a moment before Solomon realized he had not given her his full name.

"You remember *me* . . ." he began, but the sister shook her head and laughed, banking one of the oars and guiding the rowboat toward the Urizen bank.

"I'm tired," she said. "And you may be surprised to know that this story is not about you." She looked at him shrewdly, her red-rimmed eyes lancing and brilliant.

"I know this much," she concluded cryptically. "That you will have to pass through the Absence yourself. When you reach that juncture, the next step is not forward nor backward, but a strange sideways—a step not keeping with what you would expect at all, but something out of instinct, out of some source deeper than simple common sense.

"You won't know the step until after you make it. And you will never make it alone."

* * *

She had fought the Absence and won a kind of prophecy.

Or that was what Sister Enith Moneta maintained, there in the hitched rowboat on the Urizen side of the slow-moving Alph.

Since her emergence from the Absence, for thirty years in this wooded, forsaken country, she had wandered and prophesied. Poetry came to her now: when a voice at the edge of her understanding rose to taunt her, to belittle her, she brought down every deceptive fantasy, every proud obstacle, and in her battle the poetry would come.

Poetry no one believed.

She also claimed that at least part of the legends were true. The Absences *were* interconnected, rising out of Citizen Arouet's bordermetal mines, out of the hearts of hollowed trees, from caves, abandoned houses and sealed bottles, the undersides of mirrors—anywhere that air is confined, contained, reflectant, or stagnant.

Travel within them was dangerous. Enith herself had felt her faculties stripping away, in only a brief sojourn in the Absence. It was like dying, she believed. Nothing drawn to nothing, like dormant parts of you falling forever asleep.

But she had learned in the Absence, learned—and do not ask her how!—that even passing through the Borders involved tremendous risk. Right now, as they sat athwart the banks of the Alph, they could well be dissolving.

In the Borders, something grew out of nothing. But also, something reverted to nothing again.

"After all," she told Solomon, "it is the governing principle of the Absence. It is the way the Absence works, and that way touches the country around it. My new poems tell its story."

"But how do you *know* these things?" Solomon persisted. "How is an abandoned house like the inside of a bottle? It sounds like a seminarian's riddle or a problem in physics."

"It has nothing to do with physics," Enith insisted. "I am no physicist. It may be the opposite of physics."

Enith leaned forward in the boat. Solomon could smell her now—an old woman's smell, sharp and leafy. For a moment he was frightened, but the fear became fascination—the view of a swaying snake in the zoological gardens—when the old nun continued.

"The opposite of physics. Sooner or later, no matter how large, the Absence disintegrates itself. It turns on its tail like the snake you're thinking of . . ."

He sat back in the boat, astonished.

"And it swallows itself whole."

"Then what is left?" Solomon asked. He felt as though his thoughts were exposed.

"Nothing," replied the nun. "Nothing, that is, of the Absence itself. The countryside around it—what used to be its Borders—recovers in a way. But even *that* is no more than a wasteland. It takes decades, even centuries, to grow again.

"What has passed beneath the Absence is barren forever."

Passed beneath?

Passed beneath. The wake of an Absence.

The arid, irretrievable crust of a country at the river's edge.

"The Absences are moving, Solomon," Enith Moneta whispered over the slap of the water against the side of their boat. "In their wake they leave bare desolation, a salt-covered wilderness in which no animal thrives and no plant grows.

"Nothing comes out of the Absence unchanged. You dissolve, something falls away from you. And the same thing happens to the country the Absence covers."

Solomon lay back in the boat. For a moment the stars seemed to reel and tumble overhead.

The Absence was devouring the countryside.

If Sister Enith was right, all Arcady was vanishing.

Overhead a linnet circled, despairing of a place to light.

"Where is it moving, Sister Enith?" Solomon asked. "The Absence, that is."

"South and west," came the answer.

Frightened, overwhelmed, Solomon forgot where he was and tried to stand. The boat cavorted crazily against the current, gray water splashing onto the floorboards as the priest staggered, recovered balance, then staggered again.

"Row me to the bank, Sister!" he shouted.

Sister Enith wrestled the rowboat slowly about, her bracelets flashing as her strong wrists worked the oars. "Headed home now," she mused. "If an Absence had approached me every waking moment, if I could have seen the silver, whirling cloud before my eyes, open or closed, over all those wasted years at the nunnery . . . there is no telling what I might have done otherwise."

"I must get home," Solomon pressed. "I'll pass through the Absence itself to get there."

"We'll see when the time comes," Enith replied with a smile. "I expect you will. After all, you told the Blights as much.

"But don't expect to be remembered for it, to be proclaimed and published as Solomon the hero."

Solomon cast her a puzzled glance.

"For every Saint Milton that descends through chaos," the sister claimed, her wide eyes on the southern bank, "there's probably a hundred of us rowing boats on a wooded river. People history never remembers for their . . . spiritual bravery.

"If fame is what you expect to earn when you travel through the Absence, expect something else."

She set him off where he asked her, at a scarred and forsaken levee over which the Absence had passed. Barely stopping to thank the woman for his rescue, Solomon made for the banks.

Behind him, he heard the Dirty Nun reciting. Something he had never heard, neither Text nor Hymn nor Commentary. Sang, this time, in a low and beautifully brittle voice—an old woman's voice. The song was in a minor tune, the old affected intonations of seminary long stripped away from the spare melody that passed over the water.

"Out of sight? What of that?
See the Bird—reach it!
Curve by Curve—Sweep by Sweep—
Round the Steep Air—
Danger! What is that to Her?
Better 'tis to fail—there—
Than debate—here."

Solomon listened, though he did not look back. If it was her poetry, Enith Moneta was right. The Absence had done something to her words.

In the stony purchase of the old levee, he lost his footing, sliding feet first into the water, floundering a moment before clutching dry rock and pulling himself back onto shore.

For a moment as well, in the slow driving surge of the river, he had seen nothing, felt nothing. A kind of darkness rushed over him, as he imagined an Absence would do, and the next thing he knew, he was kneeling upon dry land, then standing with difficulty amid the rubble that littered the riverside.

He turned back to speak to Enith Moneta, to thank her belatedly, but she had vanished. The river rolled beneath him, and he marveled at how wet he was.

Hours wet. Miles wet.

For a moment on the bank, Solomon doubted that Sister Enith Moneta had ever passed through the river and his life. There was no sign of her on the water, and all the evidence pointed to his coming here alone. Perhaps he had dreamed through a night's blackout in which he rode the river miraculously, skirting eddy and snag until he came to this place, this morning, and awakened washed upon the banks.

It was plausible. As believable as any Dirty Nun.

The ground on which he stood was flattened, devastated by something beyond his knowing. Salt and ash covered the blackened earth, and a light smoke rose through the air like steamed breath in winter. Birds instinctively seemed to have quit the area, but in the distance, on the river's opposite bank in a crowd of dark and greenery, a solitary bird sang in an evergreen copse.

He could still cross the river and travel north.

He could still return to Lambeth, to the safety of custom and lesson.

After all, what more improbable source of wisdom, what more implausible solution to the threat of Border and Absence against his house, than Sister Enith Moneta?

Again, the lone bird whistled on the far banks of the Alph. No doubt it was a mockingbird, for in its singing it had caught a new melody, a minor melody that broke and twisted and mingled with the splash of the water.

It was the same tune that had carried Enith Moneta's song to him over the rushing current of the Alph.

Solomon Hawken stood and laughed, his clothes sodden with icy water.

See the Bird—reach it!

"Who more improbable?" he asked the smoking air, the ash and salt, the desolation around him. "Why, Solomon Hawken, of course. I am the most improbable hero of all."

There were dozens, perhaps hundreds of explanations as to what had happened to the levee, to the patches of ground up and down the banks of the Alph. But Enith's was the one he had.

There, in the midst of devastation, Solomon chose to believe that the Dirty Nun had carried him from the waters beneath the cliffs, from the lip of the Absence, all the way to this spot. But more important, he chose to believe the many things she had told him.

It was the story that made him responsible. It was the story that sent him home to Arcady, triumph or fail.

"Better 'tis to fail there," Solomon breathed, "than debate here."

Birdsong tumbled from the darkened copse, each melancholy note a redemption.

So again Solomon set his path toward Arcady. He hoisted himself up the gritty banks, scrambling and scrabbling until his fingers clutched roots, his hands furrowed through moist earth.

The Absence was approaching his childhood home. The Borders were but a foretaste of its havoc. Despite his judgment, his wisdom, and his abiding fear, Solomon had to stop it.

His resolve first wavered not a hundred feet from the levee. Overwhelmed by the sheer distance, the miles that lay between him and Arcady, he sat down where the desolation veered off into the forest—a swath of about a hundred yards void of tree and undergrowth and grass, a landscape as bare and rocky as it no doubt was in the earliest days, before greenery and water and even before soil itself. The trees at the edge of the wake were parched, uprooted, dusted; they bent in toward the emptiness as if some unspeakable force had drawn them toward its center.

The Absence had uncovered the bones of the country.

All of a sudden, Solomon felt small. He reached down and gathered a handful of white pebbles, rolling them gently in his hand. The stones were clean, blanched, as though by perverse geology.

Who was he against this devastating power?

What would he do when he reached Arcady?

He could not imagine Morgana and Mina leaving the ancestral home. They were anchored there, like the sphinxes and the mirrors, and no fear—not even that of an approaching Absence—was likely to move them.

So what would he do? Hole up with his family until the very last, seated in the changing rooms of a dying manor? Would they stare at one another like reflecting mirrors, optical transmission lines, face to face until the Absence passed over, taking them the saints knew where and leaving complete ruin behind?

Dry steam rose from the dry rocks at Solomon's feet. He was helpless to stop this kind of wreckage. Perhaps Enith Moneta was wrong. Perhaps the Absence was *not* moving toward Arcady, perhaps not moving at all. . . .

Again he fought down the temptation to flight, to ease. One way or another, he would do something definite. He would stop running, but beyond that he was not sure.

Occasionally he looked to the stars for direction. The Plow and Harrow had tilted in the northern sky, changed once again from when he stood atop the ledge overlooking the river. The river itself beckoned with a soft, feminine voice, and straying once too near its banks, Solomon saw faces in midcurrent.

The drowned, he told himself. All those of Urthona and Urizen lost in the river are rising this morning. Old Atreus himself no doubt among them, riding his daybed to eternity.

It is the Last Day, he thought fancifully.

His thoughts were disrupted by the crash and grind of machinery.

Solomon opened his eyes. A silver cloud rested and swirled on the riverside path, drawing brown leaf and twig, needle and dirt into its churning center.

Slowly, the heart of the Absence closed in upon him.

Closed in, for behind him approached the same silver cloud, and inland, shimmering through a stand of pine trees, yet another cloud emerged onto the desolate white flats, moving to the sound of thrashing and crashing.

The dark mills. Grinding the forest to oblivion. Circling around him from the south, as if it warded him away from returning home.

Solomon looked toward the beckoning water. Hands rose from the turgid current of the Alph, coaxing and urging, calling him into its flowing center. By instinct and by his youthful fears, he knew that into the water was *not* the way.

It was the way he had passed before.

Something new was asked of him.

I must get home. I'll pass through the Absence itself to get there.

After all, I told the Blights as much.

The clouds were scarcely a hundred feet from Solomon now. He could see past their reflectant surface, into a whirl of wind and fragment, a chaos of rubble and flickering stars.

Solomon turned to face the nearest Absence—the cloud proceeding over the inland rubble, thrashing through a clearing of felled poplar. His only hope, the hope of his family and perhaps of the continent itself, lay somewhere in those dark, chaotic recesses.

After all, if the Absence stood between him and Arcady, the best and only way was not around it, but *through* it.

Some of the Blights had passed through it. Constantine among them. Who, amid his violence and brutality, had shown a strange and generous faith.

Enith had been there, as well. She had survived. Had said that the journey even stripped away her foolishness. And after all, the poetry that had followed him out of the waters, riding on her raspy, bland, old woman's voice, had changed, was haunting and daring and deep . . .

She had known he would pass through the Absence. She had suggested as much.

And now, firsthand he would discover what books could not tell him, nor the feral boys nor the lapsed nun and all her poetry. Discover, in his heart and on his breath and at the ends of his fingers, what rumor and report could only guess.

Could it be worse than drowning? Than what the Blights had threatened to do to him?

Better to fail there than debate here.

A passage of the Text he remembered, a moment when Saint Milton himself had stood on similar shores. To the churning rhythm deep in the Absence, Solomon chanted the lines, aware in the chanting that the story had happened before, would happen again and again, and that he was not alone.

> ". . . the Sea of Time & Space thunder'd aloud
> Against the rock, which was inwrapped with the weeds of death.
> Hovering over the cold bosom in its vortex Milton bent down
> To the bosom of death: what was underneath soon seem'd above:
> A cloudy heaven mingled with stormy seas in loudest ruin;
> But as a wintry globe descends precipitant . . .
> With thunders loud and terrible, so Milton's shadow fell
> Precipitant, loud thund'ring into the Sea of Time & Space."

"The same story," Solomon breathed after a long silence. "In that much, the seminary was right."

He stepped forward, took a deep breath, extended his arms. The Absence billowed over him in a fierce crackle of static. His body twitched and jerked with the impact. A dull visceral coldness filled him, and he opened his eyes to a gray, swirling nothing. At once, the singing fell silent, and words slipped away from him. Immediately, almost by instinct and certainly before his will could react and silence its wavering, his body recoiled with the horrifying certainty that he had done something wrong.

He vanished into the cloud, and the long river gestured behind him.

CHAPTER 22

The borders between Urizen and Tharmas were unmarked and unguarded—long, grassy stretches of land that bisected the Alph and a chain of rounded hills that the inhabitants called the Mountains of Albion.

It was no longer an important boundary. Tharmas and Urizen were more like adjoining provinces or counties under the governance of Citizen Arouet, who ruled from Vala, his distant citadel in Luvah. Now their old, not always friendly rivalry displayed itself only in the croquet matches between teams native to each country.

So it was no surprise when the wagon crossed the border without any of its passengers noticing.

Endymion had run out of directions. Quickly, with growing urgency, he dropped the reins and searched the pages of the Text for guidance. For the first time since the departure from Arcady, he doubted his obscure, bookish method of finding his brother.

After all, Solomon was hard to figure. He subscribed to no common sense, and the intricate cause and effect Endymion had fashioned from seminary logic and Textual scholarship seemed almost absurd, given the sudden, irrational flight of his older brother.

At first there had been clues that he was on the right track: an ashen smudge of bootprints by the roadside not five miles from Arcady's western gates; the discarded lantern a mile after that, its base engraved with the small but familiar crest . . .

Full-winged hawk, red sun at his back . . .

Enough to keep him going, despite Khole's incessant warnings.

"Hunting for hares," the phoenix boded. "This is all for the chase. It doesn't matter to you whether Solomon turns up or not . . .

"Unless you are the one who finds him."

Of course, Endymion denied the accusation. It was for their mutual, familial good, he insisted, and it takes a clever man to catch a clever man.

And the Text had rewarded his cleverness. Readily, almost clairvoyantly, he had opened the book to the right page, the right passage. Verse and engraving would give him the clue, and he would continue, resting his weary eyes and thoughts in contemplation of intricate Golgonooza afloat in a dreamy, bottled light.

And after he rested, new notions and clues came to him, as though he had glimpsed them in the labyrinthine city.

But here, at the borders between Urizen and Tharmas, the clues had vanished, his guesses exhausted themselves. Now Endymion sat atop the driver's seat of the wagon, thumbing the pages of the Text, staring absently at the engravings as the horses he was supposed to guide felt the slackness of the dropped reins and ambled off the road in search of grazing.

"It has to be here," he whispered, turning the page. "Solomon *has* to be following this Text: it is so characteristic, so involved . . ."

"And so wrong," the phoenix whispered from the shadowy, fragrant wagon.

And in the absence of clue and indication, Endymion took a long look at his journey to find his brother.

He could no longer keep straight why he wanted to do it. It was not for Morgana's reasons: Faith was lost for good, Endymion reckoned, and he had no trust that Solomon could dispel the Borders around their disintegrating ancestral home.

The journey had become a scavenger hunt for him—a venture into the heart of the maze. He did not like to think that his reason for finding Solomon was what Khole had said—simply to prove that he could do it.

"But I suppose it might be," he admitted to himself. "I suppose . . . I'll know when I find him." He pushed the unsettling thought from his mind, once again rifling the Text for signposts, for clues.

Morgana drowsed in the dark of the wagon bed, mantled over by the spread wings of Khole the phoenix. Though the bird's eyes were open, his expression wakeful and alert, there was a distant turn in the absolute center of his eye, as though he kept watch on the farthest reach of the horizon.

All in all, it was a distracted, abstracted company, unprepared for the six guardsmen who stepped from cover into the riverside pasture, their rifles raised.

These men were not alone. Twelve more of the Citizen's finest lay covered on a grassy Mountain of Albion some twenty feet above the roadside, aiming a shining array of firepower down upon the travelers.

Had Endymion known what stood before him, had he not spent the last month confined to his upstairs bedroom, sorrowing among birds and gin and bottled cities, he would have seen cause for neither alarm nor fear.

It was a sore subject among the Guard commanders, Diego especially, that when a young man in Urthona, Tharmas, or northern Urizen came of age, they practically had to shanghai him into the regular army. The glamorous life was with the rebels—the breakneck guerrilla tactics, the dashing commanders like ben Ezra or L'Overture or the Lady herself. The Guard, then, received the leavings—the dutiful, less capable sons, the slack-jawed boys in the front of the classroom, the last ones chosen for sport or hunt or at cotillion.

Tharmas was the worst, the story went: next to radical Urthona, where the rebellion was strongest, the Tharman families, farthest away from the Citizen's seat of power in Vala, had the least allegiance to Arouet and the least respect for his soldiery. Consequently, it was only the most inept of Tharman youth who found their way into the ranks of the Guard.

The boys who awaited Endymion's wagon, stationed in the road or on the nearby hillocks, were unexceptional. When their commander, a whey-faced object named Scofield, leveled a pistol at Endymion, two of the lads, thinking it a signal to attack, opened fire, narrowly missing one of their cohorts who knelt twenty yards away from the wagon, clumsily trying to draw the ramrod from his musket. One shot swept the hat from his head, the other crashed into his haversack, slapping him flat onto his face in the dirt, his weapon discharging and hurling the ramrod like an arrow shaft into the side of the wagon.

Khole crashed against the side of the cage, and Morgana, wakened by the gunfire, leapt to her feet as the ramrod shivered in the thick wood.

The door of the cage burst open and the phoenix surged through, freed into the smoky dark of the wagon.

All at once the guardsmen poured from the hill. Scofield gestured wildly, trying to stop the unleashed assault, but they charged nonetheless, fixing bayonets as they ran, tripping over musket barrels and stocks, colliding with one another and sliding on the bare, frosty ground.

The attack spent itself before it reached the wagon. Three of the men in the first wave, entangled with one another at the initial blind rush, fell headfirst ten feet from Endymion's rearing team of horses, and the men behind them tripped over the wreckage.

Morgana stood in the wagon bed amid a volley of curses and a discharge of weapons. She set her hand on the latch of Khole's cage, but a soft, soothing murmur from the bird assured her that he was safe, caged or free. Meanwhile, the guardsmen fumbled to their feet. Scofield, perhaps the only man in his squadron who had not fallen, been winged by friendly fire, or been otherwise mashed and pummeled, again pointed his pistol at Endymion.

"I'd step away from that book if I was you," he warned.

Endymion lifted his hand from the painted plates of the Text. "It's symbolic," he explained. "It can't really . . . you don't think it can . . ."

The fearful, gaping stare that met him answered his question as well.

"Don't do anything . . . sudden, Endymion," Morgana warned behind him. Khole fanned his wings, filling the air with the faint scent of frankincense.

"I'm afraid we'll have to coruscate that book," Scofield announced.

"Beg your pardon?"

"Coruscate. Seize the property."

Masking a smile, Endymion closed the Text. A dozen firearms, both empty and loaded, trained on him as he leaned from the wagon seat and handed the book to the young officer.

Prisoners of the Citizens' Guard, they were guided west at a cautious pace. They were bound for deeper Tharmas, for some backwater camp and the questions of fools.

Or that was what Endymion supposed. He steered the wagon dutifully in the midst of the mounted column of guardsmen. They had traveled no more than two miles on this new, forced march, and already the troopers were approaching him, misguided by the sign on his paneled wagon, calling him "Doctor Immaculo," haggling for his *Famous Oils and Nostra.*

One of the guardsmen even slipped the Text back into Endymion's hands, hoping by this gesture to barter for a cure for hives.

The first balloon to pass over them was an observation craft. The great seal of Arouet—the sun rising over a topless pyramid—was emblazoned on the billowing canvas, and the three men in the gondola busied themselves between ballast and telescope.

Staring up at them through lenses of his own, the faceted telescope his long-dead cousin Cortez had fashioned of Arcadian window glass and mirror fragments, Endymion recognized the balloon passengers as guardsmen, no doubt as incompetent as his captors on the ground.

If he turned the lenses just right, he could release those things . . . those energies in the mirror. It had worked when the Borders had overtaken the house: he had seen a bright, prismatic light flash in the halls of Arcady, knock over tables and meridienne armchairs, pass through windows and set afire the dried rhombs of the topiary.

Of course, that was in the Borders.

But maybe . . . some of the oddness and power had stayed with them here in the Presences.

Endymion turned the spyglass in his hand, examining it from every angle. Releasing such powers among the guardsmen would be like dropping fireworks in their midst. Distraction enough, while he and Morgana escaped.

"And the bird," Khole whispered, flapping on his free perch, his voice no more audible than thought. "The bird could escape as well . . ."

But Endymion was not listening. The spyglass in his hand, no matter how he tilted it, held the light prisoner. His own eyes dazzled with reflected sun, Endymion blinked stupidly. The afterimage of a winged figure, black and green, fluttered over the field of his vision like a dragonfly . . .

Then turned, swooping toward him with a menacing shriek.

Endymion tried to dodge, nearly slipping from the driver's seat as the image of the winged creature rushed through the long reflectant tube of the spyglass. Into the open air it dived, whirling once around Endymion's face, stinging him, whining fiercely as it fluttered through the dark of the paneled wagon, turning, preparing to attack again.

At once Khole reacted, pouncing, the buzzing circling thing vanishing in his glittering maw. Then the phoenix turned serenely to Endymion, his warm, almost human eyes regarding the sun-blind inventor.

"What was it?" Endymion asked, rubbing the red welt on his cheek. The escorting guardsmen, who had apparently missed the whole incident, regarded him blankly.

They could not even see the sting.

He cleared his throat and blushed.

"Fairies. Even mistakes can free them," Khole warned, his voice again trailing at the edge of hearing. "There's hell to pay when they're loose. It's not just flesh and blood you're up against, Endymion."

"Flesh and blood cause the bruises, though," Endymion replied curtly. He was embarrassed that the reflected light had dazzled him, that . . . an illusion had sent him scrambling, even raising a welt in some . . . some psychosomatic hysteria.

For there was no injury, no sting. He brushed his fingers over his cheek, felt smooth and unwounded skin. He knew he looked like a fool to the bird, and only the fact that he was with his illiterate aunt and a score of idiots—none of whom would notice his fright and clumsiness—kept him from humiliation.

"You don't know how close to the Borders you are," Khole cautioned, perching on Endymion's shoulder. "And here you sit, measuring the sun and beguiling yourself with reflections."

"*You* are the beguiler," Endymion replied aloud in irritation. "You and your parables and double-talk."

He smelled the frankincense, the sweet, invigorating odor of the bird.

Endymion was going to say more. He was going to put the phoenix in his place with a witty phrase, a scalding indictment of all things spiritual and avian. But then Endymion realized that nobody else could hear Khole. That what they heard was Endymion's side of the conversation, addressed, it seemed, to the empty air.

Endymion swallowed and glanced furtively around. A dozen guardsmen gaped at him, and Morgana, with a sly look and soft, consoling click of her tongue, climbed into the light and took over the reins of the wagon.

"Watch out for those angels, Endymion," she warned with a chuckle. "They send people away for talkin' to figments."

Endymion coughed, pulled on the bottle of gin, and stared sullenly into the dark of the wagon, where the eyes of the phoenix glittered and the sunlight flickered fitfully off the surface of bottled Golgonooza.

In the day and night that followed, Endymion tried out every invention he had brought with him. They all had worked in Arcady, after the encroachment of the Borders had invested them with unpredictable powers. But now, in the mundane Mountains of Albion, they returned to the simple devices which they were intended to be. The spyglass was useless after Endymion's sun-blinding, and with spots in front of his eyes, the velocipede was a dangerous vehicle, and for that matter, incapable of escaping with his heavy, arthritic aunt.

The bellows were unhelpful as well. For the life of him, Endymion could not remember why he had brought them.

What remained, then, were his sole invention and his most interesting collectible: his bottled city and the hurdy-gurdy, whose possibilities were plentiful but unexplored.

Once, not long after he had bought the hurdy-gurdy from a gypsy in Shiveleigh, Endymion had set the contraption to play one of the Hymns. Standing by the banks of the tarn, he sent the machinery through the minor melodies of "The Angel," the grieving song of the girl who outgrows her guardian angel. It was a sad little tune, but already the Borders had encroached on the grounds of Arcady, and in the new suspension of physics it became much more. Now, the boxwood-edged rose beds in Uncle Raphael's garden drooped and yellowed in response to the song, though Endymion played it in the first spring of the year.

It was enough to take his thoughts from his estranged son, from the imagined unfaithfulness of his wife and twin brother.

But then the roses greened again when Endymion reversed the melody, when he turned the crank of the hurdy-gurdy toward himself in a brisk counterclockwise motion. The melody, too, was brighter, the minor notes that marked the ending of the Hymn about the angel now placed at its beginning, a darkness out of which arose a musical light.

Blessing and blight from the same machine, he had thought.

A farmer's godsend.

Until he saw that the backward motion of the hurdy-gurdy, the inverted melody, not only greened the plants but sealed the blossoms back in the green buds and brought him back into the house to the previous page of Morgana's calendar.

In the distorting climate of the Borders, the hurdy-gurdy had turned back time.

Endymion imagined the implications—mathematically, scientifically—and the prospect had left him breathless. Until he saw the limits of the machine.

For the hurdy-gurdy would turn back only a day. The reversal seemed to take something out of it, exhaust something deep in the heart of the instrument, and it would sit silent then, coaxed to music by no hand, until a week had passed and the stolen time was recovered and surpassed, never again to be relived.

It had been disappointing there, in haunted Arcady. But here in easternmost Tharmas, a day would be enough. If Endymion could find another Border, invest the machine with whatever it was that the Borders brought to its performance, a day reversed would still set his wagon somewhere back up the road, in a time before they met up with this band of guardsmen and were taken into custody.

But it would have to be soon. Before nightfall, before the cycle of a day, after which even a successful reversal would simply take them back up the road, still in custody of the Guard.

Endymion set his thoughts to the hurdy-gurdy, now guarded by Scofield and another of the guardsmen in the wagon bed. If the moment arrived, he promised himself, he would seize it.

He had idled too long in gin and in Golgonooza's transparent splendors.

* * *

There were other eyes on the Tharman frontier, watching as the wagon escorted by guardsmen and balloons moved slowly west along the Alph.

A squadron of rebel cavalry had stopped to rest and water their horses in a cedar grove that sloped down to the lip of the river. When their commander, a seasoned, lean irregular named Whitefield, heard the guardsmen coming, crashing clumsily over the trail above, he guided his green-clad troops quietly on foot into the cedars. There they watched the wagon pass, silently loading their weapons.

They stepped from cover when the wagon had trundled by, and, in a thin line spanning the river road, stood calmly and leveled their guns.

Endymion, seated by his aunt on the driver's seat of the wagon, caught a cry as it tumbled out of the air above. In the high, cloudless sky, a red balloon passed over, its gondolier gesturing, shouting, pointing back up the road.

Endymion leaned forward, turned . . .

And the first rebel volley seared through the guardsmen.

Driven through the air by the impact of the first salvo, Scofield slammed against the side of the wagon, sighing almost serenely as his blood spattered the dry wood over Doctor Immaculo's faded name. Khole cried out and took to wing, gliding perilously to the top of the wagon.

Endymion, drawing on an old, forgotten athleticism, hauled his aunt into the safety of the wagon bed, lifting the heavy Morgana as though she were a doll, a small child. Lightly he set the flushed, muttering old woman and her rumple of quilted skirts by Khole's abandoned cage. Then, scarcely winded, he burrowed into the blankets and baskets and bottles that littered the back of the wagon.

A second volley erupted, splintering the driver's seat. The guardsmen returned fire and scattered, making for the hillocks, for the woods, the rebels shooting after them with murderous efficiency. The woods blanched with a thick smoke, and Khole took to wing, circling above the melee, orbiting the Guard balloon like a bright satellite, drawing fire away from the routed guardsmen and calling out dolefully as though he, too, were wounded.

Endymion reached for the reins, but they lay slack in his hands. The horses had slipped their harnesses as well, galloping wild-eyed away into the evergreens.

"We were prisoners of the Guard, weren't we?" Morgana prompted, leaning toward her nephew in a chiming of broken glass, tugging his cutaway coat. "Aren't prisoners of the Guard friends of the rebels by some kind of . . . *default*?"

"This isn't whist, Morgana!" Endymion snapped. "Stay down!"

"I suppose, then," Morgana asked calmly, struggling to her knees, "that all that reading taught you something to do in . . . circumstances like these?"

"There have never been 'circumstances like these,' Morgana," Endymion answered, pulling her back to the floor of the wagon bed and glancing desperately for something—anything—to avail them in the withering gunfire.

Again and again his eyes rested on the hurdy-gurdy.

There was a time before this ambush. A time when he might warn Scofield, the guardsmen, the whole bloody lot of them.

Somehow he could avoid . . .

The gunfire stopped. He heard the rebels advancing.

Standing quickly in the wagon bed, Endymion clutched the handle of the hurdy-gurdy. A fierce-looking rebel ducked into the back of the wagon. Framed in sunlight, the man raised a pistol, cocked it.

Endymion turned the handle toward himself as the rebel gun exploded, driving a shot through the hurdy-gurdy. Endymion's instrument shattered, its music unraveling into cacophony, and a gray and shimmering darkness engulfed him.

CHAPTER 23

It was like swimming through quicksilver.

That was the way Endymion described it later: the thick, resistant element choking and chilling him.

What lay before him was shimmering nothingness—fog with no boundary, no bottom.

Once Endymion tried the bellows against the encroaching mist. For a moment, it seemed, the gray cloud ebbed, a pocket of welcome air forming in its wake. But it returned as quickly, and after a fierce, futile pumping of the wheezing device, Endymion gave it up and folded the bellows, carrying it over his shoulder like a grotesque umbrella.

For a while the wagon plummeted through a darkness loud with rhythmic, metallic grinding. The vehicle moved slowly, drawn by no horses, guided by no driver. The paneled covering of the wagon bed had been sheared away by some large and irresistible force, and it seemed to Endymion that all life had fled his presence—no Morgana, no Khole, not even unwelcome guardsmen or rebels. Standing in the wooden bed among his bottles and blankets and machineries, his hand tightly clutching the handle of the shattered hurdy-gurdy, he wrestled down panic, his denying, gin-soaked thoughts.

I am dead, groaned the darkest voice in his head, as a whiff of juniper rode in the mist around Endymion. *That bullet I thought lodged in the hurdy-gurdy lodged in me instead . . .*

And this is the afterlife . . .

Which is nothing like they said it would be.

Soon a slanted light filtered through the fog, and with a deep, shuddering sigh, Endymion realized he was still alive. Still, he had no idea where he was, or how he had managed to get there.

Voices called to him from the mist. Once a figure flitted at the margins of his vision, half cloud and half woman, trailing a white robe like a bridal gown of webbing.

She turned before she vanished and spoke to him, in a language whose feeling rather than meaning he caught, since all of the words were alien—sibilant, rustling sounds like a high wind through dry leaves.

It was a feeling of forlornness. Endymion could put no other words around it.

The woman vanished into the fog, and he knew that somehow he had fallen farther than the Borders.

As the light waxed and focused, darker shadows loomed amid the whirling gray mist. Endymion looked among them for landmarks, for points of reference, mapping the chaos in his mind as he would a maze, a confusing forest.

But this is chaos, something whispered. *The last place a map will do.* It sounded like Khole's voice. Mellifluous and tender, it arose from nowhere and everywhere.

"Where are you?" Endymion asked, and the fog blanketed his throat, filling his lungs, choking him.

The phoenix was far away. He knew that much.

And suddenly, he knew far more.

He was alone in the midst of an Absence.

Endymion had dreamt about Absences before, at night in his upstairs chambers, Golgonooza glittering on his lap as the candlelight passed through the glass, bent and shadowed against the cityscape of teak.

They had not frightened him then. He had decided that the heart of an Absence would be like Golgonooza, like the great ruined cities of Napolis and Ville, both of which he had seen from the air, riding silently above them in a gondola.

Stone still smoking. A tangle of bordermetal—beam and girder and wire in a skeleton of ravaged architecture.

But now he had seen the real thing, and it was less than ruin.

There was no signpost, no landmark. The Absence stretched in all directions, glacial formations of icy clouds extending like a maze of footpaths for as far as Endymion could see. Directly below him, the mist was opaque, impenetrable, rising to the hub of the wheels as though the wagon were mired in a cloud. Broad dark tendrils extended out of the fog, slanting and crossing and bending, some a step, a yard, *above* others, hovering absurdly in the heavy fog like a madman's mobile.

Endymion picked one trail and followed it with his eyes, but it ended not a dozen steps from the tongue of the wagon.

The first trail leads from nowhere to nowhere, he thought grimly. *And I am traveling it in a horseless wagon.*

Cautiously, he lifted his leg over the side of the vehicle and lowered himself. Farther and farther he sank into the mist, until his arms extended and he dangled ineptly from the wagon side, his feet thrashing invisibly below the surface of the mist.

No. This would never do. The wagon floated on a strange tide, around which was nothingness, a fathomless drop into a cloudy void.

Endymion scrambled back into the safety of the bed and lay there for a while, beading sweat and gasping in the close mist. Above him was only a swirl of grayness, indifferent and dividing, like the sky in some bleak parable.

It was a story, he decided.

Unfortunately, he had preceded Diego into the world by thirty minutes, which made him the second son and not the third.

For wasn't it always the way of a story that the third son was charmed, gifted, succeeding where his elders had failed?

First Solomon had vanished. Swallowed up, no doubt, by the same devouring nothingness that now threatened to envelop his younger brother.

The fog that was eating the wagon away.

It had started when Endymion climbed back into the wagon bed. The mist crept over the side rail, which began to unravel in his sight. Endymion blinked, brushed the fog with his hand, peered at the rail through the rising murk. Sure enough, the wood was shredding, splintering. As though the mist were made of acid, or hungry.

Alarmed, Endymion examined his hand, which had just passed through this new, corrosive fog.

It was intact, without blemish or blister. Whatever, it seemed, had destroyed his vehicle had left him curiously unharmed.

"Impossible!" Endymion muttered. "No rules, no physics here!"

Shortly, though, there would be no wagon as well. Nothing to stop his fall into the foggy abysm.

Frantically, Endymion looked around the wagon bed. Khole's cage teetered on a ledge of dissolving wood, then tumbled into the fog. Endymion strained to listen above the thrashing sound of machinery. He did not hear the cage hit bottom—no sound of impact, no clatter or crack.

Only the continual grinding of the distant machinery and somewhere, teasingly faint, the liquid sound of bells, and fainter still, the vaulting cry of a lark.

There was an end to this place, but he could not see it from his vantage.

Already, it seemed, Golgonooza had fallen into the murky void. There was no sign of the bottled city.

Inanely, possessively, as though the bellows kept him somehow from oblivion, Endymion clutched the instrument to his breast and grasped a handlebar of the velocipede. They were his last machineries.

They were what he had to show. They, and the Text that lay open in the wagon bed, its pages riffling in a warm, circling breeze.

Endymion picked up the book, his eye first settling on a lengthy, obscure passage:

> The Mundane Shell is a vast Concave Earth, an immense
> Harden'd shadow of all things upon our Vegetated Earth,
> Enlarg'd into dimension & deform'd into indefinite space,
> In Twenty-seven Heavens and all their Hells, with Chaos
> And Ancient Night & Purgatory. It is a cavernous Earth
> Of labyrinthine intricacy, twenty-seven folds of opakeness,
> And finishes where the lark mounts . . .

"This has to be the 'cavernous Earth,' " he mused, glancing at the surrounding, shadowy mists. He returned to the book, staring long at the beautiful women engraved at the top of the page, the dark and frightening creature at its bottom, extending its contorted, branching limbs like the tendrils of an ancient, dark-hearted tree.

"The Absence itself," he muttered. " 'Labyrinthine intricacy.' 'Twenty-seven folds of opakeness.' The descriptions seem to fit . . .

"It *has* to be the Absence! And then . . ."

The bells and the larksong reached him, dim in the fog somewhere off to his right.

" 'Where the lark mounts,' " Endymion breathed joyously.

Suddenly, with a leap in his deepest imaginings, he fought back a strange urge to mount the velocipede and ride into the mist.

Foolish, his common sense told him. *You saw what happened when you tried to descend from the wagon.*

But another voice, teasing at the edge of his thought, kept asking, asking . . .

Then what is holding up the wagon?

"I am a fool for doing this," he whispered to both voices, and straddled the cycle.

Foolish, the voice repeated.

Endymion ignored it.

This is a place where logic falters, he thought. *Where no physics governs the things of the world, but only what the Text says.*

Or what Solomon makes of it.

And in such a place, there had to be a different way of doing altogether.

So Endymion mounted the velocipede, breathing deeply the silvery, misted air of the Absence. He started the cycle in a sputtering of spark and steam, then with a kick to start the back wheel in motion, rode the old contraption over the brink of the wagon bed.

For a moment the velocipede tumbled, dropped. Endymion's throat tightened, and his chest clenched. But just as he was about to cry out, the wheels shuddered against solid ground—or against something solid. Endymion rocked, wrestled for control, and righted himself. Reflexively, mindlessly, he began to steer, looking back once through the rising mist and velocipede backsteam as the wagon vanished from sight—whether dissolved or covered by fog he could not tell.

So, on a trail he could scarcely imagine, much less see, clutching the bellows and trusting his own considerable ingenuity, Endymion steered the velocipede through the misty dark, away from the thrashing sound that distractingly, insistently, echoed in the darkest center of the fog.

The dark shapes Endymion had seen at the edge of his sight rushed forward and by him and vanished. Black winged figures extended insubstantial hands toward the racing velocipede, but they receded more quickly than they rose from the fog, mingling with clouds like a partially formed memory.

Once, twice, Endymion thought he recognized a spectral shape. A softening of the umbra took on the form of a loose strand of hair, a twisted tendril of mist wrapped elegantly around the neck of the dark frame . . .

Faith? Lyca?

He called them both, called them twice, but the shadow dissolved into fog and a thick, impenetrable grayness surrounded him.

Then a darker form loomed in his path, hooded and caped against the swirling mist. For a moment the figure had a face—pale and unblinking, a purple livid scar upon the neck . . .

Endymion thought of home, and puzzled as the Great Hall rose into his memory—mahogany and stairwells, the crystal chandelier and draped mirrors . . .

The portrait.

The face in the cloud smiled wickedly, then vanished.

Innocent's face. Endymion wondered why he had fashioned it out of mist and terror.

With no definite route, no destination, he drove on warily, always steering away from the harsh, mechanical sound. The pathway he followed seemed to dip into thicker darkness, but the mist seemed less packed now, more breathable.

In a hiss of steam, Endymion braked the cycle. There was something else, stationary and large, at the very edge of his sight.

Within it, the larksong trilled for a brief, exceptional moment.

"My brother," Endymion whispered hopefully. "He's nearby!"

Suddenly, something grabbed his ankles.

Endymion cried out, struggling to break free of the grip that held him, tugged him slowly into the suddenly spongy road. All around him a gibbering sound rose through the mist, a wailing and squalling like a hundred infants, abandoned and lonely . . .

In the cry was hunger as well.

Endymion pulled his left foot away, set it too firmly on the velocipede pedal. The vehicle listed dangerously, and he dismounted to recover his balance. The thing grabbed him again, tiny clutching hands shrouded in fog, sprouting from the spongy earth like grotesque plants.

The last clinging grasp of the dead.

With a preternatural, adrenal strength, Endymion wrenched his feet from the pale, moldy fingers. Kicking the velocipede into life, he began to steer, to ride.

The road surged up to meet him, and it was breathing and light and a skyline dark and defined ahead of him—one that he took for ruins, for the husk of a city at the Absence's edge.

If he could make it there, he decided, he would be free.

As he approached the skyline, more and more figures emerged from the shadow. Dryads, the willowy, pale nymphs who, it was said, inhabited the hearts of trees, flitted across his path, their mossy robes trailing bark and leaf, which fluttered in the air as though caught in a whirlwind.

The faerie, the fabled folk of the air, buzzed about his head like wicked midges, annoying him, distracting him. Though they posed little danger, no longer magnified in the lens of the spyglass, they were nonetheless irritating, persistent. Endymion batted at the whining things, rocked uncomfortably on the velocipede, then steadied himself, all the while steering resolutely toward the dark array of buildings ahead.

Ahead of him as well, framed in a foggy, slanted light, a girl wandered—too large to be a nymph, too heavily clad, her hoop skirts and petticoats billowing awkwardly in the mist as though she were . . .

A balloon? A gaudy Tharman kite?

She floated at the edge of sight, her arms extended as though she embraced the fog, as though it gathered her in, and once or twice Endymion drew nearer, could make out the slope of her shoulders, the color of her hair.

Auburn. Like his dead wife Lyca.

Like his daughter.

Still she ran ahead of him, moving quickly, half lost in the distance and the mist, stopping once to shake her hair and let fall something on the sloping path behind her. Endymion pedaled more quickly, his lungs bursting from the thick air and from exertion, but the trail his velocipede followed forked away from the dropped item.

Finally, from a high vantage overlooking the spot on the trail, he looked down through the mist upon the tiny ribbon the girl had discarded. With a soft puff of the bellows, he scattered the tendrils of fog from the curled, forsaken silk.

Pink. Faith's color from infancy.

Vainly he peered ahead into the depths of the fog. The girl was gone, vanished behind the first lofty row of wooden buildings which leaned toward him, crazily and shadowless, in a chaos of geometry and angles, as though they beckoned him in to set right the architecture.

The city was wooden, rough-crafted. Buildings crazily skewed, irregular, leaning as if in terror of a plumb line. Endymion approached its outskirts cautiously, dismounting from the velocipede and guiding it, slowly and unsteadily, pushing it on its unstable wheels like a child determined to play with a broken toy. The buildings cast green, interlocking shadows, as though three or maybe four suns illumined the disheveled skyline.

Teak. The city was made of teak.

It surprised him that he had not recognized his own handiwork. Golgonooza spread chaotically in front of him; the detail work in which he had prided himself seemed clumsy and cumbersome on this scale and from this perspective.

Yet it was his city, planned and mapped from his upstairs room in Arcady, the buildings set painstakingly in the green glass while the phoenix watched patiently from his perch.

On those nights, it seems, when the gin flowed and imaginations ranged, Endymion Hawken had created a part of the Absences.

Endymion smiled triumphantly. For lower on the page—on the very page he had been reading, that had prompted him to venture from the wagon into the abiding mist—another line had caught his eye.

" 'But travelers to Eternity pass inward to Golgonooza,' " he proclaimed, almost intoning. "It is another sign, I know! And when I pass into Golgonooza, I will find my brother. . . ."

But it became even more clear, as he waded through the fog and the jagged alleys of teak and hardened glue, that somehow Golgonooza was connected to the vast, labyrinthine system of chaoses that bored through the Urthonan landscape. Irregular windows stared down at Endymion, the doors opened at impure angles into empty interiors, and the whole city ranged in disarray before him, disappointingly lifeless and estranged.

"I thought," Endymion declared, to no one in particular, "that it was . . . better made than this."

In scarcely an hour, he was irretrievably lost.

From his new perspective, the buildings were indistinguishable. Alleys and side streets that he could have sworn he had connected to major thoroughfares with glue and needle and knife those nights in his upstairs bedroom were actually dead ends, cul-de-sacs, running up against walls and shadows.

Rifling his gin-riddled memory, Endymion tried yet another alley—a dark, narrow passage that angled sharply, promised for a moment an opening into a square, then butted into a wall of knotted teak.

Endymion sat on hardened glue, the faint smell of gelatin and milk rising from the foundations of his handiwork. Removing his spectacles, he squinted into the shadows and cursed himself, damning his conceit—that he had made the city too elaborate and convoluted to navigate.

"That is not all you convolute, old man," taunted a voice from somewhere amid the shadowy upper stories of the buildings.

Endymion squinted up into the mist. "Who are you?" he asked.

"Oh, don't you *know*?" the voice asked ironically. "You who know . . . everything?"

"I don't understand," Endymion stammered. "What—what is this . . ."

"I am here," the voice proclaimed, and a shadowy form slipped into the smoky alley. For a moment Endymion glimpsed a face, dark eyes, a scar . . .

But the shape dissolved into mist. Endymion reached out, groping toward the entrance to the alley, but his hands passed through cloud, through nothing.

"Uncle Innocent?" he asked.

Low laughter rose from the darkness—a gravelly sound like an avalanche of stones.

"Oh, so much more than your uncle Innocent," the voice replied. "Though at one time you couldn't tell us apart."

"I don't understand," Endymion said.

"I was the thing . . . that got inside him," the voice explained. "I was . . . the fire he let in."

Endymion leaned back into the shadows.

"Ask your aunt Morgana," the voice urged. "That is . . . when you see her."

Again, the low laughter.

"W-why are you here?" Endymion asked—to the voice, to the shadow, to nobody at all.

"To announce that the worst of your nightmares . . . has come to pass," the voice replied gleefully.

"My daughter! My . . . my brother Solomon . . ." Endymion began, his thoughts reeling.

"No. Neither of them figure in the *worst* of your nightmares," insisted the voice.

Endymion swallowed. "Very well," he said, masking the quaver in his voice. "If you are so certain what this 'worst nightmare' is, then why don't you . . . *proclaim* it?"

Thin laughter rang through the eaves of Golgonooza.

"You have been bested," the voice gloated, "in a battle of wits. That, my dear precisionist, is *your* worst nightmare—damn the daughter and the brother in the bargain!"

"I . . . I don't understand."

"Oh, you're quick with that confession now, Endymion Hawken. *'I don't understand, I don't understand.'* But where was this modesty when your dear stupid brother Diego declared his belief that Solomon had traveled north, back toward Lambeth?"

"But the book!" Endymion protested. "The evidence of the poetry!"

" 'More interesting,' you said," the voice taunted, coiling through the alley like a dark wind. "You never stopped to consider that Diego might be right."

"But the lines in the book led me . . ."

"Here. They led you here." By now the voice passed over him, through him. "When I noticed where you were looking, I made sure you found what you wanted to find.

"Silent? Stuck for words? Let me explain.

"When you followed the Text in pursuit of your brother, you followed nothing more than . . . your own ingenuity."

"But I saw signs at the roadside!" Endymion protested. "The footprints! The lamp!"

"The footprints were those of some other traveler, I suppose," explained the voice. "The lamp was from Arcady, but Solomon didn't drop it: perhaps a dismissed servant or a light-fingered guest. Perhaps some of Diego's self-righteous in-laws left with it, as disreputable family will abscond with the linens.

"Whatever placed the lamp in the high weeds, it was my great good fortune."

Laughter rose from the hardened glue at Endymion's feet.

"Oh, but I did my part," boasted the voice. "I relied not only on remarkable chance. As soon as I saw you would adopt this arcane, Textual pursuit of your brother, I guided the passages you read."

"How did you know?" Endymion sputtered. Despite himself, he was beginning to believe the voice. "How did you guide me?"

"Throughout your travels," the voice insinuated, "Golgonooza has never left your side, has it? The little teakwood buildings that meant more to you than the rooms that housed your family. And in that . . . fashioned proximity, I could listen to you from my Absence home. And when you looked into the depths of your own clever little city . . . I could run images before your eyes—suggestive, memorable, like those projected in a magic lantern.

"Those images guided you to appropriate Texts. Then I would decide the next image. The next passage.

"Where to lure you next."

"But why?" Endymion asked. "Why draw me away from home on this goose chase?"

The voice was all-enveloping, all-pervading. "There were places where your wit could have done some good. Arcady. East in Urizen. You could figure out things, and it seemed only fitting that I draw you away from . . . familiar terrain. To a place where your inventiveness was useless. What is it your Text—your little guidebook—says?

> "The idiot Reasoner laughs at the Man of Imagination,
> And from laughter proceeds to murder . . ."

"Murder?"

"Oh, yes. Negligent homicide. While you wandered away to the West, the time passed wherein you might rescue your daughter, your brother . . .

"Yourself."

The mists thickened, and Golgonooza fell silent. For a long time—ten minutes? an hour? it was hard to tell when there was no measure of passing day or night—Endymion waited for a noise, a sound.

But no sound came.

Alone, his back propped against the frail teakwood of a spiraling tower, his machinery leaning against the far wall of an alley, Endymion gazed up among the spires of the hand-fashioned buildings. The gin-bottle sky bent, green and tapering, above the tops of the towers, until it was lost in mist and the latticework of wood.

"I have failed," he murmured. "Failed beyond all reason."

Suddenly, around him uncanny noises rose and echoed in the cavernous cityscape. The muffled whinny of a horse mingled with a snatch of song Endymion almost identified, and one solitary bell, as clear and resonant as though it rang in a tower of the city, tolled the third hour as he climbed wearily to his feet and wandered out of the alley, into a bright intersection, a gap in the assembled buildings.

"Wait," he whispered. "I never made this."

The streets were shifting around him.

Uneasily, Endymion looked behind him, as the teak buildings slid and tilted together, swallowing the alley from which he had just emerged, his velocipede, and his surety of escape.

Had I stayed in there but a moment longer . . . his thoughts began.

"But you *didn't* stay," a voice observed, a voice unlike the other, sweet and familiar, cascading from an open window above the intersection. "You have an imagination of disaster, Endymion."

Endymion recognized the new voice at once. He stepped into the middle of the road, green light descending on him, dappling him green and black. "Where are you, Khole?" he asked. "Where are you, old flyswatter?"

The phoenix appeared on the windowsill, his once-bright colors ashen and dull in the green shade. Slowly, as though the moment had been rehearsed when the bottled city had been planned, he sang a verse from the Ninth Hymn.

"He kissed the child and by the hand led
And to his mother brought,
Who in sorrow pale, thro' the lonely dale
Her little boy weeping sought."

Immediately Endymion recognized the melody, the melancholy tune that he had heard beneath the sound of horses.

For a moment he could not speak. Silently, tearfully, he beckoned to the bird, but Khole remained perched twenty feet above him, shaking his feathers in a thin, incense-laden smoke.

"You can see above this architecture, can't you?" Endymion asked.

The bird stood silent, implacable.

"Find the way out, Khole. Fly out of here. Bring word to Morgana."

The phoenix slipped his head beneath his wing. "What can she do that your wit and machineries cannot?"

"I . . . I have no idea, Khole," Endymion confessed. "But Morgana is outside, in the Presences, and I am here. She's the closest one to me, I suppose."

Suddenly he felt overwhelmingly tired—giddy and nauseated. "She may be able to . . . figure the way out of here," he murmured.

"It will do for beginnings," Khole said. "At least, for the first time, you are looking for another's guidance."

Springing aloft, the phoenix glided lazily over the wide intersection. The building from which he had flown tipped backward and shuddered against a tower, and Endymion, confronted again with his faulty workmanship, cursed shoddy glue and bad light.

"I'll find her," the phoenix promised, his golden eyes soft and bright. "Or, better yet, I'll find someone who can help. Stay where you are, and try to stay where you are."

Endymion grumbled at the soaring bird, who vanished amid the fading green light. Now Golgonooza tumbled rapidly into darkness, the gloaming as brief as that by the seashore. Endymion drew his gin flask from his pocket, found it empty, and surprised himself that he didn't care.

"This is a story," he muttered bitterly. "And I am one of its failures."

For wasn't it always the way of stories?

The absurd story of Saint Milton, in which the hero plunges into chaos, unites with the shadowy Bard, and builds a new world on the ruined foundations of the old. Endymion wondered how he could *ever* have believed such foolishness, even as a child.

Or the fairy tales, whose eldest and middle brothers fail to find the princess, defeat the troll, or slay the dragon, and whose happy endings rest with the youngest, the least likely?

Endymion laughed harshly, leaning against the unsteady teak wall. No tale ever told what happened to the failed brothers—the ones who returned home broken or returned home not at all.

Perhaps, if storybook logic held, Diego would rescue *him* as well.

As he *rescued* Lyca on that floody night many years ago.

* * *

Diego and Lyca had claimed a hairbreadth escape from the waters.

Halfway back to Arcady from Diego's home in Shiveleigh, the Alph had overtaken them, washing the barouche up against its northern bank, its slow, powerful waters spinning the carriage like a leaf caught in a torrential spring current.

They had spent the night on opposite sides of the barouche, balancing their weights, they claimed, to keep the carriage upright in the driving water.

Endymion had believed their story, through that spring night and through the winter when his first son, Garrick, was born. And for four years more.

Until the change came over the boy.

It was nothing marked or dramatic, the sense of alienness that surrounded the child. The preference for sword over compass or caliper, the delight in picture histories of the Wars of False Doctrine.

The child's breath carried the chill of subterranean waters, and at night his father would startle, sit up in the bed, as Lyca, already pregnant with their third child, Faith, stirred in her sleep and murmured.

He would try to catch the name on the lips of his sleeping wife, but it was elusive. Once he thought he heard her breathe *Diego*.

He could have been mistaken.

Then he would look at Garrick, and think of the cuckoo. The supplanted nest.

The boy was a changeling.

Over the years, as Endymion dwelt on the prospect, father and son drew farther apart.

By the time Garrick joined the Guard, Endymion barely recognized him at table.

And Diego? By that time, Diego was a presence at reunions, a silent question in the mirror of the Great Hall.

Endymion was sorry now. Sorry for cold rage and suspicions.

Through the course of Garrick's childhood, through the layers of removal between father and son, through the death of a wife no longer loved and a hundred dark imaginings and confusions, Endymion had dwelt on the supposed betrayal as he had brooded over misleading Text, over the small, imperfect structures in the heart of the gin bottle.

All things had lain magnified and distorted in his gin-addled vision and memory. Only now, turned about and lost entirely in the whirling Absence, did Endymion wonder why he had spent seventeen years proving infidelity rather than forgiving it.

Exhausted from his efforts against the gray and stifling clouds and from long thoughts over his own unbending intelligence, Endymion drifted toward a fitful sleep. The fog covered him like cerements; his part in the story, he figured, was over.

Before his closed eyes, a pink ribbon dangled mockingly, like an afterimage, like a brief impression of light.

CHAPTER 24

Little Miles Hawken, known contemptuously by the servants as "the darling of Arcady," was complaining about his sandwiches now.

Surely Auntie Mina, who was not really his auntie but his cousin, and yet whom he called "auntie" out of respect and the difference between their ages . . . surely Auntie Mina remembered that his sandwiches were *expressly* to be carved into lozenges and stars? His sister, Flora, preferred rhombs, but she would not eat until *after* her nap, and therefore was it all that hard to remember the requests of *one* child and one only?

Why, as a sculptress . . .

"Be easy on Auntie Mina, darling," Allegra urged, noticing her husband Diego's countenance had darkened from red to purple. She had brought them both—Miles and Flora—three leagues south from her family home near Shiveleigh, hearing that Morgana was calling the Hawkens together on a matter of some importance.

Naturally, the message had reached her late, as messages always did the relatives by marriage. By the time Allegra Hawken had arrived, braving the road and its possibilities of Blights and rebels and Borders, the situation had changed entirely.

Morgana was gone. And Solomon, whom Allegra had never met.

That sot Endymion.

Why, she and Diego and the children were the only true Hawkens left in the house, which was now given over to a brace of lunatic girls, one of whom was a sick sculptress—and her sickness was her fault, the Text made that amply clear—while the other . . .

Well, Allegra was almost certain that Artemis had rebel sympathies.

* * *

Diego could be persuaded to rebel sympathies himself, he decided, if the rebels would shoot boys such as Miles Hawken.

The boy sat on a tall stool in front of his father, his dark curly locks as long as Diego's—too long for a boy his age.

Allegra had set the child in front of his father with specific instructions to *show what the grammarians have taught you.* Miles had recited, had sung, and had ciphered.

And Diego had enough.

His son sang three innocent Hymns about shepherds and lambs with a jaded, theatrical style that showed that *he*, not the song, was the center of attention. He finished in a rush, and squawked again for his sandwiches.

"I don't care *how* sick Auntie Mina is!" he exclaimed over his mother's shushing and hand-waving. "Can't she just take laudanum and bring me my sandwiches?"

Diego glared. He remembered his own reaction when Endymion lost his daughter and fled to his room, inconsolable.

He did not love himself for wishing it could have been Miles Hawken instead.

* * *

When Artemis called Diego into Mina's studio, he leapt to his feet quickly.

Willie Melmoth did not miss it. The slight flush around the ears. The way the big captain brushed back his hair when his cousin beckoned. The way he followed her behind the closed door, recklessly for a man with one good leg.

Willie had never seen him move like that. Not even in battle.

One masked glance at Allegra told him it was not lost on the Captain's wife, either. She watched the exchange, her husband trailing the Lady like a lapdog. Her gaunt features narrowed even further as she rose and huffed to the door, scanning the topiaries for the saints knew what.

Willie turned away.

No gawking. It was not his concern.

"I have not figured yet what I shall call you," the boy piped.

Willie looked up. Miles Hawken was staring straight at him. Linen shirt, stock, and cravat. Vest and riding coat. A boy dressed like a popinjay.

Had Willie dressed like Miles Hawken at that age—at any age—he would have been soundly thrashed by his mates. Why, even today, he knew a few rough customers who would thrash him for merely having spoken to a child dressed so formally.

"Come, Master Miles," Willie urged, his gaze half on the fuming Allegra. "Let's walk among the topiary, you and I."

No gawking.

"I shall do as I please," the boy insisted, with a dramatic shake of his curly mane. Nonetheless, Miles slipped from the high stool and shuffled slowly, uncertainly across the hall, his black slippers scuffing against the year-old dancing wax on the floor.

Allegra did not turn from the window.

"Go with Willie," she ordered, and the boy stared at his new companion, with a look mixed of curiosity and fear.

Willie smiled, placed his hand on the child's shoulder, and guided him into the garden. Around them and above them, the topiary leered and loomed, unkempt cedar and taxus cascading from sculptured squirrel and horse.

"You were saying, Master Miles?" Willie prompted, steering the boy around one of Mina's statues—another unidentified Hawken, his hands set to a wheelbarrow, the wheel of which had broken (or fallen off) and vanished.

The boy looked at him blankly.

"Something about 'calling me'?" Willie prompted.

They were twenty, thirty yards from the house now. Wary of sphinxes despite Diego's insistence that the creatures were strictly nocturnal, Willie watched the shrubbery and vines.

"Oh, yes. I was merely saying that I had not determined what name you would go by."

"Willie Melmoth," Willie announced. "Call me . . ."

"I shall call you . . . well, by whatever nickname your appearance and behavior suggest to me!" the boy proclaimed triumphantly. " 'Tis a practice I pursue with all my father's followers and troops and servants."

The boy flinched. The grip on his shoulder had suddenly tightened.

"I suggest, then, that the nickname which occurs to you should be

'Mister Melmoth,' " Willie muttered with a frozen grin. "As I am neither follower nor troop nor servant, but an accidental companion to your father."

The boy wriggled in his grasp. "I shall *tell* my father!" he protested, but a subtle quiver had entered his voice.

" 'Tell him'? 'Tell him' what, Little Mister Man?"

Willie tightened his grip. He could discipline no further, this not being his own child. But Miles Hawken didn't need to know that.

"Tell him . . ." The voice was trailing, tentative, faint. "That you're manhandling me. Squeezing my shoulder much too hard."

"Oh, but I would deny that, Miles."

"You'd be lying!"

"Maybe not," Willie replied pleasantly, his grip unflinching. "Maybe 'too hard' for you is no more than a friendly squeeze from me."

He released the boy. Miles lurched away, tumbling into a topiary.

"Tell your father if you like," Willie challenged. "He's as apt to believe me as he is you. But it ain't the point, Miles, who the old man credits. Or your mama or your aunts. Or me, for that matter. You're like one of those mirrors in the Great Hall, boy: you're reflectin' what they make of you, and reflectin' that reflection until you go back so far you vanish."

Miles stared at him for a moment. His eyes narrowed, and Willie caught a glimpse of something cornered and frightened in the back of them.

"I don't have to listen to you!" the boy proclaimed defiantly. Then, with a sly smile: "You just said so."

Willie turned toward the door. "Oh, that I did. You can come in with me, or you can wait around out here. Your dad says the sphinxes hunt by night, don't he?"

He was ten steps toward the door when he heard the boy approaching behind him, the rasp of the slippers on the brick garden path.

* * *

"She's gone around the bend, Diego."

The Captain sat on Morgana's wheel and stared at the cold ashes of the fireplace. He could not look at Artemis, for when he did his throat went dry and his breath caught, and he felt the hotness about his eyes as though he had faced the sun for an afternoon.

"Around the bend?" he asked.

His voice was steady. Good.

"It's the disease. It's working on her brain now," Artemis explained. "Mina claims that something's stirring in the wax."

Diego could hear her moving behind him, her voice over his right shoulder, then the left. Surreptitiously, he peeked across the room.

Artemis knelt above a broken shard of clay.

"I . . . what's this about wax and all?"

"The wax mold," Artemis said. "In the heart of the clay investment."

"It's Commentary to me, Cousin," Diego said. "Pure bowlahoola and Commentary."

He thought he knew what she meant, but in the face of unfamiliar terms and ideas he had always played the fool, let his cousin explain what he needed to know and gone from there.

Artemis had always been glad to do it.

"Never mind the details, Diego. What's important is this: Mina says the wax is moving, with a particular warmth and animation of its own; she says she can feel it through the hard clay."

"And what does this mean to you, Cousin?"

"That we should find Solomon. Quickly. If he can cleanse Arcady, turn back the Borders, then we both can endure his priestly moods and prattle. This house is not the only thing this family loves that is dissolving, falling apart.

"Neither Guard nor partisan, but *time* is our enemy now."

* * *

It was like a pulse against the cold earth.

At first, Mina had thought it was hallucinatory, at best a false sensation at the tips of her numbing fingers. For the disease was said to do just that, eating at the extremities and the nerves until the body dissolved, more or less.

But the pulse *was* there—a faint beating in the heart of the clay.

Holding the mold for the statue's right hand, its long tapered gray fingers gently placed on a carved facsimile of the Text, Mina circled the statue, wiping dried clay from her forehead. Her white smock spattered and dusty, her movements light and swift, she looked like an angel born in the back of a hearth, a wraith rising from a dustbin.

They would come to her soon—her sister and her cousin Diego—

sure that the death's-head moth had consumed her mind. And yet they were wrong.

What had consumed her was the sculpting itself—the deep knowing that whatever might befall her, whatever her family might think or say, the statue was her stand against the chaos around her. The statue was a monument to history and love, but it was more than that: part of Mina's art was mysterious to her, and she had to stay alert, attentive in the making, so that when that mystery announced itself, she could give it place as well.

Trembling, struck by a disease that left her physically wasted at noonday but still lucid and keen in her imaginings, Mina began the slow process of affixing the hand to the stub of a wrist. Her fingers wrapped around the statue's forearm. Its pulse throbbed strongly, a hint of warmth arising through the clay.

Mina gasped, staggered back from the pedestal, losing her footing and tumbling to the marble floor.

So *that* was the mystery. But what . . . why . . .

The clay hand hung for a moment in place. Then the fresh clay gave way to its weight, and the hand dropped, shattering in a dozen large pieces upon the hard studio floor.

Pale wax peeked out like bones from the gray rubble of shards.

Mina muttered a mild oath. She rose to her knees and took in the results of the accident. Three fingers were broken on the sculpted hand, which now clutched only a fractured slab, scarcely recognizable as the sculptured book she had designed only two nights before.

"Great darkened Urizen!" she swore again, and the room seemed to shudder around her.

Suddenly there was a cry from the hall. Gathering her balance slowly, her mind still on the mishap, Mina backed away from the statue, sidling toward the hearth, toward Morgana's wheel, which suddenly began to spin in an erratic, clockwise motion.

Absently brushing the dust from her smock, Mina walked into the Great Hall.

* * *

"Luddite absurdity!" Diego muttered, crossing the mirrored walkway, vainly trying to keep pace with the swift and graceful Artemis.

She spun about, black hair flickering over her face like dark fire.

"Call it what you like, Cousin. The vanishment of the countryside is not my doing. It's the fault of your . . . Citizen and his damned machineries. Stirring the Borders to disruption. All his terrible engines laying waste to our . . ."

Diego overtook his cousin, passed her in the reflecting hall. "Our *green and pleasant land*!" he bellowed. "By the saints' pimpled asses, Artemis! How many times do I have to hear this same argument?"

None of the rebels had ever proved that Citizen Arouet's activities had altered anything, Border or Absence. Artemis should have known better. And yet she persisted, railing about some obscure machinery, that the grinding sound in the heart of the Absence was Arouet's mills and looms, his winches and smelters.

"I'm tired, Cousin," Diego snapped. "Tired of riding and of Solomon's hard little bed that's no better than forest ground. Tired of three-day-old coffee for breakfast, in the field and at home, and tired most definitely of your mossback naturalism."

Artemis only laughed. "Get to thy Labours at the Mills," she said, "and leave me to my wrath."

"Quoting the Text, Cousin? I would have thought better of you."

The arguing cousins nearly collided with Mina as she wandered into the Great Hall. The girl blinked, brushed clay dust from her lip, and with a wan smile held up a fingered shard.

"I dropped Solomon's hand," she announced.

Suddenly, the hall was full of voices.

Diego recognized his mother's song amid the thronging babble. Christabel's voice soared for a moment over the murmurs, the strains of a childhood Hymn sweet in her breathy soprano.

> "And by came an angel who had a bright key,
> And he open'd the coffins & set them all free
> Then down a great plain, leaping, laughing they run,
> And wash in a river, and shine in the Sun . . ."

Diego's eyes were hot, smarting. Then another voice rose above his mother's—a stern, deep voice, demanding brandy and cigars. Then the tumbling sound of water as though the house were suddenly afloat and moored in the river, the Alph moving all about it, up on a sandbar or caught in the shallows as though someone had thrown it off a boat.

The mirrors filled with water, drowning the reflected scene. Diego gaped at the glass, standing in the dry hall and marveling as the imaged waters flashed through the imaged room, bright as foil or as melted metal, and the fish bright too as they played around the chandeliers.

He looked at Artemis.

Who saw something else entirely, her gaze astonished on the tall clerestory windows.

Now Diego turned again, and the mirror against the near wall was blank, reflecting nothing but light. Its gray, silvery surface glistened without images, neither face nor form.

A choir of mermaid voices rang in the rafters.

* * *

"I have never seen the likes of it," Diego confessed later. "Water and fish in the mirrors. Choirs in the belfry."

Artemis shrugged as she tightened the cinch on the saddle. "Border ruffles," she excused. "Surely you've seen the sphinxes."

He had. He did not see the connection.

From the beginning, the sphinxes had been a minor Arcadian hazard. When the creatures lay dormant, in the long times between Border encroachments, the children had sported with them. Kassandra and Raphael, Aristo and Cortez would dance around the greening bronze pedestals, teasing the statues as they would a large, penned dog.

Hawken adults shuddered and warned, citing near escapes that had taken place from the first time Prometheus and Innocent brushed with the creatures while laying bricks around Atreus' "burial chamber."

The sphinxes roamed the topiaries and the grounds closest to the house. Hiding in the shadow of the towers, they lay in wait for unsuspecting Hawkens. Roger and Vergil had run afoul of the creatures at least one time in their incautious youth, and Vergil, the slow, sober second child, had a scar along his right calf to show for a run-in with Ceraphis herself.

Vergil was never the same. It was as if the sphinx attack had . . . beaten him in a dim and inner place. From the time of his wounding until his untimely death at the age of twenty-five, he had followed Roger's every instruction as though his older brother were prophet, lawgiver, and father rolled into one.

Ceraphis would have laughed to see it. At last, she had riddled one Hawken into docility.

Following Melusine Stella-Maris' death, the poor relatives moved into the mill house. James, fresh from a business failure among the bordermetal mines where anyone not bent on losing money, it was said, could prosper and flourish, came home *to regroup*.

He brought along with him his two little daughters. Artemis and her daring entered the quiet games of the twins.

And this, Diego remembered well.

* * *

You can do it, 'Dimyan, she whispered tauntingly. *Touch the fountain.*

The three youngsters crouched beside a topiary squirrel, ill-trimmed by James Hawken as part of Roger's near-disastrous attempt to make his cousin useful. Grotesquely, the shrubbery creature leered toward the center of the garden, where a live, flesh-and-blood sphinx crouched by a dry fountain, gnawing a suspicious bone.

It was a game among the children. Once they spotted a sphinx somewhere on the grounds, two of them set a task before the third: touch or retrieve something near the animal, move openly toward it, taunt it—the options were many, and varied with the peculiar, competitive politics of childhood.

Endymion's task was easy. When it came to physical bravery, neither Artemis nor Diego expected much of him. Slowly, clinging like a bagworm to the edge of the topiary, the boy brushed along the squirrel to the more overgrown, geometrical shapes near the fountain. At the circumference of the juniper sphere Endymion crept, through the corner of the quadrangle and the juncture of the displayed triquetra, like a mathematical phenomenon bisecting a dozen polyhedrons, until, his path having circled twice clockwise around the fountain, he poked his hand through the shield of a taxus rhomb and touched the stone fountain daintily.

The sphinx snuffled and stirred. The black hair rose on her back, like metal shavings stirred by a lodestone. Then settled as the creature chose to return to her trophy, to forget the disturbance in the shrubbery behind her. The hot odor of decaying flesh rose briefly over the soothing, watery smell of the evergreens, then submerged, vanished.

Endymion rustled back to his companions, his yellow coat streaked with the teal of juniper, the gray-green of spruce and cedar. Gasping, triumphant, he held up his fingers, displaying the white, chalky powder he had rubbed from the dry granite with a touch.

"Good work, 'Dimyan," Diego muttered, his thoughts already on other challenges. "Now for you, gentle coz."

Artemis regarded him serenely, her brown eyes dark and immeasurable.

"You . . ." Diego whispered dramatically. "Have to touch *it*."

Artemis frowned. *"It?"*

The boys smiled.

"Why, the sphinx," Diego said. "The damned animal itself."

The girl swallowed and blinked. "Very well."

Around the fountain Artemis circled. Counterclockwise, in the opposite direction from her cousin. Briefly she emerged from the easternmost rhomb, and swiftly, her dark hair flashing once in the moonlight, ducked into the reversed triquetra closest to the monster.

"Diego, you shouldn't . . ." Endymion began, but the larger, stronger twin silenced him with a wave.

"Watch," Diego hissed.

Years later, he was still unable to say *for sure* that he saw his cousin's hand snake from the dark, triangular shrub. *Swift as a striking adder,* she had boasted later, clutching the pulled black hair, waving it in front of Diego's nose teasingly.

So quick the creature didn't feel me pull 'em.

Diego had caught a whiff of lavender and herbs in the dancing handful of hair. He had suspected his cousin at once—for after all, wasn't her *own* hair dark, almost black? But Endymion, who adored his venturesome cousin and was inclined to believe whatever she said, held the hair aloft like a trophy.

"Sphinx mane, Diego," he whispered admiringly. "Prize of the hunt."

After all, beneath the lavender and verbena, there was a lacing of an old, feral smell. Something harsh and acid—a whiff of fear, perhaps, or anger.

It remained in Diego's memory long after Endymion had ceased to believe the sphinx was anything but natural, long after Artemis confessed, on Saint Agnes' Eve twenty years later, over a third glass of brandy, that she had pulled her own hair and invented it all.

For your entertainment, Diego, she had explained.

You expected so much of me then.

* * *

Now, twenty-five years after the sport in the topiaries, Ceraphis and her brood seemed legendary, remote, as the cousins stood in the anteroom of the mansion, bundling for the crisp morning air and the long journey in search of Solomon.

"I suppose we must seek out your rebels," Diego said, draping his government-issue jacket over the banister and choosing instead one of Endymion's tattered black greatcoats.

Artemis cast him a curious glance.

"Snipers," he explained laconically. "A red jacket's no more than a target in the Lady's Land, and that's where we have to go to find an escort through the Borders. The Guard isn't going to take with you riding along. The Lady in their midst? The Great Witch?"

Artemis laughed. "The Great Witch is hungry, Diego. She conjures bread and cheese from whatever pantry won't swallow her whole. For once you're right. We'll have to join my troops. I can guarantee your safety among the rebels. You could not do the same for me among the Guard.

"And what is more," she added, winking at her tall, mustachioed cousin, "we are the ones—not you—who know the Borders."

* * *

Willie Melmoth saddled three horses and four pack mules, muttering at being rousted from bed at an early hour. He muttered the more at returning Borderward, where Blights and dryads and the mirrored angels seemed bent on disturbing the spiritual peace.

But his lot, it seemed, had fallen with the Hawkens. It no longer occurred to Willie Melmoth that he had any other option but to accompany Diego to Urthona, to Lambeth, to the edge of the Absence itself, if need be.

Their story had become his story, and despite the hour and the prospects ahead of him, Willie Melmoth had joined for the duration.

In the hay-smelling shadows the three mares flashed and whickered. Saddling them by a single faint lamp, Willie noticed how the Borders affected the light itself. Around the lamp lay a small, wavering halo, its glow fragmented into the colors of the spectrum and one color more—a metallic gray that, when Willie looked at it from different angles, was interwoven with red or green or violet.

Leutha, they called it. The color of the Absences.

In the far corners of the stables, the shade purpled and vaulted into shapes that resembled something almost human, sometimes so strikingly human that Willie would turn uneasily, thinking that some intruder was watching him from the door.

"Not a night to set out on," he grumbled, cinching the saddle on the third mare—Diego's brown Juno. "The wind up and the ruffles prowlin'."

Juno regarded him solemnly, nuzzling his Benjamin topcoat for sugar or fruit.

"But it seems just like 'em to tow me along," Willie continued, softly pushing Juno's muzzle away. "It's Hawken after Hawken ready to drag an Urthonan boy halfway through an Absence and back again on their own family business."

Juno snorted. She probably agreed.

"Leastwise," Willie resolved, speaking to the mare in urgent, serious tones, "I ain't leavin' Arcady without my aircraft. I done it once before, and was nearly rebel fodder at L'Overture's abatis."

Juno nuzzled his hand in a fruitless search for sugar, for dried apple.

"If it takes a brace of their mules and a cart to tote it," the gondolier continued, "so will it be. I'll pass off the baggage as the Lady's to Diego, as Diego's to the Lady."

The horses saddled, the mules laden, and the cart filled with a mysterious-looking bag, Willie led the whole drowsy caravan out of the stables and into the courtyard. Diego was there, his Guard uniform discarded for a black greatcoat and a gray fedora. Artemis stood beside him, cloaked in green, her long dark hair braided for the ride.

At that moment, Juno stopped suddenly. The other horses jostled against her, and Willie, on the driver's seat of the cart, his hands loosely on the reins, followed the intelligent stare of the animals to the torchlit wall of the mansion, where Diego's shadow blended with Artemis' in a swirl of leutha gray.

It seemed as though Artemis was leaning toward her cousin, as though her onyx-black hair brushed softly against his blanketed shoulder. Then the moon surged from behind a wall of clouds, bathing the courtyard in a silver, haloed light. All shadows vanished for a moment, and Willie breathed deeply, leading the horses toward their riders, the big flanks of the beasts steaming in the crisp air of the morning.

* * *

Three miles out of Arcady, they forded the Alph at Melusine's Shallows. Named for Aristo's mermaid bride, the shallows afforded the easiest passage across the river into Urthona. Here the Alph tumbled swiftly over gently sloping flat rocks, the waters clear and the footing steady.

Artemis guided them fluently, her green cloak catching moonlight. Willie brought up the rear, seated uncomfortably in the cart, cursing and cajoling the mules at each dip in the road, each bend in the maze of trails that marked the forests of southern Urthona.

In the middle of this odd procession, Diego would lose sight of his cousin for a moment. Then she would seem to emerge from the boles of trees, from juniper and taxus, weaving a dryadic trail through the woods.

By instinct Diego's hand rode softly on his pistol. Rebel country. Even Juno stepped lightly, as if she absorbed the intent of her rider.

Scarcely a mile from the river, Artemis brought her horse to a stop on a small, rocky plateau overlooking a thick nest of cedar and pine. The Urthonan woods stretched below her like a rebel's maze, and she motioned to Diego to draw his horse near.

"From this point on," she insisted, "the two of you travel blind."

* * *

He objected to the green scarf wrapped over his eyes, and judging from the string of oaths emerging from the absolute green darkness, so did Captain Diego.

From his experience as a gondolier, Willie could feel the rise and drop of the land as the trail wound over a squat, round hill and down into a leafy declivity, to judge from the nearby sound of birdsong and Artemis' warning to lean forward on the wagon seat.

Then the smell of woodsmoke laced with hemp, a muffled exchange of words (one of the voices was the Lady's), and then rough hands moving deftly under his blindfold and a sudden, flaring light that dazzled him and hurt his eyes as he was tugged from the cart and set roughly on his feet.

When his sight settled, he saw the tents and the men in green. It was a sizable rebel camp, and veteran, judging from the blacking and the beards.

A hundred or more gaunt men ranged around a dozen banked fires, talking, cleaning weapons, passing hemp pipes, drinking a hot concoction Willie guessed was coffee. They eyed the Captain warily as he passed on Juno, but Willie seemed of little consequence to them, almost beneath their notice.

Good enough, the lad thought. In far Urthona he had heard of the rebel kneecappings—a brutal discipline enacted on the farm and river boys by the insurrectionists. If a young man was judged unruly, disobedient to his parents, or otherwise delinquent (as he had been, no doubt, by jettisoning almost all provisions to make a place for his balloon in the baggage), the day would come when he would be stopped on the road or on a secluded pathway by two, perhaps three green-coated men.

A well-placed bullet, lodged in the miscreant's lower thigh, or, if the crime was grave enough, in the kneecap itself, was usually enough to discourage future misbehavior. Thus the provisional forces, of which the Lady, it seemed, was a commander, kept watch over the countrymen in southern Urthona and northern Urizen.

They were keeping watch over Diego Hawken now, who glared back at them from his high position atop the big mare. The gray fedora pulled tightly down over his eyes, he regarded his hosts contemptuously, refusing to speak when the rebel lieutenant, a certain Evander Rousseau, addressed him courteously, officer to officer.

Artemis drew the lieutenant aside and sounded him on episodes and disturbances, on the unusual occurrences over the last three days of his watch.

Rousseau was to the point with his account.

A centaur, it seemed, had tried to stray from the Borders into common land, from Absence into Presence, and the bellowing as the big creature unraveled against the edge of the Borders had rousted the men from their slumber. A solitary picket, set on sentry at the Borders' edge, had seen the beast dissolve to the strange, dissonant music of pipes.

A genie, as well, had emerged from a soldier's ill-placed Border campfire, rising in a glory of crimson smoke and promising wonders and the granting of wishes. The boy who had struck the fire, a young man whose village and family had been burned out by patrolling guardsmen, fell prey to the seductions of greed, and following an old tale, wished for an infinite number of wishes, which looped him, apparently, to an identical campsite where an identical genie arose from an identical fire, and despite himself he wished the same wish and was translated again, and once more until, weeping and distracted, he found himself on the banks of the Alph, facedown in red mud.

Then there was the third phenomenon, compared to the others much less remarkable, but worthy of note, if the Lady was interested.

The Lady expressed her interest.

Rousseau himself had seen the man, lean and gangling, a shock of graying hair bushing under a black clerical tricorn. This scarecrow of a wanderer had watched them pass, convinced of his own obscurity and seclusion, but all of them had seen him and noted him, and marked him for certain disaster unless he found a sensible guide.

Diego, standing at remove from Artemis and the lieutenant, overheard Rousseau's description of the ungainly wanderer. At once he recognized his brother.

"Where did he go?" Diego asked, then again more loudly.

Rousseau's eyes never left his commander.

"Lieutenant Rousseau," Artemis ordered quietly, "I shall need your presence, along with that of sixty troopers, horses, and supplies for a week."

"It will leave a gap in the lines from here to the Alph, Lady," Rousseau protested mildly, but the Lady's silence was convincing.

It was less than an hour from Artemis' arrival in the camp to her departure, escorted by Lieutenant Evander Rousseau and sixty weathered troopers, clad in tattered green and homespun brown. At the head of the column, her cousin beside her, the Lady steered her horse along a wide path skirting the riverbank until she vanished into shadowy forest, the line of troopers following her like the tail of a burrowing snake.

Willie brought up the rear of the winding green column, still muttering in his efforts to guide the uncooperative mules along a narrow passage. He longed for a gondola, for clear skies and a lofting wind.

For a cup of stiff rebel coffee to keep him awake in a long night of travel.

Morning found them at the Borders' edge, where birdsong ceased and the sunlight slanted crazily, as though filtered through a crystal prism. Willie felt the tensile edge of the Borders break around him with an electric crackle, and the horses ahead of him weaved through newly twisted dried willow and vine. The sound of the surging river was strangely regular in the distance, beneath the snorting and snuffling of horses and the scattered birdsong, as though a mill wheel turned upon powerful waters.

Within an hour the lead rider whistled urgently and reined in his horse. Bunched behind him, his companions milled uncertainly on the path, their horses stamping and whickering, churning the grass and raising forgotten, glittering dust.

The edge of the Absence hovered before them like a shimmering curtain. In dismay, Artemis stood in the saddle, looking back to Diego, her face a dark map of worry.

"If he came this way," she said, "he's gone into the Absence."

Willie inhaled sharply. He stared at the whirling, opaque spectacle, the gray cloud that flashed in intense variegation of red, of green, of violet.

Leutha. The color of change.

* * *

It was the color that filled Morgana's vision as, escorted by Whitefield and his rebel cavalry, she rode eastward in the night toward Arcady.

Whitefield was returning her home. He said that the Tharman road was no place for an old woman alone.

To the left of the cavalry column, the Alph stirred sluggishly in the moonlight.

Old woman alone.

Defeated and drowsy, Morgana leaned against Whitefield's back. The rebel commander guided his big roan carefully over the rough corduroy road, and the old woman, nodding toward sleep and eager to lift her heavy spirits, stared out over the glittering water.

For a brief, sparkling moment she heard music—a discordant cascade of bells.

Morgana held her breath. A dizziness, a temptation to laugh rushed over her.

None of the rebels noticed.

Out on the moonstruck water a dark shape danced over the reflections.

The angels were coming.

Suddenly, the sound of rebel hoofbeats fell away, and Morgana saw the dark vault of Arcady's attic. The other velocipede—her cousin

James' it was—bathed in moonlight cascading from a broken roundel window.

The costume jewelry on the wheels sparkled crazily, and the broken glass that littered the attic floor sparkled in response.

It was like a fire of reflected light, and deep in the corner of the attic, dark wings brushed through the shadows, and a low birdsong rose into dusty air.

Khole. Morgana knew the phoenix at once.

She tightened her grip around Whitefield's waist.

The vision burst into flames. There, in the attic of Arcady, a slow, smokeless burning rose through the racks and boxes, spread over discarded toys and ancestral clothing, the fire covering all that it touched but harming nothing, neither singeing cloth nor melting wax.

"What is it, Miss Morgana?" Whitefield called back to her, and for a moment the vision wavered, the distant light lost in the shadows of midnight and rising river fog.

"Nothing," Morgana murmured. "Nothing but change."

She caught the smell of myrrh off the river, of balsam and sandalwood, and then she saw the attic, the fire . . .

The phoenix burning, the flame passing over his wings like a glory, and "Father and Mother," she heard him say, "I return from flames of fire tried and pure and bright . . ."

CHAPTER 25

Leutha. Glittering gray laced with green and red. The color of the Absence, its signature in desolate land.

Solomon waded in the shimmering gray light through a skeletal wilderness of rock and metal towers. The ruins reminded him of Endymion's Golgonooza, or what it must be like from Morgana's description. Shells of buildings, irregular streets and alleys, but these structures were made of stone, not teak, and the profusion of bordermetal hinted at something that had once flourished and was now vanished, almost forgotten, exploited by unseen and malevolent hands.

Desolate, but not silent. A chaos of voices raged over the wasted landscape. Once Solomon thought he heard each of his brothers. Endymion called for Faith in the cavernous distance, and Diego shouted something unintelligible, the quality and timbre of his voice clear but the words within it garbled. Among the voices was the soothing, fluttering call of a phoenix (Endymion's phoenix? Of course, he could not tell) and the distant tolling of a tower bell.

Solomon stopped, startled by a movement in the mists at his feet. An entanglement of wire rose out of the shimmering gray and scuttled toward him, moving recklessly, savagely. Separate, knotting strands stretched and twitched like the legs of a spider.

He stepped back, shouted. The thing rushed by, gibbering like a frightened bat, vanishing into the haze. In the wake of the creature, the landscape around Solomon fell quiet, the only remaining sound a grinding noise that kept a regular, inexorable rhythm at the greatest distance.

It was then that the horseman lurched from the shadows.

At first Solomon thought someone had followed him into the Absence, raised his hand in the beginning of a greeting . . .

Discordant pipes began to play.

It was no ordinary rider, but a centaur that approached, as though gathered out of the mist, weaving menacingly through the toppled buildings and the wires. With a hoarse cry, the creature galloped toward Solomon, great staff arcing in its meaty hands.

The first blow whistled by Solomon's head, spangling the leutha mist with crimson and green. Solomon dove beneath the feet of the beast, who instinctively vaulted him on a breakneck path through the rubble. Finding clear ground, the centaur pivoted and charged again.

This time, windmilling his arms, Solomon tried to strike back, but a swift, glancing swat from the staff sent him tumbling backward. He evaded a more serious blow by sheer good fortune, as the centaur's weapon snarled in borderwire on its lethal downward path.

As the creature wrestled with the tangled staff, Solomon made off through the shifting mist, his destination a ring of dark wooden buildings some hundred yards away. As he approached them, the buildings seemed to recede, the sky above them glazing and catching an alien light. On what seemed to be a nightmarish treadmill, where he made no progress no matter how swiftly he ran, he soon heard the sound of hoofbeats behind him.

He turned. The centaur reared above him, staff raised for a shattering descent. Solomon fell, his hands extended helplessly in a futile attempt to ward off the blow.

Through mists and shadows, descending like a crimson sun, a bird swooped slowly out of the distance, scattering clouds and spreading light as it brushed by the centaur. An odor of ash and incense fell from the air like light.

The centaur roared, dropped its staff, and galloped away into the mist. Solomon staggered to his feet.

The bird banked in the gray air and vanished into the maze of wooden architecture. Dazed, Solomon followed, and now the buildings were closer, and closer still, moving dreamlike to embrace him.

Memories of Arcady rushed toward and by him, like the bird in the fiery crimson disk.

He thought again that he heard Endymion call. Heard the sound of a tolling bell.

Terce. Third of the Saints' Hours. His clerical ear caught the familiar rhythm of the bells, which had summoned him for years, as student and as novice, to his lectures on the Commentaries.

Here at the threshold of the first of the buildings, Solomon paused. The bells rang again. From somewhere in the woody-smelling dark a voice, distressingly familiar, summoned him.

Gathering a deep breath, he stepped over the threshold.

* * *

The hall was lit with tallow candles, the faint odor of the lamb pen wafting over the lectern and the desks.

The boys did not turn when Solomon entered the room. Instead, their gazes remained intent on the man behind the lectern, gray-haired and black-coated, his face indefinite in the distance and the slanted light.

Softly, Solomon slipped into a chair in the back row. The odor of lemon oil and wood shavings surrounded him, and he sank into a calm dreaminess, the lecture prodding at the edge of his awareness.

Something about replication. About recurrence and cycle.

He glanced at the boy beside him.

Short, dark-haired, gnomish features. A certain patrician shagginess. Then the cycle completed, the recognition flashed over the years and past the purposeful burials of memory.

Marcus. Marcus Chatterton.

The boy turned to him and winked. In astonishment, Solomon gripped his desk, tried to stand.

His hands were those of a youngster—thin, blue-veined, and circumscribed by oak and candlelight. And the lecturer, leaning into the light across the oaken podium, a torrent of gray hair spilling over the seminarian collar, was himself.

Abstractedly the lecturer intoned the lines from Saint Prometheus' Commentary. "Ere Babylon was dust," he began. Stopped, coughed, and repeated.

> ". . . Ere Babylon was dust,
> The Magus Zoroaster, my dead child,
> Met his own image walking in the garden."

Solomon blinked, leaned back in his chair. Marcus passed him a note across the aisle.

Pontus Tarn, it read. *We'll try the boat again.*

And suddenly the room dissolved into an eddying mist.

Leutha. Gray and green and blood-deep crimson.

Solomon sank into the swirling cloud. Deeper and deeper he fell, slowly, as though he were falling through water, and it seemed as though he, too, were drowning . . . drowning . . .

Out of the cacophony of voices and cries and sounds rose a great crashing of machinery, a regular, threshing sound at the heart of the cloud. Suddenly, out of its swirl stepped a figure.

A man cloaked in darkness, his face pale, ethereal.

It took Solomon a long while to recognize his uncle Vergil.

The Hawken nose, the tangle of hair early gray.

The serenity of martyrdom.

Vergil had always been simpler than the others. Solomon remembered him only fleetingly as a slow, tranquil presence in the chambers of Arcady. Remembered a sadness when Vergil washed away with Grandfather Atreus.

But here he was. Vergil, or a phantom Vergil. A ghost that hovered by Solomon Hawken, fishbelly white, almost translucent, a purple scar lacing his thick neck . . .

The sphinx bite? Solomon remembered a story . . .

The phantom's hair was dripping with water and weeds.

Not your fault, Vergil whispered. *That was a lake and a drowning a thousand years ago. Drowning is . . . always an accident. Not your fault. Nothing is your fault.*

Nothing? Solomon drifted in a glittering haze.

Nothing. It is the coalescence of a thousand causes, a thousand effects, incited at the beginning of the world, before the old ones, before the bordermetal and the standing ruins, before the Text and the Hymns and the ink that illumined them.

You could not help what happened to that boy. He was bound for it from the beginning of time.

"Who are you?" Solomon asked. The complexity of these words, this explanation, was certainly not Vergil's.

Nor was the sound. For the closer Solomon listened, the more clear it became that the voice was someone else's.

Do you like stories, Solomon Hawken? it asked.

Solomon blinked stupidly. The voice encircled him like the leuthan mists. He could no longer tell whether it came from the specter before him or from somewhere in the distance, or whether it dwelt inside his thoughts.

Indeed, whether it *was* his thoughts.

Then look, the voice commanded, and the cloud before him glowed with an unnatural light, filled with images like those cast by mirror and lamp and colored glass—the "magic lanterns" of childhood entertainments. Solomon saw Lambeth again before him, the high outer walls giving way to the lower walls of bailey and court, the squat student quarters and the three circular lecture halls which stood like windowed silos in the midst of the seminary grounds. Slowly, his eye was drawn to a moonlit grove in the southern gardens.

Solomon remembered it well. An herb and flower patch it was, planted by some wag of a gardener with jack-in-the-pulpit, monkshood, and angelica. Encircling the herbs was a solitary row of gaudy sunflowers, tall and outrageous, the delight of less seminaried students. In the midst of the herbs and flowers branched a young lime tree, which for some reason the caretakers feared dead every snowfall, only to find the hardy little plant green and thriving through the most grim and denying winter.

It was an odd little garden, ignored by lecturer and divine. So early on, it had become a place where Solomon and Marcus met, practicing their newfound spellcraft in seclusion and quiet.

Right you are. The pervading voice interrupted Solomon's revery. *The meeting place. Now watch and listen.* The image of Vergil, transparent and tattered in parts now, gestured languidly toward the garden scene, the purple scar on its neck covered by a snaking finger of cloud.

Bright forms moved through the imagined garden. Solomon and Marcus, fourteen-year-old students disguised as novitiates, slipping into the garden. Solomon watched, recalling a long-dead time, as the image of his younger self slipped through the high border of sunflowers.

He had been frail then, his skin pale and papery—almost as translucent as that of the specter beside him. It was a wonder he had survived Urthonan winter.

But the scene before him was high spring, the lime in full leathery leaf, the flowers as well casting up scape and bud.

One night in the spring, Vergil coaxed, prodded. *A particular night. You must remember.*

Solomon did not remember. Yet everything about the scene seemed possible, plausible: he remembered the garden on a hundred nights like this one, and the conjuries that would take place would be no different from those on a score of occasions, when he and Marcus had tested what they believed to be their newfound magical powers.

But listen. Listen and recollect. This night is not like any of the others.

Now the two lads stood before the lime tree, and Marcus quietly began an incantation, a preparatory verse from the Commentaries:

> ". . . Nor in this bower,
> This little lime-tree bower, have I not mark'd
> Much that has sooth'd me. Pale beneath the blaze
> Hung the transparent foliage; and I watch'd
> Some broad and sunny leaf, and lov'd to see
> The shadow of the leaf and stem above
> Dappling its sunshine!"

Under the words of the incantation, the lime tree began to shimmer and glisten. The sunflowers, drooping on their stems, lifted their faces and turned toward the new source of light.

Looking through cloud and childhood memory into the glowing heart of the tree, Solomon watched from the bower's edge. He saw the green eruption of light, while at the same time he saw himself, a pale student of barely fourteen, bedazzled by that same light. In the heart of the green light arose a double vision, a whirling series of images and insights: in the light, he saw a boat coasting over Pontus Tarn, manned by Marcus and his rowing twelve-year-old self, floating softly in a tranquil lake; in that lake was reflected a passing balloon, manned by his grown self and a young gondolier.

Melmoth. They had called the boy Willie Melmoth.

Now he stood before the shadowy dolmens, before a Border edge that somehow seemed to house a silvery, shadowy Absence before which his older self stood, contemplating entry.

Now, from his older perspective, Solomon recognized what was happening to the boy. There, in the seminary's lime-tree bower, Marcus' conjury had opened a visionary moment—a moment in which he, merely an onlooker, might have seen his past, present, and future in the glowing branches of the tree.

What good might it have been had he understood that vision as a boy? Solomon did not know. He crouched in the snaking fog and cupped his chin in his hands.

Perhaps everything would have been the same, he told himself. *Perhaps nothing.*

At least I would have known that . . . it all connected somehow. That it all had the purpose of . . .

He could not figure that purpose. Not yet.

Then the light of the tree waned, and the garden recovered its familiar shape—the flowers and herbs encircling an ordinary, sunstruck tree, the faint odor of citrus rind above the crisp smell of angelica. For a moment the boy almost remembered where he would be years later. Solomon could see it in the eyes of his youthful self.

The boy turned toward him, his young face glimmering with a hint of recognition . . .

Then the light of the tree glowed even more brightly, and the boy turned back.

Confused and disturbed by the vision, Solomon crouched in the leuthan mist. "What does it mean?" he stammered. "Why are you showing me this?"

Nothing, the image of Vergil responded. *Oh nothing. Do not let it trouble you. After all, who is to say that you really saw these things on that very night years past? Who is to say that what you are watching is not some dream you are dreaming now at thirty years' remove?*

Solomon shook his head. The words insinuated like fog, like trickling water.

He did not know what to believe.

In a kind, lethargic gesture, the phantom placed his hand on Solomon's shoulder. It felt icy, wet, like an infusion of winter rain. Vergil pointed away from the glowing scene, back toward the obscure and whirling clouds.

Solomon turned to follow, looking back once, a last time . . .

As the boy in the vision gestured wildly at the tree.

"Wait," Solomon whispered, to the beckoning ghost—to himself as well. "I want to hear what that boy says. I don't *care* whether he said it years ago or if I'm dreaming it. I want to hear it."

Be my guest. Listen.

* * *

"Didja not see it?" the young Solomon asked. "Didja not see it, Marcus?"

His friend regarded him skeptically.

"What did *you* see, Solomon?" Marcus asked.

The unnatural light about the lime tree sputtered and faded. The bower sank into shadow, and a nightingale, startled to silence by the magical false day, sang with obvious relief in a not-too-distant cedar.

The sunflowers turned away from the faintly glowing tree.

"Myself. Somebody else . . . *not* myself, Marcus. I don't know how else to explain it."

Marcus blinked, frowned. "*Try* another way, Solomon. I'm not following this."

"You mean . . . you didn't see me in the light of the tree?"

Marcus shook his head.

"How about yourself? Something of your past or present? Something that . . ."

"Nothing, Solomon. I saw a light. I felt a sense of surpassing peace. As the Commentary said, *I have marked much that has soothed me.*

"But not visions. Not prophecies. Saint Milton had those. And the Bard, when Saint Milton descended from Paradise into time and space to join him in the black cloud redounding. And those visions were real, I suppose, but they have passed from this place and time." Marcus' eyes narrowed. "You don't really believe *you* saw such things, do you, Solomon?"

Solomon swallowed hard. It seemed that the sunflowers had turned their faces toward him, that the herbs themselves were watching.

Peeping herbs. He had read of them somewhere.

The whole garden awaited his answer.

* * *

What will he say, Solomon? the taunting voice asked, as Solomon watched the scene unfold before him: his boyhood self at the edge of a vision, questioned by his best friend, his mentor, his hero.

"I hope . . ." Solomon began.

But you know how it will turn out, the voice interrupted, fulsome with a suspect compassion. *You know he will deny his vision.*

* * *

"I suppose . . . it *is* superstitious, Marcus," the boy conceded. "I suppose there's just so much physics against it—I mean, against visions and all."

"Not that it wasn't true *once,*" Marcus said with a smile, raising a comical, admonitory finger. "A consequence of our fall. You can only bend physics so far."

Solomon looked away, nodding almost imperceptibly.

* * *

Perhaps it was your opportunity, the voice maintained, as Solomon watched the boys depart the bower, head for the torchlit entrances to the student rooms.

The phantom passed between Solomon and the fading scene, as though trying to block the last light. A greenly glimmering lime branch shone faintly through his cloudy form. *Perhaps you missed it,* he urged, *in that little bower thirty years ago. Understandable. For who could blame you, a boy of twelve? eleven?*

"Fourteen."

Fourteen. Who could blame you? How could you stand against . . . the relentless prompting of your friend?

"Relentless?"

Who had the vision?

The bower was empty and dark. Already the clouds of the Absence had begun to cover the little scene, and already the neatly demarcated rows of herb and flower were lost in the rising mist.

Who had the vision? the image of Vergil insisted.

"I did. Or I *suppose* I did. I'm not altogether sure. For didn't you say yourself that perhaps I haven't remembered it all, or remembered it correctly?"

A good point, Vergil conceded. *Perhaps I am wrong. Perhaps things never happened the way you saw it now. What do you recall? What do you remember?*

"Nothing. Nothing definite, that is. I recall no particular vision, no images of older men, of lecturers or balloons. Perhaps I forgot them all purposely, when Marcus didn't see them."

When he . . . discouraged you?

"No. He never discouraged me. That wasn't it. Or . . . I don't believe it was."

It's like an Absence itself, is it not? the voice asked.

"An Absence? I don't follow."

Past, present, and future so jumbled that your own motives fall away. There's an Absence in each of us, where memory mixes with fear and desire until belief and fact confuse, and you are uncertain what you saw and what you imagined.

In the clouds of Absence, most things wither and die. Things fall away.

For a moment, the clouds lifted. Solomon saw into the distance, into ruins as vast and forsaken as those of Napolis and Ville, the great deserted cities of the old times. Rock and wire and rubble stretched as far as he could see: red steam arose from the barren reaches of the landscape.

Solomon looked out across the plains of burning sand, toward terrible mountains of marble. Indeed, it was a ruinous landscape: its pits and declivities flowing with molten ore and fountains of pitch and nitre, its ruined palaces and cities and mighty works. Its furnaces of affliction, in which angels and emanations labored with blackened visages among stupendous ruins, arches and pyramids and porches, colonnades and domes.

In which dwells Mystery, the voice admonished. *Babylon . . .*

"No," Solomon protested, quietly and uncertainly. "It's desolate, all right. Forsaken and bleak. But I don't have to stay here. The Blights have passed in and out of the Absences for years. It's a spot on the landscape—dark and terrible, but a *spot.* Stationary."

The last word came from him slowly. He had seen the devastation along the banks of the Alph, the wasteland covered with a snow of salt and silica. He had heard the warnings of Enith Moneta.

He was not sure how *stationary* the Absences were.

You are . . . uncertain, his companion said hungrily, diving through the mist like a shark after a ribbon of blood. *I can feel it in your thoughts, in your innermost fears.*

And you are right to be uncertain. For contrary to what you have been told in seminary, in childhood, in all the years and stories of your life, the Absences are moving. They have come unmoored, dislodged by the machineries of Citizen Arouet.

For he has mined for metal too deep in the Borders—too deep and too long, and the tunneling and digging, the incessant grinding and tearing of his devices, have dislodged the Absences.

Now they are moving, as an inner Absence moves within each of us, wherever we go, wheresoever we fly. We are Absences, Solomon, leaving loss and devastation in our wake.

"Why should I believe you?" Solomon asked, his heart sinking with the knowledge that, indeed, the voice was persuasive—that in spite of what his better instincts told him, he was beginning to believe the words, falling into their deception, their . . .

Difficult truth, the phantom maintained, completing his unspoken thought. *Not deception, but difficult truth. It is what I am telling you here.*

For a moment the dark shape shivered and shifted, and Solomon thought he saw an older face behind that of his dead uncle.

Innocent's face. The scar. The haunted eyes.

And yet another face behind Innocent's—a face older still. A countenance more brittle and corrupt, formed of whirling leuthan cloud, and infinitely evil.

The Absence, Solomon thought. It's not Arouet who is the villain. Not Uncle Innocent, neither guardsman nor rebel nor Blight . . .

It is the Absence in all of them. That is the evil.

But how do you stop a formless mist?

Now you know, the voice maintained, Vergil's gentle shape dissolving like smoke in a sudden wind, leaving only chaotic mist behind. *You know that the Absences are unstoppable—that as they expand to cover the continent, everything they cover will wither and die.*

Everything, that is, except . . . those who consent to carry an Absence within them.

"*Consent* to carry?" Solomon was distracted, barely listening. Through his mind flashed an image of Arcady, the smoldering frame of his childhood home and the once-green and fertile grounds.

Oh, that *will not happen,* the phantom soothed. *The desolate mansion grounds are an image of your fear only. The destruction of Arcady will not happen.*

Or let us say it does not need *to happen.*

For those who consent to carry an Absence within them are those who . . . comply with it, who enable its movement, its intention.

They will be spared. The hairs on their heads are numbered, and the possessions in which they revel and delight will remain, untouched by fire and devastation.

They will increase in knowledge and power.

And magic.

"How? How do you follow the will of . . . of a witless, arbitrary force?" Solomon asked.

You already know the answer. The Absence is . . . not witless. Not a force of nature, like cyclone or glacier.

The Absence is sentient, Solomon Hawken. It surrounds you, and it is in you.

For my voice is . . . your voice, the mist announced, solidifying, taking form again, no longer Uncle Vergil but something darker and omnipresent, spreading its cloaked arms like enormous batwings. *The inmost prompting of your true heart. And I know that you will assent. Ultimately. You will follow the Absence, and it will bring you the magic you awaited in seminary, in the lecture halls, by dolmen and by burning lime tree.*

It will bring you into yourself.

Drawn toward the dark voice of his guide, Solomon closed his eyes. For a moment, an image not of his making raced over his thoughts—of himself in a high Arcadian tower, surveying the groves and bowers and topiaries of his ancestors, a plot reaching back five generations to old Grandfather Atreus.

From that tower he would govern and dictate, shaping the grounds by magic into forms outrageous and divine. The topiary animals, uprooting from their spots in the garden, would gambol before him like living things, and the fruit trees—apple and peach and pear—would bear forth in abundance, their nectars blended into cordials and wines.

It was earthly paradise, this imagining, and his heart yearned toward it—toward the crimson sun setting bright over Uncle Raphael's grove.

So bright it seemed to burn against his eyelids, the image taking on a light and life of its own . . .

And opening his eyes, Solomon found himself still in the Absence, looking up through the glittering gray cloudbank toward a glassy green sky . . .

Where a crimson disk hung brilliant above.

For a moment, Solomon dismissed it, thought it was the sun shining through the thick leuthan clouds of the Absence. But the disk grew and neared him, red light scattering through the mist, dispersing obscurity and darkness.

In the heart of the disk was a golden-haired man, dark of visage and countenance. He was winged and robed all in purple and gold and white, the colors of spring and renewal.

Solomon looked at him curiously. His eyes were familiar, not quite human in their brilliance but more than human in their softness, their depth.

The voice that had instructed and coaxed him all along fell silent, supplanted by a far music of bells. From the crimson disk there tumbled ash and the faint smell of incense, and the dark shape of the ghost dissolved into the reeling mist.

The winged man settled on a jagged stone, resting his arms over a matrix of bordermetal wire. He looked trapped, enmeshed in steel webbing, but his brilliant eyes were calm, serene, and he smiled as he regarded the gaping Solomon.

Solomon stood. All voices had fled the mist, and the light from the winged man had cleared away all darkness.

"Who—who are you?" Solomon asked.

"Who do you think I am?" the winged man answered maddeningly. Solomon caught the whiff of gin beneath the incense.

"I . . . I don't know," Solomon confessed.

The winged man considered the answer. "I have been to that city," he announced, gesturing broadly toward a squat group of buildings in the distance, "where your brothers await your arrival."

"My brothers? What are they . . ."

"Trying to rescue you," the winged man insisted. "And in turn, you may do the same for them."

"But the Absence," Solomon persisted. "What it told me . . . or what I know . . ."

"Is true," the winged man interrupted. "At least in part. Now we can begin."

He shifted on the rock. For a moment green light, filtering through the dispersing clouds, cast his shadow on the barren ground behind him.

A huge, winged shape, birdlike and auspicious.

"You must fight the Absence itself," the winged man urged. "Its very voice encourages denial, unsays the present, renders this . . ."

He gestured across the gray, cloudy wasteland.

". . . out of the glory of creation. No, you must fight that voice, saying *no* to its *no* and *yes* to a deeper voice, buried in the clouds and chaos and nothingness around you."

Again the winged man's dark eyes met Solomon's gaze, and the priest wondered where he had seen them, why the man was familiar.

Arcady. The upstairs room.

The angels. But instinctively he knew that was not the *whole* truth. An angel this creature might be. But it was something else as well.

"But sometimes it's . . . *my* voice," Solomon protested. "The voice that spoke to me was sometimes my own!"

"Who told you this?" the winged man asked calmly.

"It's my voice," Solomon repeated, this time less assuredly. "I knew what it would say, and it in turn knew all about me."

"*All* about you?"

Solomon was silent, racing through his memories.

The angel leaned forward, curiously. "Think, Solomon. What did it say?"

Solomon slipped his hands into his pockets. There was something jarring at the edge of his memory, some place where the voice had slipped, unraveled . . .

Perhaps he had missed it.

The thought brought the words rushing back to him—word for word, as he had memorized the Text at Lambeth. The soft condemnation of the voice beneath the thick honey of a false compassion.

Perhaps you missed it, in that little bower thirty years ago. Understandable. For who could blame you, a boy of twelve? eleven?

Fourteen.

Fourteen.

"That's it!" Solomon cried out. "It did not know my age! So its thoughts were not my own—not *entirely* my own! The voice was not mine!"

The angel smiled faintly, nodded.

"But suppose," Solomon muttered, turning and pacing through a waist-high maze of bordermetal, "suppose I made that mistake on *purpose*, to make myself believe it was not my voice, but something outside of myself—something I could blame for my own failings . . ."

"You're as bad as Endymion," the angel said. "Tangled over yonder in the streets of his own making, where the Absence led him in and got him lost. He's imagined a brand-new father for his oldest son, and convinced himself . . ."

"I know who you are!" Solomon exclaimed. The image of the bird rushed through his memory—the phoenix in the aviary of his childhood, the same bird perched later in the dark corner of Endymion's forbidding room, the only source of warmth and light in that labyrinth of pain.

As he was here, amid the tangle of bordermetal, the confusion of cloud and time and motive.

"But now you know that the true evil lies in the Absence. And that its first trick is to convince all those around it that the evil they see is purely human: oppressive guardsman or insurrectionist rebel, Orthodox or Post-Millennial or seminarian skeptic, rather than the polymorphous evil that it is, filtering through everything, showing to general and beggar and gondolier alike their most frightful, most corrupting aspects. It is time for your instruction, Solomon Hawken," Khole said, brushing back his auburn hair and staring into the scholar's distracted eyes.

The gaze of the phoenix was wild and kind—a thing no Absence could contain.

CHAPTER 26

For two days Willie had watched the swirling heart of the Absence from not a hundred yards away,

The clouds seemed to swell, to ebb and flow. By the second evening he almost believed that the Absence itself had moved, shifting ground ever so slightly from west to east.

Of course, he had always been taught that was impossible. The Borders themselves were deceptive, a haven for illusion and twisted light. Surely they had made him believe for a moment at sunset that a pin oak at the easternmost edge of the cloud was now partially overtaken by tendrils of gray leutha.

For after all, the Absences were stationary. It was a law of nature, they said.

And apparently it was another law—this of human nature—that each Hawken rivaled another in a clamorous race for glory and attention.

Diego and Artemis had found contest in every event that had come to pass since the rebels camped by the Absence's side. Now, as the second night encroached on the campfires, the cousins were at it again, firing pistols at a battered canteen they had lodged in the bare branches of a poplar.

Incessantly, foolishly, the pistols rang in the Urthonan twilight. The Lady was by far the better shot: the canteen rattled and popped at her each firing, and the air bristled with the Captain's curses as he missed again and again.

Artemis' men watched the proceedings with grim, poker-faced indifference. Willie knew that they snickered about the Captain's temper around the campfires, but for the most part all of the rebels, from

Rousseau down to the elegantly named Justin St. Hyle—a beardless boy from Luvah, the butt of veterans' jokes and pranks—kept their distance from the warring leaders, watching their rivalries and arguments from the safety of other campfires.

Yet Willie could not shake his earlier impression, the unsettling feeling born in the courtyard of the Hawken estate. Artemis' and Diego's shadows had seemed to touch for a moment in the fitful moonlight there. Some electric affinity sputtered and cast its subtle light whenever the cousins disputed and vied.

Willie could not figure it. He had no way of knowing.

Besides, he could not study it for long. The rations were dwindling. What would he say to his companions when they opened the bag in the bed of the mule cart, fully expecting dried beef and hardtack, only to find silk they could not eat, cording of no use to them but perhaps to hang a young balloon gondolier who had thought too fondly of his obscure craft?

* * *

The cousins' story ranged back to their childhoods. When Cousin James, penniless and joyful, had settled in Melusine Stella-Maris' abandoned mill house with his two young daughters, Diego had avoided the place for months. He was ten years old, after all, and unsympathetic to his shiftless uncle, the nutty smell of hemp that wafted from the mill house, and especially the large-eyed eight-year-old girl who watched him cagily from the dark, watery-smelling threshold.

In the third month, Artemis had sailed a toy boat down the millrace to where Diego fished for koi on the edge of Grandfather Atreus' lake. It was a clever craft, fashioned of her father's foul papers.

On the back of a bad sonnet, Artemis had crafted a message for the sullen, oversized boy who had glared at her as he passed on horse or foot.

Pig face, it had said. *Diegoe the pig face.*

Sputtering oaths about cottagers and tenants and cousins once removed, especially female ones, Diego had hurled a stone through the mill-house window and fled into the East Woods, where he spent the afternoon hiding and snickering.

The next day another boat made its way downstream, breasting the current with another message.

Still a pig face. Glas brekin pig face.

Despite himself, Diego had smiled.

As he would smile a thousand times henceforth. Always despite himself.

Their rivalry began at once. Diego, large for his age and impressively strong, found it an endless source of frustration that young Artemis was his match and better in every contest.

She was faster, of course. She dodged the sphinxes among the topiary with a grace and facility that Diego could not manage. Brought sphinx mane home as trophies, if you could believe her stories.

She sat by the ancestral gate or by the main entrance to the mansion, laughing as Diego staggered from the garden to a chorus of whimpers and growls, his breeches and gaiters chewed past recognition. And fuming in the courtyard, Diego would laugh, too, when Artemis' dark brown eyes rested on him brilliantly and teased the laughter out of him.

Though Artemis was not as large or sturdy as Diego, she won contests of strength as well by wit and science. The gate to Uncle Raphael's nut groves, rust-frozen and immovable to Diego, she opened by setting her shoulder to a carefully chosen spot below the latch. She had lifted bales of hay, small farm animals, and pulled up the boarding in the mill house while searching for the mermaid treasure she was convinced old Atreus had exacted as rent from Melusine Stella-Maris.

It was not all science and wit, her extraordinary strength. Some of it was illusion. Once, using what appeared to be the leverage of her weight, Artemis hoisted a cow in a dramatic gesture in the dark of the barn. It took Diego a month to discern the elaborate and concealed pulley system the girl had rigged to deceive her cousin and win his wagered money.

It had taken him even longer to discover he was not her match in *any* physical contest, that mentally he was never close to her equal.

His first—and his only *real*—triumph came years later, in the lofts of the same barn that had housed Artemis' pulleyed victories.

She was thirteen then, her body shifting into a new and womanly form. She held more interest for him than she ever had before.

Oh, Diego had been cautioned over cousins who wed. The Mariners and the Hayleys had done so in Shiveleigh and regions south and west, and the results were rumored to be horrific.

Children with Border wire for hair.

Pig face.

But it never hurt to look at a beautiful girl. Artemis' brown legs, uncovered innocently before her gaping cousin, dangled from the rafter in the loft as the girl peered over the mass of baled hay ready for winter fodder.

"Only a jump?" she called down to Diego. "Why not a dive or a tumble?"

Diego sighed. It was like her. His feat of derring-do paled before Artemis' censure, as the girl clambered onto the beam and, with a graceful leap into the musty dark, flickered through the sunlight of the barn window, flipped, and landed softly on her feet in the midst of the hay. Dust and seed scattered through the loft, and Artemis laughed, certain that again she had bested her cousin.

More agile. In ways more strong.

But not more stupid, by all the saints.

Diego had planned the next step for a week, steeling himself for another challenge. With a grunt he clambered to the rafter and danced along it like a rope walker. The old pine, set in old Atreus' time, creaked beneath his weight.

"Now the other side, Artemis!" he croaked, trying to mask the nervousness in his voice.

Artemis peered from the loft.

"But there's . . . there's no *hay* there, Diego! And it's thirty feet, at least!"

Even in the shadows he could see her blanch, her beautiful brown eyes widen as she looked up to him.

"Afraid?" he asked softly, then again, louder, triumphantly. His voice rang through the loft, scattering the wakened swallows.

Artemis stared back at him, her full lips parted breathily. For a moment Diego wanted to seize her, to kiss her roughly.

Instead, he leapt from the rafter, into the still, stifling air of the loft.

Later, the doctor would tell Diego's father how lucky the boy was to have survived such a fall. Artemis' guess at the height of the rafters had been woefully short. Roger and Endymion had measured the distance by geometry and marked it at forty-five feet—the kind of fall that could kill the less fortunate, the less resilient.

When Diego hit the ground, his ankle turned and snapped beneath him. Almost seventeen years later to the day, he would lose that leg in an explosion, under the service of Arouet and the Guard. But always until that moment a dull, watery pain would vex his ankle, making it difficult to walk, especially when the weather changed.

He would still feel the old barn-loft throbbing on the day the surgeon took the saw to his leg.

But in the aftermath of his jump, as the swallows and barn mice scattered and a nervous calf moaned and kicked in a nearby stall, Diego did not know the extent of his injuries. All that he understood was that the searing pain in his foot did nothing to diminish his victory. With all his strength and bravado he stood, brushing the hay and manure from his clothing. Triumphantly, he looked toward the loft, toward his wide-eyed cousin, who peered down from a parapet of bales.

Artemis turned away and vanished into the high dark.

Diego had won, by will and sheer recklessness, over his cousin's wit and common sense. He remembered that afternoon all his life.

Remembered it almost two decades later, as he and Artemis vied with each other at the Absence's edge, before a band of rebels and a puzzled Willie Melmoth.

* * *

By the morning of the third day, everyone in the search party had begun to feel a little reckless, a little foolish. Rousseau had stopped taking Justin St. Hyle's money at cards, and Willie Melmoth had fallen from watchfulness into hour-long naps on a grassy bank overlooking the Absence. It was obvious, to Artemis, to Rousseau, to threescore rebel cavalry, that Solomon was not returning. A further stay in the Borders simply whiled away resources and patience.

On the third morning Artemis sat in the bullet-riddled poplar, looking out over the Absence, clutching the tattered remnants of the target canteen.

Diego paced below her, dark hair untied and cascading wildly over his shoulders. She could see the little bald spot at the crown of his head, strangely vulnerable and monastic amid all that bluster and violence.

Of course, he disagreed with her. Didn't he always? And after all, Solomon was his brother, and he was more inclined to persist in the search, such as it was.

Such as it was. An inconclusive wait beside an inconclusive phenomenon, its object an inconclusive priest who had fled when his powers might most have availed.

Let him *stay* lost. Waiting by the Absence had reminded her how much the mansion side of her family bored and annoyed her. Better by far to return to Arcady. To carry Mina away—by force, if necessary—and let the mansion fall apart if it was meant to fall.

Artemis dearly loved her younger sister, and Aunt Morgana was a good sort, as well. There was also something she could not place about Diego that drew her back time and again to contend and bicker with him. But as for the old dead Hawkens and their sons Solomon and Endymion . . .

Diego was the best of them, unetherized by theology and metaphysics. Yet even he was grumbling and whining like a piqued aristocrat, now that Artemis had declared the search over and ordered a return to the rebel camp.

She knew Diego. He was not done with wrangling.

"Leave me two men, Artemis," Diego insisted, breaking her revery with a voice too authoritative, too loud.

He was staring up at her, arms folded over his broad chest.

"Leave me Rousseau," he said. "And Willie Melmoth."

Artemis shifted on the bare branch. "What do you intend to do with them, Diego? Circle the whole infernal Absence?"

His smile was hard and brittle as flint.

"Just leaping from the rafters, Cousin," he replied in a low voice.

"And taking them with you. Hawkens are all alike."

Diego's gaze flickered away from hers, found a focus at the heart of the Absence. "Perhaps you're right," he conceded. "It is a waste of venture and bravery."

Artemis nodded.

She didn't believe his concession for a moment.

As the troopers saddled their horses and prepared for the ride, she remained in the tree, her eye on Diego and that Melmoth boy who followed him like an aide-de-camp.

Diego was likely to try anything. To wrest power from her in a mutiny (it would fail) or to commandeer a brace of men to follow him on a harebrained jaunt around the Absence (which would fail as well).

Whatever he tried, it would be reckless and no doubt completely irrational.

And it certainly would bear watching.

* * *

The morning was half over by the time the troop was ready to move. Deliberately, the column of horse slipped through the soundless woods, winding a path amid leafless trees and birdless branches.

Artemis rode at the back of the column with Rousseau, her eyes attuned to every shift and movement in the forest. Diego was fully aware where she was, and knew she was watching him.

"So be it," he muttered to Juno, as he guided the mare through the tangles at the edge of the path, the nearest rebel rider a good ten yards away. "After all, I'm not my cousin's prisoner. Whatever I do . . . she can't stop me."

The path circled the encampment in a wide, ascending arc. Not ten minutes from the site, the covering of trees fell away into sudden and surprising bare country, a wide swath of treeless plain that led down to the Absence itself, visible at scarcely a quarter mile's distance.

The ground was stunted, razed, as though a glacier had passed over it. White salt covered the plains and steamed unnaturally from the harrowed landscape.

A Hell of our own making. The phrase came vaguely to Diego's memory. Something from the Text, from the memorized creeds of his childhood. Not that he believed in the Hell of the Text. Nor very much in the Text itself, for that matter.

But so it might have looked, that *hell of our own making.*

He smiled grimly. He was about to make hell out of it.

When the point rider—a Corporal Manasseh—was lost in the trees around a bend in the trail, Diego slowed his mare. Willie Melmoth passed him, guiding the ungainly wagon. Then Corporal Coban and Justin St. Hyle. He didn't know the others.

Diego steadied himself in the saddle, hugged Juno's flanks with the pressure of his knees.

When Artemis and Rousseau were not ten yards from him, Diego whistled and yanked the reins toward the Absence. He kicked Juno with his cavalry spurs, felt the spiked wheel drive and dig. The mare sprang from the trail as if she had been ignited, racing in full gallop down the crusted slope of the artificial plain.

Above the hoofbeats Diego heard a solitary, plaintive cry from Artemis. It was lost at once in a persistent grinding sound that seemed to be rising from the center of the Absence.

Do not think now, Diego told himself.

Ride.

The long, confident strides of the mare propelled him over the rocky approach to the Absence. Somebody was coming behind him, pursuing. Diego did not look back. He broke through the edge of the Borders like a diver plunging into tranquil water. Currents of fire and light jangled around his face.

Now the Absence lurched toward him as though it had come unmoored and rushed to meet him. Diego lowered his head and crouched in the saddle like a rider in a rain of bullets.

Juno snorted and bucked, and an uncanny cold rushed over the both of them. Diego opened his eyes to gray cloud and swimming light.

He whistled to the horse, a low and soothing passage from one of the Hymns—he could not remember which one. Juno calmed beneath him, the first building leapt into view, and Diego, his hand and heart surprisingly steady, took a deep breath and guided his mare toward the distant sound of machinery, a lone traveler through the outskirts of chaos.

Thin tendrils of crimson-laced leutha thickened as Juno galloped toward the grinding, thrashing clamor at the core of the Absence. Her rider held tightly, his face against her mane-swept neck.

All around Diego, like a mariner's sky before a storm, lightning flickered and blazed. A hot, powerful wind coursed over his face, as though he had ridden into a furnace.

And yet he persevered. Shutting down all his thoughts, all his senses save hearing, he rode his startled mare into the whirling mouth of the Abyss, bent toward its center and guided by a strong knowing: Solomon was ahead of him, perhaps not far away.

I am like Saint Milton, Diego told himself. *Tumbling into chaos to . . . to rescue the world and myself.*

He startled. *Do not think,* he reminded himself. *It always makes for trouble.*

The emptiness of the Absence reverberated, echoing with his thoughts. *Do not think,* somebody whispered to Diego's left, and then, nearby and to his right, another voice repeated the caution, louder this time and more urgent, more shrill.

Where are they? Diego asked himself, then tried to cast down the thought, to tumble into a serene, effective blankness. But the thought was in the air, and as he wrangled with his own, jarred intelligence, Juno came to a stop beneath him. Nervously, she sank her muzzle into the pooling clouds and grazed deeply on some obscure, invisible plant.

Diego leaned forward in the saddle. The place was familiar: a fence row rising out of the mist nearby, a pair of branching maples long and far to his left. A field that sloped down to a solitary thin row of cedars, outlined against the leutha sky like gnarled towers of bordermetal.

The ground seemed to tilt in front of him, and rising from the mist, strange at this juncture of autumn, he heard a chorus of crickets.

Nightshade Vale. Suddenly he remembered it.

He was standing in Nightshade Vale, where the ambush had cost him his leg.

A man on horseback emerged from the fog, raising a gloved hand in greeting. Diego recognized the gait of the approaching gelding before he could make out the man in the saddle. Then the red uniform of the rider was defined in gray light.

Tricorn. Epaulets. Muddy black bluchers.

It was Major Hyperion Werther. Diego's old commander.

But Werther had fallen in the East, in this very vale two years ago.

And then the smell of the charnel house, the faint sweet stench of the battlefield graveside and the sanitary corps. The uniform sagged on the shoulders of the rider, the head lolled crazily, and light glinted off the wrist bones of the gloved raised hand.

The Major looked at Diego with eyes as dull as coins.

Set up position on the right flank, Captain, he ordered, in a voice so dry and lifeless that it lifted leaves from the foggy bottom, stirring them in the fetid air with a forlorn, papery rustle. *Set up position. There's a brace of pickets behind the cedars.*

* * *

For two years, Nightshade Vale had been a place on a map, a gloomy spot in the nest of Diego's nightmares.

But now, in the midst of the Absence, the nightmare was happening again.

The same Nightshade Vale had risen from the mist now, the same fences, rows of trees, the same scattered arrangement of red-jacketed troops. And now a ghostly Hyperion Werther approached Diego with the same orders, the same deployments, that had cost him a company and a leg.

Now, for the first time in his memory, Diego Hawken was afraid.

Clutching Juno's reins tightly, he guided her up the slope, away from the motioning revenant, away from the Vale and the cedars and the prospects of ambush and death. Diego turned the big mare toward the hulking buildings that had dotted the horizon in his approach to the Vale, and Juno surged beneath him like a weathered efficient piece of machinery. Together, horse and rider rode toward the distant cityscape, as the sun, green and elliptical, burst from behind the clouds like a light caught in a bottle.

Coward! the revenant screamed behind him. *Traitor!*

Diego heard the words. He would have ignored them if he could. But three decades had schooled him in a soldier's instinct, in a warrior's pride, and though a part of his mind cried out *Fool! Do not think!* he turned anyway.

A pale, spectral company had assembled in the bottom of the Vale. Some were his fellows from the old campaign. Others were more recent, their wounds dripping and fresh.

Bolingbroke Norwood was there, the top of his head sheared away by the rebel bullet at L'Overture's abatis.

Take the position, the ghastly commander urged, his dead voice rising into a breathless whine.

Torn between wisdom and honor, between fear of the dark and fear of cowardice, Diego steered his mare toward the leftmost end of the column . . .

And as it had done before, in the Luvan twilight of three seasons back, the stand of cedar blossomed with gunfire.

No *brace of pickets.* Twenty rifles at least, all in the hands of rebel marksmen.

And again the guardsmen began to drop, as snipers, perched in the far maples, added their guns to the fusillade. Bolingbroke, his arms splayed toward an indifferent heaven, fell forward in an explosion of black blood. Calvin Newton, Luther Locke—men he remembered from earlier campaigns, their names rushing back to him like a volley of bullets—fell in the withering crossfire.

Diego rose in the saddle and shouted. He drew his pistol, then thought better: he could never hit anything with a gun, anyway.

He put away the pistol and drew his sword. The feeling was strangely jubilant: the ambush had taken from him all choices but to fight, and when he could fight he was free, actual. He was at warring peace. With a whoop, he guided his mare toward the middle of the assembling, kneeling ranks . . .

And then a bullet crashed into his leg.

His one *good* leg.

Diego reeled. He clutched vaguely at the saddle horn, trying to gather his balance. The hot ball burrowed into his knee, the searing pain he remembered from the last battle rushing to meet him like the smoke from the rebel guns.

Ruined! his thoughts screamed, with the dry, condemning voice of Hyperion Werther.

Halt. Lame.

A poor Saint Milton he had turned out to be. Legless in the dark cloud redounding.

For a moment the green sky reeled overhead, and then he was falling, falling from Juno's back, the clouds and the bottle-bright air swimming above him beneath a strangely artificial sun. He remembered nothing else.

CHAPTER 27

"The rebels think Arouet had *something* to do with it," Khole conceded.

Solomon, sweating and tired, grasped the angel's wrist. Khole drew him up the rockface to a little crag where the scorched remnants of a nest lay scattered across the dry stone. The air was thick with smoke, with the faint whiff of frankincense, and Solomon rested himself in the faint, seductive fragrances, staring across the plains below him.

Darkling plains. What they had called them in seminary. Swept with confused alarms of struggle and flight.

"And his intentions were nothing more than greedy," the angel continued, his bright wings fanning away the leuthan mist until the air around the old nest was fresh, breathable. "After all, Arouet did not care if he undermined all lands, desolate or green. He wanted only to draw forth metal for his machineries, to transform everything—commerce and society, the whole unscrupulous universe, if need be. For his looms and mills, his mines and arsenals, bring more to his coffers than a nation of fishermen and farmers.

"It may be true that Arouet's mining dislodged something. Shook something that had anchored the Absences for years. But Arouet is really no more to blame than . . . Ezra ben Ezra and his fanaticism. L'Overture and his bloodthirstiness . . ."

"And this," Solomon interrupted, gesturing toward the plains below, "is the shape of our future?"

If it was, it looked grim indeed. It was a featureless plain, bare and brown. At the edge of Solomon's sight, something glowed red and orange and menacing—volcanic, perhaps, or brushfire.

If this was the future—how the continent would appear once the Absences had covered and passed over it and finally exhausted themselves—then it would be best to end it here. Why, the rockface was sheer, and the forbidding ground below almost inviting. To fall would be effortless, painless except for a brief, shocking moment followed by darkness, by sweet oblivion.

"And it would be too easy, too conventional, to tell you that such is the coward's way," Khole murmured.

Solomon startled. It was unsettling, the way all things in the Absence—whether the kindly phoenix or the sinister voice—read his thoughts.

"It would be too easy," Khole said again, his dark eyes intent on his despairing companion. "Because that is *not* the coward's way out, when the body fears death so much, so deeply. But it is still a foolish way."

"There is a better one," Solomon agreed—at first with uncertainty, but with growing confidence after he had said the words, after he had aired the statement and could not take it back. He was not sure what it was or could be, but yes, somewhere in the depths of his believing, he knew that a better way was there.

"Tell me," Khole whispered.

His eyes on the darkling plain, Solomon heard the angel settle behind him in a rustle of robe and wings. Khole's dark hand rested on his shoulder a moment, and Solomon felt an electrical warmth pass through him. Suddenly he was alert, sustained and peaceful, and his thoughts came with rapidity and clarity.

It must have been how Marcus felt when the green hand of the dryad touched his.

"Perhaps Arouet's mines are not to blame for the movement in the Absences, Khole. But perhaps his machineries—his mills and shovels and great looms—had a part in it, with all their crashing and grinding and tearing away."

"Perhaps." Khole's gaze turned toward Solomon, the deep gold of his eyes passing through him, seeing into his very depth and nature.

Solomon wanted to hide, to avert his eyes: the stare of the angel seemed to unmask the dark regions of his thoughts, his own selfishness and preoccupation. For a moment, he flushed and turned his back on Khole: little had changed—the landscape inside him was a darkling plain.

"What you do not know," the angel said, "is the nature of Arouet's machinery."

"Then *you* tell *me*," Solomon urged.

Khole rose from the lip of the fragrant nest, his bright wings brushing through ash, through charred branches and straw.

"Come with me," he said, guiding his uncertain companion down from the heights, onto the dreadful plain. "Come with me into the ruins. We will speak of machineries there. And of magic."

It seemed to be in mourning, this landscape they passed through on their way toward the distant skyline. It was no ordinary ruined town toward which they progressed. Solomon recognized the signs, the landscape.

They wandered west along a river that could be nothing but the Alph, past a shallow, rushing falls and a long chain of sandbars, littering the river like untenanted barges.

It was terrain Solomon knew, from his books and from the stories of his father and Aunt Morgana: it was the westward approaches to Ville.

Ville had been a city of substantial size in the early times before history and recollection. Border miners knew her streets, her Absence-ravaged bridges, the convolution of wire and bordermetal that littered the southern shore of the Alph.

Great she had been once, but with great violence, it seemed, she had been thrown down. Except for the rubble, the streets of stone and the gutters that ran with refuse and rusted water, there was nothing in Ville that pointed to life, past or present.

Here from the eastern approaches, three collapsed towers loomed against the sun-reddened skies—the now-dead heart of the wasted city. Khole, pacing ahead of Solomon on the paved road, turned and beckoned. Solomon had no choice: uneasily, he followed the angel toward a honeycomb of overlapping roads, ramps, and bridges, toward dappled shadows in the midst of a foggy sun.

As Solomon stepped into the shade of the first overpass, a crumbling stone structure that beetled over a road that dwindled to a footpath then to nothing in the humid, musty dark, he heard the sound of machinery again.

The regular, mechanical grinding of a loom or a mill or a reaper rumbled through the network of metal and stone like a monstrous and impersonal heartbeat. Solomon paused and listened, wrapping his greatcoat more tightly around his shoulders in a gesture not of cold, but of deep unease.

In all his times at the edge of the Borders and within their shifting country, he had heard this grinding sound ten, maybe a dozen times. And it had always seemed distant, safe in removal and faintness. But suddenly, once he had stepped into the Absence, the sound was there at all times, as regular as pulse.

"The machinery," he said, as Khole turned to regard him. "You said you would explain."

The sound grew louder as Khole passed from the collection of shadows into the light of the ruined city, its opened boulevards and side streets illumined by a faint, amber sun. Solomon followed from the shade of the overpass, blinking stupidly as the full light struck his face.

The streets extended as far as he could see—empty except for intermittent piles of rubble, heaps of scrap metal, ganglia of wire. The battered facades of the buildings leaned into the boulevards, their shattered windows opening into emptiness, into nothingness. A dry wind whistled through the facades and alleys, and scraps of yellowed, dried paper, crumbled by centuries' neglect, flitted over the streets like moths in a hot night wind.

Khole walked to an intersection of two main thoroughfares. The wind caught him, rustling his white-and-gold robes. The pinions of his wings shuddered in the amber light, and he turned to Solomon, beckoning again, standing beneath a gas lamp that bent over the street corner, the light long dead in its abandoned globe.

"Do you remember that passage in the Text," the angel began, "about the *porches of iron and silver*?"

Solomon nodded. Quietly, he spoke the lines from memory:

"Some Sons of Los surround the Passions with porches of iron & silver,
Creating form & beauty around the dark regions of sorrow,
Giving to airy nothing a name and a habitation delightful . . ."

Khole nodded. "The very lines, indeed. What do you make of them, Scholar?"

Solomon winced at the title. "Artists. The lines are generally taken to refer to artists, who take the airy nothing of thought and spirit and render it tangible. Tangible and beautiful. Like Mina does, and like Morgana . . ."

His thoughts raced back to Arcady, but Khole's clear voice tunneled through his revery, loud above the grinding of the distant machinery.

"But all the *airy nothing*, all things of the soul and spirit, are not delightful," Khole admonished.

"I need no angel to tell me that," Solomon declared.

"When Arouet established those machines on the lip of the Absences, he did so for his own selfish reasons. Mill and loom, forge and foundry—all were designed to process the bordermetal his gatherers found in the Borders.

" 'Tis an old story—one we all know—but even then the Absences were at the brink of dislodging themselves, welling and ebbing and covering things that strayed or were built too close to their edges.

"One by one, the Absences swallowed Arouet's machineries. As the mills and forges vanished in the clouds, they changed, and not in appearance only. The Absence altered the machineries, as it alters the thoughts and souls of those who pass through it.

"You will find mills and looms nearby, but they no longer grind nor weave the things for which they were once intended, having been pressed into darker service."

Solomon stood beneath the lamp now, gazing up skeptically at the smoky glass. "Darker service?" he asked.

"As the Absence eats away at the landscape," Khole explained, "dissolving the countryside, it also . . . corrodes the inner landscapes of those who come into contact with it. It is what happened to your uncle Innocent many years ago, and it is what happened to the Blights. How else could you account for them?"

"The Blights," Solomon replied. "The Absence eats their memory. It eats their hold on good and . . . and convivial things."

"That it does," Khole agreed. "And Innocent floats in the midst of the Absences—sometimes vaguely himself, but mostly a form for the cloud that consumed him. Consumed him from the inside."

Solomon shuddered. Innocent had become what he beheld.

"But there is Enith Moneta as well," Khole reminded him. "Who had, at the core of herself, something the Absence could not fragment or disperse.

"And yet it wears away at . . . at *everything*, Solomon. At *everyone*. Corporeal and incorporeal. Body and spirit."

"And the machines?"

"The machines," Khole replied, "have become the conduits between the two realms. Or so the Absences have made them. Mills that grind the substantial into the ethereal, looms that weave the spiritual into the corporeal."

"It sounds far-fetched," Solomon protested, leaning heavily against the lamppost. "Like . . . like some kind of allegory."

"Like the Text?"

Solomon nodded. "Like the Text. But these are still real machines. Not images in a book. And the Absence has taken them over? And uses them to perpetuate and extend itself?"

Khole nodded.

"Then the solution seems . . . pretty clear," Solomon ventured. "If the Absences have been unleashed by Arouet's underground machinery, perhaps some hope lies in destroying those machines. In stopping them from unmooring other Absences, even though some damage has been done already. At least that way, when the unmoored Absences finally dissolve, those that remain will be stationary, moored in balance. As they used to be."

He looked at Khole eagerly. The angel was crouched beside him, overlooking the smoldering wasteland with a gaze at once abstracted and intent.

"It can be done," Khole agreed finally, his auburn hair lifting in a hot Absence wind.

"I'll do it," Solomon declared. He stopped and caught his breath, surprised at his own boldness.

But after all, it was for the lot of them. For Morgana and Mina and Endymion, whom he had deserted in a dissolving house. He would make amends to them, to everyone, like . . .

Like Saint Milton returning into time and space.

"If I have to dismantle them," he proclaimed, "wheel by wheel, beam and cog and shuttle, I will do so."

He blushed at his own bravado. He meant very deeply every word he said, but still a small part of him, schooled in the skepticism and irony of Lambeth, laughed at him for meaning it.

"Would that it were that easy," Khole replied. "But remember the nature of this machinery. Part wood and metal, yes, but part ether and spirit as well. You could destroy the frame, the treadles and shuttles . . . but it takes far more to destroy the machinery.

"It takes magic, Solomon Hawken. It takes most powerful magic."

Solomon leaned against the lamppost. This piece of news surprised him, dismayed him. After a long silence, he laughed bitterly. "You have come to the wrong source for magic, Khole. That is, if you expect *me* to lend a hand in it."

"I am not so certain about that," the angel replied gently. "You have come a long way from faltering in a rowboat. A long way as well from abandoning a house at midnight."

"I am not afraid," Solomon agreed. "But neither am I . . ."

Khole gestured, and a faint green light hovered like a glory over the surface of the lamp. On the warm wind the angel rose—two, now three feet off the ground—until he cupped the gas globe in his dark and delicate hands.

"You remember well what you read, Solomon," he observed. "But do you remember this?"

The globe flickered with a new, internal light. White and golden, it was, the color of Khole's robes and of distant springs. Solomon peered into the glowing heart of the lamp and saw the forsaken country at the Absence's edge, the Blight encampment he had left in a flurry of adorations after he had duped Constantine and the others.

"I remember it, Khole," he murmured. "But why . . ."

"Watch," Khole commanded, and Solomon saw himself standing in front of the assembled boys, the sleight of hand and feigned incantations—words and motions he had scarcely believed—that had occasioned his freedom from Blight captivity.

He did not like to remember it. It was fraud at its worst, a confidence scam on innocent, illiterate boys. When he had fooled Constantine and the lot, Solomon had believed only that his words could veil and deceive and entangle.

But now, in the globe of the gaslight, he saw quite another scene—a glade in the depths of the forest, framed by the frosted glass as neatly and quietly as the snow-scene paperweights he remembered from his childhood. Over and around the globe his own voice weaved and sang and coaxed, as though the woods itself had filled with his speaking.

They were the words Solomon had used to dupe his Blight captors:

words of freezing and cold and gelid water, of the saint forming a living man from the icy mud. But now, for the first time, Solomon saw the genuine magic his words had effected.

The forest in the glass iced over. The pendulous branches of the evergreens sagged farther and farther still with a white, clinging glaze. One tree after another, deciduous and evergreen, shivered, cracked, exploded as the water in their sap froze solid and expanded.

The Alph, visible barely at the edge of the lamp, moved sluggishly as the cold congealed its waters.

The forest was freezing to the chanted music of the Text.

"*My* words?" Solomon whispered incredulously.

"Words of the Text," Khole corrected. "Given voice by you in a jest, a ruse."

"But those boys would have taken me . . ." Solomon began.

"To exactly where you stand now," Khole interrupted with a low laugh. "Despite your fears, you have ended up every bit as deep into the Absence as the most adventurous of Blights has ever wandered."

Despite himself, Solomon smiled.

"It's the way it was meant to be," Khole explained.

"But what about the words?" Solomon asked. "How did I do . . . what I did?"

"Not you," Khole explained. "But the Text. It's the way of magic. The mage or the priest mouths the words in the Absence or in the Borders, and the words do their work against the world itself, shaping or bending or breaking the physics as the words see fit."

"The seminary dismissed such talk as old wives' tales," Solomon mused. "Neo-orthodoxy at its most . . . most orthodox. Extremism. But I suppose it isn't."

Khole merely shrugged. "The trees are frozen."

Solomon looked long into the globe. "And the river itself was icy when I crossed it with Enith Moneta," he agreed. But the seminarians said . . ."

"The seminarians say many things," Khole interrupted. "What have you seen of their magic?"

Solomon thought. Little binding spells. Wardings and summons of peace. Unreliable and temporary.

Nothing like this blast of incanted ice.

Solomon smiled grimly.

For once in his life, he had been a mage.

"So tell me, Khole," Solomon asked, lifting his eyes at last from the scene in the globe, a new resolution in their depths, doubling and redoubling like an optical transmission line. "What is this magic, and how may I learn to use it?"

* * *

"The principle of spell-casting," Khole explained, "lies more in listening than in speaking."

The two of them, angel and priest, stood in the rubble of what must have been an enormous, multitiered structure—a strange, geometric pavilion, webbed by metallic stairwells and a huge, encircling mezzanine, that drew little or nothing from the buildings surrounding it. No doubt an anomaly when Ville was a thriving town, the building remained unusual, even in ruins.

Judging from the kiosks and cubicles that lined its bare bottom floor, the pavilion was once a marketplace, a domed agora in which the great commerce of Ville had flowed hectically. But now it was like a heath in the desert, a parched land where only the wind bargained and haggled.

Khole seated himself on the bottom of one of the stairwells, and clutching the black, enameled railing, stared into the skylight above them. Solomon followed the angel's gaze to the jagged glass, the latticework of metal beams bent and broken by the impact of some incredible force.

"Magic comes by hearing," the angel pronounced dramatically. "And hearing comes through the Text alone, muddled and ruinous though it may be. Despite your magical gifts, Solomon Hawken, you have not learned to listen, to attend."

"All I ever did in seminary was listen," Solomon snapped. Despite himself, he was irritated at Khole, at this pompous and aggressive pronouncement. "And I've listened to more of the Text than *you* know, brother angel."

Khole laughed. "I know your seminaries," he said. "I have seen them in your stiffness and skepticism.

"What I have learned above all is a deep respect for your courage and spirit. Most men would still be sleeping after your course of study."

Solomon flushed. Part of him agreed with the angel, but Khole was talking about the seminary! About his life's work! Dismissing his studies with a jest, no matter how soft and compassionate!

"I know you have cast hundreds of spells before," Khole continued. "The conjuries with Marcus Chatterton were only the first."

"For what good they have done," Solomon replied bitterly, seating himself on the cold metal step above the angel. A gray wind dove through the shattered skylight, bearing a faint whiff of ashes. A forlorn leaf of yellowed paper—a page from a book, perhaps—swirled in a whirlpool of air and dust like a small bark caught in a maelstrom.

"They have done more good than you reckoned," Khole said quietly. "But like the gifts of so many, your gifts came with an accompanying wound.

"Think of the strong man in the story, his slow thoughts unable to bear the weight his mighty arms can lift. Or the dryad, who in her great beauty and greater stealth is anchored forever to a parcel of ground within eyesight of a solitary, special tree. Diego is boggled by abstract matters; Endymion is consumed with them. Artemis and Jasmina are eaten as well, each with her own illness.

"Your gifts are not without a cost as well. For you could not believe your magic unless . . . someone else believed it for you."

Solomon leaned forward.

You have to listen! Listen before you talk. It is the first thing that you learn there.

The words of the Dirty Nun rushed back to him, and after them, the words of Constantine the Blight.

First listen, then talk. It is the bestest rule.

"I am listening," Solomon said.

Khole regarded him with a dark, glittering gaze. "That night in the lime-tree bower," the angel continued, "when Marcus Chatterton neither shared nor saw your visions."

"What of it?" Even now, from this remove, Solomon did not like to remember that night.

"You gave up after that," Khole said. "Both of you stood at the edge of new magic that night, and on a dozen nights before and since, new magic waited for you, extending its hands in the shadow of dryadic dolmens, in the replicating mirrors of your boyhood home, and most often, most urgently, in the pages of the very Text you studied—the very Text you claim to know as well . . . as the angels do."

Solomon blushed at the angel's gentle, ironic smile.

"Marcus embraced that magic," the angel said quietly, "even though he never reached it. Fate, perhaps, or something more malign, touched him one night in a boat on Pontus Tarn."

"Where my spells could not avail him," Solomon muttered hotly, standing and ascending the metal steps. Halfway up the flight he stopped.

He had no idea where he was going. It was running—running from his failures, from the night on the lake and the drowning boy. But he had no idea where his running would take him.

"Listen!" the angel called after him, his clear voice sharp in the vacant air. Solomon turned on the rusted steps, regarded the dark, glittering eyes of the angel.

Listen before you talk. It is the first thing that you learn there.

"Your spells failed," Khole urged, this time more softly. "But that was not your fault. You were no more to be blamed than . . . than Marcus was for drowning. And yet he carried his death with him to the bottom of the Tarn, while you have carried yours through almost thirty more years of breathing."

The angel paused, letting his words sink in.

"Very well," Solomon said, painfully and at last. "How do I . . . recover from this death?"

"There's recovery in new magic," Khole said. "And healing. And this magic has been at hand since first you reached for it in the early classes at Lambeth, since you saw it trapped and beckoning in the facing mirrors of Arcady."

Solomon sat again. "It's all bewildering. All double-talk. The spells failed. They continue to fail, and no amount of saying makes that otherwise."

"But listening does," the angel corrected. "And seeing."

Khole would show Solomon the ways of magic, there in the cavernous ruins of Ville. Not how to cast the spell as much as see its result: how, for example, incantations of warding and cold might not fall together in a shield of ice around the caster, but might instead freeze a shallow tributary of a nearby river, ice-locking a barge that was otherwise destined to be broken up in the rapids. Or how, perhaps, a cantation of healing might not heal the wen on your shoulder, but prosper instead the crops of your neighbor, bringing his children health at the harvest and through the privations of winter.

For magic has intent and volition. And the art of the mage is alignment with the will of magic, rather than forcing the magic to do his bidding. The difficulty lay in the purity of his motive, which magic, it seemed, respected above intellect or will.

They started small at first, angel and student there in the ruined cenotaph of Ville. It was as though the abandoned buildings of the city, no more than hollow frames for generations, awaited words and magic to fill them.

"Simple," Khole began. "Start simple. And first, above all, listen."

Solomon paused, cleared his senses, and listened.

To the creak of the rusted metal steps under his feet.

To the wind as it whistled through the desolate skylight.

To the skitter of rats and abandoned papers over the abandoned floor of this structure.

To the ever-present thrashing of machinery deep in the bowels of the Absence.

Solomon listened to all of these. And it seemed to him then that each of them asked for the same thing—the stair and the wind, the litter and vermin, and even the ominous grinding machinery deep in the dreadful abyss. They wanted to be freed. Renewed.

Below him, the angel's voice rose in soft singing:

"Calling the lapsed Soul,
And weeping in the evening dew:
That might controll
The starry pole:
And fallen fallen light renew."

"Yes," Solomon replied. "That's it! I knew it before you sang."

"You knew," the angel agreed. "Everything under the Absence cries for restoration, renewal. Now, try your spells. Use the words your seminary taught you. Long ago, in Lambeth. . . ."

The angel's voice underscored all sound. It was the voice and breath in the forsaken heart of the Absence.

Solomon closed his eyes. His thoughts raced over the Text, the hundreds of obscure, labyrinthine lines he had learned from Father Ezekiel Gordon, from the Right Reverend Catullus Wollestonecraft.

No. The angel had said to *start simple.*

So he began with a Hymn. In silence he imagined the illumined page of the Hymnal.

Light blue. What was the word? *Azure.*

"Enough semantics," the angel urged, reading his thoughts. "Try the spell."

His thoughts jogged back to the Hymnal page. Solomon recreated it in his mind. Azure. The willows draping over the margins, the figures male and female intertwined like the First Humans in the lower right-hand corner.

There. The page was clear in his recollection.

Again he listened. The regular thrashing of the machinery provided a cadence, like a metronome ticking somewhere below him. The wind lulled, and all he could hear now was the distant machinery.

Still, expectant, Solomon matched his breathing to the measure of the distant machine. Soon, listening more deeply, he could hear his heart slow, the beat coalescing with machinery, with breath.

Now all creation drummed to the same rhythm. Now was the word's time, and the Hymn on the azure page rose spontaneously from Solomon's lips.

"In futurity
I prophetic see,
That the earth from sleep,
(Grave the sentence deep)

Shall arise and seek
For her maker meek:
And the desart wild
Become a garden mild."

The Hymn passed over him and vanished. It trailed away in a dozen echoes, scattering through the Absence and over the wreckage of buildings.

Solomon smiled, filled with a new assurance. He opened his eyes, the child in him half expecting a green garden in the place of the forsaken ruins of Ville.

But the same landscape stretched before him. As desolate, as barren and bleak to the eye, as it had been when he entered it, when he had begun to conjure.

Still a *desart wild.*

Where was the magic in this?

Solomon staggered on the creaking stairway, started to speak . . .

"No!" Khole snapped, his black eyes blazing. "*Listen* first! *Then* speak!"

Again Solomon attuned his ears to the landscape around him.

"Remember," the angel prompted, this time more quietly. "Not all listening is done with the ears."

A paradox. Solomon started to question, to scoff, but a wiser impulse stilled him. Quietly, sinking into the deepest calm he could muster, he opened *all* his senses.

The landscape bare. Gray and brown.

All silent, except the gnashing of the machine.

The air warm, sharp with the smell of ash and creosote and . . .

The faint hint of honeysuckle.

"See?" Khole asked, gliding to the top of the steps where he stood on a broken railing, white wings fanning the misted air. "The smell of flowers in the deep abyss. Something has changed. Somewhere among us, the fallen light *has* been renewed.

"Listen with all the senses, Solomon. And believe."

"Believe?"

"That the magic has worked. That despite the first evidence of your senses, despite what you desired, the magic has accomplished what *it* desired. If not directly in front of you, then assuredly in another country, another time."

"I see." Solomon frowned. "That's all?"

"All for now. More and more, as you practice and believe, the magic will manifest its power to you."

Solomon sat on the rusty steps. "So help me understand. When I . . . played at magic before Constantine and the assembled Blights, my words effected the *will* of that magic in . . . in another part of the world."

"In southern Urthona," Khole agreed. "Where the woods iced over and the sap in the trees froze and exploded above your brother Diego. Delivered a besieged squadron of guardsmen from certain death."

"*I* did that?"

"The magic did that," Khole corrected. "And among those guardsmen was your brother Diego."

"Who is now . . . trapped somewhere in the Absence? Little good the magic did him in the end."

"But it is not the end," the angel insisted. "And you must learn your magic quickly, for his sake and for Endymion's. For the first task that lies before you is their rescue. From the wreckage of that town in the distance."

Khole pointed off to the west, but Solomon did not follow the gesture. His head lowered, his eyes on the cracked pavement at his feet, he blanched at the angel's news.

He had tried a rescue before—one stormy night on Pontus Tarn . . .

"But that was then," Khole said, again reading his thoughts, "and you have dwelt in it for over a score of years. Now every hour is indispensable.

"In the space of a breath you can redeem those years."

"Like Saint Milton?" Solomon asked.

"Like Saint Milton."

* * *

And so instruction began. Solomon tried one spell and another, marshaling his formidable knowledge of the Text and saying those words over the fallen scaffolding of the skylight beneath which he and Khole rested, over the wind that plummeted through its broken glass, over the marred and clouded light in the sky.

Nothing around him seemed changed by his words. The Absence had fragmented and dissolved far too many things. Still, Khole taught Solomon to rest in the belief that the change was done—by the will of the magic, and not his own.

"It will happen," the angel assured him. "And though not in the way you intended, it will happen in a way that will avail you, perhaps more thoroughly than you have knowledge or strength to expect."

And Solomon, despite years of training to the contrary, found that he believed the angel.

CHAPTER 28

For the first time in its confused and pastoral existence, Arcady was an armed camp.

Artemis' rebels manned the house. Green in every window of the mansion by Mina's extinguished lamps and cold candles. The sun glinting down on gun barrels like light on bordermetal in the deepest forest.

In the middle of guns and vigilance, Garrick was almost lost. Pacing the Great Hall, he watched himself in the puzzle of mirrors—a faceted thing in a cloudy, infinite depth. He could see the back of his head in the reflections. Could see his profile.

And even though all the angles were covered, Garrick Hawken did not know where he stood.

Was he a prisoner? a guest? a host in his family estate?

He was the only guardsman at Arcady, left by Diego because someone familiar with the mansion and its eccentricities should be on hand, on watch. The rebels, ordered to truce by the Lady, regarded him skeptically. They were eyes in the hall, eyes in the green shade of the topiary. They spoke in grunts and murmurs, occasional nods passing for *good morning* or *good afternoon.* The third floor of the house was bolted against him.

From the second-floor balcony adjoining the rooms where he stayed—his uncle Diego's quarters for family meetings or for refuge from the domestic wars with Allegra over his estate at Shiveleigh—Garrick watched the soldiers set about their elaborate defenses: green lines by the East Woods, by the orchard and mill house. Sentries amid the verdigris and bronze of Mina's statues, chevaux-de-frise on the long, level grounds south of Grandfather Atreus' lake.

For two days Garrick dined alone, scraping together bread and moldy cheese from the cobwebbed pantry, salt beef from the brine barrel in the cellar. He would meet the rebels on the stairs, would turn his head.

Then, in the dining hall, after the troops had eaten, he found a full plate set for him amid gutted candles: potatoes and bread and side meat—a soldier's ration, cold from waiting but tasty enough. A second meal followed on the next night, the same fare but still better than bread and cheese.

At first, Garrick assumed the anonymous dinners were Mina's doing. But his cousin remained in the dusty studio, rapt in the contemplation of a slowly assembling statue.

It was the fifth day before Garrick visited her.

She paced abstractedly through the studio, circling the clay investment, which stood on its pedestal like some eroded monolith. From its rough, faceless surface, Garrick could not tell that a carefully carved wax figure stood inside.

Mina looked up from the scrap of bronze when he entered, smiled wearily at her young cousin.

"May I help you, Cousin?" he asked, blushing.

Mina brushed her hair back. In the broken light streaming through the high windows and rising from the dwindling fire, she looked a dozen years older than Garrick remembered her. He startled at the deep flush across her face—the spreading, inflamed moth wings of the disease.

"Just help me move Melusine into the studio, if you would, Garrick," she replied softly, gliding toward the door.

He followed her through the mirrored hall, toward the capsized statue of the mermaid at the foot of the stairwell. "I figured . . . it was high time I was useful again," he said, too abruptly, too loudly.

Mina did not reply.

"I mean, the war and all," he explained.

Mina stood over the statue now, her hands on the handles of an old, rickety barrow. Melusine lay facedown on the floor, at the very spot where Diego's earlier acrobatics had left her.

There was something pitiful and bereft about the statue's hands. Mina touched the bronze fishtail gently, forlornly.

With a grunt, Garrick wrestled the statue onto the barrow. "I thought these things were hollow!" he exclaimed.

Mina's laugh was faint and papery. "Hollow, but still metal, Cousin."

"This is more parlous than soldiering," Garrick observed. The barrow creaked and sagged as he began to push it through the mirrored hall. "I'd sooner go to war."

"And who's to say you *aren't* at war, Cousin?" Mina asked from somewhere behind him.

Her reflection drifted through the farthest mirrors.

Garrick turned around, faced her.

"I'm a soldier, Mina. Not a sculptor's apprentice. Diego and Artemis are somewhere out in the Borders, set against ruffle and Absence in a search for my missing uncle. Father, in his own lunatic way, is about the same adventure, and he's taken Aunt Morgana with him. I'm . . . I'm *housebound*, Mina. As trapped as that wax figure in your clay."

"And who is to say, Garrick," Mina responded softly, approaching him, setting her flushed and mottled fingers to the handle of the barrow, "who is to say that you're not fighting the war . . . simply by being here?"

Garrick brushed her aside gently, and began to push the statue once again toward the door of the studio. "Heaviest damned mermaid in all Urizen," he muttered.

Mina laughed. "In the *world*."

"Why do you want her in the studio, Mina?"

"It's the war, Garrick. *My* war. The war from in here."

"I don't understand." Garrick turned the barrow laboriously, guiding it through the door.

Melusine regarded him vacantly, serenely.

"Every war," Mina said, "is a war against confusion. Against that time when everything you know and love unravels."

She coughed, stopped in the doorway.

Garrick would always remember how the midday sun seemed trapped in the mirror behind her, how she stood dark amid a halo of borrowed light. He started to say something, something about confusion and unraveling, but then Mina moved, the light faded behind her, and he forgot what he had been about to say.

"Well, that's my pronouncement," Mina said. "Set her by the fireplace, Garrick. The light on the bronze will ripple like water, and she would've liked that, I'd wager."

* * *

Every war is also a war of waiting.

After Diego vanished into the Absence, Artemis was left to wait and wonder.

It is the lofts all over, she told herself. Another one of his blind leaps from rafter to floor.

"And I am left to clean up after him," she murmured, to Willie Melmoth, to no one in particular, as she sent Rousseau, Manasseh, and Coban in a wide reconnaissance along the edge of the Absence, as she ordered the restless troops to make camp once again beside the swirling, glittering cloud.

* * *

"What do you think, Willie?" the Lady asked.

The two of them sat on the driver's seat of the wagon, staring out over the Absence. The moonlight caught on the swirling, metallic cloud, which gathered and shimmered like crushed oil.

Willie glanced at the rebel leader. For a long hour, seated beside him, she had said nothing. Through that silence, it had seemed that the whole landscape—Presence and Border, the tumbling cloud before him—had called out to him, louder and louder, in a language he could not quite understand.

Artemis looked back at him, darkness in the depths of those eyes.

It was no wonder, Willie decided, that all of them—from Justin St. Hyle to the Captain himself—were halfway in love with the Lady.

"Willie? Willie?"

He stirred on the wagon seat. "Beg pardon, ma'am?"

"What do you think, Willie?" Artemis repeated. "What would you do next, if yours were the deciding and the carrying out?"

"I don't know, ma'am," Willie confessed. His face was hot; he stared uncomfortably at the reins draped over his hands. "I . . . I . . . expect . . ."

"Go on," Artemis urged, after a long pause.

Willie took a deep breath. "I expect you're here . . . for some reason, Lady." He scratched his head, searching for words. "Do you remember much of the Text?"

"Why?" Artemis asked. She'd had enough of the Hawkens and their Text.

Willie looked away. "Beggin' your pardon, Lady. Still, there was somethin' my father told me—somethin' he recollected out of the Text, when the wars stirred up again and everybody set out becomin' guardsman or rebel. He made me put it to memory. He memorized it himself, long ago, you see, because his father had done it and his father, clear back to the Third War of False Doctrine, when it . . . *applied*, like it does now . . ."

"What was it, then?" Artemis snapped. Then, more quietly, more kindly, "What does the Text say, Willie?"

Willie closed his eyes, clutched the reins as though he were guiding the wagon team through a dream or a vision. It did not matter that the reins were slack, the horses safely tied and drowsing a hundred feet away.

"O go not forth," Willie began. Paused, cleared his throat.

> "O go not forth in Martyrdoms & Wars!
> We were plac'd here by Universal Brotherhood & Mercy
> With powers fitted to circumscribe this death,
> That the Seven Eyes may have space for Redemption.
> But how this is we know not, and we cannot know
> Till Albion is arisen; then patient wait a little while."

"Patient wait a little while," Artemis whispered, more mildly than she had expected, imagined. "Thank you, Willie."

The face of the Absence whirled before her like a maelstrom seen from a distance, from on high. Before it, walking at the edge of the campfire, a green-jacketed soldier kept a silent vigil.

She would wait here, with powers fitted to circumscribe this death, though she had no idea what those powers were, and where or if she would find them.

"Patient wait a little while," she repeated, and stared off into the dark.

She did not have to wait long. By the next night, Whitefield's cavalry had found her.

Rousseau escorted them into the camp, a dusty column of partisans three days on the road from the Tharman border.

It was a surprise to see Tharman rebels this far east, to see them north of the Alph. More surprising still was the woman they brought with them.

Artemis gasped when Morgana pushed back her broad hat, stared amiably at her niece with brilliant gray eyes.

Their reunion was brief, almost wordless. Artemis and Willie helped the old woman down from the saddle, and Morgana kissed them both, rolling wearily onto the young gondolier, whose knees buckled with her weight.

"O go not forth in Martyrdoms," Artemis muttered teasingly to the lad, who snorted, weaving beneath the struggling, protesting Morgana.

Artemis slept well that night, and rose before most of the others. Waking instantly alert, as she always did in the field, she slipped from beneath her blanket and walked toward the wagon, toward the guttering morning fire.

Whitefield had wakened before her. They spoke quietly as the sunrise flickered red on the face of the Absence.

Morgana snored in the wagon bed, and Whitefield leaned into the fading warmth and light as Artemis, having learned of the wars in the west, the ventures of ben Ezra against a pressed and marginal Guard, asked finally the question that had troubled her since her aunt's arrival.

"How did you find your way to *us*, Lieutenant?" she asked.

Whitefield frowned. The dust of the road streaked his forehead, lay heavy in his long red hair. He looked ancient, faintly prophetic, as he stretched his hands toward the fire.

"The Absence," he said. "The Absence guided us here."

It was Artemis' turn to frown.

"Not like you think, Lady," Whitefield continued quickly. "It was indirect, like the Absence was . . . *herding* us. But if it was, it was herding elsewhere than here."

"I don't understand," Artemis said.

Whitefield stirred uncomfortably. Glanced over his shoulder at the wagon, dark against the slowly lightening woods.

"Miss Morgana claimed she knew the way back to Arcady, and I promised I would see her there. I knew I would regret it up the road, when the miles turned into leagues and Tharmas turned into Urizen, but I felt it the sole and honorable thing to do, her having lost her nephew and wagon and all.

"And once the word is spoken, you live with it. You're in for the duration, the way I figure."

Artemis nodded. "Go on."

"We had not gone a mile before Miss Morgana begun to guide us in circles." Whitefield leaned away from the fire, picked up a dried branch, stirred the ground in front of him. "Seems that the nephew—your brother, Lady?"

Artemis shook her head. "Cousin."

"Seems he had steered them by the Text, and the old lady followed his directions. She hadn't paid attention to the country around her.

"So we headed east, along the Urizen Road. I figured that since it used to be a trade route into Ville, and Miss Morgana claimed that Arcady wasn't far from the ruins . . . that the road would get us closer than an old lady's circles."

He smiled faintly, tossed the branch onto the embers. It smoldered and smoked, and then the bark curled with a faint edge of flame.

Artemis imagined the scene: the gray, windswept roads, the lean cavalryman crouched in the saddle, Morgana behind him, her heavy arms encircling his waist, the smell of old clay and verbena reaching under the sharp odor of horse and the rising, metallic whiff of a coming rain . . .

"Soon as we crossed into Urizen," Whitehead continued, "the Absence was there in front of us like a storm cloud, like a storm. Have you seen, Lady, those days when your side of the field or the road is sunny, and the clouds and the rain gather not half a mile from you? So you could draw a line or build a fence between storm and sun? It was like that traveling east.

"The Absence pushing us farther south until it covered the Urizen Road entirely. Pushing us farther away from Miss Morgana's home, as I figured it."

Artemis nodded. "But *south*, not north. How did you . . ."

"Then your aunt speaks up," Whitefield said, raising his hand. His gray eyes fixed on the burning branch. "Says I won't believe what she's going to say, but I should bear with her, should believe her because it's true."

"The angels," Artemis said. Anxiously, she glanced toward the wagon. "I know what comes next, Lieutenant."

Whitefield's eyes met hers. "No, Lady," he said quietly. "I don't expect you do. Because Miss Morgana said she saw an angel—a solitary angel, she said. His wings crimson and green and edged with white."

"I'm surprised she told you," Artemis said. "They put her in a wish sanitarium once. For seeing too many angels."

"This one was . . . one she knew, evidently," Whitefield said. "He was beckoning her. To a notch of Border between two clouds of Absence. She claimed he was telling her that . . . that it was a passage. Between two sides of the Absence."

Whitefield leaned back on his haunches, closed his eyes.

"And you took the passage," Artemis prompted.

"Indeed I did, Lady." Whitefield smiled uneasily. "I don't have to tell you that commanding partisans, you decide things quickly and you don't look back."

"I know," Artemis said.

She was not sure she *did* know.

"And the way I figured," Whitefield explained, his rusty palms lifted in a gesture of bafflement, "it was follow an old woman's angels or a faceless cloud that chewed up everything it covered.

"What would *you* have done, Lady?" His gray eyes were searching, unsettled. "I know the angel didn't get Miss Morgana home. But it *was* a passage through the Absence. Rough ground and no place to rest or water a horse, and a good five miles with the Absence whirlin' and rising over you like a wall of water.

"It got us through the Absence." He smiled encouragingly. "And it got her here."

* * *

By noon Morgana had awakened. She was nursed by the gaunt, dusty rebels, plied with dried fruit and tea, and propped ceremoniously on blankets in Willie Melmoth's wagon. The wagon itself was drawn beneath the shade of thick cedars, and in the fragrant shadow Morgana drowsed, and watched and waited, her eyes on Artemis, on the leuthan cloud in the distance.

Morgana had lost weight, Artemis noted, Of course, she had never been a dainty woman, but now a certain angularity had set into her form and gesture. Morgana was large and monumental, but no longer portly, her gray hair gone from steely blue to white, almost yellow. She sat in the wagon, her gaze fixed on the hollow of the Absence, as though she awaited a miracle.

"If that's what she's waiting for," Artemis whispered, again to nobody as the sun vaulted over the camp and the shadows dwindled, "I hope she's the first to find it."

But from that vantage point in the wagon, Morgana was the first to see Marion L'Overture.

At one moment the line of trees surrounding the wasteland at the lip of the Absence was original, unbroken. Then the partisans rose from the branches like startled birds, the rebel green emerging from the deep greens of spruce and pine. The large black man with the golden eyes followed his vanguard from the forest's fastness.

Morgana raised her hand, pointed sleepily at the advancing army.

Artemis' men were taken by surprise. They fumbled for weapons, called out alarums. Then, recognizing the approaching troops as their own, they lowered musket and pistol. Rebel greeted rebel in a quiet and estranged reunion.

Artemis looked long into L'Overture's eyes. They had served together for a month in Urthona, and she knew him well enough.

He approached her over the wasted ground, the left sleeve of his green jacket torn away, revealing the golden tattoo of a tyger on his shoulder—the fierce, mysterious beast of the Hymns. The silver flute rested in a sheath sewn to his right sleeve.

Two soldiers followed behind him, their uniforms ragged and old, blightlocks adorning their belts and a smell of incense following them like a dangerous wind.

"Lady," L'Overture said quietly, his voice as melodious as the song from his silver instrument.

"Marion," she responded laconically.

They regarded each other like duelists, like lovers.

"What brings you north of the river, Lady?" L'Overture asked.

For a moment Artemis was uncertain whether to tell him. Though he was her ally, and though she counted him among her friends in a distant and roundabout way, they stood in unsteady country now, in the Borders where sight and shape, thought and allegiance varied with the wind and weather.

Diego was L'Overture's enemy. She could imagine their meeting.

No. There had been enough blood in the Lady's Land. She would lie, would send L'Overture away into the depths of the Urthonan woods. Send him after imagined guardsmen, or centaurs, or foxfire and mirages.

"Tharman partisans," L'Overture noted, casting a quick glance at Whitefield's troops. "What brought them east?"

"You want to know so many things, Marion," Artemis answered, her thought scrambling for stories, for blinds and ruses. "What brought *you* here, my friend?"

The gold eyes stared at her, unwavering.

"The cloud. The cloud brought us. We could ride no other way."

Artemis knelt by the fire. For some reason, Whitefield's words returned to her memory.

. . . an old woman's angels or a faceless cloud . . .

Her troops—Urthonan, Tharman—her aunt and Whitefield and Willie Melmoth. All awaited her words, regarded her expectantly from fireside and guardpost, from wagon and shade and blasted encampment.

Commanding partisans, you decide things quickly, and you don't look back.

Well, then.

"Marion, you had best be leaving. We're awaiting the arrival of my cousins from the depths of the Absence, at which time they shall be taken into my custody. Placed under my protection."

L'Overture's face broke into a handsome, dangerous smile. "Is your cousin the guardsman among them? The one-legged captain?"

Whitefield moved slowly, cautiously, to a spot by Artemis' left shoulder. Rousseau moved to her right. Buoyed by their presence, the Lady answered.

"He is, indeed. He is alone. No doubt weakened from his journey."

"All the better," L'Overture purred. His men were gathering behind him now, hands moving slowly, lightly, to the butts of pistols, to the sword hilt.

Artemis glanced around her. Coban and Manasseh emerged from the shadow of the cedars, where they had been attending Morgana. The old woman shambled along between them, her weight resting heavily on their shoulders. Slowly, with incredible, ungainly ceremony, they approached the assembled leaders at the fire's edge.

Whitefield moved aside for the approaching woman, who smiled and wrapped her pale fingers around his dusty hand.

"You are not alone, dear," she murmured to Artemis. "The angels stand with you."

"Thank you, Aunt Morgana," Artemis replied curtly, "but I think that . . ."

A quiet glance from Whitefield stilled her dismissive words.

L'Overture's eyes stared beyond her. The eyes of a lion, of a great predatory bird. For a moment he glanced into the tops of the trees, into the whirling air at the Absence's edge.

The faintest uneasiness crossed over his broad, handsome features.

"Very well, Lady," he said at last, his smile forced now, unsettled. "As a favor to you, we will go on. After all, Captain Hawken *is* your cousin."

Artemis heard a long sigh of relief rise from Lieutenant Rousseau, heard Whitefield sniff nervously.

And then, over her shoulder, she heard the rustle of invisible wings.

L'Overture was gone as quickly as he came.

After a moment of strained amenities with some of the Urthonan rebels whom he knew, he turned and vanished with a wave into the forest, the silver flute catching a flicker of sunlight as he and his green-clad troops blended with the deeper shade of the evergreens.

For the first time in hours, it seemed, Artemis breathed deeply. Something in her yearned for a cheer to rise in the ranks of her soldiers, for Rousseau and Whitefield to lift her to their shoulders and carry her exultantly around the campsite to the tune of the great songs of the rebellion.

Instead, Whitefield nodded and joined the Tharmans at their campsite. Rousseau supervised as Coban and Manasseh escorted Morgana back to the shade and the wagon.

Artemis was left alone. Nothing had moved, it seemed, since Diego plummeted into the Absence. And yet it was not the same.

For a moment a shadow passed over the sun, and she looked up, expecting . . .

She was not sure what she expected.

But a feathery cloud, its edges stained red and green by the high sun, passed over and vanished above the deep forest.

She had done all to stand, and she had stood.

And in the wind that had borne the cloud south and away, Artemis heard the wings again.

The whirlpool of the Absence seemed to mask, to beckon. Walking toward the shade, toward the wagon where her old aunt rested in vision and memory, Artemis closed her eyes.

"Patient," she breathed. "Patient wait a little while."

CHAPTER 29

Solomon's instruction was wearisome, insistent.

There, in the ruinous tangle of bordermetal and stone, Khole taught him the rudiments of magic.

"We haven't long," the angel would urge, hovering in the damaged windows of honeycombed buildings, his bright eyes intent on Solomon. Khole pointed to the misty horizons of Ville, where another series of tilted shadows lay bunched against the grayness of the Absence.

A city of wood and nightmares. According to the angel, it was the next destination.

And yet, despite his listening, despite his attempts to purify thought and motive and despite his spacious memory, which included the Text and Hymns and many of the Commentaries, Solomon had yet no evidence that any of his fledgling spells were working. Vainly he would set snatches of Hymn or Text to work on the smallest of things: to drown the noise of the incessant mechanical grinding from somewhere in the depths of the Absence with a new sound, any sound. Cautiously, tentatively, Solomon set forth the words, his first spells little more than questions asked over the tattered stone landscape:

> "Can such an Ear, fill'd with the vapours of the yawning pit,
> Judge of the pure melodious harp struck by a hand divine? . . ."

He stopped. He listened.

The machinery persisted, rumbling and gnashing around him, beneath him.

The spell had not worked. Or it had not worked to his expectations.

He had to remember that—to remember what Khole had told him about the effects of spells.

Perhaps light, then. The dispersal of the thick pervading mist. Solomon closed his eyes. Thought of the Hymn about the little lost girl. There was something in it about light. . . .

Solomon pictured the illumined page, the deep blue on which the words were printed, the twining foliage of the margins . . .

And the words came to him.

"Frowning frowning night,
Over this desart bright,
Let thy moon arise,
While I close my eyes."

It was an old favorite of his in a scarce-remembered region of his childhood—a lullaby sung to him by his mother? By Cousin Amelia?

Perhaps it would work as a spell.

Triumphantly, he opened his eyes . . .

To unchanged, pervading mist.

And yet, like a coin dropped to the bottom of a shallow, murky pool, something flickered dimly for a moment, or seemed to flicker, deep in the leuthan fog. Had he not said the words and hoped for their success, he might not have noticed it.

He decided to believe that the dim, fitful light was a flowering of his spell. Oh, it could be coincidence, could be a hundred things.

But Solomon decided to believe.

"At last," he breathed, brushing back his gray, matted hair. It was somehow important to *say* that the spell had worked. "Something. Not much, but something to begin . . ."

"It is time," urged a voice behind him.

Startled, Solomon wheeled and stared into Khole's golden eyes.

"Yet a little while," he protested. "I'm . . . I'm not ready . . ."

The angel smiled. "It is time," he repeated.

"And you are ready, Solomon Hawken."

There was no more to be said. At the angel's coaxing, Solomon set out through the network of littered, paved streets that divided the ruined city. Great, monolithic structures loomed over him, shadowing the alleys and squares. The landscape was marred by broken statuary, clutches of bordermetal, by stairwells leading up into the vacancies of mist.

It was more than the ravages of time. Mist pooled in the hollowed walls, spouted and curled from fissures in the broad, broken roadways.

The Absence was eating the city away.

Scarcely three blocks from the site of Solomon's instruction, the pavements fell away into rubble and dirt. In the western distance lay the leaning buildings of his destination—the buildings Khole had pointed out when his instruction began.

He could look at that destination now. Now, as the ruins of Ville dwindled into the mist behind him, he paced toward the wooden city.

Solomon knew the voice would return: the sinuous, accusing voice that had rehearsed his cowardice in the lime-tree bower and at Marcus' drowning, the horrible prospect of his brothers broken and lost. And yet he awaited as well the other voice—Khole's own—that lifted and restored him in this cloudy country.

But for now, he was left to his own.

The teakwood city, its buildings askew and crumbling, seemed distant indeed, the road to it steep and arduous. And yet the leuthan mist of the Absence must have distorted space and the time that it took to get there, for Solomon had not traveled a hundred yards when the shadows of the first buildings surged around him, filled with wizardries and broken science. The grinding of other machinery, the chittering of gnomes, and the insistent gnat-whine of genii filled the murky air.

All that was unimportant now. Solomon steered through transforming alleys, following one sound amidst a chorus of rising noises.

The cry of his brother Endymion.

He wished he had time to practice the spellcraft. His memory raced over volumes as he ran, leaning against buildings and stepping into squares and courtyards, following the sound of his brother's cry, then the fainter sound of Endymion's ragged breathing, which meshed with the grinding of machinery until once Solomon feared he had confused the sounds—feared he would lose his brother in the maze of teakwood and ivory.

Now he paused, caught his breath in the skewed arrangement of tilted and toppling buildings. The upper stories of the building against which he rested had snapped away, broken with the sheer force of something in the higher air. Now topless, the spiraling, rough-cut tower was like a huge felled tree in the midst of a grove, its collapse an avenue for new wind and light.

On the base of the building, carved by rough hands into the foundation, lay a passage from the Text. The green light danced over it. Solomon read:

> here is the Seat
> Of the Enemy in its Webs: for in brain and heart and loins
> Gates open behind the Enemy's Seat to the City of Golgonooza

Golgonooza. He stood at the outskirts of Endymion's bottled city.

Golgonooza. Either the model city of midnight, gin-soaked fashioning, named in sacrilegious sport by his despairing brother, or the genuine item, the great city that the Text had prophesied.

Or both, or neither.

Solomon touched the rough engraving with a trembling finger. Dazed, struggling to remember, he leaned against the teakwood building, setting his feet against its glazed foundations.

His brothers might be dead. After all, had not the Absence masqueraded as Uncle Vergil, adopting a sweet and sympathetic form to entrap him? To lure him into confusion and despair?

This might be the most cruel deception of all.

Nonetheless, *if* Endymion and Diego were alive, Solomon would risk everything to find them.

Everything, a voice seemed to murmur at his shoulder. The angel's voice, borne on a whiff of balsam.

An angry, pained roar thundered out of the mist, bellowing like the furnaces of Bowlahoola.

Diego. Solomon knew that voice.

He must wade through the fog for both of them, proceeding on the evidence of things unseen.

The price may be everything, Khole murmured, his voice enmeshed with Solomon's ranging thoughts.

"But I will lose all Arcady, all the world, for my brothers," Solomon said aloud, and struggled to his feet. Breathing prayers to Saint Enitharmon, to Saint Los and Saint Palamabron for protection, like a child who calls on the magic of saints, Solomon waded toward the sound of his brothers through the thickening mists of the Enemy. The braying laugh of a genie startled him, but the blue flame that followed the creature's path through the air flickered briefly in the mist and vanished at a fortunate safe distance.

Solomon stopped, listened to the echoing laughter. "Ye Genii of the Mills!" he whispered, recalling words of the Text he had memorized in his first year at Lambeth. "The Sun is on high, your labors call you." He searched his memory for the rest of the words . . .

But those verses were no longer there.

Solomon shuddered, knowing somehow that the spell he had imagined was no proof against powerful creatures who swept through the Borders like firestorms. For the first time he regretted having left the ruins and trusting his angelic guide.

Then he remembered the summoned light, dim in a whirl of fog—that he had decided to believe it was the working of his fledgling magic.

He decided again. And with each step into the crumbling city, he decided over and over. Each time it became easier to decide, and his confidence rose and flourished.

It was a good thing, he told himself. For on his faith and confidence his spellcraft would depend.

* * *

Later, when he tried to explain to Artemis, to Rousseau and Morgana and his brother and Willie Melmoth, Diego was never sure he had it right.

He lay in Nightshade Vale for hours. Or perhaps days. The pain in his leg was immense, disorienting, and light in the Absence was so murky that day and night were indistinguishable. Dragging himself up the slope toward the maples from which the second rebel volley had come, preparing to end it all absurdly, in a crawling frontal assault against an entrenched enemy, he was astonished to find that the rebels had disappeared.

He emptied his gun into the haze. The crack of the pistol echoed dismally through the gray mists.

All his weaponry had failed him. The strong body, the armaments, the soldiery. In the midst of mystery Diego lit a cheroot. The lucifer match glinted briefly in the shadows, casting a sickly light on his face.

"I should've listened to her," he muttered, blowing smoke into the noose of clouds around him. "Artemis was right all along. There's knots out there you don't untie with a saber. If I ever get back . . ."

He laughed bitterly. "Not that I'm getting back."

His teeth clenched on the stale cigar, on a tangling pain.

Lying there beneath the trees, the pain and delirium dancing through the edges of his thought, Diego thought Solomon was a memory at first.

His older brother. In a greatcoat. Standing sternly above him.

What did I do this time? Diego asked, tried to ask, but the words unraveled into a gurgling, barking sound that pain had stripped of almost all its humanity.

Lo! I am with you always, he heard his brother say. And though his leg still burned with the angry fire of the bullet, now Diego could stand. Now, with Solomon's shoulder to support him, he could make for the high ground beyond the trees.

As the two men moved up the gentle incline, the mist around them flared with gunfire. Two shots whined by Diego's head, and for a moment he reeled against his older brother, his courage weak and tattered.

"Get down, Solomon," he muttered. "We'll wait . . ."

Solomon's shoulder seemed to give beneath him. Pockets of mist entwined with cloth and flesh and bone. Behind the whirling veil of mist, Diego heard the shouted orders and oaths of a rebel squadron reloading, the ominous clatter of rods in the musket barrels.

For a moment he was about to give in, unfamiliar fear settling over him like a shadow.

Then Solomon spoke, his deep voice flickering through the clatter of weaponry and the grinding of metal and stone. Diego did not hear all that his brother said, but the words he caught touched him like medicine, like magic:

> ". . . trembling I stood
> Exceedingly with fear & terror, standing in the Vale
> . . . but he wish'd me health,
> And I became One Man with him arising in my strength . . ."

Diego steadied himself. "Then let's do it, old boy! Those rebels couldn't hit a wagon in this fog!"

He broke from Solomon and, surprised by the health of what he thought was a shattered leg, staggered recklessly up the hill as gunfire churned the ground at his feet. On the crest, in a pocket of strange silence and stillness, Juno grazed absently and greeted him solemnly, rolling her long nose in his cupped hand.

Diego could not even remember how he mounted the horse. Solomon was there and not there, a cloudy presence rather than flesh and bone and blood. Perhaps he boosted his brother into the saddle, or perhaps Diego climbed there under his own strength and power.

Whatever the case, it no longer mattered. As the leuthan mist rushed by Diego, he marveled that it was no longer important to save himself. To *be* saved was enough, by whatever means necessary.

"Thank you, brother," he breathed into the thick, passing air. He said it without resentment, without jealousy, as Juno surged toward the edge of the Absence, her strides more certain now.

Now powers beyond his strength and knowing carried Diego toward a distant light. For the first time in his memory, Diego gave in to a greater strength—the sure ripple of the mare's back beneath him, the mist rushing by him in a harmless current, and the knowledge that something and someone, in a landscape filled with pitfalls and betrayals, had singled him out for protection.

There was a Hymn about it, but he could not remember.

Now, riding toward a dim light at the edge of the Absence, Diego thought for a moment that he heard the choiring of birds above the fading crash of Arouet's machinery, but it was only when the sunlight struck him full in the eyes, when the country resolved itself into Urthonan woods, afternoon sunlight, a mule-drawn wagon, and a column of horsemen, that his memory returned to him positively, that the events of his long adventure became as clear as they would ever be afterward.

* * *

Nor did Endymion remember much of his own rescue.

He lay in a tightening room, the teakwood walls closing inexorably upon him. The designs of his own making, the delicate carving and lacy inlay of ivory, loomed large and clumsy from this perspective. Nearer and nearer the walls came, the thin grain of the teak swelling in the moist air of the Absence.

"What is it like," Endymion asked, taking a long draft from his flask, "to be smothered in your own creation?" He laughed, coughed suddenly as the warm gin washed over him.

He pushed against the wall. The soft teak gave only a little, closing inexorably.

O the better to smother me with . . .

"Could the house I contain withstand the house that contains me?" Endymion muttered again, his words and thoughts tunneling into one another until he could not recall what he was trying to say, to think.

Then the words from the Text echoed faintly from the other side of the closing walls, borne on a voice he barely remembered.

> "Golgonooza the spiritual Four-fold London eternal,
> In immense labours & sorrows, ever building, ever falling . . ."

"Solomon!" Endymion cried out. "This way!"

And his brother appeared in the mazed heart of the city.

Standing above Endymion, Solomon looked like anything but a hero. His gray hair in its usual tangle, a stubble of beard, silver and dark brown, crusted with mud and streaked with dust and sweat. The hooked, oversized Hawken nose had been scuffed in a fall or a struggle. But Solomon's eyes were the glittering green of distant ice—green drifting now to gray, as if the sojourn in the Absence were changing their very color.

Solomon recited something from one of the early plates—the Tenth or Eleventh, Endymion recalled.

> ". . . We behold it is of Divine
> Mercy alone, of Free Gift and Election that we live:
> Our Virtues & Cruel Goodnesses have deserv'd Eternal Death."

Now Solomon looked at his brother, smiled, and waited, examining the ivory inlay of the walls as if something momentous would follow in the wake of the words.

Endymion rose to his feet, bracing himself unsteadily against the wobbly teak.

"Well?" he asked.

Solomon turned to him.

"Are you expecting magic, big brother?" Endymion asked. "Because if you are, you're no better off here than you were at your blessed seminary."

Solomon smiled again. "Let's suppose . . . I'm here to get you out. And whether it's magic or wit or elbow grease that avails me, let's suppose I'm willing to try it."

Endymion winced. He knew the recited passage as well—more from the Commentaries than from the actual Text itself, since he had hated the tough honesty of those lines, could never bring himself to recite them and could only bring himself to read them when fueled by half a bottle of gin.

"So what of these lines?" he asked, his voice hoarse and broken.

"I'm willing to try anything to save you, Brother," Solomon urged. "What will you give up to help me?"

"Give up? I—I don't—"

With a groan the ceiling above the room's far corner cracked and sagged.

"Your own cruel goodnesses cannot save you, Endymion," Solomon coaxed. "Please. You have to help me."

"I don't understand!" Endymion's thoughts raced over the prospect, the intricate city whose map he had long forgotten, the towering maze of teak and ivory and shadows.

They would never find their way through it. Never.

Damn these ramshackle, unstable buildings and what they stood for. And most of all, his own pride—in his intellect and his ingenuity—that had fashioned a flimsy teakwood village as a lasting monument and led him on a too-complicated chase into the heart of the Absence.

In anger and despondency, Endymion doubled his fist and struck the wall behind him.

The teakwood gave, cracked, shattered.

"Exactly," Solomon breathed behind him. "If you can't find your way through, be like our brother Diego. Beat, kick, and claw your way to the outside."

Endymion laughed. What did he have to lose? And a strange exhilaration rose in him, as he struck the wall again and again, a great gap forming as the teak splintered and gave way.

It was a magic of sorts, Endymion decided, as he crashed through the ruins of Golgonooza, toppling walls, buildings, a spiraling rickety stairwell, an elegantly carved encircling wall. Behind him building fell into building, crashing soundlessly in the green bottled light. A cloud of dust whirled around Endymion as he thrashed and kicked his way toward a distant light.

The dust smelled of soured milk and gin, of teak and creosote.

Endymion laughed again, this time more loudly. He set his shoulder against a tower and pushed gleefully as the structure crashed into a tilted line of buildings.

"I have let go of my strategies," Endymion announced soberly, absurdly, kicking over the wall of a huge pavilion. The wall crashed into a frail minaret, which toppled as well, splintering yet another structure, and another. A roof floated through the green-gold air and thundered down upon him, but he brushed the light wood away effortlessly, gleefully.

This was his magic. The best magic he could understand—the liberation of dismantling all that he created and owned, firm in the faith that something would replace the losses.

Endymion turned from the wreckage and paced toward the distant light that marked the edge of the Absence. For the first time in his life, he admired his brother Solomon.

In fact, when he emerged into sunlight and birdsong, when to his astonishment he saw Artemis and Diego, saw his aunt Morgana amid a rebel escort, Endymion looked over his shoulder like Orpheus in the Commentaries, breathing his first prayer in years, that Solomon would follow him out of the silvery revolutions of the Absence.

They would all be together. Solomon would join them, and armed with his new magic, they would return to Arcady as a family, purging its halls and rafters of chaos and noise . . .

Recovering Faith from the pantry of her disappearances, Aristo from his swarm at the Borders' edge . . . Garrick from the long night of conjecture.

They would be free. All of them. He would have his children once more.

Endymion started to call out, to laugh aloud. But no one followed him into light.

* * *

His brother lay deep in the clouds of the Absence, wearied by the long struggle, by the running.

In the midst of ruined country, Solomon fell roughly to the ground. Curling, clutching his knees, he felt his energy, his life, dwindling. It was a weariness unlike any he had ever known, as though all this believing and conjury, whether or not it worked, had taken from him every single resource.

And yet he had come this far. It was as far as his strength would take him. And yet, as the darkness closed about him, as the long-dead faces of Christabel, of Marcus, of Atreus and Roger and William and James and, oddly, Professor Ezekiel Gordon, flashed through his memory, he prayed to the assembled saints that, despite what it seemed, this was no ending, that somehow the true adventure had begun.

The leuthan clouds encircled his exhausted body, spinning a cocoon of gray and scarlet and green as he slept and waited and slept.

CHAPTER 30

For some time the cousins waited by the lip of the Absence. Artemis placed her hand on Diego's shoulder, whispered something to him about *nightfall* and *return.* Still they watched, as the evening closed in and the silvery clouds began to move, and, surprisingly, seemed to recede.

Still, no Solomon emerged from the Absence. And when the depths of night had surrounded them, the shroud of leutha dwindling to faint tendrils of mist over a desolate, scorched flatland, Endymion consented to Morgana's urgings and climbed into the wagon behind her and the cloud-dazed gondolier, Willie Melmoth.

Diego waited a little longer. He had given up something to his older brother deep in the cloudy chaos. If it was possible to help Solomon through his old ways of muscle and valor, Diego was ready to stand in the gap.

But nothing lived on the flat and vacant plain, and nightfall spread unbroken across the wasteland. So Diego, rubbing his surprisingly restored leg with drowsy amazement, climbed into the wagon as well. From her seat on horseback his beautiful cousin leaned toward him, smelling of honeysuckle and sleep, whispering something else to him, something about loyalty and rest. And Diego entrusted himself to her guidance, agreed that the time for awaiting Solomon had passed, that his brother would never return.

They returned toward Arcady weeping and downcast, their ambitions and weapons at rest. Stunned by the hush in the valley of the Alph, neither guardsmen nor rebels would ride tonight, and in all the riverlands, Urthona and Urizen, there were no unnatural sounds.

* * *

Lieutenant Actaeon Peacock, stalwart and orthodox as ever, lay belly-down on a southern rise overlooking his captain's ancestral estate.

A dozen, maybe more, rebel sentries patrolled the topiaries surrounding the mismatched towers of Arcady. A silent quartet of pickets crouched in the reeds beside the pond, and ten or so kept their far-flung outpost at the borders of Raphael's nut grove.

Someone of moment was inhabiting the house. The lieutenant was not sure, but with an escort like that, he'd wager that the Lady had come to call.

He was ready for that contingency. Twoscore guardsmen waited at the other side of the nut grove, fifty more around the mill house and the thick East Woods.

And here on the hill, the lieutenant had set up a brace of artillery pieces—*bull pups,* they called them, guns light enough for cavalry transport but powerful enough to level the mansion below them, if need be.

The lieutenant was sure that need would arise.

Actaeon Peacock had dreamt too often of field command. Of the crash of cannon, and the movement of armies. Now, when the possibility seemed to form itself in the nebulous light of an overgrown and decrepit estate, he was ready for heroics, for the summons of the Citizen and the battle that would follow the summons.

The Lady was Captain Hawken's cousin. The lieutenant had not forgotten. Nor did he fail to recall that Diego was more than protective of his rebel kinswoman.

But the Captain had left Actaeon Peacock in command.

He whispered dire instructions to his gunnery sergeant, and stared through the spyglass at the ancient house. From this perspective, Arcady looked frail, vulnerable, as if it teetered in the path of a leveling wind.

* * *

Five miles away, the stunned brothers sat beside each other in Morgana's wagon.

What was left of the Absence hovered over the river now. They watched as the dark waters of the Alph churned and eddied beneath the passing cloud, and almost without thinking, Diego laid a rough hand on his twin brother's shoulder.

"I need to tell you something," Endymion murmured.

"No," Diego replied, anticipating his brother. "The answer is no. She stayed on the other side of the barouche." He smiled ruefully. "At that time, for good or ill, I still loved my . . . *termagant* of a wife. Who, I suppose, is cannonading the Alph by now, searching hopefully for a drowned husband. No, Garrick is your son, Endymion."

"I know that now. Have known it for some time. It was his behavior, his . . . his . . ."

Diego smiled again, this time more softly. "His behavior is a mystery. Which we cannot sway, much less control."

Endymion frowned and nodded. The brothers understood each other no better than before, but they had the Absence in common, and the fate of following cloudy women. In the open bed of Willie Melmoth's wagon, Endymion drew forth his flask, opened it, and offered the remnants to Diego.

Artemis watched them from her seat atop the little roan mare Willie Melmoth had saddled. Her gifted and favored cousins were smaller now, humbled as perhaps the Absence had been humbled, squatting in blankets behind their aunt and the gondolier.

Yet the watery smell of lightning encircled them, and silver mist clung to the fibers of the blankets. They had been in the presence of the Enemy and beaten in their best fights. But they had returned.

"Look," Endymion murmured, his voice scarcely more than a whisper and yet strangely audible above the stirring and whickering of the horses, the rush of an autumn wind, and the faint, grinding sound of the Absence's machineries.

"Look. 'Smoving toward Arcady."

He was right. The cloud had cleared the river now, and was skirting along the southern banks of the Alph. The country behind it lay parched and bare, except for a fine film of salt.

Slowly it moved south and west, leaving expansive ruin in its wake.

"Mina," Artemis breathed quietly.

"And Garrick," Endymion echoed, saying the boy's name as if he had heard it for the first time.

"Arcady," Diego said. "Arcady is in danger."

* * *

In the studio where clay dust swam and eddied in deflected sunlight, Mina paused over her work.

There was not much left to do, and that was good.

She was so tired, so fragile. Always the voices were prompting her to lie down, to give it all up.

The house itself was coaxing her. From the rafters of Arcady, where angel and pigeon flocked in a nest of ghosts, to old Innocent's wine cellar, where only yesterday she had found a dozen gnomes lying drunk, tumbled from the Borders into an all-too-mundane stupor, Mina had heard from the inhabitants.

The statues were the most insistent of all.

They had spoken to her from their pedestals among the geometric shrubbery. Old Atreus first, frozen in mid-puff of his bronze cigar, seated atop the pooled verdigris of the sculptured daybed. A bronze Vergil floated beside him, a look of simple serenity across his tarnished face.

The two Hawkens—the most shrewd and conniving, the most guileless and dense—had urged her to bring the statuary out of the gardens and into Morgana's studio.

Bring us all home, they seemed to say. *That we may witness your last work upon your last sculpture.*

And Mina had seen no harm in the request. She enlisted first Garrick, then a squadron of rebel soldiers to cart and carry the statues into the studio. Now Melusine Stella-Maris, the mermaid foremother of the Hawken brothers, swam in a current of bronze near the fireplace, her dolphin's tail flickering urgently. And Atreus and Vergil not far away, the bronze daybed cleaned and polished now, reflecting the crimson light from the furnace.

And the vacant pedestal, her standing joke, the base for the imagined statue of Innocent, lay closest of all, scarcely ten feet from where she stood now, her chisel digging, faceting the quickly drying clay.

Give it up, all the statues seemed to say, choiring in unison through the cobwebbed studio. *Sleep, and forget your labors.*

Most present, most persuasive, was Mina's own father. The statue of James Hawken remained in the Great Hall, far beyond the door and her direct sight. She could see it from the studio only in the farthest recesses of one of the nearby hall mirrors, reflected from reflections in the maze of facing mirrors.

Mina met her father's glance through an infinity of frames. James looked more disheveled than he had in life, magnified and monumental. His beveled hair was unkempt and bushy, his right hand scuffed and shiny. His waistcoat, carved and chiseled in broad, almost geometric planes, was scarred and ash-stained to a vague silvery color, shot with crimson light and verdigris.

A strange, whirling light played over his brow, and when she stood at a certain angle, Mina wondered if the image had anything to do with her father at all, or whether James' form was a coalescence of strange, glittering clouds.

Lie down, the figure of her father seemed to urge. *Work no more. You are tired and ill. You will not finish, for your illness has made you depend on them all.*

On Morgana and Artemis. On Diego. Even on Endymion.

And none of them are here.

You cannot, will not, finish.

"Who are you?" Mina asked.

She knew it was not really her father's voice.

Then the voice was gone, vanished into the reflections, its last words echoing from rafter to polished floor in the great Arcadian hall.

Lie down. Work no more.

Mina felt suddenly tired, her tools heavy in her grasp. Slowly, as though moving itself were painful, she set the chisel on the floor, the dark blade of the instrument visible through a new translucency in her hands.

* * *

From a mountainous overlook at the edge of the Alph, once a little maple-covered knoll but now a huge, bare precipice torn and shaped by the passage of the Absence, Diego and Artemis stared down over northern Urizen, over the salt-rimed wake of the swirling cloud, over the groves where the last leaves hung on poplar and oak.

Over Arcady, visible at three miles' distance, the small tower-shadowed pond glowing with the first touch of sunrise and the muffled campfires that encircled the estate.

Guardsmen. You would never see the rebel fires at dawn.

"I can talk to them," Diego insisted. "After all, I still have a commission in the Guard."

"One you resigned," Artemis replied, "when you rode off with me. Do you think that any guardsman—your old friend Actaeon Peacock especially—would welcome your return from the Lady's service?"

Diego followed her gaze to the plain below. "You're right. It's over for me, Artemis."

He sat back heavily in the saddle. Old Juno stirred under him.

"Guard or rebel," he continued, this time quietly, even humbly, "Tharman or Luvan or Border or Absence, what matters to me is my brothers' house. My nephew and your sister, as well. They're all in danger, Artemis."

He gestured toward the border of the estate. At the edge of Uncle Raphael's nut grove the Absence had slowly encroached on a line of pecan trees farthest from the house. As though they fell before the blades of a huge silver whipsaw, the nut trees splintered, toppled, and vanished into the boiling cloud.

Already, the house itself had begun to shift and alter. The old towers leaned and distorted, as if the cousins glimpsed them through a prism. The color of the grounds as well was prismatic, multicolored and motley in the fractured light.

"We're too late," Artemis said. "Lifting this . . . government siege and freeing Mina and my soldiers will take until nightfall, and by that time . . ."

It was Diego's turn to fall silent. As Artemis looked toward the dark brow of her cousin, she was struck for a moment with a slight estrangement—wondering at first glimpse who this man was on the horse beside her. Then her thoughts caught up with the apprehension, her experience threw light on the moment, and she recognized Diego Hawken.

Her cousin and girlhood companion. Her . . .

What *was* Diego, anyway?

Artemis watched as the mystery slipped from the saddle heavily, staggered slightly as he found his footing on the bare, rocky ground. Already the sun had vaulted high into midmorning as he began the descent of the bluff on foot, his thoughts warring, she imagined, in a wrestle of final loyalties, despite what he said.

* * *

But he had come out of the Absence, and no longer was there any doubt, of loyalty, intent, or even of a grand and general strategy.

Diego sat in the midst of his rebel staff, drawing a map in the dirt with his knife.

Rousseau crouched beside him, observing solemnly the plan of the grounds, the carefully arranged and defensible orchards, the yards over which a rescue party would have to move, in full sight of government riflery and the saints knew how many border ruffles.

The rebel lieutenant was ready to call it off, to cede all Arcady to the Guard.

How long could they hold the mansion, with these changes in the Absences?

Let the redjackets have it. They were welcome to it.

Endymion leaned against the wagon, regarding Diego's map through his faceted spyglass. His brightest machinery was gone, the velocipede and hurdy-gurdy left in the clouds of the Absence, the rest of his collection imperiled in the attic of the mansion. All that was left him was the bellows, which had promised wonder and magic those years ago when he gathered them, but now seemed disappointing, mundane in the midmorning sunlight.

Endymion wondered if he could help at all.

Artemis stood behind the three pensive men, her dark hair crackling with the electric emanations of the Borders, and yet in all this fire and light she seemed curiously cold, distant, as if something had passed by her understanding.

They intended to decide, the male and the wealthy. And because it had been that way for generations, the rebels would follow their orders.

It was going to be as it always was.

But she was still the Lady. Still the Mistress of the Borders, as skilled with the manipulation of ruffle and emanation, of Absence and leuthan cloud, as anyone who was not a Blight or a prophet.

"Smoke and mirrors," she whispered, as Diego drew a battle map with his knife in the dirt. "Smoke and mirrors and sleight of hand. But if you only ask me, I will set you a table at the front steps of Arcady."

* * *

"A tactical nightmare," Evander Rousseau argued. "The enemy outnumber us, and they have the vantage of terrain and concealment."

Endymion, rolling the faceted spyglass in his hand, turned expectantly toward his twin brother.

Diego mulled through the possibilities as he had ranged through the thick clouds of the Absence. He would wander awhile, would grope his way through his old military learning, won in the field more than the schools, until he found the opening, the option, the key.

The mind was a more unwieldy weapon than pistol or sword, arm or squadron of lancers.

But the answer was there. He would not stop believing for it.

"Perhaps a diversionary tactic," Artemis suggested quietly from over his shoulder.

Diego did not move.

" 'Twould have to be a diversion, indeed," Rousseau maintained with a sniff, winking at the Captain, at Endymion.

Morgana grumbled something scarcely audible from her seat on the wagon. Something about *blowhards* and *masculine apes.*

Slowly, Diego turned toward his cousin. When their eyes met, it was a muted sparkle they exchanged, void of the acrimony and rivalry that had marked their twenty years together. Void of the passion as well, for Diego looked into the Lady's eyes for the first time without reeling in their brown and fathomless depths.

A new quiet had emerged. Something settled and even disappointing, but peaceful in an odd, unfashionable way.

They were family once more. Together they would take the house.

"Diversion is the Lady's home, Lieutenant Rousseau," Diego said quietly, his eyes never leaving Artemis. "I myself have seen her lift a cow on a wager. The question remains what we will be . . . diverted to do."

Morgana grunted as the driver's seat of the wagon tilted in her direction. Willie Melmoth had stood, had scrambled back into the wagon bed, leaving her alone on the bench.

"Perhaps a select band of guerrillas," Rousseau urged. "Partisans who could take vantage of the Lady's illusions and find a way through the lines into Arcady, to relieve our troops and your cousin."

"It remains to discover the way," Diego replied tersely, his gaze riveted to the makeshift map. "Oh, it's there to be found. It's a matter of perspective, is all."

"And a matter of time," Rousseau insisted. "The cloud is moving. We haven't . . ."

"Captain Diego, sir," Willie Melmoth called, his head buried in canvas and bags.

Diego raised his hand. "A matter of perspective. Give me time and I will see it."

"Captain Diego!"

The second, more insistent summons caught Diego's attention. Gripping the side of the wagon, the Captain rose to his feet, peering into the bed to where the young gondolier thrashed and rummaged in the rebel supplies.

"Here they are!" Willie Melmoth exclaimed triumphantly, drawing the balloon silks out of the leavings. The gray-green fabric was tough, intact, though wrinkled and soiled by the long trip.

Diego frowned. "What is . . ."

Then he remembered the woods of northern Urizen. His brother passing over in a rain of gunfire.

What Solomon must have seen from that height!

It was the direct route to the roof of Arcady.

"There ain't a gondola," Willie started to explain. "That's at the bottom of your granddad's lake. But . . ."

"Do what you have to do, Mister Melmoth," the Captain ordered crisply. "I have my change in perspective."

"Sir?"

" 'Tis the vehicle that will drop me into my home," Diego said. The rebels glanced at one another in consternation, until Artemis, stepping in front of Lieutenant Evander Rousseau, addressed them with her old dark fire, her brown eyes flickering.

"Then you'll be needing that diversion, Captain," she maintained. "Gentlemen, accompany me back up the hill. I shall show you the new lie of the grounds, and our pathway to Arcady."

"Help me build a scaffolding, Lieutenant," Willie said to Rousseau, his words almost an order, and the lieutenant found himself obeying them swiftly, reflexively, as if they had come from the Captain himself. "And guide the wagon into that far field. We've less than an hour to sprout wings."

Now the camp was a bustle of men and horses. Morgana steadied the team that drew the wagon, looked up into the cloudless sky past the sight of drudges and unbelievers, to a squadron of bright wings pivoting in the glitter of the morning sunlight, the cloudy backdrop of the approaching Absence.

The battle was preparing, and it was not of flesh and blood alone.

CHAPTER 31

Mina could see the fire through her fingers.

Leaning against the furnace, she lit the flames that would eventually, ultimately melt the bronze for the statue. The metal lay in place in five stone crucibles, apportioned for weight and wieldiness. When the time came, the temperature raised two thousand degrees and the bronze molten and ready for pouring, she would start the process of filling the clay mold.

Ghost and gnome, sphinx and genie would try to deflect her from her work. The statues themselves would conspire against her, for Mina could hear them whispering at the edge of her hearing.

She regretted having brought them into the studio.

"But what of it?" she whispered quietly, returning her attentions to her work. "No remedy now."

Already the shadows in the room had lengthened, surprisingly gray and gloomy for midmorning as if a cloud were eclipsing the sun. In the shadows she could see shapes moving, and voices rose out of the shimmering dark.

They were bent on telling her how ill she was, how weary, how incapable of the last steps that lay before her. Whistling over the bronze of the statuary came a hundred voices. Old Atreus and slippery Melusine, sweet Christabel and Vergil, gentle James, joined now by little Faith—all urged her quiescence, her rest, her easeful death.

It is too much hurting, they said. *It is too late for heroics. Other work is worthy, too.*

Mina knew the coaxing for what it was—a great distraction. For some reason, whatever reason, the voices did not want her to finish the work.

Now, in the cloudy sunlight, the fire began to glow in the bottom of the furnace. It would be hours—six, perhaps even eight—until the bronze began to melt.

Mina had time to reckon this mystery of voices. Provided she had time at all.

* * *

"Three is the most the wagon can hold," Willie Melmoth explained. His ragged scarves billowed and sparked in the fire as the balloon filled and began to rise, the gondola fashioned from the wagon lifting beneath it, the bed rising above the bending axles.

Diego glared at the young balloonist, as if just enough glowering and dark countenance would cause the lad to change his mind, to say, *Oh yes, Captain Hawken, the damned thing will hold a dozen well-armed rebels and a howitzer.*

And by the way, Captain, I've found how to make it bulletproof.

"Stand away from the smoke, Willie," the Captain muttered at last. "You're comin' to stink, and if we're traveling in close quarters shortly, it'll render you unpleasant company."

There had been no doubt since the rebels raised the scaffolding. The balloon would sail over Arcady guided by the young gondolier, and deposit Diego and one other seasoned fighter on the roof of the building. From that point, the Captain would rally the rebels and break the siege, issuing forth from the mansion and heading for the East Woods, where the remaining troops under Artemis would meet them, covering their escape through the pecan groves, right at the lip of the Absence itself, where the gunsights were cloudy and the guardsmen dared not follow.

Now all that remained was determining the third man in the craft.

Lieutenant Rousseau was the obvious choice. Lean and wiry, he would take up little space, provide less ballast. And after his surviving a dozen fierce battles against the Guard—most of which were against the very officer he sought to accompany in flight over enemy lines—his physical courage was unquestioned.

" 'Sall well, Evander," Diego replied finally to the pleas of the lieutenant. "I expect you'd be the best man up there, except for the Lady, who'd be the best man of us all . . ."

He winked at Artemis, who smiled in spite of herself.

"But I need the both of you on the ground." Diego looked to the swelling balloon. "To support my troops in the wood. Or to assume command."

He brushed the last statement swiftly, darkly.

"So I'll take with me Justin St. Hyle," Diego concluded. "Or Corporal Coban."

His eyes scanned the ranks of the expectant rebels. One of them would show him, he knew. Would take his gaze and return it with a quiet fiery stare that would whisper, *I am your man, Captain Hawken. I know there are times when each man rises to something lonely and splendid, and this is my time, whether I have chosen it or it has chosen me.*

He knew that look from a hundred battles. He expected it.

But he did not expect his brother.

"You'll take me, Diego," Endymion said, stepping away from the wagon. In his spectacles and his long waistcoat tattered by Absence and wandering, he looked more schoolmaster than warrior. He clutched the spyglass and the bellows like foreign objects. And yet the look had settled in his eyes and dwelt there. The rebel soldiers parted to let Endymion step forward.

Willie Melmoth, sensing the older man's resolve and his new, desperate courage, led Endymion toward the gondola, which was rising now, straining at its moorings as though it longed for uncertain skies.

Despite himself, Diego nodded. For a moment, he glimpsed in Endymion the gallantry that had blossomed, in a different generation and on far fields, when his son Garrick had first taken to battle.

The child is father to the man, Diego thought, though he could not place whether the line was Text or Hymn or Commentary.

The child is father to the man.

And about damned time he is.

* * *

The first of the gunfire reached Mina faintly, as the temperature in the furnace passed the first thousand degrees.

It came to her ears as a rustling, the sound of a navy of doves arising from the far gardens or branches breaking in the distant peach orchards. Scarcely an insinuation under the pleading of the ghosts, it rose in volume until she was certain she heard it, until she lifted her eyes from the contemplation of the glowing bronze and looked toward the rafters.

Where angelic shapes warred among the dust motes, wrestling in a silvery infiltration of cloud.

* * *

Above her as well, stationed on a second-floor balcony overlooking Grandfather Atreus' pond, Garrick Hawken trained his spyglass through the tall surrounding pin oaks out onto open ground, toward the borders of the estate, toward a scarcely detectable movement of green among the poplars.

He knew it for what it was instantly. His uncle Diego leading a column of rebels.

And was it not fitting? After all, here he stood on the balconies of Arcady, the one lapsed guardsmen in a garrison devoted to the Lady.

His life paralleled his uncle's. Perhaps it would do so in heroism as well, in skill and accomplishment on the field of battle.

Garrick smiled ruefully. It would take a victory like the Citizen's first brilliant campaign in eastern Luvah, like the greatest of the Lady's victories along the Alph, to win what Garrick Hawken was after. To erase the puzzlement and disappointment with which his father regarded him.

The green line twisted through the poplars. With his trained soldier's eye, Garrick saw nearer movement. Someone, perhaps his uncle, was skirting the grounds and headed for Uncle Raphael's nut grove.

Where a line of red uniforms had gathered, the midmorning sun glinting blue off gun barrels, immaculate and blinding white off the raised blades of sabers.

And another line, stalking north from the nut grove, threescore strong at least. Already they were crossing the trace, the mill house blocking his view of the advance. Nor would the rebel leaders see this flanking line. It would wade through the hemp fields, circle around them like a slow, silent mill wheel. Close off their path of retreat.

There, between two armies, the rebels would be crushed like grain between cold, grinding stones.

And yet, beyond those troops there was another line—a line of mist and cloud. Gray, shot through with green and red. Garrick had not seen the likes of it before, but he imagined that the green and red were the uniforms of soldiers, mingling and passing one another in the smoke of gunfire.

Funny. He had heard no report of riflery. At least not enough to raise smoke like that.

But the time for speculation was over. A company of guardsmen was planted in a place of defense and vantage, another on the way to flank the rebels, to bring mayhem and needless slaughter.

Surely Diego saw them. Surely . . .

Garrick shook his head. The grounds of Arcady were deceptive. Add the Border encroachment to a tricky landscape, the smoke in the distance . . .

He turned from the balcony into the adjoining room—his uncle's quarters when Diego visited Arcady. There, in an opened armoire, amid a spill of clothing and boots, he found a black frock coat, tailored for his broad-shouldered uncle, that fit him like a tent. A black fedora, slipping over his ears and eyes, completed the makeshift disguise.

He could reach the nut grove before his uncle, could warn Diego . . .

Could avert a bloodbath, effect a rescue . . .

The story played through his head like a heroic ballad. He returned to the balcony, leaning across to the nearest of the oaks. The dry leaves rustled as the branch sagged with his weight, and Garrick Hawken began his mission of espionage for the safety of his uncle . . .

And the heart of his father.

CHAPTER 32

The shooting had begun when the balloon, aloft on the first northern breeze, rose like a sullen moon above the bare rocks and lumbered toward Arcady, three forms dark and visible in its unnaturally heavy gondola.

The wagon bed was not made for transport and flight. Yet it had to serve when the rebels raised the balloon, and now it careened at the end of the ropes, the most awkward gondola imaginable, thick black smoke smoldering at its center as the balloon dipped perilously near the peach orchard, then rose again, startling a squadron of guardsmen and drawing the first musket fire.

Diego leaned over the rail. The guns of the guardsmen sputtered below him, filling the ancestral grounds with mist and light. For a moment he lost sight of Arcady, then the towers emerged from the veil of smoke.

Then the noise, and the first rounds whistled by the balloon. One shot rocketed into the wagon, splintering a wheel and burying itself in the underside of the bed.

Endymion, standing above the spot where the bullet hit, cried out, nearly dropping the bellows into the fire. Willie reached through the smoke and grabbed him, pulling him away from the blaze.

"You keep usin' that contraption to stoke us aloft, Mister Endymion," the gondolier urged. "It don't do us no good facedown in the nut grove or the tarn."

Gently, he took the bellows from Endymion's hands. Shunted to the side of the wagon now, his head at rest against the hard wood of the wagon, Endymion watched helplessly as Willie Melmoth coaxed the low fire to a steady glow, and the makeshift aircraft rose higher, higher, until the bullets spent themselves below.

"Now," Willie said, wiping wet ash from his forehead. "Supposin' you take this implement back, Master Endymion. Leave the guidin' to me and the maneuvers to Master Diego."

"And what should *I* do?" Endymion asked, holding the bellows awkwardly, like a bucket of water or a newborn infant.

"Exercise this thing, sir," Willie suggested. "Raise the hot air."

Diego smiled grimly at the veiled order.

"Well," Endymion stammered. "I . . . I suspect I've raised hot air in my time before."

Diego laughed. Slowly, as though the laughter were coaxed from him, Endymion began to laugh as well.

Now the troops at the nut grove opened fire on the passing balloon. Briefly the shot whizzed and rattled by the wagon, and the three men crouched low in the safety of the bed. But then the volley of musketry was answered by another volley, deeper in the grove, moving deftly between the guardsmen and the approaching Absence.

Diego peered over the wagon side. "The Lady!" he muttered in relief. "Diversion's a-brewing."

* * *

It was all Artemis could do, guiding the troops along the edge of the whirling cloud.

From this close range—not twenty yards at the most—the Absence seemed to beckon. *Do not look into it,* she had told the men, and Rousseau, riding double on his burdened horse, Aunt Morgana seated nervously behind him, policed the column of rebels. He called out names if a man was tempted, if he wavered, if his gaze turned toward the cloud they all knew was coaxing or beckoning. Each time, his voice snapping like a rider's crop, Rousseau turned the men from too closely contemplating the leuthan abyss.

The rebels moved north, skirting the grounds of the estate, the Absence always to their right. The mansion bobbed in and out of view through a net of walnut trees. Then, through an edge of smoke, part gunpowder, part leutha, red uniforms emerged from between the thinner, leafless pecan trees.

Guardsmen. In formidable numbers.

"No closer, Lady," Rousseau urged. " 'Tis self-slaughter to attack those numbers, even with surprise in our wake."

"It's our order to provide diversion," the Lady argued.

"So be it," Evander Rousseau replied, the resentment thick in his voice. "Throw a score of lives away to cover your cousin's approach. They always claimed that they would die for you: keep them to their word, Lady."

Artemis stared into the faint turmoil of black and red. It would not do. She could not butcher young lives to save . . . a house she had grown up hating, resenting.

And yet Diego was overhead, and poor Mina waiting inside.

Artemis leaned toward the smoke, catching the faint hint of powder in the air. Something would come to her. Something had to come.

* * *

Behind the rebel lines, secreted in the cover of a blood-red stand of bishop's holly, his path winding toward the column of green at the edge of the curious smoke, Garrick did not notice at first the encroaching cloud, the humming in his ears like a choir of gnats, the song in a slow crescendo as the cloud approached and settled not ten feet away.

Consulting his compass, its whirling needles unreadable as glyphs, then giving up all geography and relying on memory, on his intimate childhood knowledge of the nut grove and surrounding evergreens, Garrick caught the first of the music, as the droning in the cloud descended into lulling music, into lulling words.

> There is sweet music here that softer falls
> Than petals from blown roses on the grass,
> Or night-dews on still waters between walls
> Of shadowy granite, in a gleaming pass;
> Music that gentlier on the spirit lies
> Than tired eyelids upon tired eyes;
> Music that brings sweet sleep down from the blissful skies.

It was probably from the Hymns somewhere. Unlike his father, Garrick was not drawn to theology. And yet, whatever its source, the music was serene and plausible, and the compass slipped through his fingers, its needle twirling as it struck the weedy ground.

In a moment he would have been drawn into the beckoning cloud, had not the rebels discovered him.

Justin St. Hyle, posted at the southernmost fringe of the East Woods, saw Garrick drop the compass, saw him teeter at the edge of the gray cloud. It was St. Hyle who sprang from cover, sprinted across the level ground, weaving through the dried and abandoned hemp plants.

He reached Garrick just as the Absence's song stilled in the boy's ear, just as Garrick began to step into the vortex of leutha and lost light.

"Git away from it, y'damn fool!" the rebel lad muttered through clenched teeth, grabbing the black-coated boy by the shoulders and pulling him away from the churning cloud. For a moment, charmed by something in the heart of the Absence, Garrick wrestled with his rescuer, broke free . . .

And Evander Rousseau, slipping stealthily through the tall tobacco plants, tackled the boy before the cloud devoured him.

There, facedown in the red Arcadian soil, Garrick was stripped of the black coat, of the ill-fitting fedora. The rebels discovered the hated red jacket beneath, its epaulets and gold buttons a sign of an officer's aide.

Justin St. Hyle drew his knife to finish the work. The blade was at Garrick's throat before Evander Rousseau, jarred by something familiar in the terrified face of the boy, wrestled the blade away from the petrified boy, from his equally petrified assailant.

"I knew I was left here for something," the lieutenant murmured. "If this boy ain't a Hawken, I'm the Citizen Arouet."

* * *

"But it's not only the guardsmen in the East Woods, Artemis," Garrick insisted.

He stood between two ragged, rough-looking rebels who had dragged him before his cousin and who regarded him skeptically now, like barnyard rat terriers surveying a lady's lapdog.

This Lady, however, was as cagy as the partisans she led. Artemis sat in the bare notch of an oak tree like a life-weary dryad, her green jacket muddy, tattered, and powder-stained, her fabled dark eyes ringed with fatigue.

Garrick was a good lad. Honorable and truthful.

And yet, the information he brought might well betray the Guard he had served faithfully, gallantly.

"Why are you telling us this?" she asked, her eyes focused on the distant brown fields, where the leutha cloud approached, scattering brush and dried leaves. "Why are you . . . informing on your people?"

Garrick's gaze never left her. Twice she settled a veiled glance on her cousin, but his eyes had not moved.

That gunmetal-blue Hawken stare. Diego's eyes.

"You *are* my people," Garrick said again. "You. Uncle Diego. My father and Cousin Mina. Beyond Guard and rebel, Urthona and Urizen, all those boundaries the soldiers and statesmen set. *You* are my people."

"That's sweet sentiment enough," Artemis replied, waving her hand dismissively. "But if you're right, we've two companies of guardsmen to deal with, and deal we must in the next hour."

She looked at Rousseau, who looked away.

"So . . ." the Lady drawled, an ironic smile spreading across her dark and lovely face. "What strategy do *you* propose, Garrick Hawken?"

The lad frowned. "I've . . . I've been thinking about the estate, Cousin. How it's set up, and how the wind's blowing."

"East to west," Artemis noted. "The gondolier was troubled by it."

"Exactly," Garrick said, his young face intent, urgent. "East to west. Think of the fields, Artemis.

"Think of the lay of the land."

* * *

She gave him only Justin St. Hyle. Could spare no more men for a harebrained venture. And after all, she could not countenance the destruction.

And yet Garrick was convinced that two men, torches, and prevailing winds could stop the long line of guardsmen he watched from the shelter of dried tobacco and hemp.

Three dozen. Perhaps forty. In a forced march with muskets at the ready.

Garrick twisted away the parched tip of a tobacco leaf, cast it into the air. It floated on a gust of easterly wind and sailed over the field toward the guardsmen and the woods beyond. Garrick watched the dried leaf fragment flutter past unnaturally stationary fingers of cloud, scud across the low pasture until it vanished from sight in a haze of mist and red uniform.

"Good," he breathed, and nodded to Justin St. Hyle.

Who, some twenty yards away, set torch to the first of the dried hemp plants.

When the smoke reached the guardsmen they thought nothing of it, the almondine smell of hemp masked by the sharper, more familiar smell of tobacco. Maybe one or two of the red-jacketed men looked to the east, saw the brown fields burning.

It was a phenomenon of war. It was the soldier's terrain.

So the hemp smoke reached them in disguise. None of them, not even the boys from the Lady's Land, who no doubt had experience with the honorable, deceptive weed, recognized the danger until all prospect of danger had fled their imaginings.

Some of the men sat down in the fields. Others yawned and trailed off into the southernmost fringes of the woods, their orders forgotten in a thick, pleasant haze of smoke.

Garrick laughed from the upwind side of the burning. He was his father's son after all, ingenious and phantasmal, more devious by far than his uncle Diego.

"I would make a good guerrilla," he whispered. "A partisan with illusions and sleights of hand. My father shall hear of this, if we both survive the coming storm."

And for once, he was sure his father would approve.

* * *

On the hill overlooking Arcady, Actaeon Peacock prepared the bull pups for the first salvo.

Government artillery was unreliable. So they had told him in military school. Explosives were highly variable, accuracy virtually unheard of.

And adding in the encroachment of an Absence . . .

Wiping soot and smoke from his brow, Actaeon leaned against a walnut tree, its black bark rough against his back. His thoughts brimmed with numbers.

Range and trajectory. Factoring in wind. Blowing heavily from the east now, the faint smell of burning hemp in its wake.

And at the back of the wind, the Absence. The great uncertainty.

Actaeon Peacock hated uncertainties. The moving void, the Lady somewhere in the nut groves.

He pondered an array of figures, rejected them. Victory was a number he could reach. He could find it through the proper calculations.

Peacock closed his eyes. He blocked out the sound of the milling gunners, the rifle fire from the groves below him. It was there, somewhere. The equation, the vector, the range.

And he was calculating still when the sphinx crept out of the woods behind him, her eyes unnaturally bright. Slowly she stalked him, the final factor, his gunners turned to stone by her cryptic gaze, the fur on her back bristling with incalculable hunger, with mystery and sly cruelty.

* * *

Artemis knew the smoke for what it was. When the faint smell of tobacco reached her over the misted fields, she took it as her signal and raised her hand. The rebels dismounted silently, losing themselves in the foliage like ghosts blending into the ruins of an ancient house. In a thin line they crept west toward the company of guardsmen, loading their muskets as they moved.

Artemis could see the insignia on the red uniforms of the guardsmen, the dirt on the blucher boots, the muskets uplifted and firing into the unlikely aircraft or not firing at all, lulled and lowered in the encroaching cloud of hemp smoke. Slowly, as though each gesture registered and echoed in a distant arrangement of stars, the Lady lifted her hand again. Evander Rousseau, in the middle of the thin rebel line, followed suit, and the men around him leveled their guns, aiming low as the great rebel leaders—ben Ezra, Westley—had taught them years ago, at the beginning of the conflict . . .

Leaders who had taught them everything but mercy.

L'Overture's golden eyes hovered like suns in Artemis' remembrance.

No. The instructions of cruelty would stop here.

Gently, the Lady lowered her hand. The rebels approached the drowsing red line, a young man in the vanguard stooping, almost lovingly lifting the musket from the hands of a sleeping guardsmen.

Merrily, listlessly, the flower of the Citizen's army surrendered.

* * *

Fifteen hundred degrees, and Mina, weakening rapidly, circled the clay investment, imagining the wax figure buried inside.

It would be Solomon in bronze, emerging like Saint Milton from his rocky forms.

As she drew near the end of her work, all her faculties seemed to be leaving her. Her hands trembled, and the eyesight failed that once spotted sermons in stone, that imagined bronze figures in the topiaries.

Her will as well seemed to fade. For the first time Mina welcomed the rest, and the choir of angels and ghosts in the rafters seemed to sing a pleasant music.

She had forgotten why she began the statue in the first place. Surely there was something in the earliest inspirations—a grand idea or noble purpose—but it had long vanished. Perhaps she would recover it, would remember when the completed statue stood resplendent and polished before her.

Somehow Mina did not believe that memory would return.

She stopped at the back of the statue. The clay had hardened. Now she could pour the metal.

Memory and grand purpose did not matter now. All that mattered was completion, was seeing the statue through. She had fought a good fight and finished her course.

She was ready to be offered.

Two thousand degrees was all she knew of a future, and the temperature of the furnace climbed as the room clouded further and the racket of gunfire grew closer, louder, and more unavoidable.

* * *

Over the roof of the house the balloon swooped—low, narrowly missing one of the towers. Willie guided the craft as best he could, but the artificial gondola was unwieldy, and the wind currents conspired against his navigations.

"This way," Diego ordered, pointing toward the gabled roof that covered the main attic of the mansion. He remembered the open skylight, the broken window wide enough to climb through the chaotic defense of Absence and guardsmen. "Through the edge of that silver cloud," he urged, pointing into the glittering mist.

Endymion looked up in alarm from the bellows. The path his brother proposed glided between two of the towers and over the main attic—a formidable challenge for the best gondolier—but the cloud, which Diego did not seem to recognize, was an encroaching Absence.

An unmoored Absence, moving malignly over the mansion itself.

* * *

The song of the Absence, the same song that had nearly lured Garrick into a whirling, disintegrating death, reached Mina in her studio as she drew the first crucible of molten bronze from the furnace.

As always, the fiery light washed over her as she grasped the crucible with the long iron tongs. Even from six feet away, the furnace heat crackled the hair on her arms. She could feel it even through the thick gloves, and weakened, she reeled at its power.

It was all she could do to lift the tongs.

The leuthan smoke of the Absence mingled freely with the smoke from the furnace now, and when the song reached her, it seemed to come out of the molten bronze, out of the orange-hot flame.

Where they smile in secret, looking over wasted lands,
Blight and famine, plague and earthquake, roaring deeps and fiery sands,
But we smile, we find a music centered in a doleful song,
Like a tale of little meaning, though the words are strong.
Surely, surely slumber is more sweet than toil, the shore
Than labor in the deep mid-river, wind and wave and oar.

Yet another song—Commentary? Hymn?—another call to slumber, and the crucible and tongs wavered in her gloved grip.

Her skin smarting with the radiant heat, Mina took a deep, scalding breath. She closed her eyes, but the eyelids were now translucent, and she could see the crucible, glowing like a lamp behind a veil of silk, as she walked toward the statue and poured the first of the bronze into the clay investment. For a moment the molten metal popped and sputtered over the wax, coating the sides of the earthen mold, settling at the heavy base of the slab.

In the rafters, the ghosts screamed hysterical warnings. The banister in the hall shuddered, its railings scattering like the teeth of a broken comb. Morgana's wheel began to spin crazily, first clockwise, then counterclockwise, as the sun rose and set twice in the clerestory windows.

But now, given over to work, having emptied the first container into the steaming investment, copper–white bronze extruding from little flaws in the base of the statue, Mina Hawken forgot the ghosts and the music, the gnomes and whispering statues and her beckoning father. She scarcely heard the thunder in the attic directly above her. Foremost in her mind was swiftness, efficiency, the clean transfer of the next crucible from furnace to statue. Forgetting her fatigue, moving briskly while the right heat remained in the furnace, she turned back to the glowing light, to the second crucible of molten bronze, and to the end of her steadfast and lonely impulse.

* * *

Steadfast and lonely, Diego leaned out of the wagon bed as Willie guided the balloon awkwardly through a shifting wall of smoke.

"It's here somewhere," he muttered to Endymion, to no one in particular, as Willie, all movement behind them in the midst of the wagon bed, steered one slowly spinning wheel over a chimney with all of six inches to spare.

"Stay back, Diego!" Endymion warned. "The cloud! You don't know whether . . ."

He stopped in midsentence. Diego stood on the driver's seat of the wagon, crouching unsteadily as the dark shingles surged below him, rippling and changing like a sea of slate. A wave of leuthan cloud curled slowly toward the balloon, its path converging with Willie's headlong course over the roof of the house.

Endymion rushed to his brother's side, pumping the small hand bellows absurdly. And yet the cloud whirled away from them, leaving smoke and fresh air in its wake.

In a long passage over the roof they stood together, the soldier prepared for a deadly leap into battle, his scholar twin protecting him with wind and machineries. Endymion squeezed the bellows until he was red-faced and gasping, looking for all his efforts like some sedentary, inexperienced piper.

And yet each time the clouds parted, the balloon sailed through safely, and at last, on the far side of the roof, the open casement of the skylight came into view, the broken glass scattered across the slate. Now Diego, perched on the driver's seat like an enormous predatory bird, slipped a loaded pistol into his belt, gripped his menacing long knife between his teeth, and, with a bladed, glinting grin at his older brother, leapt to the roof.

His footing was not good. For a moment the cracked wooden leg skidded on the slate, and Diego flapped his arms for balance. The edge of the roof seemed uncomfortably close, and he fell to his knees, grasping for purchase on the dark shingles. Then, clambering back toward the skylight, he slung his good leg over the casement, down into the darkness . . .

And with a muffled cry, fell headfirst into Arcady.

Endymion leapt from the balloon and, unsteady himself with exertion, clambered up the side of the roof. One desperate look back told him that, despite Willie's efforts, the craft had moved out of reach and was sailing sedately over the topiaries, bound for the northern borders of the grounds.

It would take the lad an hour to turn the thing around.

Endymion scrambled to the skylight and peered over. His younger brother, artificial leg wedged between casement and sill, dangled headfirst into the dark attic like an enormous long-haired bat. Diego wriggled and writhed, muttering garbled oaths.

And meanwhile, the Absence seeped into the roof.

"Diego!" Endymion called down to his brother. "Are you . . ."

"Meowt oviss, nammit!" Diego growled.

"What?"

"Me*owt* oviss!"

"You'll have to . . ." Endymion began. Then he heard his brother spitting, and the long knife clatter to the attic floor.

"Unlace the leg, Endymion!" Diego snapped, this time far more clearly. Endymion fumbled at his brother's thigh, feeling foolish, a bit embarrassed . . .

"Here, dammit!" Diego exclaimed, untying his pants.

Quickly, no longer thinking of a propriety that no longer mattered on the roof of a dissolving house, Endymion pulled away his brother's pant leg to reveal the leather corset, laced like a shoe, that held the prosthesis in place.

The pistol fell into the attic and went off, the gunshot echoing through the upper stories of the house.

Drawing up his brother's bunched trousers to where they tangled with wooden leg and window, Endymion reached into the hip pocket, found the canteen that was government-issue to regimental officers.

Usually water or tea. But this officer was a Hawken.

"By Saint Ololon, Brother!" Diego shouted. "What's keeping you up there?"

Endymion opened the flask.

Whiskey. Not his drink of choice, but given the circumstances . . .

Taking a deep breath, he used the bellows to gust away an approaching billow of Absence. Then, draining half the canteen, he set about the work. Fueled by the liquor, with the same tipsy dexterity that had set a score of buildings in bottled Golgonooza, Endymion deftly untied the wooden leg, forgetting all consequence in his intent on the job at hand. Thus freed, Diego Hawken, braced for the fall, dropped unarmed, pantless, and one-legged into the darkness.

Endymion called out twice to his brother. He looked up: the glittering clouds of the Absence had surrounded him, were moving closer. With a silent, surprised prayer to Saint Milton, Saint Ololon, and Saint Palamabron, and a deeper prayer that he had not wasted his time in the praying, Endymion Hawken dangled his feet through the skylight.

Then, downing the rest of the whiskey in one monumental swallow—after all, it might well be the last call of his life—Endymion leapt into the darkness, and the cloud covered all of Arcady.

* * *

Through the back of her hands, she could see her family beckoning.

Mina was transparent now, her skin as ruddy and clear as rose-tinted glass. The tongs were heavy in her hands, the last crucible almost impossible to lift from the furnace. Across the reeling room she staggered, talking to herself—old snatches of Text and Hymn and remembered conversation, shored fragments that she repeated now like a litany to lift her thoughts from fatigue and despair. The Chimney Sweep was there, and the old Leech Gatherer; Melusine Stella-Maris sat side by side with Saints Michael and Adonais and Saint Milton himself.

Soon they were all words, these legendary figures, these venerated saints, sounds and syllables that formed a backdrop, a soothing white noise in which Mina's thoughts could settle on the sculpture, on the task at hand. The family, from old Atreus to little Faith, called to her from the rafters, urging her away from the pedestal, the investment, the final pouring, but she moved resolutely across the studio, clay dust swirling in gray eddies at her feet.

It was almost over, and she would see the mystery face to face.

Mina redoubled her recitations, the words blurring into obscurity, dancing on the edge of nonsense, as she hoisted the tongs for the last time and poured.

Molten bronze flashed into the clay, a continuous red-gold stream, as the ghosts cried out and the angels of the Absence—angels far darker and more malign than any Morgana had seen or fancied—flickered from shadow to light, the sudden auburn glow of the room exposing their bat wings, their gloomy and sharp-toothed visages. With a cry, the angels dissolved back into the cloud that had spawned them, had thrown the illusion through the house and bothered the visions and dreams of a generation of Hawkens.

Now, suddenly, the clay mold stirred on the pedestal. The hard clay flushed, softened . . .

Transformed . . .

And Solomon Hawken staggered down from the pedestal, dazed, shaking the clay dust from his black greatcoat.

Mina opened her arms to her cousin in welcome, in love, but now she felt herself floating, lifted toward the rafters of the studio by unseen hands. All of the bat-winged angels had fled, and many of the ghosts. The faces around her were welcoming and kind.

Only gentle ghosts remained. Melusine and Christabel. Mina's own mother, Amelia Darkling, Cousin Faith and her pink ribbons.

They sang a song of the sea, but not like the sirens of a nightmarish house. They sang a song of wide expanses, of a violet and engulfing sky.

For a moment, before she was entirely transparent, before her thoughts turned to large and celestial matters, Mina Hawken looked down on her cousin Solomon, on the little bald spot in the midst of his nest of hair. She marveled, just before her old thoughts failed her and her new thoughts vaulted into an even wider marveling, at how frail Solomon was.

How frail they all were, in fact.

How each of them, wounded, had found strength in spite of and because of their wounds.

Mina's thoughts tumbled over the fragments she had spoken, saying goodbye to each name and phrase and consonant with a caress, a loving, brief enshrinement. There was one last sentence—she could not remember, but fancied that it marked the end of the Text which had sustained and vexed her family, her country, for so long. It seemed fitting to remember it now—the last words for the last words.

"Father and Mother," Mina breathed, as amiable James, free entirely from the leuthan clouds and surrounded by a choir of ghosts, smiled lovingly on his returning daughter, "I return from flames of fire tried and pure and bright."

CHAPTER 33

"Father and Mother," Solomon said as well, in unknowing unison with his departing cousin, "I return from flames of fire tried and pure and bright."

Stepping down from the pedestal, he stumbled, righted himself, and glanced about the dusty studio. The air was filled with specters—leuthan shapes that fluttered like strange, silvery banners in the hot air.

How he had arrived in Arcady he did not know. Perhaps it was the mysterious workings of his new spellcraft—the intent of the magic. Or perhaps it had something to do with the statuary, with air contained and enclosed, like that in an abandoned house or behind the glass of a mirror.

Whatever it was, there was no time to worry over it or even question it. Solomon believed he had rescued his brothers.

Now was the time to rescue Arcady.

Solomon closed his eyes, abolished the fear and misgivings, the disastrous imaginings that he knew would bring his spells to ruin. He thought of the mansion half-eaten by the gloom of the Absence, and replaced his fear with healing, affirming thoughts.

This was Arcady. However he had come here, he was home.

And home would survive the onslaught of darkness and disintegration. The spells would see to it.

"Youth of delight," he began, singing the Hymn called "The Voice of the Ancient Bard." Then stronger, with more confidence, as his voice filled the shadowy room and the ebbing coals in Mina's kiln glowed with a new and expectant light.

"Youth of delight come hither,
And see the opening morn,
Image of truth new born.
Doubt is fled & clouds of reason,
Dark disputes & artful teazing . . ."

For the first time, the effect of the spell was manifest.

The ghosts, the resident spirits of the dusty, disheveled room, scattered into the smoke and shadows like clouds before a purging wind. Genii, circling the dying flames of the furnace, winked out like snuffed candles, and gnomes roiled and crumbled on the clay-strewn floor.

It had begun, this cleansing of Arcady.

Still, it was only beginning.

Solomon stalked toward the Great Hall. He knew that the Enemy would be there, arrayed against him in legion, multiplied by mirror and bordered light. Dust from dried clay eddied around him, and Morgana's wheel, set turning by strange and unseen forces, slowed to a stop and spun in the other direction.

Statues of his ancestors stirred in the rippling bronze. Behind him, nearly hidden by the shadows and the leuthan cloud, a dark form slipped from the empty pedestal and followed him toward the mirror-struck light.

As Solomon stepped into the long room, the walls themselves seemed to glitter like broken glass. Trapped in the mirrors of the Great Hall were things older and deeper than ghosts.

Solomon moved through a maze of reflections, a shapeless, almost amoebic darkness hovering at the vanishing point of the images in a dozen mirrors. Something back there was watching him, haunting his steps through the ancestral gathering room.

Solomon called out once, twice. His voice echoed in a surprising emptiness, redoubling on itself until his cries were garbled, an immense, chaotic chorus.

No answer.

Solomon turned his attention to the first of the mirrors. The thing—whatever it was—pulsed at the far edge of sight. His own thoughts wrangled and bucked when he looked into its churning darkness, as though something were filtering into his soul, distracting him, inclining him to listen.

That . . . poetry you speak . . .

Solomon stopped. Reluctantly paid heed.

You should know.

"Know what?" Solomon asked, regretting it instantly.

An image formed in the center of the mirror, taking on shape and substance as though it emerged from an absolute, effacing cloud.

A hooded form, pale beneath a black robe. A face in a portrait, a shadow coursing down its neck like a scar.

"I know you!" Solomon exclaimed. "Uncle Innocent!"

Oh, but I am not merely Innocent, the hooded specter sighed. *I am every other ill you have known.* It waved its silvery hand, and a cavernous room seemed to open in the farthest reflections, an image in the heart of the mirror's heart.

A subterranean place. Solomon had no idea how he knew the imaged room was below ground, but the knowledge entered his thought and stayed there.

A table stood there. An opened copy of the Text the sole book upon it, the light from the image circling the book like a halo. The book lay open to the central plates, to the engravings of two men bent backward, in adoration of a fallen star . . .

In worship of a disaster. The thought seemed to take its own words.

Solomon frowned. He remembered the plate well, but he had never looked at it in quite that way.

A mishap. The voice was audible now. Solomon recognized it as Innocent's, as Vergil's, as his companion in the journey through the Absence. It was his guide and narrator through the melancholy of his seminary past.

I will show you more, the voice confided gleefully. *Let your eye follow down—what is it?*

Optical transmission lines . . .

Now, in the imaged room, a hand lay on the book. Solomon started to ask a question.

"Who . . ."

Nobody in particular. A student, perhaps a lecturer.

You know the type.

A hint of a smile traced over Solomon's lips. He knew such insinuations all too well. And something in him had moved beyond injury by this kind of diminishment.

And it was many years ago, the voice continued, undaunted. *Before Arcady, before the families. Before your family.*

Before the names of places.

Now the scene in the mirror expanded, revealing a study, a library. Other books filled the reflected room—walls and walls of shelves, dark mahogany, volumes bound in leather, in cloth.

Solomon could not see the end of them.

One of many, the voice observed, its dry irony echoing in the mirrored hall. *Your revered Text one of many that might not have been preserved, might have vanished as these did, were it not for sheer accident. . . .*

When this library was destroyed, before Arcady, it could have been any volume saved from the fire and explosions, from the Twelve Disasters that tore down the stone and surged up metal, that tore holes in the fabric of what is. . . .

Why, any volume might have been saved. An herbal. The life story of a thief or a grammar-school primer. A funerary register.

By accident, it was the book you revere. By blind accident. Nothing more.

"There is no accident," Solomon whispered. "This is the book that was saved, not the others."

The voice sniffed dismissively. The scene of the library, the Text on the table, reflected into the facing mirror and back until an infinity of libraries and texts filled the brimming room. Solomon knew that the voice was repeating itself, trying the same old dodges of doubt and uncertainty for a reason, a specific reason.

Perhaps, at last, it was afraid.

Afraid, because Solomon Hawken had passed through flames of fire tried and pure and bright. He had returned to his ancestral home, for the first time bearing the priestly powers that no Urthonan seminary could bestow upon him.

He was close to victory. He knew that.

But nothing in the Great Hall—not the angeled and ghosted rafters nor the scattered images in the dozen mirrors—could guide him now.

You are at a juncture, Sister Enith Moneta had told him. *At a crossroads yourself.*

He remembered the night on the water, the nun's stories and reminiscences, the cottage whose silvery, reflective windows had spangled its own interiors with light . . .

Mirrors. The windows had been mirrors.

And the seedy sister, the Dirty Nun . . .

When you reach that juncture, she had told him, *the next step is not forward nor backward, but a strange sideways—a step not keeping with what you would expect at all, but something out of instinct, out of some source deeper than simple common sense.*

You won't know the step until after you make it.

And you will never make it alone.

* * *

The floor of the attic pooled with silver clouds, as Endymion helped Diego to his feet.

All around them, the keepsakes that the Hawkens had stored in this house for generations—the memorabilia, the cedar chests, old clothing and toys, portmanteaus and dressmaker's models—winked out as the cloud surrounded and devoured them.

Diego barely had time to snatch his pistol from the encroaching cloud. Holding up the weapon, he inspected it stupidly, as though all of a sudden he had forgotten what it was used for.

Slowly, the Absence closed in on the two brothers. Now Khole's nest vanished in a whiff of frankincense, and the roof above the brothers yawned open, revealing nothing but silvery cloud from the rafters to the edge of infinity. Oddly, through the skylight, the sun shone in a blue sky, but around them the clouds turned, and boiled, and beckoned.

Diego teetered on his one leg; Endymion rushed to support him. Steadied by his twin, the Captain recovered his balance.

Once more, Endymion aimed the little bellows at the approaching cloud. Now the puff of air was ragged, ineffectual: the cloud rolled back on itself, but then surged forward again like spindrift on an inexorable tide. Now the skylight vanished, the framed sun eclipsed by the shadows.

Together, as though they were a single creature, four-armed and three-legged, the brothers staggered toward the trapdoor of the attic, still visible between the spreading pools of cloud. They reached the ladder and descended, Endymion following right after Diego, the rungs above them vanishing as they clambered down. They tumbled into a heap at the head of the stairs, then down a flight together, to the second-story landing, itself besieged by a narrowing cloud.

Diego leaned against the banister, then pushed away as the cloud crept over. Losing his balance, he fell onto the landing, followed by Endymion, who had tried vainly to hold him up.

"Nobody will ever know," Diego muttered, pushing his brother off him as the clouds closed again around them.

"Know what, Diego?"

"That what we did was . . . was *heroic*,"

Despite the situation, despite himself, Endymion smiled.

"Why does it matter, Diego?"

Diego shrugged. There was no place to go, and they both knew it.

"It doesn't matter," he conceded. "Doesn't matter at all. Kind of makes you think, though, don't it?"

"There's a way out of this," Endymion muttered, ignoring his brother's more philosophical speculations.

"What's that?"

"I'm not sure," Endymion conceded. "Dammit! I have no idea! I'm out of ideas entirely and . . . and it isn't nearly as horrible as I thought it would be, even though we're right at the shores of . . . of . . . disintegration. But I believe the way out *is* here, if we could think of it."

He pumped the bellows listlessly into the arriving cloud.

"This way," Diego muttered. "You're my legs in this venture, 'Dimyan."

Laughing softly at hearing his childhood nickname, Endymion followed the Captain's orders. Leaning down, slipping his shoulder beneath Diego's arm, with a stagger and a grunt he hoisted his brother. Diego tucked the pistol in his belt and balanced his weight as he had done with his wooden leg for years, becoming suddenly lighter against the shoulder of his scholarly twin.

For the first time in their recollection, Diego had become the brains and Endymion the muscle. Together, the brothers descended the last flight of stairs, and stood together, unsteadily, at the edge of a world of mirrors.

As the floor of the house tilted and rocked like a ship in storm, Endymion lurched to the entrance of the Great Hall, dragging his brother with him. The dozen or so candles Mina had lit and set in the room's four candelabra reflected and magnified in the labyrinth of mirrors, until it seemed as though a hundred thousand flames fluttered and winked in the hall, that the walls themselves were burning.

Instinctively, Diego brought forth his pistol.

The hall resounded with a chorus of voices, a ghostly choir that teemed in the rafters and mirrors. Like streamers they fluttered in the drafty mansion, sometimes assuming human form, sunken eyes and haggard faces, sometimes simply swaying, as featureless as light.

Melusine was there, and old Aristo. Prometheus and Atreus on his wheeled bed. Christabel and Roger, James and William . . .

Endymion choked back a sob when a slanted beam from the clerestory, filtered through the pink light in the garments of Saint Ololon, settled into the form of a young girl, her wisp of hair drawn up in delicate ribbons of light.

"Faith," he murmured, and for a moment Diego sagged in his arms.

Solomon as well stood at the center of the room, spinning in a barrage of light, which splashed over him and sparked against his coat. Of all the figures in the Great Hall, his was the most troubled, recoiling at a vicious assault of flame and ember. His image passed through each mirror, his smoldering back caught in one reflection, his profile in another, in another his face a map of weariness and dismay.

He was solid. Too solid for ghost and reflection.

"Solomon!" Endymion called out, and as his brother turned, a blast of shimmering leuthan light erupted from the mirror in the far corner. It rushed into Solomon like a wave, like a force, and in that far mirror a darkly hooded form hovered in the midst of a lamplit library, rumbling and laughing.

The twins knew the hooded face at once. Some thirty years ago, like any curious boys, they had noticed the painting turned to face the wall, the chipped frame, the back of the canvas.

At night they had sneaked a look at the portrait of Uncle Innocent.

Which was how they recognized him now.

With a laugh surprisingly quiet and sweet, the first murderer reveled as Solomon fell to his knees.

You have failed, he said, his soft voice lifting out of the choiring ghosts. Each of the brothers heard that voice, and each thought the message was for him alone.

Do not judge yourself harshly, soothed the dark man in the mirror, as his caped form wavered like a reflection on a troubled pond. *Let the world, let those you love, do that.*

Diego raised the pistol, aimed it at the dark, indefinite shape in the far mirror. It was not Uncle Innocent—that much even he could tell.

Whatever it was glided with hallucinatory speed from the form of Innocent, through Vergil, through L'Overture and Hyperion Werther and a bat-winged angel, repeating the forms in the rafters and mirrors, all of them composed of one substance—a brilliant, flickering leuthan cloud that took all shapes and retained none, settling at last for the first shape of its choosing, the Uncle Innocent of Diego's darkest boyhood imaginings.

It was a long shot, a hundred feet or more, and Diego had proved beyond doubt his incompetence with the weapon.

And what if you were to shoot? the image of Innocent asked tauntingly, turning dead eyes toward the great-great-nephew he had barely known or noticed until this moment. *The shape before you is not the villain.*

Your uncle is thirty years dead.

This shape is my mask, the form I have chosen to take. I am Arouet, L'Overture, the Absence itself. I am beyond you, larger than you all . . .

"But there's part of you I can shoot at," muttered Diego. "Hold me steady, 'Dimyan."

The floor tilted beneath the brothers. The shape of their villainous uncle dissolved into leuthan cloud. Solomon struggled to his feet, and another darkness—a whirling darkness like a maelstrom in ink—gyrated in the heart of the far mirror.

"I can't hold you up, Diego!" Endymion protested. "I—I can barely stand myself!"

"Don't think about it, 'Dimyan! Stand!"

And for a moment—no more than a second or two—the violent chaos of the house found a balance, stilled.

Solomon gained his footing as well.

Endymion steadied and stood, supporting his lamed brother.

And Diego pulled the trigger, firing a single bullet into the black epicenter of the mirror.

A wide crack spread over the surface of the glass, crazing in a flaring, spiderweb pattern. For a moment the ghostly choir fell silent, and the Absence itself seemed to gasp, to lose voice.

Then, all caution thrown behind him, Solomon stepped toward the broken mirror.

The next step is not forward nor backward, but a strange sideways.

He had first seen the table, the library, the Text, in the heart of that glass.

It was the place to start.

With one fearless stride, a moment as close to physical heroism as a Textual scholar had ever come, in Arcady, Urizen, or elsewhere, he vaulted against the surface of the mirror . . .

Which bent, crackled, and closed around him, as he entered the heart of the heart of the Absence.

CHAPTER 34

The leap through the mirror had been the substance of children's stories, the long fairy-tale dream before the interventions of science. The kind of thing he had imagined before Endymion had told him of its impossibility.

He had leapt into the mirror because it seemed right at the moment, and for no other reason than that rightness.

Now he lay in a dark mahogany chamber. Windowless and doorless, lit only by the faint, guttering light of a lantern on the lowest shelf. At first, Solomon thought it was the library imaged in the mirrors of the Great Hall, but the light revealed a narrow cubicle, furnished only with a cot and small night table, upon which a glass of gin sat, half full, and a cigar smoldered, its long ash hovering precariously over the table edge.

Dust motes hovered in the lamplight, stationary in the motionless air. Solomon felt something like recognition.

Relics from his familial past lay scattered in the narrow room. Prometheus' spectacles, and Aristo's oar, with which he had rowed out onto the Great Lake to court Melusine Stella-Maris. A necklace of seashells, no doubt the dowry of the mermaid bride.

Innocent's signet ring, its skull and crossbones *ominous*, as Solomon's mother used to say, *but not entirely incriminating.* His portrait leaning against an empty shelf, this time face to the room.

It was a collection to rival Endymion's, each oddity freighted with a shared past. All through the room, the smell of stale tobacco, the underlacing of juniper.

Old Atreus. Whose house this was, and for whose final chambers this room had been intended. Atreus, small particles of whom flickered like sand in the deltas of the Alph, scarcely a memory of the old tyrant whose spirit once animated their carbon, their bone.

From the beginning . . . the voice insinuated, the voice no longer Innocent, but something darker, more resonant and strange. *From the beginning your family has been like this.*

Artifacts in an abandoned room. Over which the wind blows according to its circuits. Each remembered for a shell, a ribbon . . . a nut grove or an odor on that same silent wind.

Solomon glanced through the leavings of his family—some scarcely recognizable, lost to memory, like the spindle leaning against the little night table. The lamp was rusted, the pink ribbon, though more new than other belongings, had already seen the first of the moth's corruption.

Was it true what Innocent—or the thing incarnated in Innocent—had said about the family? If so, the Hawken line was like the path of the Absence. Which passed over fertile country, leaving desolation and salt behind.

"But still," Solomon said. He prepared himself for spellcraft.

Then the face in the portrait began to change.

Solomon did not *see* it as much as sense it—a movement of pigment and shadow in the corner of his vision. He knew better than to look in the face of the portrait, for it was transforming, he knew, into other faces, other forms . . .

Arouet. Ceraphis. L'Overture and ben Ezra. Constantine and the gibbering boy in the branches . . .

The Absence had passed through them all, had touched their edges, had set up residence in their corrupted hearts, had shaped each of them into monsters. Solomon did not need to see to understand.

The villains in his life were only forms of this larger evil.

Now the voice came to him again, insinuating in a language below words, offering him empire and magic, women and riches and all the knowledge veiled for generations . . .

The other books in that room, it seemed to say. *I can set them all before you, their wisdom spilling into your soul like . . . like . . .*

It was his own voice speaking to him, coaxing him, seducing him. But Solomon fixed his mind on the Text, his memory on its shimmering plates, his heart on the words he had read and memorized over years of study.

He knew the passage he searched for would suffice: that indeed, despite Absence and winnowing and fire, he would find the Text he searched for tried and pure and bright.

Then he recalled it. Opposite the Thirty-ninth Plate, the vividly inked portrait of the lovers asleep by the seashore that lay near the end of the Text itself. The bird rampant above them, on the facing page the lines he sought.

He recited them aloud, with a fierce joy.

> Such are the Laws of thy false Heav'ns; but Laws of Eternity
> Are not such; know thou, I come to Self Annihilation.
> Such are the Laws of Eternity, that each shall mutually
> Annihilate himself for others' good, as I for thee.
> Thy purpose & the purpose of thy Priests & of thy Churches
> Is to impress on men the fear of death, to teach
> Trembling & fear, terror, constriction, abject selfishness:
> Mine is to teach men to despise death & to go on
> In fearless majesty annihilating Self, laughing to scorn
> Thy Laws & terrors, to put off Self & all I have, ever & ever. Amen.

The words thundered in the narrow room. For a moment Solomon felt drained, as though something large and essential had been sapped from him by speaking.

Now I must stand, he told himself. Even to the death. I must not believe that the Absence is winning.

For a brief, flickering second he thought of Khole on his bed of dark ashes, how, shrouded in incense, the bird had awaited the miraculous change to angel, to teacher.

How Solomon had awaited that change himself, as the leuthan clouds had covered him at the edge of the Absence.

It was an image to which he clung as his strength and virtue dwindled. He focused on it, excluding the other images the Absence hurled at him.

For the guttering flame of the lantern began to move, to alter shape in the dusty, distracted globe. With each movement it enlarged and grew, and in its depth Solomon saw disturbing things.

A collapsing house.

The death's-head moth on Mina's face.

The leering face of a Blight, and his silvery breath.

Now a wind lifted through the room, edged with the glittering red and green of leuthan mist, scattering papers, rifling the flame, lifting Solomon precariously off the ground and spinning him, as though he had been caught in a small but powerful cyclone.

Below him, a stairwell opened, leading down into darkness. Like a whirlpool, the leuthan wind circled around him, spiraling, funneling, sucking him down . . .

Solomon closed his eyes. Dreamlike, he thought, *this has happened before . . . a story old as . . . old as . . .*

Saint Milton himself . . .

And as he lost consciousness—for a second or an hour, he could never tell—a phrase of the Text swam through his last waking thoughts:

so Milton's shadow fell
Precipitant, loud thund'ring into the Sea of Time & Space.

He awoke in complete darkness. The thrashing sound of the deep, subterranean machinery was loud here. Like the heartbeat of a monstrous, cornered beast it crashed and thundered through the shadows. Somewhere beneath the floors, the earth and the stone of a century's foundation, Solomon decided, buried by years of neglect or design, lay one of Arouet's deceptive machineries.

A mill, perhaps. A loom or a great steam engyn, devised for the portage of bordermetal out of the depths of the earth.

Whatever it was, it had worked beyond the Citizen's design. Solomon was nearly convinced of it. The machinery was a wild horse which the Citizen had mounted and which now carried him away.

The dark mills of the enemy. Which as they ground and thrashed, no doubt tore the Absence further from its original anchoring.

"I will follow it," Solomon breathed to himself. "Even to the depths of earth and the end of time . . ." Even though the wind that rose to meet him out of the depths was warm, unnaturally warm, he wrapped his greatcoat tightly about his shoulders—protection, perhaps, against what awaited him in the epicenter of the Absence.

Solomon stalked into the darkness, his strides more confident, anointed.

Soon the darkness rushed over him and engulfed him. Solomon felt as though he were wading through nothing, as though everything he knew and could sense had evaporated before him, leaving pure Absence in its stead.

Slowly, shapes began to emerge from that darkness. At first Solomon believed that his eyes were adjusting, that the gloom in these subterranean passages was not as total, as complete, as he had supposed. Around him columns loomed out of the blackness, and heaps of ruined metal, as though some ancient intelligence had placed bordermetal in orderly piles within these deserted catacombs. Glass cases, most of them shattered, were arranged at eye height intermittently along the walls. Some of them contained axes, one of which, almost by reflex, Solomon lifted gently from its casing.

Armed now with a bladed weapon, Solomon knelt beside one of the hulking metallic carcasses. It was scratched with old designs, obscure writings, a sort of impenetrable cuneiform he could not see well in the darkness. He shifted, letting the source of light tumble over his shoulder . . .

And discovered that the radiance came from Khole, who stood glowing behind him, arms extended in a gesture of acceptance and embrace. The angel's face was serene, innocent, and wise, and his raiment was glistening.

"Khole!" Solomon cried out joyously, leaping to his feet in the shadows as the light from the angel, green and golden, spilled through the cavernous room. "Where . . ."

"Waiting for you," the angel replied.

"But how did you know I would come *here*?" Solomon steadied himself, hoisted the ax to his shoulder.

"I was not sure," Khole confessed. "But if you were to win through, against cloud and Absence and the darker regions of your own fear . . . this is the spot where I knew I would find you."

"But why did you leave me? Why didn't you help?"

"You're here, aren't you?" the angel asked.

Solomon bristled. He could have been swallowed, dissolved, the Absence consuming the best of him in his own ancestral home, while Khole . . .

But the angel was right. Solomon *was* here, wasn't he? Aligning himself with the magic's intent, he had rescued his brothers and passed through the first of the Absence's ambushes.

It was something he had to do alone.

Now he was bound for the transformed machinery in the great depths of the evil itself, for that spot where the insubstantial took shape and habitation, if what Khole had told him before was true.

And why shouldn't it be true? After all, the magic had brought him this far.

Heartened, Solomon Hawken rose and continued, his path breasting the shadows, sloping down toward the crashing noise in the heart of the earth.

"Are you sure of this?" Khole called after him. "That this is what we must do?"

"It is what I must do."

Khole sighed deeply. "Then I must follow," he whispered. And he took up the cup and followed, bright wings folded against his golden robes.

* * *

"So all of this lies beneath Arcady?" Solomon asked the angel, as the two of them waded deeper down the winding tunnel, their path illumined by the angel's light.

"Yes, but we are beneath the ruins of Ville as well, and outside Lambeth and in the eastern mountains of Luvah where the wish sanitarium lies, and on the borders of sunless seas. Space collapses in the Absences, and reckoning by reason becomes . . . impossible."

Solomon smiled sadly. "Endymion always claimed you were a puzzle."

"Endymion is well, Solomon," the angel assured. "You saw him in the Great Hall, and it was no image, no illusion. He's well for now, and for days and months to come. Oh, he'll endanger himself again and again, because he'll never learn the lesson completely—that figuring out things doesn't always fix them."

"And Diego?" Solomon shifted the heavy ax to his other shoulder.

"Rest assured *that* one will seek his own danger willingly," the angel replied with a soft, musical laugh. " 'If you can't wrestle it or kick it in the face, it doesn't exist,' or so he's bargained for thirty years. But I think he's learned that the stuff of battle is not only steel and shot and fire, but smoke and distances, as well. Sometimes strength and courage aren't enough, but they're still his best allies."

"So they're both safe," Solomon said. "Or as safe as can be expected. Now for the house. For Arcady."

Khole fell silent, but still he followed, as Solomon steered an ill-lit path through the wreckage of collapsed stone and tattered bordermetal, his eyes on the darkness ahead.

It was not long before another light rose to meet him.

Here in a deep entanglement of stone, any light at all was a surprise, but Solomon stopped short at the green-golden glow ahead.

Green and gold. The colors of natural summer. The colors of Khole's radiant wings. And yet, in contrast to Khole's radiance, this light appeared deadly and artificial—the flat color of a serpent rather than a blossoming branch.

All the while, the thrashing, mechanical sound continued, closer and more insistent, drowning out words and echoes and even thought.

Now Solomon clutched the ax apprehensively. He could hear nothing behind him, and the winglight of the angel seemed to have dwindled and faded. But he knew by faith that Khole was nearby, that though their paths might extend to the ends of the earth, the angel had chosen to be with him.

He was not alone. At rest in this knowledge, Solomon took a deep breath and stepped into the unhealthy light at the bottom of the tunnel.

It was like a scene from the Hymns, like an illuminated plate he remembered from that ancient accompaniment to the Text. The chapel, the tombstones, the gravesite brambled over by a century's neglect. But despite the buildings, the signs of habitation, the landscape before Solomon felt unoccupied, void of a recent human touch.

The thrashing sound was deafening now, emanating from somewhere in the chapel's shady interior.

With a last, furtive look over his shoulder at Khole, Solomon walked toward the chapel door. The angel seemed to dwindle into smoky light behind him, but Solomon was not alarmed.

After all, his magic sustained him.

As the shadow of the little steeple crossed over him like a strange eclipse, Solomon first saw the loom through a hole in the stained-glass window. Its frame was a tattered combination of wood and metal, the wood having rotted and chipped away to reveal an iron undergirding, a dark, rusted skeleton beneath the ragged pulp.

And yet wood and metal were not its only elements. A glittering mist covered the loom, sometimes seeming to buoy and move the shuttle, sometimes knitting together frame and beam and handle. The machine lay in a juncture between the material and the immaterial, so that at one moment it seemed to be emerging from the leuthan cloud, while at another it seemed to be swallowed by it.

Despite its disrepair, the loom had kept something like its original purposes, the shuttle weaving rapidly from one end of the web to the other and back, the treadles driving with a regular, stamping rhythm, as though invisible weavers guided and propelled them.

Surrounded by mirrors and statues of saints, the contraption wove, out of apparent nothing, a leuthan fabric that tumbled to the chapel floor, folded, and dispersed into the Absence itself. Solomon knew it on sight: a Penelope Loom, the mages of Lambeth had called it, a sturdy machinery whose original intention was to draw energy from the air around it, converting moisture and light into motion and weaving what remained into nothing. The contraption was usually large, a principal device in the steam weavers of Luvah and of southern Urizen, but here, in the subterranean folds beneath an Absence, its function had altered.

Perhaps Arouet had once used it to create energy to empower the bordermetal mines—as a dynamo that provided light for the murky caverns, locomotion for cart and winch. But now the Absence had taken it, and its task was different.

He remembered Khole's words, spoken far above, in the ruins of Ville.

Looms that weave the spiritual into the corporeal . . .

Yes, that was it.

And when it lay exhausted, the chapel, the garden, and the whole subterranean labyrinth would fall into complete and permanent darkness.

The movement of the loom reflected off the chapel walls, where a score of mirrors framed the strange transference of nothing into thick, sentient fog. Like an object caught in the Great Hall of Arcady, the loom receded infinitely into the heart of the mirrors.

Optical transmission lines. Endymion's term came back to him.

A last assurance. For when the machine itself ran down, it would take centuries, perhaps eons, for the mirrors themselves to forget its motion. A thousand looms, perhaps a million, would continue to wind and weave in the redoubled reflections, and the motion itself would create cloud upon cloud, enough . . .

To detach the Absence for good. Or spread it across the face of the world.

That is, if it was not stopped in time.

His jaw clenched, plumbing his memory for the right verses, for the right spell, Solomon gripped the ax and ascended the stairs of the little chapel: the stone crumbled beneath his booted feet, and a small, whistling thing—live borderwire, perhaps, or a wayward gnome—sprang shrilly from his path.

If he had come in time, the Absence would hang in place—perhaps by a strand, by a tendril, but in place nonetheless, its silvery cloud stationary over the same spot through Eternity . . .

And of all people, Solomon Hawken would have stopped its spread.

As the last thought crossed his mind, the chapel was rocked with a gleeful, sinister laughter. Blocking out the sound, Solomon raised the ax slowly, resolutely.

But at the topmost step to the chapel, he staggered. He slipped and fell to his knees. The stones beneath his feet began to fade, to melt and contort, to liquefy.

Solomon cried out, sure that the stones were turning to water, that he would drown in the depths of the Absence.

But instead, the pavement turned into a steep, glassy incline, the dim glass rippled with fire and age. Solomon could not regain his footing. He slid backward, desperately, absurdly, as though he had tried in vain to scale a mountain of ice.

He was sliding down a long, ash-stained mirror.

"Khole!" Solomon cried. But the angel had vanished in fierce, reflectant light.

Desperately, Solomon tried to regain his balance. His boots scrabbled hopelessly over the slick surface. The ax clattered against the mirror beneath him until, with a last twist of his hand, Solomon dug its blade into the glass. Using the ax like a piton or pick, he pulled himself unsteadily toward the chapel.

The door ahead of him clouded and swirled. Solomon pulled himself to the threshold, his arms burning with exertion. The light boiled and steadied, and suddenly he saw himself in the doorway, ash-smeared and scratched, ax in hand.

The chapel door was a mirror as well.

Within its clouded reflection, he could see the distances behind him.

The leuthan clouds, the sickly green of the garden, the dark maw of the tunnel, bright writhing light . . .

Alarmed, clinging to the ax handle, Solomon pivoted and looked behind him. All he could see was cloud—shimmering leuthan cloud, that approached him billowing over the green-gold garden, taking on the hues of snakeskin, of beetle wing, of all things glittering and lethal.

Solomon cried out—for Khole, for anyone—and sprang toward the chapel door.

You have lost your home by your trespass, a voice urged, the same voice Solomon had heard as he watched his childhood self in the lime-tree bower. Somehow it had changed from Uncle Vergil's assuring tones into the more reptilian, more accusing voice of Innocent, then deeper still, until it stripped itself of all humanity and became only words and discordant, seductive music. Sweet, insinuating, it played beneath the thrashing sound of the loom in a syrupy, poisonous counterpoint.

And of all people, Solomon Hawken would have stopped its spread, the voice proclaimed ironically. *Solomon Hawken, who would have been Saint Milton, or the Bard, or both. You have sacrificed your family to such vanity and cowardice. And to no real avail—that's the sad part of it all.*

For the Absence will dissolve you as well.

Gasping, Solomon pulled himself onto the chapel floor. He ransacked his memory for the words from the Text, from the Hymnal—the groundwork for a destructive spell, an incantation to dismantle the churning monstrosity of metal and wood before him. But the thrashing was louder still.

It was the only sound in the chapel, in the entire Absence.

Solomon closed his eyes, shouted Text and Hymn, but the words of his incantation slipped from his memory like water through his fingers. Something about veils and deaths and the silent shuttle . . .

And then, he stopped and listened.

Again the deafening sound of the loom rose to throttle him, to blot out words and voice and thought. But Solomon closed his eyes and listened, again matching his breathing with the slow, regular pulse of the machinery, as he had done in the great pavilion under Khole's watchful eye. He tried to imagine the illumined pages, but the gnashing of the loom was too loud, and the whirl of leutha and light so dazzling that, even with his eyes closed, it seemed as though he looked at the sun through the thinnest of clouds.

He could not think of the pages. Could not imagine their colors and illuminings.

You will lose your magic . . . the voice warned.

The magic! For a moment, Solomon had forgotten it entirely. Straining to remember snatches of Text or the Hymns, he began once, twice . . .

And, as though the voice was prophetic, each time his voice faltered, lost completely in the crashing, shrieking sound of the loom, which continued to weave its blank, chaotic fabric out of the heart of the Absence.

Desperately, his eyes clamped shut against the chaos of light, Solomon tried to remember a page, any page, of Text or Hymn. Nothing came to his mind's eye but shadow, the dark paneling of the Great Hall of Arcady . . .

Home . . .

And the image of Christabel Whitford Hawken, his sainted mother, passing before his eyes like an afterimage of light. And the simple song she had taught him, before he could read and when he could barely remember, flickered in his memory like an image at the far vanishing point of a mirror.

> And by came an Angel who had a bright key,
> And he open'd the coffins & set them all free . . .

Solomon sang the snatch of the old Hymn. Sang it again, in defiance of the crashing sound that engulfed him.

So be it, he thought, as the words vanished into the noise. *It is the best I can remember.*

Firm hands grasped him by the shoulders. Strong arms lifted him. Solomon felt the swift brush of a wing over his face.

He opened his eyes. He stood in the nave of the little chapel, the loom grinding and clattering before him like a carriage stripped of its team and racing down a steep hill.

Khole was beside him. The angel's arms held him up, the angel's wings covered him in protective shadows.

Heavily, Solomon stood, the whole chapel rocking around him.

In the deafening noise Solomon turned toward the angel. Khole's wings were shabby, ragged, as though he had picked this time, this place, to molt or die. He stared at Solomon, a look of simple pity and compassion in his glittering eyes.

"Th-thank you," Solomon breathed.

"Do not thank me yet," Khole replied. "It is not yet finished."

At the front of the church, the altar shifted. Uprooted by the tremors in the chapel, it began to scoot, then sidle toward Solomon with quick, jerky motions, crawling past the loom, the mourner's bench, the neat rows of pew and kneeler, as though it were some monstrous, galvanized parody of a living thing.

Solomon lifted his ax. Khole fluttered and murmured beside him.

Now the pews themselves shook and tilted in their places. The mirrors on the chapel wall began to slip, to fall from place, to shatter on the stone floor of the building. Bright shards of mirror reflected the green light in absurd, fragmentary patterns, and Solomon, growing dizzy in the kaleidoscope of mirror and stained glass, struggled for balance, for footing.

Now the Text deserted him entirely. He remembered no passages, no lines.

"Khole! Do *something*!" he shouted, but his cry was lost in the tremor and crash of the mirrors, the hysterical grinding of the loom. The angel appeared to be in six—no, *seven*!—places, reflected in a dozen mirrors, his image fragmented like a saint in stained glass, like an icon in the tesserae of a battered mosaic.

But I am alone, Solomon thought. The beams above him cracked, spilling tile and stone from the chapel roof.

I am alone, and I must make something of this.

Cautiously, he approached the loom. Now, out of the spinning heart of the machinery, the sinister voice returned, this time as though he were hearing it through a glass dome or a baffle of water.

You have lost your angel, your last companion and hope, the machine sang, almost gleefully, as the cloudy skeins enveloped Solomon, choking him, smothering him. *You have lost your angel, and you are nothing without him.*

Drawn by the music in the voice, trying not to listen, Solomon raced his hands across the frame of the loom, searching for a switch, a lever, a gear—anything that might shut down the roaring, the clamor.

His hand passed through nothingness, and for a moment he felt the white-hot evil of the spirit that the loom was weaving into being.

Suddenly the clouds eddied and dispersed beside him. Khole was there, ragged wings flailing, the same look of serenity and innocence and wisdom filling his countenance as in the tunnels, spangling the air with a new and unexpected light.

Seraphic. That was the word.

But the machine ground on, thrashing and shrieking, as Solomon fumbled for the lever, his feet resting vainly on treadles that continued to move with their own harsh volition.

Then Khole reached toward the loom.

At that moment, in a knowing deeper than thought, Solomon recoiled. A malign intelligence, dark as a subterranean river, chuckled through the harness and heddles of the loom.

You will lose your angel . . .

"No!" Solomon cried. "It's what the machine wants! To weave you into . . ."

But it was too late. Khole's ethereal hands fastened upon the frame of the loom, and suddenly a scarlet light flashed over him, his wings bursting into a heatless flame.

He was caught between the worlds of substance and ether.

In the core of the fire Khole turned, regarding Solomon calmly, painfully. There was no accusation in those angelic eyes, and for a moment, reaching out for his friend and mentor, Solomon recalled the waters of Pontus Tarn, closing over another bright and innocent gaze.

The angel slumped smoldering to the floor, his hands still fastened upon the frame of the loom as though he were nailed to its wood and metal. Now his ethereal substance wound and raveled through the dark machinery of beam and shuttle and mottled cloud and vanished into a leuthan mist.

"No!" Solomon cried. Enraged, he stepped back from the screeching machine. In his anger he could hear no voices, neither song nor coaxing. Lifting his ax high above his head, he brought it thundering down upon the loom, the splinters flying, the terrible ratlike squeal as ax tore into metal, blindly, relentlessly, flickering up and down in a thousand shards of mirror.

Out of the loom a skein of mist curled and writhed, catching Solomon about the arms, about the neck. Slowly, inexorably, it pulled the priest toward the whipping shuttle, toward the central, consuming works of the machinery. It was trying to draw him in, to consume him, to entangle him in the long garment of darkness, pull him into the void more absolute than the Absence itself.

With his last remaining strength, Solomon cast aside his own dark imagining of dissolution and destruction. He struggled with the Absence, and thought, oddly, of Saint Milton. Then a strange passage of Text rose up from nowhere—from his absent thought, from the weaving loom. Abstractly, carried away by the words into some sort of painful ecstasy, Solomon recited them, out of his fitful memory.

> "... Silent Milton stood before
> The darken'd Urizen, as the sculptor silent stands before
> His forming image; but within that portion
> His real Human walk'd above in power and majesty,
> Tho' darken'd, and the Seven Angels of the Presence attended him.

"The Seven Angels of the Presence," he whispered reverently now, as the loom shuddered and stopped, shuddered again.

The angels. Solomon was sure he had met them: not the likes of Khole nor his winged, ethereal beings in the mirrors and chambers of Arcady, but the everyday angels who had crossed his human path when he needed them. Morgana and Mina, Artemis, Diego, Endymion.

Marcus, of course.

Perhaps others he did not—would never—know.

And perhaps what he had done today would stand angelic for someone, as he vanished into the absence of memory unheralded, alone ...

But having done what he could.

With a lurch, the loom resumed its weaving, but it seemed somehow weaker. Indeed, the clouds seemed to thin around Solomon, to scatter on his arms, to recede ... and as if that moment were a stopgap, a key, other words returned to Solomon Hawken in a cascade of poetry newly remembered. A passage from the Text, a passage of weaving and renewal:

> "Her Looms vibrate with soft affections, weaving the Web of Life,
> Out from the ashes of the Dead ..."

Solomon pulled the ax from the clinging leuthan strands and kept hacking, his ax flickering and flourishing above the fracturing machine. Part by part, fragment by fragment, the loom broke up and away, frame skittering across the floor, spindle tumbling, unraveling a stream of cloud as it crashed out through a chapel window, one of the treadles coming to a halt but the other churning, rising and falling, propelled by itself or by something far more knowing and fiendish, rising and falling again and again, each time more slowly. Solomon, his energy nearly spent, hammered the wreckage until something deeper than muscle or thought or feeling was all that was lifting his arms, and, with a last pathetic sigh, the loom ground to a halt, the exhausted Solomon lying atop it, weapon still clutched in his bruised and bleeding hands.

The Absence settled to a strange calm. For a moment, the leuthan mist curled gently, almost lovingly, through Solomon's gray mop of hair, as he lay at the foot of the loom, so entangled with frame and skein that he seemed hammered to the spot.

Nowhere was there any sound. Solomon's free hand, dropping the ax, moved in a graceful gesture over the ruined machine, quartering the air above it, scattering cloud and mist.

"And tears fell down like dews of night," he whispered.

Tears for Diego and Endymion. For little Faith and vacant Aristo. Oh, for all the vanished and changed.

It is over, Solomon thought, with an odd admixture of relief and grieving. Quietly, he let his hand play down the hot frame of the demolished loom.

Oh, it is not over, a dark voice told him.

It rose unexpectedly from the crumbling statuary of the castle, from the twisted mouths of the saints in the stained glass. *Oh, it is not over. Weep for them all. All your little "Angels of the Presence." For you have killed them.*

Solomon stood, the loom dissolving at his feet, sawdust and rust black on his fingers.

The loom was broken, and he was free from its dark skein, but the voice was still present, weaving yet darker insinuations into the mouths of the icons. Saint Ololon glared down at him from her place in the western lancet window. Her skin and purple robes jaundiced by the changed light, she was a lamia, a mother of sphinxes, rather than the Virgin trembling on the Porch.

The man-sized statue of Saint Los had become the Enemy. Miller of Eternity, Prince of the Starry Wheels. His was the form of the Citizen, glimpsed through poster and coinage, but the Citizen's face moving into abstraction, the geometry of its features heightened and angular until the statue seemed to be carved of gray gem, shaped by a sinister lapidary.

An empty pedestal, not far from the broken loom, shimmered with a dark cloud. It was like Mina's incomplete statue among the topiaries, the invisible sculpture of vanished Uncle Innocent. Its emptiness was more ominous, more threatening, than the scowling faces on the stone saints.

Solomon shuddered, and the cloud on the empty pedestal spoke.

Weep for yourself, it said. *For you will be the first to die.*

Stones fell away from the eastern wall of the chapel, crashing behind a veil of dust.

Vaguely, bumping against the mourner's bench, Solomon made for the door. A fitful light wavered in front of him, dancing through the shadows of the chapel. It hovered for a moment like foxfire above the doorway, then danced away, darting through the shadows and rising dust toward a little side entrance, a candlelit alcove uncovered by the collapse of the eastern wall.

Follow the light, urged a voice descending from the face of Saint Milton. Solomon blocked his ears, shouted defiantly, trying desperately to drown the voice, the threat . . .

Then realized this was a different voice.

Khole's.

Like welcome rain it tumbled from the statuary, sweet and melodic, the voice that had sustained him in the early despair of the clouds, had taught him the first steps of spellcraft. Solomon had believed that voice once—believed it enough to rest in the knowledge that spells were changing something despite the evidence of things seen.

It was a hard choice, and against the evidence.

But it was his own.

Follow the light, the voice repeated, this time more urgently, no longer falling from the statue but rising up inside Solomon himself, weaving itself gently through his thoughts until the prompting of the voice was indistinguishable from his own believing, wed to his own desperate heart.

Now the light danced over the surface of the fragmented mirrors.

Solomon followed it, shuffling through glass, through rubble. The alcove toward which the light maneuvered seemed distant, unapproachable, and then suddenly nearer, swelling and receding as though he glimpsed it through a haze of heat, as the wavering margins of a mirage.

A lectern sat in the alcove—or perhaps they called it a pulpit, considering where he had found it. Solomon approached it apprehensively, to find that it was falling apart as well, beehived with little widening holes, as small whirlpools of leuthan cloud opened and swirled in its burnished wood.

Atop the pulpit sat an ancient copy of the Text, as it sat customarily on a thousand pulpits from easternmost Luvah to the farthest reaches of Tharmas, where the land tumbled into the ocean of night. Its leather cover was cracked and dried, its pages dissolving as quickly as the pulpit, blossoming with Absences.

Solomon circled the pulpit, bathed in a light the color of verdigris. He did not touch the wood: it seemed too fragile, as though it might crumble or explode with a simple brush of the finger. The Text lay open to the Fourth and Fifth Plates: long verse paragraphs, their dark ink fading against the wash of blue that colored the facing pages, the Fourth Plate displaying a bone-white drawing of a dolmen, a tilted gibbous moon, and a panoply of shadows.

The pages were falling apart. Already great holes lay in the Text. The verse was garbled, unreadable, partially erased.

Solomon blinked, cleared his throat. Such gaps the scholars called *lacunae*. And of all the pages of the Text, these were the most disputed, for at the top of the Fifth Plate were the notorious erased lines.

At last and once again, Solomon Hawken was alone with a Text.

Suddenly lucid, the priest compared the ravaged passage before him to the original—the passage he had studied and committed to memory from seminary. The original he remembered readily: first he recited it aloud, in a whisper that shut out the rumbling in the chapel, the creak and crack of the rafters, the warring, insinuating voices.

> "Here the Three Classes of Mortal Men take their fix'd destinations,
> And hence they overspread the Nations of the whole Earth, & hence
> The Web of Life is woven & the tender sinews of life created
> And the Three Classes of Men required by Los's Hammers and woven
> By Enitharmon's Looms & Spun beneath the Spindle of Tirzah.

The first, The Elect from before the foundation of the World:
The second, The Redeem'd: The Third, the Reprobate & form'd
To destruction from the mother's womb. . . . follow with me my plow."

Tracing his finger lightly over the crumbling page, forgetting the threats of the Absence, the danger to his life, Solomon watched in consternation as remembered verses vanished before his eyes. Lines faded, eddied, and disappeared, dwindled slowly from view like eclipsed moons or winked out like rushlights.

And what was left was fragment only, but its ink more fast and lasting than drawing or stain or even the vellum of the page itself, the letters hovering in the dusty air even after the paper that had backed them was gone.

from before the foundation of the World

read the first extant passage.

The second was shorter still.

from the mother's womb

These solitary lines and the stark outline of the engraved dolmen were all that remained of the original pages. Yet the words slashed through Solomon like a two-edged sword.

"From the foundation of the world I have been chosen," he breathed. "From my mother's womb I have been called."

Briefly, sharply, the image of Christabel Whitford, floating sorrowfully in the mirrored halls of Arcady, rushed again to his recollection. It was the first thing he had seen upon entering the house with Willie Melmoth: the ghost of his mother draping the mirrors. Closing his eyes as they brimmed with tears, Solomon lifted his hand, tried again to touch the shade of his vanished mother . . .

The vision faded, as quickly and completely as the penned Text on the page before him. He opened his eyes and looked into the facing pages, tattered and blank.

Except for the two phrases.

From before the foundation of the world. From the mother's womb.

Quickly, carefully, Solomon thumbed through the Text. The pages were thick and powdery between his fingers, and a thin breath of dust rose from the turning.

All were the same. Lengthy passages vanished and vanishing, the occasional line or phrase or even word remaining despite the Text's disintegration.

What is left will endure, the new voice—Khole's voice—inside him said, and indeed the words that remained were enduring, stable, marked indelibly in the winnowing pages around them.

Will endure to the end of the world.

On the Nineteenth Plate, near the bottom of the page, only a handful of words remained:

Watch over this World, and with your brooding wings
Renew it to Eternal Life

Solomon thought of Khole as he read, and again on the Thirty-first Plate, where six words remained, facing the fast-fading engraving of the souls rising from the sundered earth.

hidden under the shadow of wings

It was Khole he remembered, but the drawing as well sparked his memory and compassion.

Diego and Endymion. Souls rising from the sundered earth. He would not rest until he had seen them again.

But you will not see them, the Absence boded, its alien, darker voice outside him entirely now, residing in the leuthan cloud, in the shadow of the chapel, in the sickly verdigris of the light. *You will share no victories with your brothers, and they will mourn you awhile and forget you, and the world will continue as it always has . . .*

You have thwarted me twice. But at last I have you.

Lifting the book from the pulpit, Solomon scrambled out into another landscape. No mansion lay above the chapel garden, no network of tunnels; instead, as Solomon had expected he would, he stood by the side of a shadowy Pontus Tarn, in the depth of forgotten autumn. A dark form stood beside him, the abandoned shapes of Innocent, of Blight and sphinx and rebel guerrilla still ever so slightly visible in his countenance, so that the spectral companion looked like his portrait and . . . like every other entity that Solomon feared or had feared.

You said once, it murmured, its cloudy hand resting on Solomon's shoulder, descending, passing through him with an insubstantial cold like a sudden icy wind, *that the time on Pontus Tarn when you lost your friend Marcus was . . . the closest to hell that you had ever come.*

"When did I say that?" Solomon asked, his own voice echoing, insubstantial.

The ghost beside him blended into the mist and out again, halfway substantial and halfway ethereal, like the loom it had employed. And it laughed—hollowly, harshly.

Why, back on another body of water. When you rode with that fool of a nun.

Solomon remembered the cloudy night, the rushing of the Alph and the plash of oars in the strong, indifferent current.

"Wh-what of it? What if I said such a thing?"

The ghost laughed again. *I will give you more of hell than your imagining,* it claimed. *For all the hells of your fancy have beginning, middle, and end . . .*

And true hell is not like that at all.

Suddenly Solomon felt the ninth-month chill in his bones, and smelled the weedy, metallic odor of the lake. As on that night a quarter of a century before, scarcely a ruffle of breeze disturbed the waters as he rowed again toward the southern shore of the lake.

He was back on Pontus Tarn. No longer was he simply an observer, watching his youthful self move through the events of his life at the seminary.

He was *there* on the lake. There in the flesh, the smooth, oily wood of the oars cool in his palms.

His passenger was hooded, lost in shadow at the stern of the rowboat. The passenger lifted a bottle, and the moonlight glinted green-golden on the slowly tilting liquid inside.

Tharman Amber. Marcus' wine. They had found the bottle washed ashore on the next day.

"She will look the same from the north," Solomon found himself saying, surprising himself with the words, as the moonlight bathed the long brown hair, the gnomish, mischievous face of his passenger.

"You look green yourself from this vista," Marcus proclaimed. "Seasick, perhaps?"

It was the same conversation. Just like the time before.

Above them, the birds wheeled again toward the face of the waters, and the clouds raced across the face of the moon. The dried leaves swirled from the near shore like ghosts fleeing an enchanter.

"She is all there is," Marcus whispered. "Ultimately, there is no more than that girl."

I am going to have to do this again, Solomon thought, his fear and sorrow rising.

Oh yes, an insubstantial voice gloated, riding with the clouds over the water. *You will have to do this again . . .*

And again. It is the best of my victories.

The waters roiled and churned, and despite Solomon's efforts at the oars, the rowboat turned athwart in the middle of the lake, rocking dangerously as the air swirled around it.

"She's all there is," Marcus repeated, raising his voice above the splashing, above the wind's whine and whistle over the lake. "Nymph of the forest and the rising waters. This tempest will blow over, and again we can go to her."

"Nonetheless, we'd best find a way to steer this tub to the nearest shore before the storm takes us in," Solomon found himself saying before he thought. "Whether it blows over or not, we are in for it now, and an hour on the lake is passing deadly."

Why am I saying this? Why can't I stop?

Again, the hollow laugh, as Solomon headed the rowboat toward the same shadowy, tree-lined cove he had glimpsed the night of the storm, knowing full well this time that he would never reach it.

Now the sky blackened, the stars winked out, and the shore vanished. When the lightning flashed, revealing no shore, no haven—nothing but water and cloud—Solomon knew he was trapped, was doomed to repeat the shipwreck, the drowning, in the cold, inhospitable waters of Pontus Tarn.

The events rumbled on, through the lightning-crazed skies and the downpour, through Marcus' fall from the boat and the failed spells, through the last sight of Solomon's closest friend as the long brown hair billowed and spread and vanished atop the dark, rising water . . .

And then they were both in the rowboat again, rowing across the lake with the storm brewing, approaching from a distance. The scene was unfolding once more, Solomon speaking and acting before he could think, and the events winding toward the storm and the wreck and the drowning once more.

But now the dreadful prospect that this would go on forever.

Do you understand hell now, Solomon? asked the cold voice, and the boy in the bow of the boat shuddered inwardly, though outwardly he could not change.

When the lightning struck the third time, beginning a third drowning cycle, Marcus lifted the flask from his pocket—brandy or whiskey, Solomon never knew, never *had* known. For a moment Solomon's fear and grief fell away, replaced by an unfamiliar curiosity. For a moment he ceased to dwell in the old, familiar anguish, watching and listening before he sorrowed and spoke.

What *had* that been, in the flask?

Not important, the voice urged. *Wasn't important enough to ask him then . . .*

"Pass me the flask, Marcus," Solomon said.

It was a wild impulse. He surprised himself that he had said it.

For a moment his thoughts harkened to his memory of the drowning. He had rehearsed the tragedy for years, gone over every moment, every detail, in the dark corridors of his thought and self-pity.

And not once, not ever, had he asked Marcus for the flask.

Not important. Perhaps you even forgot doing it the first time.

"Pass me the flask," Solomon repeated, filled with a fierce exhilaration.

Marcus handed him the silver flask, and he lifted it to his lips, and drank.

Whiskey. He could taste the faint seasons of corn and peat, and a giddiness passed over him that had nothing to do with the drink itself, but everything to do with the drinking.

He was free of the Absence's cycle.

He could choose what came next.

Again the storm clouds rushed across the moon, and the lake boiled and dappled. Again a sheet of rain washed over the boat. Again Marcus sputtered and sat upright, then again the boat itself was engulfed in darkness as the second wave doused the little lamp.

As it had always done.

When the surge of water off the port side wrenched the oar from

Solomon's hands, he turned, just in time to see Marcus tumble over the side.

Solomon rushed aftward, somehow more assured, less desperate. Marcus floundered in the tarn, calling out for his friend, and then the whirling, eddying waters took him. He looked up to Solomon, his frightened eyes expecting something . . .

Magic?

But instead, this time Solomon dove after him.

Only when he hit the water did Solomon remember his own fear of drowning.

This is the most stupid . . . a voice began, but whether his own or his spectral tormentor's, Solomon could no longer tell.

But it was too late to scramble back on board, as the dark lake closed over him and he surfaced with a gasp, a good twenty feet from the drifting rowboat. The dark sky spun above him, and he went under again, swallowing the cold, muddy taste of water and algae.

Breaking the surface again, he flailed in the rocking waves, his hands vague, clutching . . .

Grabbing something . . .

Corduroy.

Marcus.

Solomon clutched and pulled his friend toward him.

Now the two of them wrestled in a whirlpool of stormy waters, Solomon suddenly lucid, grappling with Marcus and his own fear as the waves washed over them once, twice.

At last he broke to the air again, sputtering, coughing, refusing to let go of his thrashing friend. The lightning flickered through the southern sky, and there, not three yards away, the rowboat rocked on the storm-battered lake.

With a cry Solomon pushed toward the boat, towing Marcus by the jacket. With his lungs bursting, he reached out desperately in the stormy dark . . .

And grabbed the gunwale of the tottering rowboat.

Twice he tried to pull himself aboard. The boat tipped dangerously to receive him, but he could not pull his friend in behind him without capsizing the craft.

Marcus sputtered once, then lay heavy, silent, his long hair matted and dripping over his pale face.

Not again, Solomon thought. It will not end this way!

With his last strength he rolled into the water, burrowing deeply below his drowning friend. Setting Marcus on his shoulders, he kicked and rose from the lake, lifting the lad into the boat, then fell back, bludgeoned by a high wave.

The waters closed over Solomon Hawken, and he felt himself sinking into a cold, abiding nothingness, the hands of dryads clinging, pulling him down . . .

May the saints bless you, Marcus Chatterton, he thought. May you find safe passage to shore.

And the waters waved and surged around him, spiraling upward like a typhoon, a waterspout. At the edge of unconsciousness, he felt himself spinning and tumbling, heard beneath the rush of water the outcry of a dark voice angry and thwarted . . .

And as he sank toward drowning, Solomon smiled in the water. The enemy was already defeated, his power dwindling over the damaged countryside. The destruction of Arcady was a desperate stab in the darkness, a revenge vicious and personal.

Solomon smiled. The enemy could not hurt him. Not now, perhaps not ever.

"Such are the laws, Marcus," Solomon breathed with his last breath, as the water rushed into his throat, his lungs . . .

> Such are the Laws of Eternity, that each shall mutually
> Annihilate himself for others' good, as I for thee.

A warm wind coursed over his back, and the faint smell of honeysuckle. In serenity he waited, buoyed by the flicker of light he had just seen, had chosen to remember with all his power of remembering.

He was back in Arcady. Back in the ancient central room—old Atreus' mausoleum. Solomon heard brick tumble behind him, dry wood splintering, and a dark voice urging him to turn around, to see his ancestral home tumbling, collapsing . . .

No, he thought. Winnowing. The old world falling away . . .

> Then down a green plain leaping laughing we run
> And wash in a river and shine in the Sun . . .

The angel's bright key had unlocked the coffin.

Freedom. The will of magic is freedom. In the face of the Absence, the thousand agendas that had bent the Text to their service, the even more numerous agendas of each day, each family, each province and nation . . .

Against all of these stand magic and the heart of the Text, whose great impulse has been concealed too long.

Now the wall behind Solomon yawned open into the outer morning air, and a fresh breeze lifted through the scattering clouds. Something lifted from Solomon as well, as a last, dark thought scuttled meanly through his memory and vanished into impermeable light.

Above him, in the sunstruck, brilliant rafters, all Arcady blossomed in birdsong.

Epilogue

As the smoke lifted from Arcady, it revealed three bedraggled forms, standing in the midst of the skeletal western wing.

Two of them, leaning against one another, stood on the bare waxed floors of what had once been a ballroom, the stairs leading up from them weathered and fragmented, balusters and newel posts like a line of headless trees, the mirrors that surrounded them toppled and splintered. The stairs spiraled into nothing, as though both figures stood at the base of a helix or gyre, points in a mathematical problem.

The other form, some hundred feet away from his companions, stood in the rubble of a library. Shelves leaned inward precariously, their shadows wavering over the solitary form, and yet the man stood his ground, standing curiously behind a lectern, holding a lantern above him as though, despite the commotion and the redeemed sunlight that bathed the ruinous mansion, all he wanted to do was continue his reading. It was as if something further—dramatic or perhaps disastrous—would happen if he moved.

Slowly the warring factions stopped shooting. The few guardsmen upwind of the smoke held off for a fierce and desperate hour, then, at the Lady's third order, laid down their guns. The air spoke less of peace than of hemp and stupor, of a weird cessation of hostilities. Both armies, exhausted and lulled, recognized that a change had come for which the old factions and issues had not prepared them.

Artemis weaved slowly through the drained ranks of both armies, lying spent and bloodied among the dark walnut trees. Her left elbow had been cracked by a stray Guard bullet, her hair was singed, and her eyes smarted from the settling smoke.

Two dozen of her own she counted dead, three times that many among the guardsmen. All of her tenets and strategies not worth the least of them.

"Lay down your arms," she commanded hoarsely, stepping from cover into a clearing suddenly sunstruck, where a dozen hemp-dazed guardsmen blinked, hoisted their weapons, then lowered the guns again as though their arms were suddenly too weary to support the instruments of war. Although they regarded skeptically the green column that emerged from the nut grove, led by the woman with her left arm in a sling, there was a difference in the glances.

Nothing would be the same from this time forward. The former things had passed away, and all things were made new.

Morgana shifted uncomfortably on the driver's seat of the wagon. Far to the north, on a turning breeze, she could see Willie Melmoth's daring balloon circling and returning, approaching Arcady buoyant in a marvelously clear sky.

The mansion before them lay less in ruins than in a state of incompletion. It was as though a clock had been turned back fifty years, a century, to a time when the wings of the mansion were beam and girder and blueprint. What the cloud had done was less destruction than a reversion to what had come before.

And yet Morgana knew that no erasure is simple, no damage of the enemy without its lasting consequence. Mina was gone: she knew that as certainly as she knew that the three disheveled forms in the ruins were her nephews Solomon, Endymion, and Diego.

Silent, her countenance pale with pain, Artemis rode up to the wagon, reining in her horse and setting her good hand on her ancient aunt's shoulder.

Morgana regarded the girl with concern. It was a wound that would need attendance. Not now, but in the hours to come, when guardsmen and rebels camped beside one another, and the many versions of this story were told, interwoven, and set before them all in one lasting version that would pass for the truth.

Pass for the truth, because it, too, would be partial. Filled with gaps and lacunae. With absences, if you would.

* * *

Nor was the book itself the same.

It would never be the same, each page tattered by the passage through the Absence, culled of inessential phrases down to a core that it would take Solomon years to decipher and understand.

Perhaps he would never finish the job. Perhaps the understanding would remain the task of the generations who followed—in Arcady, in Lambeth, in the hundreds of places where the new Text would be received, reconsidered, studied, and applied.

But he had come into a priesthood of sorts.

Solomon knew this as he helped Endymion guide their massive and lamed younger brother from the half-finished western wing of the mansion. Out on the grounds a company awaited them—fourscore guardsmen, perhaps, and half as many rebels. A half-mad novice, a guerrilla commander, and an innocent aerial daredevil who had been swept along by the whole tide of events as readily as his balloon was swept by the high currents of the air.

The first witnesses of a new time.

Endymion eased Diego onto a topiary rhomb flattened by the passing of the Absence. Rousseau, singed and powder-stained, stepped forward and offered his flask to the twins. Endymion brushed it away, and Diego took only a swallow of the gin before handing the flask back to the rebel lieutenant.

Solomon blessed them all silently, unsure that the old language of poetry and saints had the words for his blessing. Perhaps the new language would have something to do with the rivers and the trees, or with the disembodied transparencies that floated away above them all, scarcely visible now in the eastern sky, trailing ribbons and cigar smoke and a stream of sparkling milled water behind them. Perhaps it would have within it something of farewell, but he knew deeply that most of the new words remained in the book he carried like a talisman. They would be welcoming, anticipatory—a new language for a world stripped of its evident magic and wed to a deeper, more enchanting truth.

As the brothers stepped into the topiary, Morgana looked above them into the recovered sky, where a solitary balloon sailed over the border of her ancestral lands and sunlight danced, though visible only to her, off the wings of a hundred angels.